THE FORGOTTEN FLAME

BOOK TWO OF
THE FORGOTTEN EARTH SERIES

BRILYNN O'NEAL

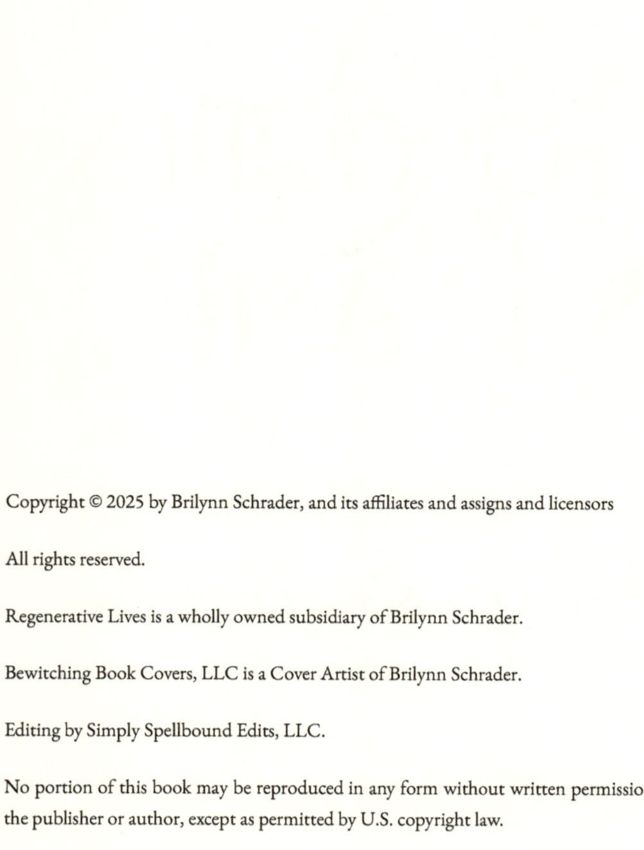

Copyright © 2025 by Brilynn Schrader, and its affiliates and assigns and licensors

All rights reserved.

Regenerative Lives is a wholly owned subsidiary of Brilynn Schrader.

Bewitching Book Covers, LLC is a Cover Artist of Brilynn Schrader.

Editing by Simply Spellbound Edits, LLC.

No portion of this book may be reproduced in any form without written permission from the publisher or author, except as permitted by U.S. copyright law.

To all the fiery women out there. May you burn the world with your rage so that a better one can emerge from the ashes.

To my daughter. You burn the brightest. Never let anyone snuff out your flame.

Author Note

This novel contains mild violence, attempted rape, talk of abandonment and grief, death, brief description of premature birth (no child death), and open-door romance.

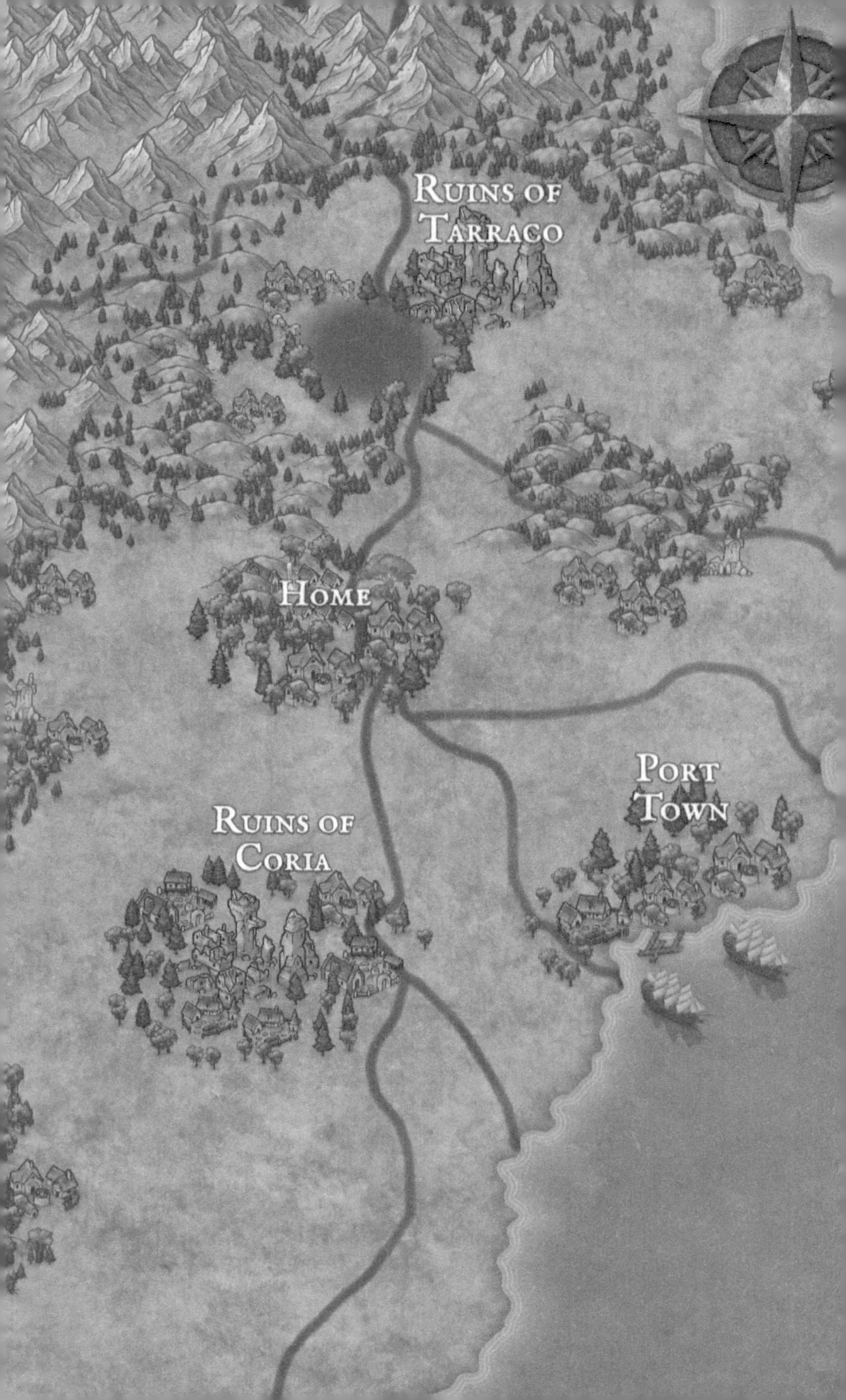

RUINS OF TARRACO
HOME
RUINS OF CORIA
PORT TOWN

Tir Na Eabha
Port City

Prologue

Willow

Sacrifice was my life.

I wanted nothing more than to disappear with my family. To forget the responsibility that came with my magic. To forget that only I could restore what was lost.

I walked through life in a haze of exhaustion, not really living the life I dreamed of after the fall of the Elite.

I had spent too long traveling around the world, restoring the dead Earth, and in the process, I'd forgotten what it was like to live a life of my own.

My family kept me going. I'd have given up long ago if it weren't for them. Everything I did was for them.

While I spent the last ten years re-growing the earth, Liam worked with local communities to establish democratic systems and train peace protectors. Our community both grew and shrank, as newcomers came in, and our most trusted soldiers were sent to neighboring villages to set up protection.

The only ones who stayed were Olivia, Kat, Leeann, Elise, and Lily.

I didn't include Marcus because he had recently disappeared. He had been living with us, recovering from the trauma of injuries inflicted on him by the emperor, and through it all, he became like a second father to our children.

He held a particular soft spot for our eldest daughter. The two of them were thick as thieves, and though he indulged her far too often, I admired their bond.

I'd even encouraged it.

I had fooled myself into thinking he was happy, ignoring the melancholy I felt anytime I was near him. He acted happy, but underneath I knew he wasn't.

Because of me.

He left without a goodbye, leaving no hint where he went or how long he'd be gone.

As the months wore on without any communication or information about his whereabouts, we all came to accept that he was either not coming back, or he was dead.

That didn't stop me from keeping an ear out for any indication of him along our travels. But, with each trip, I grew less and less hopeful.

The days away from home, away from our children, were both rewarding and agonizing. I found myself stuck between wanting to help heal the world that humans had destroyed almost two hundred years ago and just wanting to exist. To be normal. To be a family. No magic. No weight on our shoulders.

Liam felt it too. I could feel it within him and in the slump of his shoulders as we sailed to yet another part of the world to restore the barren land.

My magic knew me now. It responded without thought, as if it were truly a part of me. The channels were everywhere and within everything—a constant web of life, elemental energy, and connection.

When I created new ecosystems from dead land, new channels were brought up from the earth, weaving together to form a beautiful tapestry of pulsing life. It still gave me a thrill to see what the land would become. I didn't force it. I didn't manipulate it. I let it be what it wanted to be.

Sometimes the land would transform into what it was before it died, but sometimes it wanted to be something entirely new.

"I know that look," Liam said, coming to stand next to me on the deck of the ship as we headed back home to our children. This was our tenth long trip since our daughter had been born, and that didn't include the trips we'd taken closer to home.

I glanced at him out of the corner of my eye, all muscle and glowing blue eyes. My protector. My partner. My *everything.*

"The pirates make me worried," I responded, turning my body to fully face him.

"They aren't the Claeg."

No, they weren't entirely dead monsters intent on killing all humans. Not yet at least. But they were close. Too close.

"They feel the same."

Liam stepped into me, lightly running his thumb along my chin. "We'll figure out where they're coming from, how they're made, and why they're still here despite the living world."

"I'm afraid there are forces we do not understand, the Claeg being one of them. I still haven't figured out why this magic was given to me, or the kids, and I believe that question might be the most important one of all."

Liam's eyes softened, and I felt the anxiety in him, mirroring my own. "One step at a time. The Elite are gone, new democratic leadership is arising, and you are healing what we believed was lost to us. Resources are now available on a larger scale, and children are being born again. We've come so far. It deserves a little celebration."

I scoffed. "Who has time to celebrate?"

Liam chuckled, pulling me into his warm embrace.

"There's another thing," I whispered into his chest.

He tensed, sensing what I was about to say. "I can't find anything about her blue flame. There's no trace of it in history, and I have no idea how to help her."

It kept me up at night. I was failing her.

Liam ran his hand through my wild hair. "And the village you found?"

I shook my head. "They refused to help."

I hadn't explained the full story to anyone, not even Liam, and hoped one day I wouldn't come to regret my decision to remain silent on the topic. He knew the gist of what I'd found in that forest, but I had left out key details.

We had so many enemies, and I felt the uncertainty of many people when I was around. The hesitancy to trust me.

The fear.

A decade of peace wasn't long enough to eliminate that fear. It had been written into our DNA.

It wasn't something I knew how to change.

I feared the fear most of all.

That's why I kept the secret of that forest—for the safety of my family. For the safety of humans. We were too fragile, standing on a house of cards. What this forest was could change everything.

It could also crush us.

"Her flame appears harmless," Liam said after a beat of silence, interrupting my thoughts.

I shook my head against his chest. "It's not. I can *feel* the energy when she uses it. I can *see* it. It's more powerful than anything I've ever come across. Might even be more powerful than my own magic."

He lowered his head until his chin was resting on the top of my hair. "You're afraid."

It wasn't a question. Just like the forest, I was terrified. But not terrified for her. I was terrified of what it might mean for all of us. What it might mean for a world that was only beginning to heal. Only beginning to *trust*.

"Land Ho!" A sailor shouted, and both of us stepped back from each other and turned to the sea, forgetting my fear in anticipation of something greater.

Through the fog was the outline of the docks, and standing on the docks was the most beautiful sight.

A brunette. A blond. And a redhead. All with glowing blue eyes.

My fire children.

I was home.

PART I

Chapter One

"I think she has him," my oldest brother, Aiden, commented from the sidelines of our daily training routine, which our father, Liam, had been putting us through since birth. It was simple swordplay. Something I should have been able to do in my sleep.

"She'll find a way to blow it," my youngest brother, Aelius, responded, not even paying attention to the fight in front of him. Instead, he was juggling two flaming fireballs, trying to make them defy gravity.

Stepping back from my opponent, I allowed myself a small moment of reprieve and found that annoying smirk plastered on his face as he watched me. His muscular chest was bare and heaving, slick with sweat, as he held his sword in a ready position.

I tried not to stare too long, but clearly I failed, as his thoughts drifted into my head.

"What I wouldn't do to that pouty mouth of hers—"

"Ew! Mason! Get out of my head!" I shouted into his mind.

His smirk grew, revealing a single dimple on the left side of his mouth. *"I'm not purposely in your mind, Red, but I can be if you want."*

Rolling my eyes, I decided not to let him bait me further into this little game of ours.

"Get on with it already," Aelius whined.

I went to flip him off, but it was just enough of a distraction to give Mason an advantage. He came at me with an arcing swing, and as I went to block it, I somehow tangled my feet and went crashing into Mason's chest. We both tumbled to the ground, Mason losing the grip on his sword. It flew a few feet away, and he grunted as he took the brunt of the impact.

With my face plastered to his sweat-soaked chest, I felt the laughter before I heard it. "Well, Red, that's one way to win."

I squeezed my eyes shut. My brothers knew better than to let their thoughts drift to my ineptitude, but their rolling laughter spoke louder than their thoughts ever could.

I didn't want to move, already anticipating the look on my father's face.

"What's the verdict?" I asked Mason instead.

Mason placed his arm gently across my low back as he turned his head to where my father watched from his usual rock. *"Not surprised."*

Cracking open one eye, I squinted up at my father as he walked to the two of us, still tangled up with one another. My brothers were desperately trying to stop their laughter behind him. Strangled sounds poured from their throats in their futile attempts. I wanted to smack their smug faces, but my father crossed his arms, waiting for me to stand up.

When you're the firstborn in an extraordinary family, expectations run high. Unfortunately for me, I didn't even come close to those expectations.

My two younger brothers, however, were practically gods reincarnated. They had oozed power from the moment they were born and haven't let me forget it.

We were all fire children, our birth months exactly four months apart, forming a triangle within the wheel of the year. Though we all possessed the power of fire, our magic was very different.

Groaning, I finally pushed myself off Mason. His arm fell away, and I missed its comfort. I shook my head, disappointed I'd even let myself think that, let alone notice the feel of him against me. He was Aiden's best friend and my training partner since we were young. He'd always been off-limits.

Standing, I dusted off the dirt and met my father's gaze with my head held high.

His blazing blue eyes were a mirror of my own, and his unsurprised face soon melted into a soft smile. "You have two left feet, Solana."

"Yet somehow she still manages to win half the time," Mason added as he stood up, patting me hard on the back. So hard that I fell forward, my father catching me before I face-planted in the dirt.

My brothers both snickered.

"*Assholes,*" I mumbled into their heads.

"Back to the house, boys," my father barked, sensing the silent warring in our heads. Both of them didn't hesitate to comply, waving for Mason to join them.

Mason glanced at me before grabbing his black shirt off the ground and throwing it over his head. I pretended not to watch the muscles on his torso flex as he pulled the shirt down.

Mason caught my gaze. *"Careful, Red, I might get the wrong impression."*

Shaking my head, I chose to ignore him, returning my attention to my father.

"Sol—" he started.

"I know, I know. But has it ever occurred to you that maybe I'm just not cut out to be a soldier? Have you looked at me?" Sweeping my hands around my body, I motioned to every part of myself. It wasn't that I didn't look athletic. I was built tall and elegantly, even a little muscular like my father, but I wasn't graceful like he was. On the other hand, my brothers were born fighters, and they looked the part too.

My youngest brother, Aelius, was said to be the son of the Sun God himself. He was born with blazing blond hair, a physical prowess that was arguably more powerful than our father's, an easy ability to manipulate fire, and an annoyingly charming, albeit immature, personality. He was the golden child.

If my youngest brother had the fire of the Sun God, my middle brother, Aiden, had the fire of the God of the Underworld. He was just as powerful as my youngest brother, but his fire was darker, as if it were born from the center of the Earth itself. He had dark hair, like my mother, Willow, and was very tall, like our father. His sensitive constitution usually won him many points with the ladies. He rivaled my youngest brother at any physical feat.

I, on the other hand, had none of their power. I could barely light a candle with my flame. I had long red hair streaked with gold, legs that stretched on for days, light skin, and freckles that dotted my nose and cheeks.

My father chuckled. "Has it ever occurred to you to *use* your abilities?"

"Against Mason?" I asked incredulously, shaking my head. "There's nothing but dirty thoughts in that boy's head. I'm surprised he can even lift a sword for how little he actually thinks about his next move."

My father laughed in earnest this time. "I'm not talking about Mason. The two of you could fight in your sleep with how well you know each other's bodies."

I wrinkled my nose, unsure of what, exactly, he was implying.

"I'm putting you with Hewitt tomorrow," he continued.

I went to interrupt him, but he held up a hand to stop me. "He's new. He doesn't know your fighting style, nor do you know his. It will be a good test."

It's not that I didn't want to prove to my father that I could protect myself, it was that most people who didn't grow up around me and my brothers tended to keep their distance once they experienced our magic for the first time.

I wondered if that was my father's plan to keep men away from me. It worked, whether on purpose or not.

Mason, on the other hand, never once made me feel different or unwanted. He never shied away from my uncontrollable magic, clumsiness, or my family's intense power. He always acted as if it were normal. As if my parents hadn't changed the world, and my brothers and I weren't some freak anomalies, able to manipulate fire.

"Fine," I mumbled, resigning myself to the fact that I wouldn't win this argument.

My father gave me a broad smile. "Go," he said, nodding his head toward the house, knowing I was dying to be finished so I could go paint.

Not hesitating, I sprinted to our house.

The house was built into the side of a cliff that overlooked our small village. If you didn't look closely, you might miss it. Made of stone and glass and covered with plants, it blended effortlessly into its surroundings. To the left of the house was a waterfall that fed a large pool and stream that meandered its way through town, feeding the ecosystem that nourished our village—an ecosystem my mother had created with her magic.

The house was a legend, and not just because of its looks, or even because my mother and father were the most influential people on the planet. It was a legend because it was alive. Fed, we believed, by our magic.

It was a real bitch, though.

Racing down the stone hallway, I registered the voices of Kat and Olivia in the kitchen, and the barking of instructions from Leeann down the hall.

The din of the everyday. The only thing I'd ever known.

When I reached the door of my art studio, it was blocked by a wall of thorny vines. There was no way I was getting past it without help. Halting, I chewed on my bottom lip, debating if I wanted to get into yet another fight with the house. I also contemplated calling for my brothers who had a much better relationship with the magical dwelling.

But I didn't want to have to owe them anything.

I settled for asking nicely, untangling my lip from my teeth. "Will you please let me in?"

The vines made a small movement, winding in and out of one another, and I thought maybe my request worked, but then the vine stopped moving, presenting a single white flower bud.

I should have seen it coming, but I was too caught up in the fact that the house may have actually listened to me, that I didn't duck in time when the flower opened and sneezed yellow pollen all over me.

Trying to reign in my anger, my blue flame ignited in my palm without warning. The flame did nothing to my skin. In fact, it did hardly anything at all. It was useless beyond flickers of pain it caused when directed at my brothers. But it did like to randomly appear in times of stress.

"Going for a new look, Red?" Mason's voice came from right behind me, and I wondered how much he'd seen of the encounter.

Spinning around, I found him casually leaning against the wall on the opposite side of the hall, and holding in a laugh, his chiseled features tense with the effort. But, instead of making him look stiff, he looked soft and relaxed. Familiar in a way no one else was.

My hand swept through my hair and came away yellow.

"The house hates me," I grumbled, wiping my hand on my mud-caked fighting leathers, dirty from the tumble we'd taken.

"Can you blame it?" An undercurrent of amusement filled his voice.

I rolled my eyes. "Is there a reason you're bothering me too?"

Mason pushed off the wall and took a few steps closer.

"Aelius was supposed to remind you that your parents are hosting a large meeting later today."

"Shit, I forgot."

I was always swept away from large crowds because of my inability to control whose thoughts I could read. With too many people in one room, I'd end up with headaches that could take me out for days. Not to mention the torture of hearing some people's thoughts.

"If Aelius was supposed to warn me, why are you here?"

"He got in a fight with Aiden on the way in. Something about his hair? I'm not sure, but they burned one of the kitchen tables, and Olivia wasn't happy."

"I'm sure the house fixed it for them." I huffed.

Mason smiled, his dimple appearing. Why did I even bother with the question.

"Are you going to the meeting?" I asked, subconsciously stepping closer to him.

Mason nodded. "And you'll hide away in the treehouse?"

"Likely."

"Fuck, I wish I could go with you."

Thoughts didn't always drift into my head, and I couldn't control when they did. Sometimes, I could go through an entire conversation without hearing a single thought. Other times, I couldn't turn them off. My family had learned to control their thoughts enough around me that I rarely heard them. Mason had learned that skill, too, but I think sometimes he purposely let some drift into his head, so I'd hear them.

"Come with me," I said into his mind, and it was his turn to take another step closer to me.

"As much as I'd love to, your parents requested my presence. Something big is going on."

I sighed. "I know. They've been tense lately."

"You think they're leaving again?"

"It wouldn't surprise me."

"Will you go this time?"

I snorted, and when his facial expression didn't change, I said, "Oh, you're serious." I ran a hand through my hair again, forgetting about the pollen. "They won't let me."

"You're an adult, Red."

I shook my head. "Doesn't matter. The world isn't safe for me—I'm a walking disaster." Throwing up my hands, I waved them around like an idiot.

Mason's face lit up, finally stepping so close I had to tilt my head back to meet his eyes.

"I happen to like this walking disaster," he whispered, ghosting his fingers along my nose, wiping away the pollen.

"I almost killed you by tripping on my own feet."

Mason chuckled. "But you didn't."

I blew out a deep breath. "I'm clumsy, terrible with weapons, have a useless blue flame, and a single group of people can take me out with their thoughts. Remind me, again, how traveling would be a good idea?"

"It's your dream."

There it was. Something everyone knew about me, but something I could never have. Not unless I could prove I could protect myself and control my mind-reading powers.

I would steal you away to the stars if I could.

Cocking my head to the side, I narrowed my gaze, ignoring my increased heartbeat.

He knew I'd heard his thoughts, and his responding smirk lit me up. I forgot to breathe. Mason reached out, tilting my chin until our lips were so close I could almost taste them.

The sound of someone clearing their throat had us separating so fast that I tripped, falling against the vines. A single thorn tore at the leather on my ass, piercing through. I yelped, jumping forward, bumping into the hard wall that was Mason's chest.

He caught me around the waist, steadying me.

I heard Aelius' laughter, but all I could focus on was the strong hands that seemed reluctant to let go. Hands, maybe, that I didn't want to let go of me either.

"Thanks," I mumbled to Mason, stepping out of his arms and turning to glare at my brother. "What do you want, Aelius?"

"Family meeting in Leeann's office."

Mason's brows were pinched as he stared at my brother.

"You know something," I said into his head.

"I'll see you later, Red."

And then he turned on his heel and was gone.

Chapter Two

Mercifully, Aelius kept his mouth shut as we walked down the long, dark hallway that led further into the cliff. The house lit the hallway with bioluminescent flowers. If it had just been me, the house wouldn't have bothered. I'd have been stuck in the dark.

"What's going on?" I asked Aelius.

"I'm right here, Sol. Get out of my head."

My brother always hated when I spoke to him mind-to-mind, which was why I always did.

"Tell me."

Aelius stopped, considering my question. "I honestly don't know." He said it without looking at me, and I could tell, just like with Mason, there was something they were keeping from me.

Aelius opened the door and ushered me in. I stalked over to an empty chair and practically fell into it. Aelius walked around to the other side and sat beside Aiden.

Olivia, Leeann, Kat, Elise, and my parents sat opposite us. Everyone was silent as they tracked us to our seats.

My father watched until he was certain we weren't talking to each other in our heads. I knew better, though. The silence alone was telling. No one in this family was ever quiet.

Taking a deep breath, he reached for my mother's hand. "We received alarming news from overseas earlier this week."

My eyes swept over the group. This information didn't seem surprising to any of the adults, but what caught my attention was that my brothers didn't seem surprised by this news either.

I leaned forward as my father continued. "There is an unknown threat amassing. They are clear-cutting and burning newly grown forests and killing anyone who stands against them."

"But that's illegal," I said.

My father nodded, glancing at my mother's reaction. It was the trees she created that were being cut. It had to be devastating, but she held her head high. Determined as ever.

"It's as if people are coming in, cutting trees, burning the rest, killing at will, and then disappearing into thin air," he continued.

I shook my head. "People can't just disappear."

"That's why we're needed," my mother said. She was the only one who could sense and feel the energy channels of living things. If there were people disappearing, she would find them.

"And you're here to tell us we're staying behind again." It wasn't really a question.

My parents looked at each other as if they could also speak mind-to-mind.

I waited, hoping for a breath of thought from anyone at the table. Everything remained frustratingly silent in my head.

"We're asking for your brothers to join us," my mother said, cautiously, as if I were a bomb ready to explode.

Perhaps I was, but instead of letting that bomb explode, I simply stood and left the room. I didn't know when the years of anger and disappointment I held back would finally pour out of me, but it wasn't today. So, I pushed it down like I always did, picking up my pace through the, now dark, hallway.

"Solana!" my mother called after me, which I ignored. I didn't need to know whatever else they were going to discuss. I wasn't a part of it anyway.

I was the disappointment.

People from all over the area trickled into our house around midday. I stayed well away, locking myself in my art studio until I could no longer ignore the intrusive thoughts and ache in my head.

It was time to hide myself away from the world, yet again.

I intended to pass the time in ignorant bliss at the top of a Mother Oak tree on the edge of town, in a treehouse my father made just for me to escape the noise in my head. But a single thought trickled through the doorway and made me halt.

"Soon, the world will be rid of their kind."

I couldn't focus on the thoughts of that single person, as a jumble of others invaded my head. Instinctively, I rubbed my temples, I wanted to relieve some of the ache. I needed to escape, but I also needed to figure out whose thoughts I'd overheard.

The door where the meeting was being held clicked open, and my head snapped in that direction.

"You're still here?" Kat asked, coming to stand in front of me.

"I was just leaving."

She narrowed her gaze as if she didn't believe me.

"I'm already getting a headache."

She nodded, satisfied. "I'm grabbing refreshments."

As she went to leave, I asked a question I wasn't sure was a good idea. "Is everyone in that room a trusted ally?"

Kat faced me, her features twisted in confusion. "They are our *most* trusted allies. Is there a reason you're asking?"

I wasn't positive I wanted to say anything about the thought I heard. It wasn't a complete thought and could have been taken out of context. Furthermore, I had no way of knowing who it came from, or who it was referring to.

"I saw some people I didn't recognize."

That seemed to satisfy Kat's worry. "Some of these people we haven't seen in years. They came a long way to be here."

I nodded. "I'll be on my way, then."

Kat didn't move. She searched my face as though she could read my emotions like my mother could. "If you want to come in?"

I shook my head. "It's already giving me a headache just standing here."

Kat stepped closer, putting a hand on my shoulder. "We'll figure this out."

I smiled, but it wasn't sincere. The truth was, I'd been trying most of my life to control it. Nothing worked, and no one had devised any ideas for a solution in years. It's like everyone had given up. Maybe they had.

I certainly had.

"We'll fill you in when everyone leaves," Kat added, sensing my dismay.

With a smile still on my face, I nodded and then scrambled for the door, needing the silence and fresh air. Kat let me go without another word.

Stopping at the bottom of the steps, I glanced left toward the vines and stones decorating the wall of our house below the window where the meeting was taking place. I couldn't hear anyone's thoughts from here, but it would only be a matter of a few feet before those thoughts came racing back in.

I contemplated ignoring what I had heard and heading for the treehouse, but my feet wouldn't move. I could have snuck back into the house to eavesdrop, but I didn't want to run into Kat and have to explain myself. I inwardly berated myself for what I was about to do but saw no other immediate option.

Curling around the staircase, I came face-to-face with the vined wall of the house.

"I swear to the gods I will find a way to make your existence miserable for all eternity if you decide to blow my cover," I practically shouted at the outside of the house. Then I waited, anticipating retaliation for my tone of voice or some other nonsense.

When the house remained still, I gingerly reached out and grabbed onto a sturdy vine, pulling slightly to test its strength.

It would hold me.

I only needed to climb up a few feet, as I could already hear whispers of thoughts brushing my consciousness. I was careful with the first pull, but when the vine held and the house didn't move to disrupt my little scheme, I pulled myself up a few more feet. That's when my brain flooded with voices, and I almost lost my hold.

Gods, it was excruciating trying to decipher between streams of thoughts just to understand what was said.

After a few disorienting moments, I finally caught onto some stray sentences.

"They will regret ever getting involved."

I concentrated hard on that voice. It wasn't familiar to me, though I supposedly knew everyone in that room, even if it had been years.

"They have no clue what's coming."

As I was just figuring out how to block other voices in my head, the damn house finally decided it had humored me long enough.

I felt the vine give way a second too late, and my hands slipped off. Falling backward, I should have landed on my head, but apparently, the house didn't hate me enough to kill me. Instead, the vines snaked around my ankles, up my legs, and pulled taught around my arms until I was hanging upside down, my skull only inches from the ground.

Wiggling, I tried to get out of the vise grip, but once again, the house decided not to respond.

"Fuck you!" I shouted, swinging helplessly in the breeze.

The house only twirled me around until I was hanging in front of a surprisingly attractive man I'd never seen before.

He bent down and angled his head to the side. Blue-gray eyes stared at me. Into me might have been a better description.

"Need some help?" he asked in a deep and oddly alluring voice.

I squeezed my eyes shut. This was not happening.

He was still staring when I opened them, waiting for my answer.

"Nope. I'm good," I said, still hanging helplessly like an idiot.

"You sure?" He asked, and this time, a hint of a smile crossed his full lips.

Did I just notice his damn lips?

"I know this may sound a bit unbelievable, but the house and I don't exactly get along. If you try to help, you'll likely end up on its shit list too."

The mysterious man stepped toward the house, and the vines beside my head unfurled and presented him with a single rose.

"Are you fucking serious?" I shouted at the house. "Where's your godsdamn loyalty to family?"

The man reached out and took the rose, smiling in earnest now as he tucked it behind his ear.

I snarled. "Unbelievable!"

Did I realize how unhinged I sounded to a complete stranger? Yes. But was I so mad and embarrassed that I didn't care? Also, yes.

Without looking at me, the stranger addressed the house. "Please let her down."

"*Psht.*" That would never work.

To my absolute horror, the house complied and laid me down gently on the soft grass. The man came and stood over me, a half-smirk on his too-attractive face.

I groaned, not wanting to get up and face this person. "Thank you for the help," I said begrudgingly.

"I'd ask what you were doing, but I'm not sure I want to know." There was amusement in his deep voice.

"The house tricked me," I responded miserably, still not making any move to get up.

The man reached out a hand. It was dark-skinned and covered in tattoos, as was the skin peeking from his shirt near the top of his chest. He wore a white button-down tucked into form-fitting black pants.

The top few buttons were undone, and the sleeves were rolled up his forearms.

I suddenly wanted to know how much of him was covered in those tattoos.

Shaking my head, I chased away the thoughts and accepted his help. He easily pulled me to my feet, and true to form, I stumbled and fell right into his hard chest.

"Oops," I mumbled, planting my hands on his abdomen and pushing away.

I felt his abs contract as a low laugh escaped him.

"Sol! There you are!"

Turning away from the mysterious man, who I now realized might be even larger than my father, I found Lily, racing up the path. She stopped a few feet from us and put her hands on her legs, trying to catch her breath. She looked between us and jabbed a finger in the man's direction.

"Who's this?" she asked, but in her head, she thought, *"Damn. I'd do anything to see that man naked."*

Narrowing my eyes, I shook my head at Lily, who only shrugged, knowing I had heard that thought.

The man raised a brow at my reaction.

"I don't know who this is," I said, addressing Lily.

"I'm Kai. Captain Fraiser's son. It's a pleasure to meet you both," he offered quickly.

He was the son of the ship captain who took my parents around the world.

"Double damn. Imagine that voice praising you in the bedroom."

"Lily!" I shouted, unable to keep my reaction from slipping.

Instead of embarrassment, though, Lily looked smug. I'm sure my cheeks were red as beets, even though those weren't my thoughts.

Kai looked between us, clearly waiting for an explanation I had no intention of giving. "Excuse the outburst."

I seethed at Lily, but she only chuckled, luckily not intent on blowing my cover.

"Aren't you late?" I blurted to Kai, desperately wanting to change the subject and feeling the need to either learn everything about this man or run in the opposite direction.

"I had to take care of some things on the ship so my father wouldn't be late."

I nodded like a dumbass. It was a very reasonable explanation.

Lily smirked, letting her thoughts drift into my head, yet again. *"You must admit, there's something about him . . ."*

Lily was ten years older than me, but you wouldn't know it. She was easy-going most of the time, only switching to seriousness when the circumstances required it. Along with her mom, Elise, she often traveled with my parents. If information was needed, those two could find it. Steal it, might have been a better word for what they did, though. But they were the best of the best at what they did.

I scowled at Lily's thought. It's not that I didn't agree. It's that I didn't know how to respond.

Kai didn't miss a thing, catching the looks on both our faces.

Fuck, he was observant.

I smiled sweetly, but I could tell he didn't buy it.

"She talking shit behind your back?" Mason's voice came from the top of the stairs. The meeting must have just ended.

I shook my head violently behind Kai as he directed his attention to the intrusion.

"Shut up. He doesn't know."

It didn't deter Mason in the slightest. "She can read people's thoughts and speak mind-to-mind. Any awkward looks or silence means those two are talking shit or talking dirty." Mason winked and started down the stairs.

"Fuck you," I said to Mason.

"Yes, please."

I rolled my eyes.

Mason only laughed, reaching the grass and extending his hand to Kai. "Mason."

Kai took his hand and gave it one firm shake. "Kai."

Mason pulled away and met my gaze over Kai's shoulder. *"He's nice on the eyes."*

"You think everyone's nice on the eyes."

Mason shrugged. *"I don't discriminate."*

"Why don't you bug him with your dirty thoughts instead of me then."

"Perhaps he could join." Mason waggled his eyebrows.

It suddenly felt rude to exclude Kai. "These two think you're beautiful."

With that, I stormed up the steps, Mason's voice echoing behind me. "Hard to keep secrets around that one."

The most infuriating part was that Mason wasn't embarrassed by my revelation of his thoughts. So then, why was I?

"Hey, Sol, what's Kai thinking?" Lily asked as I reached the front door.

Halting, I went over the events of the last ten minutes.

"I have no idea."

Chapter Three

___

Mason raced to catch up to me. "Don't you want to wait until everyone's gone?" His voice easily switched to one of concern.

I glanced at him sideways, not stopping. "I heard some thoughts that were concerning. I need to talk to my parents."

Mason grabbed my arm, twisting me toward him. "What did you hear?"

I shook off his hand. Lily had raced ahead of us, and was now talking to a tall, blond man with angular features. He would have been attractive if he wasn't creepy. He leaned in just a little too close to Lily, bending his head so he could whisper something in her ear. She didn't seem afraid, but she also wasn't amused.

Kai had followed behind us, but his focus wasn't on us, it was on Lily and the mysterious man. I couldn't read his face, but whatever was there had me tensing.

"What's wrong?" Mason whispered, noticing my darting eyes.

"How could my parents associate with these people? At least this one isn't too bad to look at. I wonder how she is in bed . . . "

My first instinct was to warn Lily, but at the same moment the thoughts around me created chaos and searing pain. Putting my head in my hands, I rubbed my temples.

"Sol?" Mason said louder, grabbing onto my elbow. "You need to get out of here."

I shook my head, unable to speak.

"They're coming."

My head snapped to Lily and the man again. Lily now had a scowl on her face, and his hand was wrapped around her upper arm.

That's when Kai moved.

He didn't get far when an older man stepped in front of him, blocking his path. The man looked just like Kai, except strands of silver wound through his black hair, and slight wrinkles lined his dark eyes. Kai reeled back, and they exchanged a few words before he reluctantly made his way back to me and Mason.

With so many things happening at once, and the noise in my head, I couldn't focus or ask Kai the question that was burning in my mind.

I tried to home in on the stranger's thoughts, instead, blocking out everything around me. But I was failing and the pain in my head continued to grow to an almost unbearable level.

Kai's deep voice caught my attention. "What's wrong with her?"

"She can't be around a lot of people. The thoughts give her blinding headaches," Mason explained.

Everything felt scrambled in my brain. Even their faces were blurry as I continued to uselessly massage my temples hoping to alleviate some of the pain.

"Sol," Kai's voice cut through the noise in my head.

Looking up, I found depthless blue-gray eyes staring into my bright blue ones. I'm sure mine were glowing. That happened whenever my magic was being used, with or without intention.

Kai didn't seem to notice, or didn't care about, my eyes. "Can you focus on my thoughts?" he asked, so quietly it felt like it was only the two of us.

"I can't hear your thoughts," I replied, the sound coming out as little more than a squeak.

He narrowed his gaze, confused. As was I. "Focus on the nothingness, then."

There was a joke in there somewhere about his empty soul, but my head hurt too much to utter a word. Taking a deep breath, I lowered my hands and locked onto the steadiness of his stare. It was as if I were floating in the infinite sea with nothing but the steady waves.

There were stories in his eyes. Locked in the ocean depths.

I didn't know how long we held our gaze, but suddenly I shook my head and averted my eyes, surprised to find nothing but silence. The only voices I heard were the murmurs of the many conversations happening around us.

"Sol?" Mason asked, still gently holding onto my arm.

I smiled at him. "I'm OK." Scrunching my nose, I contemplated what had just happened.

Mason reached up and flicked it. "It's a good thing, Sol."

Scowling, I rubbed at the spot on my nose. "I know. I just don't know why or how that worked."

"Perhaps Kai has some secret power we don't know about," Mason mused, glancing over at Kai who stood a few feet away, eyes locked back on the tall stranger, seemingly oblivious to our conversation.

Though I doubted he was unaware. He didn't seem the type to let down his guard.

"Yeah, the power to make every girl's panties wet."

Lily had abandoned the stranger, rejoining our group in the middle of whatever Kai had done to me. I wanted to ask her what had happened, but her sudden thought broke through the silence.

"Well, it didn't erase everyone's thoughts." I glared at Lily, who only laughed.

"Will you excuse me?" Kai suddenly said, and then disappeared among the crowd, heading for his father.

"That was strange," Lily observed.

"Very," I agreed.

"You still good?" Mason asked me.

I nodded. "Perhaps I just need an empty mind to follow me around for the rest of my days."

Lily chuckled. "Oh, I doubt that mind of his is empty."

"So then why can't I hear him?"

Lily shrugged.

"I'm more concerned about his reaction to that tall, blond guy hitting on Lily. And the blond was why I needed to speak to my parents in the first place."

Lily frowned, but it was Mason's growling voice that made me pause. "What thoughts?"

Grabbing Mason's hand, I gave it a reassuring squeeze. "I need to speak to my parents, and then I'll fill you in."

Mason remained concerned but resigned. He released my arm, and I addressed Lily next. "What did he say to you?"

Her brow furrowed. "Nothing out of the ordinary. Just another man whose advances I had to shut down."

"He didn't hint at anything?"

"Like what?"

I shook my head. "Nothing. I just get a weird feeling about him."

"Weird isn't the correct term. Creepy is more accurate."

"How so?"

"It wasn't just the fact that he touched me without my consent. It was something more sinister. Like he holds power. But not power in the sense of leadership. Like he holds power *over* something."

I knew exactly what she meant. People like that weren't rare to come across in my family's line of work. What worried me, though, was I didn't think anyone knew. Not even my parents.

My gaze drifted to them. They were in conversation with a friendly looking man who, ironically, looked like the mysterious man's father. The only difference between them, was the older man was built much bulkier than his son.

"Excuse me," I said to both Lily and Mason.

They both let me go, their stares following me across the crowded room.

As I approached, the mysterious man in question turned his gaze on me, surprise flashing across his features, before schooling them into one of disinterest.

I concentrated, desperately hoping to catch a thought from him.

"Solana," my mother said, alarmed to see me among so many people.

"I'm fine, Mom," I tried to reassure her.

My parents stared at me as though I had two heads.

It was the man beside my father that cleared his throat. "Solana, a pleasure to meet you," he stretched a hand toward me.

I grabbed it, and he added, "I'm Marc, an old friend of your father's."

"Gross."

The one word thought floated into my head, but I didn't move my eyes away from Marc.

"He was part of the original group of peace protectors here," my father explained.

Marc dropped my hand. "And this is my son, Rob." He motioned to the man, who stood frozen, not willing to shake my hand, even though I held it out like a fool.

Without warning, I heard the familiar buzz of a honeybee and turned to find it landing on my outstretched arm.

My parents acted as though it were normal for a bee to land on me. It *was* normal, but Marc and Rob didn't know that. The former studied it but otherwise seemed unperturbed. The latter, on the other hand, watched the bee in disgust.

I pulled my arm close to my body, afraid Rob might swat at it. He seemed the type to kill smaller, innocent beings.

"Solana has an affinity for bees," my mother explained with an awkward laugh.

Bees had always followed me around as if I were their sun. It didn't bother me. They didn't have any thoughts that gave me headaches, in fact, their sound comforted me. Soothed me. Made the noise feel more bearable.

Marc nodded, as though that little fact wasn't out of the ordinary. But if he knew my parents, he knew to expect oddities. His son, on the other hand, continued to stare at the bee, before glancing up at my face, as though he didn't know which one was odder.

"That hair."

I cocked my head to the side.

"Marc and his men will be accompanying us," my father explained.

My mother kept shooting me concerned glances, clearly sensing my emotions, but I ignored her, determined to figure out why Rob's thoughts seemed hostile, when his father was clearly one of my fathers most trusted warriors.

Our parents continued to speak about the logistics of moving an army across the sea, but I kept my focus on Rob. He never changed his expression, and only fleeting words passed through his mind. At least, those were the only ones I caught.

By the end of the conversation, I hadn't learned anything new, and was resigned to let them go.

"Solana, meet me in the library once everyone's gone," my mother whispered, squeezing my arm, before following the rest of the people out of the house.

I watched as everyone left, my eye catching on Kai. His brows were pinched, and a slight frown painted his lips, as he watched Rob exit the house.

Kai must have felt my stare, because he glanced over at that exact moment. There was something in the look—like he already knew me—that made me want to open the man like a book and read every word.

"Sol!" Lily shouted from down the hall. She was flanked by Mason who stood with his arms crossed, smirking at me.

"Don't turn around. I like staring at that ass."

Flipping him off, I turned back to find Kai, but he was already gone.

I stood on the balcony of the great room as most people left the meeting and parted ways with my parents. They drifted in all different directions, and I watched as they disappeared out of view.

"So, why do they keep you hidden?" The voice belonged to Rob, and I shivered at the harshness of the sound.

Turning slowly, I tried to smile, but I'm pretty sure it came out more like a scowl. "I'm special." I didn't hide the sarcasm.

He sneered. "Or powerless."

It wasn't a question, and that one word hit me where I was most vulnerable. Heat rushed to my cheeks, and I fought to keep a straight face.

Rob noticed, though, and his satisfied smile had me wanting to hurt him even more.

His eyes bounced from me to the railing I was leaning against.

"It would be so easy."

I cocked my head to the side, studying him, tamping down the visceral reaction I had to this man. "I thought you were leaving?"

"Seems my father wanted a private meeting with your parents." He didn't hide his annoyance.

I didn't know what to say to this man. What else was I missing? What role did he play in all of this? How much of a threat was he? What power did he really hold?

"And you just thought, 'Hey, might as well go bug the daughter who I clearly don't want anything to do with'?"

Rob glared at me. "What makes you say that?"

"Where do I start? Your tone? Your body language? Your th—" I cut myself off, catching myself a second too late.

Rob took a step forward, eyes narrowing. "My what? I didn't catch that last one."

Every warning bell in my body went off as he took another step toward me. I was trapped between him and the railing that separated me from a two-hundred-foot sheer drop.

Without waiting for my response, he grabbed my wrist and held it tight. Tight enough to leave a bruise.

"Get off me," I growled.

He leaned in until he was practically spitting in my face. "You all are hiding something."

Three things happened at once that prevented me from my retort. One, a loud buzzing sound filled the air around us. Two, the vines from the house reached for Rob. And three, Kai suddenly appeared in the doorway, looking ready to rip apart the entire world.

The bees got to Rob first. They encircled his head, and he dropped my arm, swatting the air around him and sprinting into the house, his screams echoing through the valley below.

Kai plastered himself to the side of the door frame as Rob passed, but the bees didn't touch him. They were only protecting me.

Kai locked eyes with me. His were wide with shock and possibly a little bit of awe, but before I had a chance to ask a question he disappeared, following Rob.

Slumping against the railing, I rubbed my sore wrist.

Rob's words echoed in my mind, picking at an old wound.

"Powerless."

I knocked lightly on the library's large double wooden doors a few hours later. It was intricately carved with a fascinating depiction of the Tree of Life. Animals, plants, and fungi of all kinds were delicately carved as the leaves of an ancient tree. The carving covered the entire double door, its farthest branches reaching fifteen feet high, and eight feet wide to the edges of the frame.

"Come in," my mother said distractedly.

Slowly opening the doors, I was hit with the scent of old books and rich soil. The scent that always reminded me of my mother. Taking a deep breath, I worked up the courage to walk over to the couch she was lounging on in the center of the library. It was red velvet and its legs were wooden, carved like vines. The red stood out against the greens and browns of the rest of the room.

If the house ignored me, it *adored* my mother. The library was always spotless, always smelled good, and always had the best vining and flowering plants winding their way along her precious books, as if protecting them.

She didn't look up, clearly absorbed in what she was reading. Along with growing ecosystems, she also had a habit of bringing back ancient texts that she would spend hours reading and interpreting. I never bothered to ask her what she was researching or what she might be searching for. Though I adored reading, I was more like my father. Fantastical novels were the only thing that held my attention.

I ungracefully fell onto the couch beside her and slouched into the cushions.

"The paint's dry, I hope?"

I snorted. "Yes, Mother."

She finally closed the book and looked up at me. "Is there something you want to say, Solana? Or should I start?"

I shrugged like I didn't care, even though she could feel my emotions.

She sighed. "The decision was not made lightly."

"So, instead of including me in this decision, you kept me in the dark for *weeks?* And on top of that, you decided to tell my brothers first, not me?" I said incredulously, still not looking at her.

"You're right, Solana. We should have told you."

I looked at her then, surprised by her response.

My mother threw up her hands. "What do you want me to say? What *can* I say? I'm doing my best . . ."

Now, it was my turn to sigh. I knew the truth in those words. I knew what she did for the world and what it cost her. I knew she always came home exhausted and still put all her remaining energy and effort into being a good mother. She *was* a good mother.

She shifted toward me on the couch, the book in her lap forgotten. "I know you won't understand my reasons, but there is so much more to what is happening than is shown on the surface. I *feel* it, Solana."

"But what does that have to do with me?"

"There are bigger forces at work here that even I cannot understand. I set out to rebuild our world, but it's so much more than simply growing plants and restoring clean water. The entire foundation of a stable Earth rests on people and our ability to work together and form strong communities and bonds. *We* keep this Earth in balance without even realizing our impact most days. What we must do is complicated, and I wouldn't be able to live with myself if I thrust you into a conflict you weren't ready for."

I couldn't help frowning.

My mother gave me a sad smile. "Solana, you are meant to create a new world—a world where there is no fear or hatred, where the Earth thrives along with its people, and where every creature is created equal and treated as such. You know how I know?"

"How?" I mumbled grumpily.

"Because I look at your paintings and see the world you're going to build. Your vision for this world is possible, Solana. I believe that with every piece of my soul. You will get your chance to build that world. Just not yet." She looked at me with those sympathetic-mom eyes, and I couldn't help but yield my anger just a bit.

"What if I don't want that responsibility? What if I just want to paint?"

"Then your paintings will inspire others to create the world you envision."

Inhaling deeply, I resigned myself to the truth she spoke. I didn't want to fight. I just wanted to paint and see the world. Maybe she was right. Maybe staying here would lead me right where I needed to be.

But how many times could I stay behind while it felt like the world was spinning on without me?

"Have I told you the story of the day you were born?"

I nodded. This story was well-known to *everyone*. "I was born under the Mother Oak tree, under a fire sun, and the bees swarmed the moment you held me for the first time."

"Well, that isn't the whole story," my mother said hesitantly. "You also came out covered in blue flames. You seemed unhurt by them, so I did nothing. When you cried out for the first time, the bees . . ." She trailed off, clearly struggling to explain. "The bees, well . . . they came out of your flames."

I just blinked.

She continued, "I had never seen or heard of any magic like that. I didn't say anything because I wanted to figure out what had happened, but I've spent all twenty-two years of your life scouring the world for any information that might help explain your powers."

"Another thing you decided to keep from me for *twenty-two years*." I regretted the words the second they slipped from my mouth.

My mother's face fell.

I sighed. "I take it you didn't find any answers?"

She shook her head, tears threatening to fall. "I thought it would happen again, and then we could figure it out together."

I stared at her for a while, unsure how to respond.

When she raised her head, she reached for me, and I let her pull me into a hug. "Your blue flame is unique, Sol. I just haven't been able to find anything about it. Your brothers' powers are well-known in folklore. But you . . ."

I pulled back, remembering something else that was bothering me. Something else that was different. "My hair?"

My mother blew out a long breath. "Red hair used to exist before the world broke. It was rare, even back then, but the gene disappeared probably a hundred years ago."

My mouth fell open. "You're telling me no one has red hair like I do?"

My mother shook her head. "As far as I know, you're the only one."

I had no idea how to respond to that. No wonder Rob looked at me as though I was an alien. I had every intention of telling my mother about the rest of Rob's thoughts, when my brother burst into the room.

"Dad sent me to get you," he panted, as if he'd sprinted here. "They've destroyed an entire village. The forest around it has been incinerated."

Chapter Four

Leeann pulled off a miracle. What was supposed to be two weeks of preparation got condensed into two days. Everything happened so fast, I didn't have time to process any of it, as I helped prepare for my entire family to leave our home—leave me.

Mason was given the choice to go with my brothers, and true to his nature, he agreed. He would follow Aiden anywhere. Even to death.

I didn't let myself think about him and avoided him as much as I could. It was enough that I had to say goodbye to my family. It was too much to say goodbye to him. There was so much that we hadn't figured out. So much we hadn't said. I was too much of a coward to face it all.

Even with the effort of purposely avoiding him, he cornered me in the treehouse, when the house was too full of people for me to comfortably be present. It was the evening before everyone was to leave, and I was escaping that fact more than I was escaping the noise in my head.

"You're avoiding me, Red," he said as I looked over the railing toward the wildflower field beyond the oak grove. The sun was setting, creating a rainbow of colors across the sky and illuminating the sea of green that covered our village.

I didn't face him. I didn't want to see the look on his face. "I don't know what to say."

He came up behind me, stopping only inches from my back. Despite my height, he was almost six inches taller than I was. "Perhaps you start with what's going on in that gorgeous head of yours?"

I took a deep breath. "I don't know what's going on in my head. It's a jumble of thoughts that I'm not even sure are mine."

"Red." His voice was low, commanding.

Reluctantly spinning around, I came face-to-face with his broad chest. He gripped my chin, raising it so I was forced to look him in the eyes.

"Tell me what I'm thinking," he whispered, an inch from my lips.

Shaking my head, my eyes filled with tears I refused to let fall. I didn't want to know. I was terrified.

He gripped my chin harder. Another command.

I had already caught wisps of thoughts from him the moment he set foot in the treehouse, but I refused to focus on them. I refused to hear them. What was the point? When he'd be gone in the morning.

I will find my way back to you.

I shook my head again, not wanting to hear any of it.

It's always been you.

In this lifetime or the next, you're mine.

"Stop," I said, squeezing my eyes closed. "I can't."

"What are you afraid of, Red?"

"That we will never have the time," I confessed, my words barely audible.

"Time for what?" He leaned closer, his lips brushing mine, and I felt his smirk.

Opening my eyes, I stared into green ones the color of emeralds. Eyes that refused to let me escape my fears. Eyes that held me captive.

"Time to let you fuck me properly."

Mason's eyes widened, and he released my chin, almost tripping over himself.

I laughed. "You wanted to know what I was thinking."

Mason rubbed his hand along the side of his face, smirking like a child. "Now I want to know more."

I shook my head. "Take what you can get."

"Fair." He stepped closer again, this time reaching out and tucking a fiery strand of hair behind my ear and lingering a beat too long, before slowly running his fingers down my neck.

I shivered. "Mason," I warned.

"Red," he echoed, leaning into me, until I could feel every inch of him pressed against me.

"Kiss me, idiot."

He didn't hesitate as his lips crashed into mine. I had imagined this kiss thousands of times. What it would be like. What it would feel like.

I had sorely underestimated it.

It was like I'd been lost until this moment. Like a piece of me had been missing. Our lips moved as though we'd had lifetimes to memorize each other. As though we already knew that our souls were entwined for eternity.

It felt like home.

Parting my lips, his tongue swept in, as though he wanted to devour me, and a breathless sound escaped.

His answering moan had me running my hands across every inch of him.

"Fuck, Sol, I need you."

"Mmm," I mumbled against his lips.

"One night. I just want one night."

Reluctantly pulling away, I found a look that terrified me. A look I'm pretty sure I was mirroring.

"We only have one night left," I said, still breathless.

"Spend it with me," he pleaded. "Please."

He didn't need to beg. I'd already made up my mind long before he found me in the treehouse. "I'm yours," I whispered against his lips.

That's all it took.

We spent our last night together tearing down that final barrier that existed between us.

Mason carried me back to my room in the early morning hours, his lips brushing against my forehead as his tear landed on my cheek. I held my eyes shut, unable to face this final goodbye.

He pulled back, and I knew that despite his tears, he was smiling down at me.

"You'll always be my light, Red. My way home." He sucked in a ragged breath. *"Keep that little blue flame burning. Let it light your way too."*

With that, he was gone before I had a chance to say anything.

It was then that I let the tears fall, until there was nothing left. Until I was worn out from it.

When the sun rose above the horizon, I stumbled out of bed, one more set of goodbyes left.

"You look hungover," Aelius commented as I fell into a kitchen chair. Olivia had made quite the goodbye meal. I inhaled the sweet smell of pancakes and syrup, bacon simmering on the stove, along with the scent of veggie omelets garnished with fresh herbs.

My father placed a cup of steaming coffee in front of me, and I breathed in its scent, sighing contentedly.

He sat next to me, placing a warm hand on my shoulder.

I took a long sip, coming up for air when I finally realized my entire family was staring at me expectantly.

"What? Do I have something in my teeth?" I asked, running my tongue over them.

My mother shook her head, tears glistening in her eyes.

"Mom felt you last night," Aelius mentioned casually.

My eyes widened as my heart rate picked up to an unhealthy level. "What?"

Aelius burst into laughter, slapping the table, and Aiden joined, winking at me.

"I hope you're not fucking serious," I said to both of them.

"No, but the look on your face was one hundred percent worth it," Aelius replied, still unable to stop his laughter.

"I'm going to fucking annihilate you," I said, rising and putting my coffee down, silently calling the bees that were just outside the window. Always nearby. Always listening.

Aelius and Aiden both shot to their feet, nervously glancing between me and the increasing hum of the hive growing closer.

"Mom!" Aelius shouted, as if she would save him.

Smiling, I crossed my arms.

I heard my mother's laughter as the swarm of bees entered the kitchen and clumped together on a hanging vine above their heads.

They kept their eyes on the bees as they settled, waiting for my call.

"Solana," my mother warned, even though her eyes were shining with mirth.

Huffing, I sat back in my chair, and the bees lazily made their retreat out the window.

"So, how was it?" Aiden asked, smiling like a child who just discovered a candy jar.

I shook my head, shooting daggers at him with my eyes. *"None of your fucking business."*

"Enough you three," my mother's voice cut through our silent conversation. "We're going to be late."

We all shut our mouths, the weight of the moment finally settling on our shoulders.

My father grabbed my hand and squeezed it. "This isn't war, Sol."

I wanted to believe him. I wanted to think it was nothing. But a force big enough to destroy a forest and village without consequence? A force that seemed to disappear without a trace?

It didn't feel right.

My mother stood, finishing the last of her breakfast, and motioned for us. We all followed, surrounding her and wrapping ourselves in a large group hug—something we had done since we were kids. Something I was glad hadn't changed.

"There is nothing more important than the three of you, do you understand?" she said, choking on her words as she squeezed us all a little tighter.

It didn't take long for Aelius to begin elbowing Aiden for grasping him too hard. "Let go, asshole."

That was typically how these hugs ended.

Aiden smirked, not letting up, and I reached around and pinched Aelius, who howled, "Ouch. Get off me!"

My parents chuckled, releasing us.

"Oh, how I miss this when we're gone," my mother whispered, and Aelius stopped his whining.

"It's time, boys," my father said, motioning for them to get their stuff that was piled by the front door.

They both grabbed me one last time, lifting me off my feet. They didn't say anything, just held me for a few moments, before they released me and raced to the front door, shoving each other to make it there first.

I wanted to memorize them in this moment. I wanted to remember them as they'd always been because I was terrified this would change them. I was afraid it would change us all, and I wasn't sure I was ready for that.

"Don't break an ankle while we're gone, Sol," Aiden said, already out of view.

"Yeah, watch out for those invisible cracks in the floor," Aelius added.

"Assholes," I replied, shaking my head, but I was smiling.

"But loveable ones," Aiden answered.

"Love you, assholes. Don't die. And, Aiden, I'll personally kill you if anything happens to Mason."

"Don't worry, Sol. I'll protect him with my life."

"I know you will."

That was it, as the front door opened and the two of them descended the stairs on their way to the carts that would lead them to the coast and across the sea.

My mother stepped in front of me and planted both her hands on either side of my cheeks. "You'll find your way, Sol. I know you will. And we will come back to you. That's a promise."

"You always do," I replied, though I still couldn't shake the feeling that this time was different.

"You are my sun, Sol. All the hope of the world embodied in one person. Never forget that."

I felt the tears, but they wouldn't fall. I'd dried up a well of them already.

My mother gave me one more hug, then released my face, lightly touching my father's arm. They exchanged a look I'd seen so often that I wondered if they were even conscious of it—a look of love, adoration, and hope. Always hope.

My father grabbed both my shoulders, forcing me to watch him, instead of my mother's retreating form.

"Continue to train, Sol," my father started, and I couldn't help my eye roll, which rewarded me with my father's bright smile. "You are so much more than you believe you are."

He'd said that many times, and I wanted to believe it, but it was hard to trust there was more to this life.

It was as if my father understood what was going on inside my head, and he squeezed me tightly. "There's a burning fire inside of you. Let it out," he whispered into my flaming hair.

"You only say that because my eyes burn like yours do," I mumbled, dismissing his words.

He was used to my obstinance. "All the more reason to believe it if you've got a little of me in you."

Pulling back, I rolled my eyes again. "The ego of the men in this house. It's a wonder mom and I haven't left."

My father chuckled, but the smile faded quickly, his eyes glowing slightly. "No matter what happens, promise you'll keep going. Promise you'll protect what we've built. Promise you'll find a way to *live.*"

I didn't want to think about never seeing my family again. It was something I just couldn't stomach. They were coming back, and I was going to learn to control my mind reading. Anything else wasn't an option.

Despite those thoughts, the tears finally spilled as I whispered, "I promise."

My father pulled me into one last hug, nodding over my shoulder at Olivia and Kat, who stood silently by—our chosen family.

And then they were gone, and everything changed.

Chapter Five

What was supposed to be a few months turned into two years. Two long years of painting, training, waiting for letters from my family and Mason, and learning to control what I allowed into my head.

It turned out Kai, the curious man I had met before my family left, had given me a gift I could never repay. He taught me how to fall into the deep ocean abyss, a place where people's thoughts couldn't touch me.

At first, the thoughts became softer as if spoken through water, but with practice, I was able to block them completely. It was an effort that took me two years to master.

I had never had silence in my head. Kai gifted me peace that day.

The real test came the day before a fateful letter from my parents.

"I want you to try something," Leeann said. It wasn't a question; it was a command.

Nodding, I waited for my breath to slow to its normal pace after a brutal training session. Our sessions had gotten progressively more demanding. It was as if Leeann knew something was coming.

"I want you to try to fight someone while also listening to their thoughts," she said, and as I went to protest, her hand shot up. "Hear me out, Sol. You would be able to anticipate every move. You'd be unstoppable."

I'd mastered blocking out thoughts but hadn't learned how to let them in when I needed them. I had tried a few times but failed miserably and ended up in bed with a migraine.

"Leeann," I started to say, but she stopped me again.

"Let's try to turn your mind reading into a superpower, shall we?" I almost laughed as she waved over the young man my father wanted me to train with before they left.

The man ran over. He didn't say anything, and his stare was frank—calculating. He'd likely heard about me and had already formed an opinion. One I probably couldn't change, no matter how hard I tried. It was such a common phenomenon, I rarely tried to make new acquaintances.

"Hewitt, this is Solana, Solana, this is Hewitt," Leeann said before launching into her directions. "Hewitt, I want you to try to beat the shit out of Solana, and she's going to simply try to stop you. She isn't going to fight back."

Hewitt must have had the same reaction as I did because Leeann laughed. "Don't worry, Hewitt, you aren't going to hurt her, and Sol," she said, turning to me, "just do as I asked. What's the worst that could happen?"

"I end up in a coma?" I said, even as I prepared my defensive stance.

Leeann crossed her arms, a corner of her mouth turned up. The only indication she was getting a kick out of the situation.

Hewitt stood there as though he felt the same way I did—unsure this was going to end well.

"Well?" Leeann said to Hewitt as she backed away from the two of us.

Hewitt took his position in front of me.

"Don't hold back Hewitt," Leeann instructed.

"Thanks, Leeann," I replied sarcastically as Hewitt began to circle me.

Letting the empty abyss in my mind relax, I was instantly flooded with thoughts from the handful of people still in the training area. I shook my head, trying to focus solely on Hewitt's thoughts, but he took a swing at me before I had a chance.

His fist collided with my lower jaw.

"Fuck," I shouted, rubbing my face and trying to regain my composure.

"Focus, Sol," Leeann barked.

"I'm trying," I shot back, "but there's too much noise." Hewitt circled me again, but hesitated, as if he was unsure if he should punch me a second time.

"Try visualizing a connection between the two of you," Leeann called to me as Hewitt quickly closed the distance between us.

I imagined his channel. The channels of energy my mother could see, and even if I couldn't see them like she could, one stream of thought trickled through.

"Her arms are protecting her face, so go for the gut."

Just milliseconds before he struck, I was able to block his punch to my stomach and sidestepped out of his line of momentum.

"Good!" Leeann said, before Hewitt went to make another move.

"Get her off balance, then hit her right side."

Moments before Hewitt struck again, I easily moved out of the way, and he stumbled awkwardly to the side of me.

When he turned around, annoyance morphed his features.

"What the hell?" he asked himself, and I couldn't help but chuckle.

My laugh didn't help his sudden frustration, and he advanced on me quicker this time.

"One-two punch to the face, that'll shut her up."

Not having much time to react, I barely ducked away from his first punch. As he anticipated my duck, I dropped to the ground and rolled out of the way of his second punch.

"Quickly, before she gets up."

Gracefully, or maybe not so gracefully, I stood from my roll and faced him. I waited for his thoughts, but they didn't give him away this time as he plowed into me with his full weight.

We both crashed to the ground, and I yelped before he rose on his knees above me, poised to punch me in the face.

"Left, right, then break her nose."

I jerked my head out of the way, and his hand hit the dirt. He let out a sharp breath between gritted teeth. I decided I probably wouldn't be able to dodge the next blow. Instead, I grabbed his balls with my hand and called my fire. Though I couldn't burn down a house, my fire was strong enough to hurt, and it was just enough pain that he screamed and leaped off me, where I was able to pin him to the ground.

"OK, that's enough," Leeann said, walking toward us.

"What a bitch," I heard Hewitt think before I released him and sank into the peaceful abyss in my mind. I had been called that more times than I could count.

Hewitt stood and faced Leeann. He didn't acknowledge me. It's as if I disappeared the moment the fight was over.

"You're dismissed," she said to him, and he raced off to rejoin his group of friends without a word to either of us.

"Listen, Sol. Work on focusing your attention on individuals. If you can do that, then there's nothing holding you back anymore."

She was right. I just didn't know if I was ready.

"They're coming home in one week," Leeann said, still staring at the letter in her hands. Olivia, Kat, and I were all packed into Leeann's office. I had sprinted there when I heard we'd gotten a letter from my family.

Leeann's face made my heart speed up, and I clenched my fists, waiting for her to say more.

"There's no other information?" Kat asked her.

Leeann shook her head. "No. One sentence. I don't believe that's good news, but we won't know until they return. I'll alert everyone's families." Leeann quickly got up and walked out of the room. The woman was efficient, that was for sure, but she wasn't one to waste time on coddling or speculating on questions that didn't have answers.

Kat and Olivia watched Leeann leave, their brows creased.

Kat sighed deeply, and Olivia squeezed her hand. "This can't be good."

"Why?" I asked.

"It's very unlike your parents to write with so little information and no explanation. They either did that because they thought the letter might get intercepted by someone they don't trust, or something big happened, and it's too much to explain in one letter, or the situation changed quickly, and they had to flee. All those possibilities are concerning," Kat replied, sounding exhausted as she let out a long, slow breath and ran her hand through her hair.

"We won't know until they're back. There's no point in guessing," Olivia said.

My excitement grew along with my terror. They were right, something was wrong. But they were finally coming home, and it was enough to temporarily keep the fear away.

Chapter Six

"Sol," Olivia nudged my arm, and I looked up at the deck as my parents came into view.

The last week went brutally slow, but we had made it here. The moment I'd finally get to hold my family again. The moment I'd get to make up for every minute lost with Mason.

I waved excitedly, like a small child, and they gave me tired smiles before making their way down the causeway.

Racing to the bottom to meet them, I crashed into my mother. She let out a startled grunt, before wrapping her arms around my waist and burying her head in my hair, inhaling deeply, as though she wanted to remind herself I was real.

My father came up behind us and wrapped the two of us into his arms, and I hadn't realized how much I needed them until now. I held on for dear life, their familiar scents wrapping around me, reminding me that no matter where I was, or where they were, they would always be my home.

I pulled back just enough to study their faces. They looked as though they hadn't aged a day, but there was exhaustion in their smiles. A bone-deep exhaustion that I rarely saw.

"Where are Aiden and Aelius?" I asked, too afraid to ask about Mason.

My parents stepped back from the hug and gave each other a look I couldn't read. "They're right behind us, but Sol . . ." my mother started to say.

I didn't let her finish because my brothers finally came into view, and I raced to them, anxious to give them hell.

When they finally spotted me, they froze, staring. I paused too.

Something wasn't right. They looked older, which was expected, but there was something deeper. A deeper wound that wasn't visible on the surface. I kept the emptiness in my mind, suddenly shaking.

"Where's Mason?" I asked, even though, deep down, I already knew the answer.

No one said anything.

"WHERE. IS. MASON?"

Aiden's face went ashen, and Aelius looked as though he might be sick.

"Sol . . ." my mother said, placing a hand on my shoulder.

"I'm so sorry, Sol," Aiden whispered, choking on his words.

"No. No. No." Emotion threatened all sanity.

"Sol," my mother tried again, trying to turn me toward her, but I didn't hear her as I collapsed to the ground.

A keening howl left my body. The grief, anger, and shock trying to escape. There was no shoving it down this time.

"How could you!? You promised me!" I yelled at Aiden through my sobs, who still looked white as death and hadn't moved.

"Mason told me to tell you . . ." Aiden tried to say, his words stuttered and filled with a mix of grief and guilt. His fists clenched and unclenched, itching to hold me. To comfort me. But my anger and grief were too strong. I didn't want him to touch me. I didn't want him to say anything. I didn't want to even see him.

He had made me a promise.

I cut him off. "I don't want to hear them. Those are *his* words. Words *he* should be saying. Here. In my arms."

Aiden stepped back as if I'd punched him, leaving me to fall back to the ground, curling up into a tight ball and letting the grief consume me. My breath became shallow and labored as I tried to suck in enough air between sobs.

The reality was, it was me, not Aiden. I hated myself. I hated waiting so long to tell him how I felt. I hated that we didn't even have a chance to find out what was between us. I hated that I would never get that chance with him, and I hated that I would spend the rest of my life regretting all of it.

I didn't know how long I lay in the dirt sobbing before my father bent down and gently picked me up. Instinctively, I curled up in his arms and leaned against his shoulder. I kept my eyes closed while the tears continued to fall. He carried me to a horse-drawn cart, and instead of setting me down, he held me close. I remained curled up in his lap like I had as a small child, and I let the world disappear as his warmth seeped into me.

I must have fallen asleep on the journey home because when I woke, I was in my bed, my mother curled up next to me, fast asleep.

Flipping onto my back, I stared at the ceiling. I was so wrung out from sobbing for so long that I felt physically exhausted and emotionally numb, so I just watched the shadows dancing across the walls, waiting for some semblance of myself to return.

"Aiden . . ." I reached out into the darkness for him.

"Sol?" His voice sounded surprised.

"I'm sorry."

Aiden didn't respond right away, and I was afraid he wouldn't.

"I failed him, Sol. And you too."

I couldn't help the tears that began to fall again. *"Aiden, it's not your fault,"* I barely choked out.

"It is, Sol. I could have saved him." Aiden was crying now.

"Where are you?"

"My room."

"I'm coming," I said, gently lowering myself off the bed.

Slipping out of my room, not wanting to wake my mother, I walked quietly down the hall. Aiden's door was closed but unlocked. I opened it slowly. The room was pitch black, but after a childhood spent sneaking into each other's rooms in the middle of the night to plan mischief, I knew where his bed was. I tiptoed over and lowered myself on the blankets beside him.

He stiffened, but I reached for his hand anyway and squeezed it. He didn't move.

"I don't, for one second, believe any of this was your fault. No one does. You stop that nonsense right now, you hear me? Or I'll kick your ass with my newfound grace and skill, OK?" I whispered to him in the darkness.

He didn't laugh, but with the slightest hint of sarcasm, he asked, "Grace? Really?"

I elbowed him. "Well, maybe not grace, but I have been working with Leeann every day."

Aiden didn't respond, and I wasn't sure if I was helping or hurting.

Finally, after what felt like eternity, he said, "I missed you, Sol," but his tone was so sad, I almost started crying again.

I nudged his arm. "I missed you too. Aiden?"

"Mmm?"

"We'll survive this, right?"

Aiden inhaled deeply, and I could tell he was trying to gain some semblance of composure before responding so quietly I could barely hear him. "I hope so."

I nodded into the darkness above, but I didn't have it in me to say anything else, so we both lay there in silence.

Before I knew it, we had fallen asleep, and when I woke, Aiden was gone.

No one told me what had happened with Mason, but I picked up bits and pieces from conversations and thoughts. After two years of peaceful negotiations with local leaders about resource allocation, my family was unexpectedly attacked by a large force of unknown origin. No one saw it coming, not even my mother. She had failed to notice any energy channels in the area. And no one knew why they attacked when they did.

The ambush came during a peaceful tour of a small village outside an ancient forest. When Mason was lost, Aiden went lethal, essentially sprouting a volcano from the earth, decimating everything. There were no survivors.

We still didn't have answers.

I was a shell of myself over the next year, as was Aiden. Each of us grieving in our own way, and though we had gotten back to some semblance of normalcy, nothing felt quite right. The world no longer felt so alive and vibrant and full of hope. Nothing I did changed that. There was no amount of routine, jokes with Olivia, fighting with my brothers, or even painting that could pull me out of the darkness his death created. Even the arguments with the house seemed less important, though it gave a valiant effort, tripping me up at every opportunity, in an effort to get me to laugh again.

Perhaps, one day, I would.

I couldn't bring myself to go back to the treehouse, not after what had happened between Mason and me there. The memory from that day left me haunted.

Furthermore, nothing had come of the attack, and everything seemed as though it had gone back to normal. Everyone seemed to have forgotten.

Except, Mason was still gone.

"Sol?" Lily's voice drifted to me from the doorway, as I immersed myself in my art.

This painting was of the forest that was being threatened by the mysterious army. My mother had described the forest in detail. Though she hadn't described a stone archway, I added one that led into a dark forest beyond. My imagination wrote strange words on the archway, ones I didn't understand, but they seemed important somehow. In front of the archway was a beautiful wildflower field. Shadows crept out from the forest as if reaching for the flowers. As if they wanted to steal their light.

"Mmmhmm?" I replied, continuing to stare at my latest painting.

"I'm going away," she said softly.

"Oh, yeah?" I replied, not really registering what she had just said.

"Sol, look at me." Her tone was firm.

Doing as she asked, I found her brow furrowed, the concern obvious. I waved her off.

"No, Sol, I need to talk to you. This is serious. Don't act like shit doesn't exist anymore. It isn't fair to the rest of us."

I looked at her for a long while. "I'm not acting like shit doesn't exist, Lil. I'm trying to figure out how to navigate everything. I'm sorry if I'm fucking it up."

Lily sighed as she approached me. "You aren't fucking it up, Sol, I just need you right now."

I raised my brow.

"Your parents are afraid there will be retaliation for what your brother did. Though the enemy's army, and all of their supplies were wiped out, and it will take them years to rebuild, there are rumors of small-scale planned attacks overseas. I'm going over there to see what I can dig up."

This was the first I'd heard of any rumors.

"There are also strange things happening near where . . ." She trailed off, not wanting to say the words—where Mason died.

I perked up. "What kind of things?"

"Trees that look like they've been struck with lightning, but there haven't been any storms. People disappearing without a trace, in alarming numbers."

"No bodies?"

"Nothing. Just . . . gone."

My heartrate picked up. None of what happened to my family, or what Lily was explaining made any sense. Unless we weren't the only magic users.

I shuddered at the thought.

"There's more," she continued, pausing to take a deep breath. Her eyes wandered around the room, making sure no one else could hear us.

"Messages written on stone, trees, and the boat docks." She paused, her eyes searing into mine. "They want you dead or alive. All of you."

The information wasn't shocking, but it also made my heart pound. This was a direct threat. What else didn't we know?

"Do my parents know?"

Lily nodded. "I told them before coming to you."

"And why exactly have you come to me?"

Lily smiled coyly. "Sol, get yourself put back together, and then come find me, will you?" Lily asked, slowly backing away.

My eyes widened.

"I heard that mind reading of yours makes you quite the asset. Use it. Like I said, when you're ready, join me." With that, she was out the door on silent feet. Disappearing like a phantom in the night.

There was tension in the air when I entered the house after spending time in town. My parents and brothers had taken a weekend trip to a neighboring city to address a conflict of which the details were fuzzy in my head. I'd often zone out when the plans didn't involve me. Which happened a lot.

But the feeling in the air had me freezing just past the threshold. My body prepared for a threat, though there were no outward signs of danger or conflict.

The house was unusually quiet.

I stared up at the ceiling. "Care to point me in the right direction? I already know something's wrong."

The house complied. No pranks.

That didn't bode well.

A vine unfurled, pointing toward our makeshift infirmary that Olivia had created and kept running through the years. She attended to all manner of people from our own village and beyond.

I sucked in a deep breath, trying not to think of worst-case scenarios, but apparently my brain had other plans. By the time I reached the door to the infirmary, I was almost in a full-blown panic attack.

Placing one hand on my rapid heart and the other on the handle, I twisted and pushed.

The first thing I noticed was the tense silence. Then the *drip, drip* of blood falling from the bed, which was concealed from view by the forms of my entire family. The feel of my mother's magic.

A vine curled up my spine and pushed me forward, temporarily distracting me from my terror.

As I carefully stepped toward the head of the bed, the familiar sight of Aiden's wild brown hair caught my attention, sprawled across a white pillowcase.

Kat stood next to Olivia at the head of the bed, her arm clinging to Olivia's waist. She was rigid against her. But it was Olivia's face that made me halt once again.

It was white, and it wasn't grief, it was fear written across her features. A look I'd never seen from her.

Aelius' blue eyes caught me from across the bed. His young face was streaked with tears.

"What?" was all I could manage to choke out into his head.

His eyes softened and he beckoned me to his side. *"He was intentionally attacked. But he'll be OK. Mom got to him quickly, and Dad and I captured the assailant."*

I didn't know what to make of that information as I stepped to Aelius' side. Blurry eyes from around the bed rose to meet mine as I finally lowered my gaze to Aiden.

He was still, his eyes closed as though fast asleep. A sword stuck through his chest, straight through his heart. Blood dripped from the wound, staining the sheets crimson. The linens were so saturated with his blood, that it dripped to the floor.

I audibly gasped.

"Mom has it under control. She's replenishing his energy channel before she pulls out the sword."

I nodded, unable to tear my eyes away from his heart, aware that my own heart was slowly bleeding out from the inside.

Aelius reached over and grabbed my hand, squeezing lightly.

Why were the people we'd been trying to help for years suddenly turning on us? It didn't make sense.

Everything was too much. Like the rug had been pulled from under me and I was free falling, unable to control the descent. Unable to control the landing.

As I watched my mother repair an injury that should have killed my brother, one thing became abundantly clear: I could no longer remain hidden. I could no longer be complicit. I could no longer remain silent.

As the tears fell, and my family stood, united, for what felt like hours while my mother worked her magic, I devised a plan. A plan I would see through, even if I had to go against my family's wishes.

As Aiden recovered, I found my parents in the library, wrapped up in one another on the red velvet couch. They spoke in hushed whispers, my mother looking as though she was about to fall asleep.

They both lifted their gazes at the same time, waving me over to join them.

I fell next to them, and my mother grabbed my hand. They were quiet for a long time.

It was my father that broke the silence. "It was retaliation for what he destroyed."

That information wasn't a surprise. I had guessed as much. But what did surprise me was that it had happened so close to home.

My father finished my thought for me. "We never anticipated what was happening across the sea would reach us here. We were naive."

My mother cut in. "We believed we were invincible. That no one would dare try to harm us."

My father sighed. "We still don't understand where the threat is coming from or who oversees it. It's not a single town or city or even country."

"It's clear that the threat is everywhere," my mother finished for him.

"So, what do we do?" I asked, uneasiness creeping into my voice. But it wasn't so much their words, which I had already figured out for myself, that worried me. It was their tired faces.

Though I couldn't read their feelings, it was very clear that they'd been fighting too long, and it was wearing them down. They were husks of themselves, and I felt my heart breaking further at the sight of their defeated appearance.

My father gave my mother a sympathetic look before turning to me. "The man who tried to kill your brother informed us there will be more attempts. I am heading north again in a few days with your mother and Aelius to hopefully head off the problem and find the source."

"And I'm going to meet Lily," I blurted.

Both their eyes widened, but they didn't look as surprised as I thought they would.

My mother sat up straighter, staring into my eyes. Hers filled with moisture. She brushed my wild hair out of my face, tucking it behind my ear. "Your father and I have discussed extensive options, and we are inclined to agree with your request."

I sputtered. It was not what I was expecting.

My mother smiled through her grief and exhaustion. "Only you will be able to get the information we need. Your skills could prove invaluable."

"You're letting me go by myself?"

My father put a hand on my knee. "We had planned for Aiden to accompany you, but his recovery is more important, and we cannot wait until he's fully himself again. We need Aelius for our mission up north, for the protection of innocents."

"They will not anticipate your presence overseas, since we've been attacked so close to home. At least for a time. They will think we are too busy protecting ourselves and our home," my mother said.

"Captain Fraiser will make sure you make it safely to Lily. Many of our allies are working alongside her and are aware you will be joining them. You will not be alone, and we intend to join you once we've secured our home and the villages surrounding us. If anyone can figure out this mystery, it's you. We have complete faith," my father finished.

I didn't know what to say. It's everything I'd ever wanted, but I still hesitated. I'd never wanted to go alone.

As I watched their tired eyes and weary souls, I became resolved to relieve some of their burden. I had made my decision long before this conversation, and me going without them didn't change that.

My mother released my hand and pulled me into her chest, my father's arms encircling both of us a second later. And, to my complete surprise, I heard the rustle of leaves before the house's vines wove their way between us all.

Maybe the house did have a heart after all.

Chapter Seven

The week before I was to leave, I locked myself in my art studio to pass the time and started painting the image that was permanently etched in my mind: Mason in the treehouse looking out across the wildflower field. For whatever reason, I believed that if I could get it down on paper, it would leave my brain, and I would finally be able to breathe.

Maybe I'd be able to go back to the treehouse.

The day before I was to leave, I finished the painting. It looked *exactly* like the day he left. It was as though he were so close—so real—yet just out of reach.

Extending my hand, I lightly ran my fingers across the dry paint, tracing the shape of his face I had already memorized. Remembering how he looked at me. Remembering how he smiled at me—like I was the only person in the world for him. Like I was *everything*.

My fingers lingered on his lips, and without intention, my blue flame sparked to life.

I didn't know what I was expecting. To burn the painting, maybe? But I definitely wasn't expecting to be transported into the painting itself.

It felt like being sucked through a small tube, and there was nothing I could do to stop myself. As I was falling through space and time, all I could think was, "*Well, fuck.*"

It felt like an eternity before I fell unceremoniously on the floor of the treehouse, and immediately choked, holding back nausea. A moment later, I found him standing there, real as the day I said goodbye.

I froze, not daring to move from the floor. I was unsure of what to do, say, or what the hell had just happened.

He turned his head, and that oh-so-familiar mischievous grin formed on his face as he looked at me.

I had to stop myself from sobbing.

"Hello, Red."

"I don't understand . . ."

Mason walked over to help me up. He felt so real. His hands were warm, his rough calluses scraping along the skin of my palms. He was just as I'd remembered him. He even smelled the same.

"From what I gather, there are alternate realities and different realms through space and time. We are in one of those different realms," he explained, chuckling nervously.

"But how?"

"You and your mother probably know the answer better than I do."

Shaking my head, I closed my eyes, thinking he'd disappear when I opened them. That this was all a dream.

He didn't. In fact, his grin only grew in the same familiar way I was used to.

My brain struggled with his presence, and I wanted to cry, to kiss him, to pull him back with me, but instead, I just stared at him like an idiot.

"Other cultures call this place the Otherworld. Seems you found a way into it," he continued, yet he didn't seem nearly as surprised as I did.

That always seemed to be the case.

I shook my head again and dropped my face into my hands.

Mason reached out and gently pulled them away. He stared at my hand in his, and when his gaze met mine, he had tears in his eyes. It was as if he didn't believe I was real, either—as though his hand would pass right through mine.

"You can't stay here, Sol. I can't explain why, but if you don't go back soon, you'll never be able to return home."

I wanted to stay with him. I wanted the chance we never got.

Mason brushed away my tear with his thumb as he had the day he left. As if he knew the war going on in my head, he whispered, "I'm so sorry we didn't have more time."

Anger bloomed in my chest, along with shock and grief. I wanted to punch him. Instead, I pushed against his chest. He didn't budge, standing firm and grabbing my wrists, holding them firmly against his body.

He let me struggle against him for a moment until I finally relaxed, my head dropping to his chest. "I hate you."

"I know," he whispered, pulling me closer until my body was flush against his.

We both knew my words were a lie, but he let me have my outburst and held me through it. He was solid, warm, whole, and *real*.

"Our souls will find each other in another place and time, and I'll be waiting. That's a promise," he finally said, his breath skating along my ear.

"I don't want to wait. You were *stolen* from me."

His hand came up and brushed a stray strand of wild hair out of my face. His eyes were soft, understanding, and absolutely devastated. "I know."

I wasn't sure what I was expecting him to say. What could he say? But, somehow, it wasn't good enough for me. I wanted to rage against him. Force him to come back with me. Consequences be damned.

He saw all of that in my face and had the audacity to chuckle. "I feel like I'm about to get my ass handed to me."

"You are."

Without giving me a chance to let my anger free, he lowered his mouth to mine and placed the gentlest kiss on my lips.

My tears began to flow in earnest. "It's not fair."

"It's not, but you must *live*, Sol. You must do that for me, but more importantly, you must do it for *yourself*. I'll always be with you." He brushed his fingers lightly against the inside of my wrist. "Here."

A faint white image formed on my skin. A small jasmine flower, barely visible, covered the skin over the pulse of my beating heart. "A reminder of me, with a sprinkle of hope for the future," he whispered into my lips as he kissed me again.

This time, the kiss wasn't gentle. It was binding. It was a promise.

Mason stepped back, leaving me to reach for nothing but air. "You must go; the way is only open for a short time. Tell Aiden it wasn't his fault. Tell him I chose it. I chose it for him, for you, and everyone. I have no regrets."

I nodded, sobbing now, completely unable to speak, unable to let him go, and yet I had no choice. There had never been a choice.

He pulled me into one last hug. I inhaled deeply, trying to memorize him.

"Burn that painting, as much as it will pain you to do so. Keep the image in your heart, but don't let it consume you," he said into my hair.

"I can't," I choked out. "It feels like it's all I have left of you."

"You have always had, and will always have, all of me. All you have to do is look for it. There is no place you can travel that my soul won't follow. Remember, energy is never lost. Mine will follow you until the end of time."

"I love you," I breathed into his chest, wanting to say so much more but unable to. Unable to speak past the tears. Unable to speak the truth that was in my heart. He was my beginning, and I wanted him to be my end too. That my soul would never leave him, even when we were separated by worlds.

It was the only thought that allowed me to close my eyes. The only thought that allowed me yet another goodbye I wasn't prepared for.

A moment later, I was falling, and I opened my eyes to blackness, as the feeling got stronger. Shutting my eyes tightly, I tried not to think about the rising nausea in the pit of my stomach.

I didn't know how long I had fallen, but eventually, I stopped. Seeing light behind my eyelids, I opened them and blinked a few times. I was lying on the floor of my art studio in front of the painting. Right back where I had started.

Rising slowly, I dusted myself off, before looking at the painting one last time. I didn't want to destroy it, but deep down, I knew Mason was right. I couldn't let it hold me back anymore.

The painting had changed. Instead of staring at the back of Mason's head as he looked out over the field, he had his head turned toward the viewer, and that mischievous grin was plastered on his face.

I laughed and sobbed all at once.

"Fucker," I said into the void, and I swore I heard him chuckle in my head.

Remembering my wrist, then, I glanced down. If you hadn't looked closely, you would never have seen it, but there it was—a beautiful white jasmine flower. Whatever had just happened was real. Here was the proof.

Holding my wrist over my beating heart, I whispered, "Thank you."

"OK," I said, louder this time. "I'm ready," though I sure as hell didn't feel ready. I would never be ready.

Taking a deep breath, I torched the painting. As I watched it burn, the ashes falling to the floor, I decided it was about time I finally cleaned my studio.

"Holy shit," Aelius said from the doorway, hours later.

"Where's the painting of Mason?" Aiden asked, searching the room.

"I torched it," I replied, bending down to sweep up the last pile of dust, dirt, ash, and dried plant matter. The house had been oddly silent through the whole cleanup process.

"What?" I could hear the shock in Aiden's voice.

I paused my cleaning. "It's a long story . . ."

He tilted his head in question, and I sighed deeply. Then I walked over and deposited the last pile of dirt into the trash basket by the door.

"Better get comfortable," I told them, and they found a seat by the window.

Pacing back and forth, I tried to explain what had just happened.

When I finished, I turned to Aiden, who had tears in his eyes. "He told me to tell you that he chose it. It wasn't your fault, Aiden. You can't let it eat you up," I said to him, my voice beginning to break.

"Fuck," Aiden replied, burying his face in his hands.

"So, let me get this straight," Aelius finally chimed in, "you're leaving tomorrow, and you traveled to the Otherworld and talked to Mason, and then torched your painting. And *then*, on top of that, you decided that *now* was the time to finally clean your art studio?"

Aiden and I glanced at each other, and then we all burst out laughing and sobbing simultaneously.

I managed to squeak through my laughter, "I don't think it's ever been clean."

"Well, Mom and the house will certainly be pleased that they don't have to do it after you leave," Aelius replied, a smirk still on his face.

It took us all a few minutes to settle ourselves, and then we sat in companionable silence for a while.

"What now?" Aelius finally asked.

Aiden and I looked at each other and shrugged.

"We move forward together?" I offered, and they nodded solemnly.

Chapter Eight

The next day came quicker than I expected, and before I knew it, I was standing in front of Captain Fraiser's ship, looking up at the large wooden boat and white sails. It looked like all the pirate ships I'd seen in my fairytale books.

Inhaling the sea air, I closed my eyes. I'd been waiting for this moment for a long time. I was always the one standing on the shore watching everyone around me sail away.

Not this time.

My father put a hand on my shoulder, pulling me from my thoughts. He gave me an encouraging wink and a flash of glowing blue eyes, before leading me up the causeway to the deck. I brought only one bag with a few changes of clothes, some feminine products, a sketchbook, a small pallet of paint, and a few paintbrushes. I groaned when my father handed me a bag of weapons that weighed almost as much as I did.

"Don't give me that look, Sol. I hope you won't need them, but if you do, you'll have them."

I rolled my eyes but didn't protest as I threw the second bag over my shoulder.

"Liam!" a voice boomed from across the deck. Captain Fraiser walked toward us, smiling brightly. He gave my father a quick hug and slap on the shoulder before turning his attention to me.

"Ready?" he asked, and I nodded, as Aelius and Aiden raced across the deck and threw their arms around someone I couldn't see.

"I have you in your parents' cabin," the captain said as I peeled my attention away from my brothers and whoever they were talking to. "As there are no other women on the journey, this time, I thought you might want your privacy," he added, taking the bags from me and handing them to one of the crew members who raced off across the deck to a wooden structure on the far side that had a small wooden door.

"Thank you," I said, and he stared at me. I swore he wanted to say something else, but my father stole his attention.

"So, we'll hire another ship to meet you at port," my father began as I glanced in my brothers' direction again; they were talking to the captain's son. They were all smiling and laughing.

"Since when were you friends with Kai?" I asked Aiden.

"We spent two years with him, Sol."

"Oh."

"Come over here, idiot," he said to me, and I politely excused myself from our father's conversation, and slowly made my way over.

They were catching up on what had happened over the last year since returning. I watched them, and my attention drifted to Kai. He looked the same as he did at the meeting almost three years ago. He was still tall and muscular, dressed in what I only assumed was his everyday crew outfit: a white button-down cotton shirt with the top few buttons undone, revealing tattoos scattered across his muscular chest. He wore black pants, and black boots made for the water and rough seas. His hair was still long and dark, and pulled back, with a few stray strands falling across his angular face. If Lily were here, she'd be drooling all over him.

Shit, maybe I was drooling. I snapped my mouth closed but couldn't avert my eyes.

There was something different about him, though. Something I couldn't quite put my finger on. He held himself as though he'd lived a thousand lifetimes and emanated a presence that no human had a right to. Even my brothers, who could burn this ship and everyone on it, somehow seemed small compared to this man.

Kai paused as I approached, locking eyes with me.

"I can't read his thoughts," I said to Aiden and Aelius simultaneously, and that's when I tripped and fell right at Kai's feet.

My brothers burst into laughter.

"Always tripping on those invisible cracks," Aelius commented as a tattooed hand reached down. There was a pattern of waves etched along his skin that I hadn't noticed the first time he helped me up. An illusion of movement flashed across his hand, as though the waves were rolling.

I stared at it for a beat too long, before sucking in a deep breath, and accepting his help. He easily pulled me to standing, releasing my hand once he was sure I wouldn't tip over again.

The slightest hint of a smile graced his full lips.

"Ignore these assholes," I said sweetly, tearing my eyes away from his mouth, trying to pull myself back together.

Aelius rolled his eyes, and Aiden bumped me with his shoulder. Kai watched the whole interaction with quiet amusement.

"I take it these two dumbasses told you all about me?"

Kai nodded but didn't say anything.

"Yes, Sol, we told him you were a clumsy asshole who doesn't know how to keep her mouth shut," Aelius said, trying to bait me.

Aiden laughed. "Yes, he knows about your powers. Except you may want to fill him in on the one you discovered yesterday."

"You think that's a new power?"

"Are you serious, Sol?" Aelius asked incredulously. "You literally traveled through space and time."

Kai raised a brow but remained oddly silent, not commenting on the strange phenomenon or any of my other powers—not even acting surprised.

"Don't let her push you around, Kai. She's a softy at heart," Aiden chimed in.

"Do they ever let you speak?" I asked Kai.

He shrugged. "Sometimes . . ."

"Good luck with this one," my brothers said in unison, giving him a sympathetic pat on the shoulder.

I rolled my eyes, ready to make some snarky retort, but at that exact moment our parents approached from across the deck.

I watched from the corner of my eye as Kai backed away, giving us our space. He turned toward the sea and stood frozen as the wind whipped at his dark hair. I wondered how someone who grew up on the water could still be as enamored with it as he seemed to be.

"Time to go," my father said to my brothers, and they both nodded, their smiles fading.

No one was ready for another goodbye, least of all, me.

My mother came up and wrapped me in a hug, my father and brothers joined her shortly after. We stayed there for a while, and no one said anything. I felt the strongest desire to hold on to them forever, but I also felt the pull that called to me from across the sea and knew I had to let them go, no matter how much I wanted them to always be by my side. I think my mother felt it, too, because she squeezed me tighter.

"Well, shit. Our little Sol is all grown up," Aelius finally said in his best "mom" voice.

I elbowed him, and he released us, yelping.

Aiden chuckled and shook his head.

Tears welled in my mother's eyes, and she ignored all the pushing and shoving.

"I'll be fine, Mom," I said to her.

She nodded. "I know, but I hate this part."

"Me too," I said, pulling her into one last hug, trying to memorize everything about her. Her scent—leather bound books and the earth, her curly brown hair that always seemed a bit wild, just like her, and her petite size that was always shocking, seeing as all her children were much larger than her.

"Time to go, Willow." My father placed a hand on her shoulder, and she finally pulled away, her eyes still glistening with unshed tears.

"Be safe, my little sun."

I nodded, unable to say anything, as my own tears gathered.

I waved at the three of them as they slowly walked back down the causeway. They had stayed until the very last moment, and I watched until they were out of sight, my heart squeezing in my chest.

They were all I'd ever known, and part of me would always want to stay within arm's reach.

"You're lucky to have them," Kai said behind me. I hadn't realized he was still there.

"I am," I said roughly, realizing my emotions were closer to the surface than I thought.

I watched the shore as the ropes were untied; we were suddenly on our way. Kai stood silently by my side, watching with me.

There was something comforting about his steady presence.

"Kai!" the captain's voice boomed from across the deck. "I need you!"

Kai politely excused himself, leaving me standing on the deck, staring at the vanishing shore. I watched as my home disappeared into the distance.

When the coastline completely vanished, leaving nothing but a gray sky that blended into the blue-gray of the water, I finally turned to make my way to my private cabin.

I didn't make it a step before Rob appeared on the deck opposite me.

Well, shit.

Plastering a sarcastic smile on my face, I watched him walk toward me. Unlike Kai, Rob's presence had every cell in my body on high alert. I could still feel the bruising grip of his hand on my wrist. My body didn't forget.

Rob was very clearly angry, but I casually leaned against the railing of the ship waiting for him to come to me.

I instinctively opened the channel between us.

"I'm going to kill her!"

I almost laughed at the absurdity of it all—his anger and the fact that he was here in the middle of the sea, on the same ship as me.

"How lovely to see you again, Rob," I drawled.

"I'm going to smack that smirk off her face."

"Say, Rob, why don't we just drop all this and pretend like each other doesn't exist? You go your way, and I go mine?" I shrugged for emphasis.

"I know you set those bees on me," his voice trembled with anger.

I stared at my nails. "How exactly do you think I could've done that?"

"I'm going to throw this bitch off the boat."

I'll admit I didn't really try to defuse the situation. I found it all too amusing, and I wanted to teach him a lesson; I didn't think he got the message the first time.

Some crew members were watching us now, sensing the tension. It caught Kai's attention, and I watched him cautiously move closer. He was staring at Rob with murder in his eyes. It was the same look he was giving him at the meeting where we all first met.

What was their story?

"You set those bees on me, and I'm going to make you pay for it," Rob growled at me, inching closer.

Easing myself off the railing, I shuffled to the side, moving toward the center of the deck. I trusted my ability to kick Rob's ass, but I still didn't want to be trapped against the railing and accidentally get thrown off the ship.

"I have no idea what you are talking about, but I can sympathize. I've been stung many times in my life. One time my whole leg swelled up, and I couldn't walk for a week." I was rambling. It had its desired effect.

"She's a fucking liar."

"Listen, Rob," I went on, inching further away from the railing. "I understand why you might think it was me, but weren't you the one who said I was powerless? So then, how could it have been me?"

The mocking tone in my voice was hard to mask, and Rob clearly caught my meaning. I didn't have much time to react as he launched himself at me. His thoughts were loud in my head; I easily sidestepped his lunge, and he stumbled awkwardly toward the railing.

I turned to face him, as he regained his composure.

"Can we just skip this part?" I asked him casually.

Everyone on the deck stopped to watch the two of us. I wasn't proud of that, but it seemed inevitable.

"Never," he growled.

I shrugged, and this time he went for my head. I easily ducked and punched him in the gut. He grunted and took a few steps backward. A moment later, he had regained his composure and this time he went for my legs. I anticipated his every move, his mind was an open book, and I couldn't help the laugh that bubbled up my throat.

"You bitch," he said, advancing on me as a blade emerged from his shirt, and he lunged for my throat.

Barely dodging it, I heard someone shouting for Rob to stop, that it had gone too far. Some of the men started to converge on us, as I wheeled around Rob, grabbing his arm in the process and pinning it behind his back. I stomped on the back of his knee, and he fell to the ground. Twisting his arm further, he dropped the knife and let out a grunt of pain.

"Don't touch me again," I spat into his ear.

I twisted, until his arm was seconds from snapping. Pained sounds rumbled from his chest. That's when I finally dropped him. Rob fell against the wooden planks, and I kicked the knife out of his reach.

When I turned, I was surprised to find Kai right by my side. So close that his arm brushed against mine, but he didn't seem to notice. All his attention was on Rob.

"Touch her again, and you're a dead man," Kai said in such a low, menacing way, that even I shivered at the threat.

Rob glowered at Kai. "You have no authority over me, sea rat."

Kai stepped forward. A challenge that Rob was more than happy to meet, given his smug smirk, as he pushed himself up to standing using his good arm.

"That's enough," Captain Fraiser boomed.

The captain stopped before the three of us and looked around at his men. "Show's over."

Some of the men snickered as they walked away, but didn't hesitate to obey.

"Not you, Kai," he barked, and Kai halted. He didn't seem surprised by the captain's request, but anger was radiating off him, despite his stoic face. I thought I'd burn from the heat of it.

The captain looked between Rob and me. "You're not to go near each other for the rest of this trip, do you hear me? If anything else happens between you, you will both be locked up."

I nodded. "Yes, sir."

Rob nodded too, but his head remained lowered.

"Fists are fine, but we draw the line at weapons. Do you hear me, son?" he asked Rob.

Rob nodded again, but didn't say anything. He still didn't raise his head.

The captain studied Rob for a few tense, silent seconds before finally dismissing him. Rob left without a word. He never looked back, but his thoughts were still loud.

"This is not over. She will pay. Her whole family will pay."

The threat made me shiver. It felt different, like there was weight behind it, like there was something I didn't know. Something I was missing.

The captain considered me for a moment. "You're a lot like your mother, Solana."

"Really?" I asked. "She's always so composed."

"I take it you've never seen her in action?"

I shook my head. "Only on the training field. Though I've heard stories."

"Listen, I'm glad you were able to show everyone what you're made of. It'll make them think twice about going anywhere near you, but you also opened a door, and I don't think a man like Rob is going to let it go very easily."

"No shit," I replied, and then remembered the company I was in, and gave the captain an apologetic look.

His lips turned up slightly, in a similar way to his son's. "I want Kai to keep an eye on you at all times."

Both Kai and I went to protest, but the captain cut us off, "If anything happens to you, Solana, your parents will quite literally kill me. You're the only woman on this ship, and despite your particular skills, it still makes you a pretty large target. I won't comment on that mouth of yours"—he laughed—"but as much as I enjoy it, I'm afraid there are many who don't. Rob is a powerful enemy to have, as Kai knows."

I shot Kai a questioning look, and he just stared blankly at his father. I had no idea what he thought about all of this, or his past with Rob, and I was frustrated I couldn't hear his thoughts.

The captain continued, "I would just sleep better if I had an extra pair of eyes watching out for you, and I don't trust any of the other men." The last part he directed toward Kai, who nodded.

The captain waited for my confirmation.

I nodded too.

"Good. It's settled then. Kai, you'll move your stuff into her cabin right now."

The captain turned to leave but stopped at my words. "Excuse me? I don't need him sleeping with me too."

The captain chuckled. "He'll sleep on the floor, and he won't disturb you. You'll still have your privacy."

I nodded, because I didn't know what to say. It wasn't that I didn't want Kai there, it was more that I felt it was completely unnecessary and unfair to Kai. He didn't need to babysit me.

Captain Fraiser inclined his head and then left Kai and I standing there by ourselves. A few crew members chuckled, talking to each other quietly. They had clearly overheard at least some of the conversation.

"Why you?" I asked Kai.

"I'm his son." He said it matter-of-factly, as though it explained everything.

A grin split across my lips. "That's the only reason?"

Kai caught my smile, raising a brow.

"There has to be another reason."

He studied me with a sharp intensity that caused shivers to run down my spine. "I suppose he knows I'm the best fighter on this ship. Aside from you, of course."

"Interesting," I said, walking toward the edge of the ship.

Kai followed me. "Is it?"

Turning, I leaned a hip against the railing. "What makes you the best, and how come I'm just learning this information now? You're friends with my family after all."

Kai shrugged again. "Pirate attacks are common. I've been fighting since birth."

He said so little; I was intrigued by this man.

"You didn't fully answer my question."

"I didn't?" he said, coming to stand next to me, his gaze on the horizon.

I studied him for a minute, unable to help my roaming eyes. He was built like a fighter; there was no denying that. However, there was something harsher about him than my brothers or Mason.

He angled his head toward me, studying *me* now. Heat rose to my cheeks, and I looked away. He seemed to see way more of me than others did, and the fact that I still couldn't read his thoughts made his stare even more unnerving.

"You'll have to show me what you're made of, then," I said, pushing off the railing.

"And if I refuse?" He crossed his arms across his broad chest.

It was my turn to shrug. "It's your choice, but I won't believe it until I see it."

He angled his head, his lips tipping up as if he was amused. I didn't allow him a chance to reply as I stalked off to my cabin.

I guess *our* cabin.

Chapter Nine

"How'd your dad become a captain?" I asked Kai later in the mess hall, as I ungracefully stuffed food into my mouth. Growing up with two brothers, being shut away from most of the world, and being trained to fight men, I had to admit, my manners weren't exactly ladylike.

The mess hall was crowded, but no one joined us at our table. Most kept their distance, though that didn't stop their curious glances. One large man kept staring at the two of us with a rather mischievous grin.

He seemed harmless, but I kept an eye on him while we ate.

"It's in his blood. His mother is from an island in the southern seas. They were explorers, nomads, sailing from island to island. Eventually they made their way north, and my grandmother met my grandfather on the island we are heading to now." He stopped and took another bite.

That's the most words he'd ever spoken to me at once.

I waited for him to say more, but when he didn't, I asked through another mouthful of food, "And your mother?"

"Ouch, rough subject." The comment came from a small crew member that walked with a slight limp and was missing at least one tooth. Though he was about my age, he was much smaller, and it was apparent he lived a hard life. He took a seat close to me.

Probably a little too close.

"Mouse, get the hell away from her. Sit over here," Kai said, pointing to the seat next to him.

Mouse chuckled and dipped his head. "Apologies, lady, didn't realize you were so heavily fortified."

I couldn't help my laugh. "I'm a big deal."

He chuckled again, not taking his eyes off me.

"Mouse?" I said, as he sat down next to Kai.

"Nickname, though I don't think anyone has called me by my real name since I was a kid. I suppose the nickname is apt, given this," he said, sweeping his hand from his head to his toes.

Kai laughed, and the sound caught my attention. It was a deep laugh, but it wasn't so much the sound as the fact that he didn't laugh often.

"Well, what's your real name?" I asked through my own smile.

Mouse looked between Kai and I. Kai nodded, as if permitting him to tell me.

"Archer, my name's Archer," he replied almost sadly.

"It's nice to meet you, Archer. That's a badass name. You good with a bow?"

Mouse's eyes lit up, but he shook his head.

"Well, I'll have to teach you. Help you live up to that name of yours."

An awkward silence ensued, and I filled it by displaying more of my abhorrent manners.

"Mouse is a good friend," Kai explained, breaking the silence.

Mouse cocked his head to the side, staring at Kai as though he didn't believe what just came out of his mouth.

Kai seemed oblivious to whatever Mouse was trying to convey with his eyes.

Mouse eventually turned back to me when it was clear Kai wasn't going to say anything. "I enjoyed the show this morning."

"You saw that?" I asked, grimacing.

"Mmmhmmm." Mouse nodded. "Made my whole day."

"Glad I could offer some entertainment." I winked. "He won't fight me, though," I mumbled, jabbing a thumb in Kai's direction.

"He's afraid to lose."

"I'm sitting right here, you know." Kai's voice was low, deep, but strangely not annoyed.

"It's easy to forget you're here. You barely say anything," Mouse stated.

"He's not wrong," I commented after swallowing.

"I'm not afraid to lose to her."

"What is it, then, I wonder?" Mouse sounded amused, like he already knew the answer.

"I don't want more attention on Sol. It puts her in danger." His confession and his deep, rumbling voice gave me the sudden chills.

Mouse laughed mockingly. "Or you don't want the attention on yourself?"

Kai's gaze sharpened.

"Or perhaps you're afraid to touch me." The words sounded less strange in my head, but the instant silence from Mouse and Kai was telling.

Mouse grinned, trying to hold back a laugh, but Kai looked like I'd punched him.

I shrugged. "You wouldn't be the first."

"Excuse me?" Mouse asked incredulously.

"Because I have magic people don't understand, they're sometimes afraid of me, and other times . . ." I searched for the correct word. "Disgusted?"

Kai didn't utter a word, but his hands clenched tight, knuckles turning white.

"Who in their right mind would be disgusted? Look at you. You're stunning." Mouse sounded downright affronted.

I laughed at Mouse's confession. "Thank you, but I don't think it's my looks they're disgusted with."

"I'll fight you," Kai announced, which had me swinging my head in his direction.

"But you just said—"

"I know what I said," he growled. "I changed my mind."

With that, he stood and stalked over to the sink, deposited his half-eaten meal, and walked out of the mess hall before I had time to process it all.

Mouse and I both watched him go.

"What was that about?" I asked.

Mouse sighed. "I was hoping you'd be someone he'd allow in. Perhaps I read that wrong."

I had no idea what he meant by that. "Maybe I should go talk to him?" I offered.

"No. Best to just let him cool off for a bit."

Just then, a bell rang, and Mouse stuffed the last of his lunch down his throat and stood up.

"Been a pleasure, Lady," he said to me, bowing.

That afternoon, as Kai worked on helping repair a torn sail with a few other men, I found myself staring out at the bright blue sea. The afternoon was warm, and the sun shown off the ripples of the waves, creating, what my family always referred to as fairy dust along the surface of the water.

"Nice day," a burly voice said, and I swiveled to see a huge man leaning against the wood of the railing. It was the same man staring at me and Kai in the mess hall earlier.

I nodded, eyeing him suspiciously. Oddly enough, I still wasn't afraid of him. He seemed more like a teddy bear than a threat.

"I see the Cap gave you a babysitter?" It was more a question than a statement.

Pulling off the railing, I crossed my arms. "I don't need a babysitter."

The burly man chuckled. "Not disagreeing with you there."

When he didn't say anything further, I finally asked, "Is there a reason you're here?"

"No reason."

Narrowing my gaze, I watched the man inch closer to me, trying to be discreet but failing miserably. I was more curious about what the crew member was up to rather than worried about his proximity.

"I'm Eric," the man said, leaning even closer.

Offering my hand, I said, "I'm Sol."

Eric threw a glance over his shoulder, then turned back to me, smirking like a child. He grabbed my hand and gave it a firm shake, lingering longer than necessary.

I knew exactly what Eric was doing now, knowing who was across the deck from us, watching us with an icy stare.

Kai had stopped his work on the deck, never taking his eyes from us. Eric chuckled again, and I couldn't help but grin.

"You're doing this to rile him up." It wasn't a question.

The man raised a brow, but the corner of his mouth kicked up into a conspiratorial smile. "Want to play along?"

Blowing out a breath, I uncrossed my arms and leaned my hip against the ship. I may have also inched closer to Eric. "How long until he comes over here, you think?" I asked.

Eric chanced a glance over his shoulder, quickly assessing the situation. "I give it two minutes."

"That seems generous."

The man winked. "Perhaps you're right. If it were me, I wouldn't have let me come within a hundred feet of you."

"He's really committed to his duties, isn't he?" It wasn't really a question, but Eric answered as if it were.

"Yes, but I'm not sure it's *all* duty that drives him." He paused, one more quick look over his shoulder. "Not with the way he's looking at me—like he wants to gut me."

My chest hollowed out at his comment, but I refused to read into it.

"Also, you were Mason's gal," Eric continued.

My smile fell. Conveniently, I had shut away the fact that everyone on this ship knew Mason, my brothers, and, through association, me. They all had heard some version of me that I wasn't aware of. Some version of me and Mason together too.

A version that perhaps wasn't even me. Or a version that was no longer me. Not after I'd lost him.

Eric must have sensed the change in me because he nudged my shoulder, smiling. "I know our man is coming over here right now, about to drill into me for touching you. But I did want to say you won't find a more *loyal* man on this ship."

Another thing I couldn't ask him to elaborate on because Kai finally stepped in front of us. His eyes shone with icy daggers at the burly crew member still standing too close.

Eric chuckled triumphantly and took two large, exaggerated steps away from me. He then saluted Kai and meandered off.

I slapped my hand over my mouth to stifle my laugh, as Kai stalked off toward our cabin, not giving me a glance. He didn't utter a word about the situation.

"What?" he finally asked when we stopped by the door. "You're smirking like a child."

I purposely diverted the conversation. "I was just thinking about my idiot brothers and all the shit they stirred up about me."

"It's all lies?" he asked, sounding genuinely curious.

I shook my head. "No, it's all true. I'm just going to kill them for it."

The corner of Kai's mouth rose as we reached the door, but he didn't comment on my confession.

"Dinner's at six," he said, turning to leave.

"Sorry you have to be my babysitter."

He stopped and faced me, looking at me long enough to make me uncomfortable. I shifted on my feet, desperately wanting to know what he was thinking.

"You can take care of yourself far better than I can. My dad is doing it to make a statement."

I couldn't gauge his tone. I couldn't read anything about this man, which irritated me. Not only did I have no idea what he was thinking, I had no idea what to think of him myself.

"What kind of statement?" I asked though I could guess the answer. Eric had all but confirmed it.

Kai grimaced, looking like he didn't want to answer. "That you're off-limits."

"As in, sexually? Or . . ." I smirked, trying to coax that smile out of him. The one that lit up his eyes.

"In every way." He didn't smile, but his voice got impossibly deeper.

"Even to you?" I was toeing the line. I just had the strangest desire to see where that line was with him.

Kai stared at me as though trying to figure me out, and I caught his gaze as it drifted slowly down my body—agonizingly slow.

"Even to me," he finally repeated, turning on his heel without another word and stalking off.

I let out a breath I hadn't realized I'd been holding.

Chapter Ten

I woke the next day to the sound of a loud bell. Kai abruptly sat up on the floor. The blanket fell from him, exposing his torso. I couldn't help but stare at the myriad of tattoos etched across his body, covering far more muscles than any man should realistically have.

"Pirate attack," he mumbled, reaching for his shirt.

I sat up, suddenly wide awake. "Excuse me?"

"That's the alarm for an approaching pirate ship." Kai bent down and rifled through a bag, pulling out a pistol, a few daggers, and strapping a long sword to his back. He moved as if this were a regular occurrence.

I went to get out of bed and help, when Kai held up a hand. "Stay here."

I scoffed. "Absolutely not." Standing up, I aimed for the weapons bag my father made me take.

"Sol." Kai sounded conflicted, and I caught him running a hand through his disheveled hair.

"Kai," I shot back mockingly.

He shook his head.

"It's settled then," I said, pulling out my thick fighting leathers and a similar amount of weapons as Kai had just strapped to himself.

As usual, Kai didn't utter a word. Instead, he turned around as I threw on my clothes, and when I finished, we both headed for the door.

He stopped, his hand on the doorknob. "Stick close to me."

"I'll stick to you like glue."

Kai glanced at me sideways, eyes lit like I'd never seen before. I didn't know if it was the anticipation of the fight, or me. Perhaps both.

When he opened the door, we were met with complete silence.

"What?" I began to ask, and Kai put his finger to his lips as he walked to the center of the ship's deck.

There was nothing but the sound of light wind through the sails. All crew members seemed as though they had disappeared.

"What?" I asked again into Kai's head.

"It's our strategy. To make the enemy feel as though they outnumber us. They get cocky and sloppy."

"Just you?"

Kai winked. Actually winked, but said nothing as he drew his sword, the sound deafening among the silence surrounding us.

The early morning fog snaked around the ship and settled close to the water. I had no idea how they knew a ship was out there with all the fog.

Standing among the white mist, sword drawn, Kai was a god among mortals. I shivered, watching as he stood utterly still, listening. Waiting.

When the sound of a flying arrow pierced the silence and landed with a thud on the wooden deck, Kai moved, severing the rope attached to the end of it. I moved with him as fifty more arrows plunged into the ship. Like my father, my physical skills were more than human, and I quickly severed every rope within seconds.

Kai paused, watching me with something resembling amusement.

I rolled my eyes. *"You gonna help?"*

"Why? You're doing so well on your own."

Shaking my head at the jest, I went to stand beside him.

"It's not over," he said.

"I didn't think it was." I shot back.

"Watch out." Kai said far too casually as a large wooden ladder appeared out of the fog above, aiming to crush me.

I barely sidestepped as it crashed into the deck.

"Didn't think to warn me a bit earlier?" I snapped at him.

Kai just chuckled. *"They're coming."* Once again, it was far too casual, as if he were getting a kick out of this whole situation.

The pirates were on us quickly. Luckily, they had to scramble over the ladder one at a time and were easy to pick off. Kai almost looked bored.

"Is this it?" I asked, almost laughing at how easy it was.

Kai dropped his sword, leaning against the hilt, looking as though he were contemplating my question. I continued to send pirates to their watery deaths below the ship, their eerie screeching the only sound around us.

"No."

"Could you be any less informative? For fucks' sake. I see why Mouse gives you hell," I said, throwing another pirate off the ladder.

"You know, you could just shove the ladder into the water instead of going through the hassle of picking them off individually." Kai's

amusement swimming through my head made me want to smash the smug look off his face.

I huffed, grabbing the ladder and pushing it until it fell with a splash into the sea below.

"It's about to get a lot harder." Despite Kai's teasing tone, he wasn't joking.

At that moment, it seemed as though fifty ladders appeared out of nowhere, and pirates scampered quickly across them, looking for blood.

"My brothers rubbed off on you, didn't they?" I accused, sidestepping a rather large pirate that reeked of alcohol and practically killed himself.

"I have no idea what you're talking about." Kai feigned innocence.

I scoffed, twirling out of the way of two identical pirates.

"Why are you taking all this death so lightly?" I ground out as another burly, bearded pirate stumbled toward me, brandishing a sword as if he were a toddler.

It wasn't that I hadn't seen death before, but I hadn't ever seen so much in such a short amount of time. Part of me knew Kai was baiting me to take my mind off it.

"With pirates, it's them or us. Plus, these pirates aren't even human anymore."

He was right. These people didn't even look human. Their eyes were glazed, and their movements sloppy. They snarled and spit but never spoke. Some were covered in angry welts. Others were missing eyes and limbs. Their clothes were torn, and most were already at death's door.

I also couldn't hear their thoughts. But unlike Kai, it felt as though it wasn't that I couldn't; it was more that they had none, as though there was nothing in their heads. As though they were almost like the Claeg—the monsters my parents eliminated when my mother regrew the earth. Beings of death and destruction, only able to exist because the earth was dead or dying.

The thought had chills running down my spine. We weren't living in a dying world. We were living in a growing one. Weren't we? So, where were these half-dead pirates coming from?

"That's why none of the crew is helping?" It wasn't really a question. It was obvious that even without me, Kai would be able to protect the ship on his own, which was why he had barely lifted his sword and now leaned against the far railing, just watching me.

"Looks like I have the morning off too." I heard the amusement in his voice again, and it did something to me that I didn't even want to think about.

The pirates kept coming, and I slipped into a trance-like state, dancing around them and picking them of one-by-one.

"Enjoying the show?" I asked, clenching my teeth as I took on five stumbling pirates all coming at me at the same time.

"Very much. Surprised you haven't tripped yet."

At that very moment, as if he had predicted it, I tripped over a dead pirate while trying to block the clumsy swing of another sword. I rolled just in time, so I didn't land on my face, and instead landed on my shoulder. The pirate's sword swung above me, and if I hadn't fallen, I might have had a sword stuck in my side.

I scrambled to my feet, finally registering the booming laugh from behind me. The sound moved through me like wine, igniting me.

"You knew I was about to trip," I accused, taking on three more pirates. The middle one seemed the most human, and his sword swung with more accuracy, not allowing me any more thought or time to continue speaking.

Kai was at my side in an instant, though, helping me with a new onslaught of horrid pirates. I didn't have a chance to watch him, but I felt his presence never wavering from my side.

"The hulking shape of the pirate at your feet was a bit of a giveaway."

I huffed, as we both continued fending off the bumbling pirates.

"What is their goal with these attacks?" I asked. We fell into a rhythm.

"At first, we thought it was to steal our cargo. Now, we believe it's just to kill us."

I sucked in a breath. That sounded far too much like the Claeg.

"Looks like they're giving up." The moment Kai's words hit me, I saw the pirate ship turn into the wind, and a moment later, they were speeding in the opposite direction. They had left a few stragglers, and I finally got to watch Kai as he corralled them against the railing and then threw them over.

"I thought this whole operation was for me to see what all the fuss is about you. You barely lifted a damn finger," I said as the sound of the last body hitting the water met my ears.

"Why would I lift a finger when you did such a thorough job?"

I rolled my eyes, yet again, and stalked toward the cabin to clean myself up. I didn't mind that he didn't help much. It was nice to get some of my restless energy out, but the way Kai baited me threw me off. I didn't think he was capable of that, and now that I knew he was, I didn't want him to stop.

Mouse met us for dinner, and we talked and laughed. It was the same as the last meal. Everyone avoided us, though I could have sworn some of the crew members had slid closer to our table; Eric was the likely instigator of that little detail.

Kai was mainly silent through the whole thing, but he smiled more than I'd seen since meeting him.

"Heard about the pirates," Mouse said, looking at me as though I was more than I felt on the inside. An unexpected lump formed in my throat as I swallowed the food.

I shrugged. "It was no big deal."

Mouse snorted. "Not what Kai said." My head shot in Kai's direction, who was watching me. "He said you could take them out in your sleep," Mouse continued. "For someone who's an incredible fighter, you're awfully—"

"Clumsy. I know," I finished for him. "Fighting has mostly trained the clumsiness out of me. It comes out when I'm not paying attention."

"Those invisible cracks your brother spoke of?" Kai's mischievous voice surprised me.

I glared at him.

Mouse chuckled. "I get it. Fighting is natural for you. Normal human stuff is not."

I laughed, setting down my fork. "Well, I can't disagree with you there."

Mouse smiled wide. "If I were a great warrior and didn't look, well, like a mouse, I would marry you, Sol. We would go on great adventures together."

Kai choked on his drink, eyes widening. I'm sure my reaction was similar.

Mouse pretended not to have noticed.

"I'm honored, Archer, truly. I just don't think I'm the marrying type."

They both studied me before Mouse asked, "Is that because of Mason?"

Kai punched Mouse in the shoulder, and Mouse yelped.

"It's OK, Kai, I don't mind." I paused for a moment, trying to find the words. "Yeah, I suppose it's a little bit Mason and the fact that I don't want to feel tied to anything. I crave freedom."

"What about a partner, then?" Mouse asked seriously.

Kai chuckled. "Are you trying to propose, Mouse?"

Mouse turned a slight shade of pink. "No. Well, maybe. But mostly I'm just curious."

Kai laughed. "That is the worst proposal I've ever heard, and you've known her for how long?"

Mouse shrugged, his face showing signs of frustration.

"I'm honored, Archer. I could always use a travel buddy," I interrupted their conversation, which quickly spiraled into something uncomfortable.

Mouse grinned, and Kai went back to staring at me. I couldn't read the look on his face, which was becoming irritatingly common.

"You're much more of a lady than people give you credit for," Mouse commented.

"Don't tell my brothers." I winked.

Mouse pretended to seal his lips and throw away the key, offering me a grateful smile.

Kai had gone oddly still all of a sudden, not looking at either of us.

Mouse either didn't notice or pretended not to. "I'm sorry about Mason. He was a great guy."

"Thanks," I mumbled, still watching Kai and his odd change in demeanor.

Without warning, Kai stood and walked off. Mouse seemed unfazed by his abrupt departure, but somehow the whole situation didn't sit well with me.

I watched Kai until he stopped next to the sink in the corner, addressing another crew member.

Somehow, through all of it, it didn't even occur to me that he had also lost Mason. He had witnessed it. Lived it. Yes, I'd lost my best friend and the person I likely would have spent the rest of my life with, but I wasn't there. I didn't see it. Kai had. He was right there the whole time.

What else had he lost?

The man was confounding, and all it did was intrigue me. And why the hell did my heart rate pick up anytime he was near?

Standing up, I carried my plate to the sink. Kai was still in conversation with another crew member who was a few years older than us. The man stopped speaking as I neared, eyeing me with curiosity. Just like the rest of the crew had been doing since I set foot on their ship.

True to form, I tripped and would have fallen, spilling my dinnerware, but Kai grabbed my elbow, steadying me. He hadn't even looked at me. His reflexes were so fast that I didn't realize what had happened until I was standing upright, shoulder to shoulder with Kai, a dumbfounded look on my face.

The sailor looked between the two of us.

Shaking my head, I awkwardly patted Kai on the chest. "Thanks. That was a close one."

The sailor smirked, his eyes crinkling in the corner.

Kai cleared his throat. "No problem."

The sailor's eyebrows rose.

"Are you going to introduce us?" I asked Kai.

"No."

The sailor laughed this time, the sound was deep and joyful. I liked this man.

"He's grumpy," I explained to the sailor.

The sailor nodded but kept glancing at Kai, clearly waiting for some reaction Kai had no intention of giving either of us.

Narrowing my gaze at Kai, I crossed my arms. "One day, you'll crack."

"I have no idea what you're talking about," Kai said, acting bored.

The sailor appeared to be holding back another chuckle.

"Don't act dumb. It doesn't suit you." With that, I walked away.

I felt them both watching me, but one word trailed after me, and the deep voice that spoke made my whole body come alive like a spark.

"Chaos."

Chapter Eleven

S tepping out of the mess hall, I was met with the silence of the wind winding down the wooden staircase, ruffling my hair. Most people were still eating and chatting, but I needed air. And maybe I needed a little space too.

Despite my ability to keep out thoughts, some still tried to barrel their way in. I'm not sure what made those thoughts so different that they were able to get past my barriers. The thoughts felt as though they were traveling through water, sounding far away and so muffled I couldn't make out a word.

That phenomenon happened in the beginning of learning to control them, but I'd gotten so good at blocking, that it rarely happened anymore. Mostly, my head was silent unless I consciously allowed the thoughts in. And I rarely let them in. I found very little need to know what was in people's heads after a lifetime of hearing too much.

But occasionally, I still heard the faint whispers of thoughts. When I did, I couldn't help my curiosity. What made those thoughts different, that they might break through my walls?

The muffled sounds had me dropping my control, and it took a mere moment for my heart rate to kick up.

"Where is Mouse? So glad I won't have to see that useless fucker after tonight."

Swiveling on my feet, I raced back down the stairs and into the mess hall, my eyes frantically searching for Mouse. Every alarm bell in my body went off. I didn't know what was about to happen, but it wasn't good.

As dinner neared its end, there was so much commotion that I struggled to sort through the blur of people attempting to clean up their food and move on to their evening chores.

"He will rue the day he ever had contact with that bitch."

That bitch could only be me.

Dodging people, tables, and dinnerware, I searched for Mouse's familiar form.

"Sol?" Kai's concerned voice pulled me out of my search. He must have spotted me when I came back into the mess hall.

"Mouse is in trouble." It was all I could say, returning to my search, knowing I was likely two steps behind whoever's thoughts I was hearing.

Mercifully, Kai didn't question me. *"I'll take the left side. You take the right."*

Nodding, we split up.

It felt like a lifetime but was likely only a minute when I finally spotted Mouse's familiar limp. He was clearing tables, stacking dishes in his arms rushing to finish before the bell rang. My eyes darted around his table, looking for the person whose thoughts kept invading my head.

"Take out their allies. Cut the legs from under them."

Two things happened at once. First, the man in question approached the table Mouse was at. He was ten steps ahead of me. And second, I noticed the glint of a dagger at his side.

With all the commotion, the man could slit Mouse's throat without anyone noticing.

Pushing a disgruntled crew member out of the way, I ran. With all the strength and speed I could muster, I threw myself at the man with the dagger. Mouse was still blissfully unaware of the blade headed for his neck.

Colliding with the man, we both tumbled to the ground, the dagger flying across the wooden planks. The sound echoed through the mess hall. Silence followed, and movement halted at the sight of the impact and the weapon skidding along the wooden planks.

The man under me froze from the shock of the impact, but only momentarily. Using his size advantage, he flung his hips and bucked me off. I flew into the leg of a bench, where Mouse was standing, staring in horror at the scene.

The force of the impact stole my breath, and I curled in on myself.

Mouse glanced between me and the dagger, trying to decide which was more important. The other man did the same.

Time slowed.

Neither had a chance to choose, though, as a black boot covered the handle of the dagger, and a tattooed hand reached down to grab it.

Everyone stood, still frozen. No one dared even to breathe.

My screaming ribs throbbed, but my breath returned, even though every inhale felt excruciating.

Kai's eyes locked on mine, and he tilted his head in a silent question.

"He was about to slit Mouse's throat."

Kai's eyes widened almost imperceptibly. No one else would have noticed. Turning away from me, he directed his attention to the man. "What happened?"

The man stood up, dusting off his pants. "The bitch tackled me."

"Obviously. But *why*?" Kai's voice was authority mixed with a little malice. It sounded like he was seconds away from slitting the man's throat.

"Beats me. Why don't you ask her?"

"I already have."

The man's brows wrinkled in confusion as Mouse set down the plates in his hands and reached down to help me up. He wrapped his hands under my arms and lifted me onto the bench, falling next to me. His body acted as a support, and I leaned my full weight against him, clutching my bruised, but hopefully not broken, ribs.

"So, I'll ask you again," Kai said, stepping closer to the man, still holding the dagger. "What did you do?"

"Nothing." It was a simple word, yet that one word betrayed the man. It trembled as it spilled from his lips.

"You will be stripped of all your weapons for the remainder of the trip, and you aren't to go within a hundred feet of either of them," Kai said, inclining his head in our direction.

"That's bullshit." The man's words were whispered under his breath but loud enough for Kai to hear.

"Let me be perfectly clear," Kai growled, loud enough for the entire mess hall to hear. "This dagger wouldn't have gone flying halfway across the room if it had been sheathed, which means it was in your hand."

The threat was obvious.

The man didn't offer a retort, instead he turned on his heel and stalked out of the mess hall. Every eye in the room tracked his movement until he was out of sight.

When no one moved, Kai shouted, "Dinner's over."

That's all it took for the commotion to start again as people scrambled to obey.

Kai lowered himself onto the bench on my other side. I felt his eyes assessing me—assessing my injury.

"I hate to ask," Mouse began to say, but Kai cut him off.

"Sol says he was about to slit your throat."

Mouse looked down at me as I continued to lean into him. His eyes were full of warmth I probably didn't deserve.

"Who is that man?" I asked through clenched teeth.

Kai and Mouse exchanged a glance. It was Mouse who answered. "He's a traveler."

So, they didn't know him.

"He's after you because of me," I admitted to Mouse.

He shifted, causing me to almost fall off the bench. Kai reached out and steadied me. "Because of you?" Mouse asked.

Instead of answering, I addressed my question to Kai. "Is he traveling with Rob?"

Kai ran a hand through his long hair, watching as the mess hall cleared. "I don't know."

Mouse cleared his throat. "Why would Rob want me dead?"

"Something about my allies and cutting the legs from under me. I think they're trying to get to me by getting to you," I explained, exhausted from the day, the injury, and my uncanny ability to put those I love in danger.

"How can I help?" Mouse asked, and my heart tightened in my chest. Not many people would offer to help me after finding out they were almost murdered *because* of me.

Kai sighed. "Keep an eye on the travelers," he said to Mouse.

Mouse nodded, then looked down at me. "You need to get that checked out?" He pointed at the ribs I was clutching.

"My father sent me with a bag of weapons, and my mother sent me with a bag of herbs."

Mouse chuckled, his entire body vibrating. "Seems they know you're trouble."

I winked, slowly peeling myself off Mouse. "Well, that was fun. Let's not do it again, though."

Mouse winked back. "Deal."

Kai helped me stand, and Mouse escorted us back to the cabin so I could fix my sore ribs. Kai remained silent but tense. His eyes scanned every person on the ship, as we climbed the narrow wooden steps from the mess hall to the deck, and then to our cabin. Most were smart enough not to draw his attention, but the travelers didn't know Kai as the crew did.

"See the group standing by the mast?" Kai whispered to Mouse. "See if you can find out if they're connected to Rob in any way."

Mouse nodded almost imperceptibly, then peeled away from us, headed for the storage room close to the mast.

Keeping my gaze focused on the cabin, I held my body as straight as I could, given my injury, aiming to look unaffected by what had just happened. But inwardly, everything hurt. And not just my ribs.

"I don't want him in any danger," I said to Kai as he unlocked the door to our cabin.

Kai didn't answer as he went straight for my bag of herbs. If he had an opinion, he certainly didn't share it.

Grabbing the herbs, he met me at the bed, where I'd managed to lower myself. He stared down at the open bag, his brows pinched.

"I'll find the correct ones," I said, reaching for it.

"Some of these would be useful for our crew," he commented, relinquishing the bag.

"You don't have medical or first aid herbs on the ship?"

Kai shook his head. "Just the basic wound care supplies."

"I'll ensure my mom fully stocks your ship when we return."

That one statement felt loaded. Like perhaps I knew, deep down, there might not be a return.

When Kai didn't respond, I looked up from mashing comfrey in my mouth and spreading the paste along my ribs. He made nothing of my half-exposed torso. Instead, he watched me complete my task as if he was memorizing my every move.

"I can teach you," I said.

His eyes snapped to mine. He nodded, standing, and headed to the door without warning. When he reached for the handle, he stopped. "I'm sorry."

"You have nothing to be sorry for. I'm the one who should be sorry. Seems I cannot go anywhere without trouble following me." I said as I wrapped a clean piece of cloth around my ribs, now covered in green paste, and tied a knot to secure it.

"Your brothers made it seem easy. But it's not much of a life." With that, he pulled the door open and stepped through it without another glance, not waiting for the questions he must have known I'd ask.

After he left, I stared at the door for a long time, wanting desperately to ask him about his time with my brothers. His time with Mason. But I knew he wouldn't talk about it. Or, maybe, he *couldn't*.

I wanted to know why he seemed to care so much. And not just about me, but about my whole family. It wasn't like he really knew me, and yet, it felt like he did. As if he'd always been there, and somehow, I hadn't noticed him until now.

There was so much hidden in him. And, for the first time, I wanted to know *everything*.

Chapter Twelve

---

*"*__D__*ead wind. Full moon . . ."*

"Bad omen . . ."

"The sirens are near . . ."

"Too many of them . . ."

"No sleeping tonight . . ."

"Maybe it's the girl . . ."

Shutting off the channels of thoughts, I shook my head. I was standing on the deck of the ship, helping Kai with the monotonous task of sweeping. The afternoon sun was warm, and without wind it felt divine just to soak it up. I didn't realize I'd stopped sweeping, tilting my head to the sky.

When I came out of my trance, I found Kai staring at me, and somehow, without saying a word, I knew he knew I was listening to the people around us.

I waved him off and continued sweeping. "Just wanted to figure out why everyone is so spooked."

"And did you?"

I shrugged. "Full moon, no wind, mythical sirens luring us to our death." I paused for a moment and then added, "Some of them think it's me." I focused back on my sweeping, not waiting for Kai to respond.

He didn't for a while, but I felt his eyes on me. They were always on me. "They really think it's you?" he asked.

I shrugged again, still sweeping, not knowing what I was so afraid of in his eyes. "I'm used to it."

"That's not something you should ever have to get used to, Sol."

If his voice held a hint of anger, his face held no indication of that anger.

"It's all I've known." Kai never broke his stare, his eyes darkening, and I quickly changed the subject. "Hasn't this happened before?"

"Full moons and no wind? Yes, they've both happened many times, just not usually at the same time."

"What happens on those nights?"

"No wind means no work, which usually means everyone gets drunk and makes fools of themselves. Everyone has their superstitions about full moons, of course, but it is usually just a normal night for us." I could tell there was something he wasn't saying.

"What are your superstitions?" I asked.

Though he looked serious, something in his eyes changed. "Don't have any."

"Oh, come on. You spend your whole life on a boat, listening to everyone's stories, and the sea itself, and you have no thoughts on the subject?"

He finally smiled at me, and I swear my heart kicked up at the sight. "Are you asking if I believe in sirens?"

"Sirens, selkies, mermaids . . ." I shrugged.

He laughed, the sound deep and rich and playful. Goosebumps erupted on my skin. "Well, since meeting you and your family, I suppose anything is possible, but if you're asking if I've seen any of those magical creatures, then no, I have not."

I rolled my eyes. "I'm not asking if you've *seen* them, I'm asking if you *believe* in them."

"Well, I suppose I do. I guess I have no reason not to, especially with you around."

Shaking my head at his jest, I found myself smiling. We fell into a companionable silence after that, staring out at the calm ocean.

"I don't like what you're thinking," Kai suddenly said, glancing at me out of the corner of his eye. I wondered how long he'd been watching the thoughts roll through my mind.

I angled my head toward him. "How do you know what I'm thinking?"

"I don't have to read your thoughts to already know it isn't a good idea." His casual amusement was back, and damn did I want it to stay this way forever.

I waved him off. "You've heard too many bullshit stories from my brothers. Plus, they're majorly biased."

Kai laughed. A deep laugh, that I felt everywhere, despite the fact he wasn't touching me. "Fair enough. But I still don't like what you're thinking."

"Oh, I *always* like what she's thinking," Mouse said, coming up behind me.

I whirled around and gave Mouse a huge grin. "See, Kai, nothing to worry about."

"Even more to worry about now." Kai crossed his arms, his muscles straining against his tight shirt, but his tone was still teasing.

Mouse pointed his thumb at Kai. "How'd you get him to smile?"

"I have that effect on people."

"Well, there's no denying that," Mouse replied, walking over next to Kai and plopping himself down on the planks of the deck and resting his back against the side of the ship. He placed his hands behind his head and closed his eyes.

"Done with work?" Kai asked, lowering himself down next to Mouse.

"No wind. No work. Thought I'd kick up my heels for a while and give the lady some more lively conversation. She's likely bored out of her mind hanging with you all day."

I couldn't help but chuckle, and Mouse grinned behind his closed eyes. Sitting down on the other side of Mouse, I relaxed against the wooden beams.

"I take it you didn't tell her?" Mouse asked without opening his eyes, his face still turned toward the setting sun.

I waited for Kai to respond, but he didn't say anything.

Stealing a glance, I noticed his face had returned to its normal blankness—as unreadable as his thoughts.

"I don't bite, you know," I tried.

Mouse snorted and opened one eye to look at me.

"Mouse determined that the man that attacked him, was, in fact, one of Rob's traveling companions," Kai said, avoiding the comment completely.

Leave it to Kai to change the subject when the subject was himself.

"Not surprising," I replied, sighing, as I leaned against the side of the ship next to Mouse, resigned that I wouldn't get anything else out of Kai, and I didn't want to think about Rob.

Somewhere, deep down, I knew I'd have to face Rob. I'd have to learn what he was really up to, and how deep his influence was.

How powerful he really was.

But, for now, I'd enjoy the evening with the rest of the crew.

The three of us sat in comfortable silence, listening to the soft creaking of the ship, and soaking up the warm sun on our faces. My thoughts soon drifted to my silly plan, and I smiled to no one in particular.

Though my eyes were closed, I felt Kai's gaze.

After dinner, the crew met on the deck, and everyone found various places to sit or lounge. Drinks were passed around, and before I knew it, crew members stumbled over one another, laughing and chatting. I watched them with silent amusement, slowly sipping on an amber ale that tasted like piss, but it was the only option, and I found I liked the buzz that eased my anxiety.

The moon rose on the horizon. On the water it looked twice its normal size. It lit up the night in an ethereal glow that softened the hardness of the ship and crew.

"It's beautiful," I said, walking up to the ship's railing, where Kai had planted himself and was staring blankly across the glassy water.

He turned his attention to me. Always assessing. Always watching. Always curious. Always far too observant.

"Nice dress," he finally said, turning his gaze back to the sea.

"Thanks," I replied flatly. I had changed into a rather plain looking dress. It was ivory and form-fitting down to my waist, and then it fell loosely to my ankles. The skirt was lightweight and flowed like mist when I moved. Kat had embroidered small ivory flowers into the skirt; it was my favorite dress. The *only* dress I ever wore. It lit up in the moonlight.

A whistling noise behind us caught my attention, and I found Mouse who, as promised, had dressed in his best outfit.

Kai held back a laugh when he saw him.

Mouse had put on a clean white shirt, much less frayed than his usual ones. The shirt was tucked into finely pressed black slacks, and his feet were bare. The outfit didn't stand out, but on a ship where function often overrode fashion, he looked a little out of place—just like I did.

Mouse glared at him before bowing his head in my direction. "Lady?" he said holding out his arm.

I couldn't help but giggle as I took it. He beamed at me proudly. I was easily a head taller than him, even in my own bare feet.

And then the music started, a lively tune making its way across the deck of the ship. Mouse and I grinned at each other.

"You didn't," Kai said, rolling his eyes, but a smile lit up his entire face.

With the moon behind him, he looked like something from a dream. Too beautiful to be real.

"Oh, yes we did," Mouse and I replied in unison.

"You should join us," Mouse said to Kai.

"I'm good, thanks."

Mouse shrugged before leading the two of us toward the center of the deck.

Everyone was staring at us now, but I was used to it, as Mouse and I took our positions. I had let Mouse choose the musicians, the music, and the dances, as I didn't know what the crew enjoyed.

We moved and twirled around the deck to the music. We both laughed at my clumsy movement and Mouse's awkward hopping due to his limp, enjoying the pure joy of the moment.

I let everything fall away when I danced. I lived solely in the music and the movement. Shutting out every other sound and thought, I let my body intuitively move. It was similar to how I fought. Nothing else existed but the movements my body had memorized.

Soon, there was laughter behind me as Captain Frasier came up behind me, grabbed my hand, and spun me into the next dance. I beamed back at him as we both fell into step beside each other.

After that, others got up to join, and their laughter was more beautiful music to my ears. I caught the captain wink as I spun past him.

We laughed and stumbled, and at the end of the song, the captain bowed. "Thank you for the dance, Sol."

I bowed my head. "The pleasure is all mine."

"Look what you started," he replied with a laugh as more music began to play.

"That was the intention."

The tension on the ship had completely melted away. The crew stopped thinking about bad omens, and whether I was a witch sent to doom them. For the moment, I wasn't what everyone feared. I was just me.

He stood there and looked at me for a moment as more dancers began to move around us. "I will leave you to it," he finally said, bowing his head. Then, abruptly, he turned and walked toward his cabin—in the opposite direction of his son.

There was something he wasn't saying. Something he wanted to tell me. I didn't know if it was about Kai, or about me. I guessed it was the former, though.

Like father, like son, I thought to myself with a chuckle that was most definitely brought on by the slight buzz of the beer.

I spotted Kai out of the corner of my eye, but instead of watching the growing dance party, he was staring out at the sea, as if there was something out there.

"What are you looking for?" I asked him quietly, so I didn't startle him.

"Just looking."

I dropped it, though he wasn't telling me truth. There was something in his eyes that I recognized now. Something that made it obvious he was hiding something.

"Don't want to join the party?" I tried.

"Not really my thing." He still wouldn't look at me.

Fine. If that's the way he was going to be, I'd find someone who wanted to dance with me.

As if hearing my thoughts, a large man stepped in front of me, and I almost barreled right into him. My eyes traveled up his torso to his face. I found it lit with a knowing smirk.

"Eric."

"Sol," he said with a wink. "Care for a dance?"

"Is this because you actually want to dance with me, or is it because of a certain stubborn ass?"

"Can't it be both?" he asked, holding out a hand.

I grabbed it. "Good enough for me."

Eric yanked me against his chest, holding me far closer than he needed to. The music had slowed, and we both swayed, turning every few seconds.

It was as though Kai had some magical sense of when I wasn't alone. It took ten seconds of dancing for Kai to notice. His eyes narrowed as he watched us.

Eric caught on, too, and I felt his chest rumble with laughter.

"You're trouble," I said, smiling up at him.

"Trouble tends to attract trouble." He winked, spinning me unexpectedly.

Almost tripping at the sudden movement, Eric grabbed my waist tugging me back into him. Our bodies were flush when the familiar deep voice that caused my whole body to light up, interrupted.

"May I cut in?" Kai asked, his voice so low it almost sounded like a death threat, not a simple request.

Eric winked again, then spun away from me, removing his hands from my body. "Of course." Eric backed up slowly, watching the two of us, and grinning like an idiot.

"You don't have to dance with me," I said, trying to walk away, but Kai grabbed my wrist, halting my movement.

"I want to."

Looking down at the hand that remained firmly wrapped around my wrist, I nodded, lifting it and placing it on my waist instead.

His hand flexed against my back, and he held himself stiff and unmoving as I reached for his other hand and put it in mine.

I stepped closer to him, and he took a small step backward, as if I'd sent a bolt of electricity right through him.

I chuckled. "Don't worry, I don't bite." I started moving, pulling him along.

It took him only a moment before he relaxed and fell into step with me.

"You aren't half-bad," I commented.

"I said I didn't dance, I didn't say I *couldn't*."

Laughing, I pulled him closer, and this time he didn't step away. It was the first time we'd ever been this close, and his scent washed over me, smelling of jasmine and the sea. The smell was familiar, somehow.

We danced for what seemed like hours but was likely only a few minutes. A slight gleam of sweat covered our brows.

When the song ended, Kai didn't hesitate to drop his hands, taking one giant step away from me. "Thank you for the dance," he said, his tone flat and half-whispered.

He didn't wait for my response, so I shouted at his back, "You asked me! Shouldn't I be thanking you?"

He acted as though he didn't hear. Mouse came up next to me, shaking his head in Kai's direction.

"That man is impossible," I said, as we watched him post himself up at the railing of the ship, back to watching the water.

"Try living on this ship with him for the last ten years."

"Ten? I'm surprised his sour mood hasn't spoiled yours."

"Never."

A few shouts of glee caught our attention. A few crew members plunged into the cold sea. Their clothes sat by the railing, and I grinned despite Kai's cold shoulder.

I looked to Mouse, who knew exactly what I was thinking, and we made the decision we wouldn't let Kai ruin a good time.

Mouse stripped, but I kept my dress on, and we both ran to the side of the ship and climbed up onto the railing. We shot each other a glance, nodded, and then jumped hand-in-hand into the ice-cold water.

I heard Kai shout as we fell, but I ignored it.

As I hit the icy water, I let go of Mouse's hand and let myself sink below the surface. When my body slowed, and I was suspended just below the surface, I opened my eyes to the blackness. Except, it wasn't complete darkness. Illuminated by the moon, inches from my face, was a seal, its eyes wide and knowing.

It tilted its head, the blue-gray eyes so familiar I almost choked on the water that made its way into my mouth. The seal made to move closer, its fin held out in front, as if it wanted to touch my face.

Bracing for the touch, but not afraid, I held perfectly still. Inches from my cheek, the fin transformed into a human hand, the skin pale in the moonlight.

The rest of the seals body had also transformed, and now I was staring at a small woman with pale skin, long blonde hair, and deep, knowing, blue-gray eyes.

I didn't have much time to register what was happening as Kai dove in after me. When the bubbles cleared, the selkie had backed up a few feet, staring at Kai who had swum up beside me.

Kai stiffened when he saw the woman, and the woman did the same. They remained still for a long moment, staring at one another.

I began to run out of breath and had to tear my eyes from the two of them, kicking frantically upward.

Breaking the surface of the water, I gulped in fresh air, panting frantically. Mouse noticed my panicked breath and swam for me.

"Are you OK?" he asked, concerned.

I nodded, remembering Kai was still underwater with the selkie, and I searched for their shadows beneath the water. Mouse followed my line of sight, his eyes wide in sudden understanding.

We didn't have to search long, as Kai's familiar shape moved toward me. He surfaced a second later, and though he didn't say anything, I could feel the anger in the way he practically dragged me to the side of the ship.

"Are you going to explain?" I said to him.

He stopped abruptly, inches from the ship, and turned to me. "Am *I* going to explain? Are *you* going to explain why the hell you would throw yourself off the ship into freezing cold water in the middle of the night?" he hissed.

"Kai," Mouse said, treading water next to us, but Kai shot him a glare that had Mouse snapping his lips shut.

"I assume you can climb," he added angrily as he turned and grabbed onto the ship and started climbing without looking back at me.

I sighed and then began climbing right behind him. Mouse followed silently.

The music on the deck had stopped, and if I had thought everyone was staring before, they were *all* staring now.

"Shows over," Kai growled at everyone before grabbing my hand and guiding me toward our cabin.

I didn't argue with him, and I didn't try to pull away.

When we reached the door, he dropped my hand and pulled out a key to unlock it. He held the door open but refused to look at me.

Walking into the room, I kept my fiery anger in my clenched fists, the blue fire itching to be released.

This wasn't about me.

Kai lit some candles, but the ice still burned in his eyes.

"What *exactly* are you so mad about? Is it that I don't follow rules? That I'm reckless? That I'm naive and don't know the ways of the world? Or are you mad because I now know your little secret?" I asked, trying to keep my voice from betraying my own exasperation.

Kai's gaze finally met mine, and there was something behind the anger in his eyes. He held my stare without saying a word, before throwing me a towel.

"Are you going to say anything?" I shouted into his mind.

A wave of surprise came over his face for only a moment. "No."

"Have you told your father?"

"No. And I've no intention of telling him."

"You don't think he deserves to know that his wife visits every full moon?"

"I'm done with this conversation. You need to change. The dress does nothing to hide anything when wet," Kai said, abruptly leaving the cabin, and slamming the door shut behind him.

Looking down at my dress, I muttered, "Fuck."

It became embarrassingly see-through when wet. I clawed at the wet buttons on the back of my dress. It was surprisingly difficult to unfasten them without help.

I should have heard them coming.

But I had let my guard down.

Chapter Thirteen

A handful of men swarmed my cabin and easily overpowered me, pinning me to the wall. They held my arms above my head, and one of them pressed his leg between mine, forcing me to widen my stance, so I couldn't get any leverage to kick.

They were the same group of men from last night, standing by the mast. The unknown travelers. Well dressed and alarmingly clean, they didn't look as though they'd seen a hard day in their lives. Except, they clearly knew how to subdue a person.

"Well, well, well. Not so tough when there is more than one opponent," Rob's voice drifted into the cabin ahead of him.

Guess that confirmed our suspicions.

I struggled against the hands that held me; it was no use. They had clearly prepared. All the men wore fire-proof gloves to hold me. And they clearly knew tonight everyone would be too distracted to notice.

What I wouldn't have done for an ounce of the firepower my brothers had at this moment.

"Need others to do the dirty work for you?" I spat at Rob.

"They were happy to help. Not sure if you've heard the rumors, but not everyone is happy you're here."

"Yeah, well, get in line."

Rob walked over, bending until his face was only inches from mine. His eyes spoke of hatred so deep I wondered how someone could possibly harbor such animosity for someone they didn't even know. Where was this sickness coming from? Was it brainwashing? Magic? Something more sinister?

He trailed a finger from my cheek down my neck and stopped at the neckline of my dress.

"Get your filthy hands off me!"

His response was to rip the dress down to my waistline, exposing my chest. I was helpless to do anything. I stood there. Exposed. Unable to stop the leering eyes of all three men.

"You sick bastard," I spit in his face, and he backed up a foot or so, wiping his cheek with the sleeve of his shirt.

"I'm going to enjoy watching you die."

The men holding me didn't move or say a word. They waited for Rob's directions. He was the leader here, and for the first time, I realized just how influential and powerful Rob was. Why the captain had made that comment about him. Why Kai looked as though he wanted to kill him.

"Kai!" I screamed into the void, before Rob ripped the rest of the dress off, and I stood there naked and shivering from both the cold and my own fear.

I'd never been in this situation and I had no way of defending myself. I had never been alone. I had the most powerful family always at my side.

They couldn't save me this time.

Not able to use my pathetic flame, and without bees in the middle of the sea, I had no way of defending myself. I was trapped. Helpless. Dead.

I struggled in earnest now, but the men held me firmly, clearly stronger.

Rob laughed. "Powerless without the help of your precious family. How does it feel knowing you're *nothing*?"

His words hit a nerve, but I kept my face passive.

"You should know," I spat, and unlike me, he didn't hide his reaction.

I'd also hit a nerve, and his face twisted into fury.

Maybe I didn't know everything about Rob, or why he hated my family so much, but I did recognize something—he hated that his father was held in such high regard with my family. He hated that, compared to his father, he was nothing.

He was a man that had something to prove.

Those men were always the most dangerous.

As the glint of a gun appeared in Rob's hand, his anger blotting out all reason, I closed my eyes and called something deep inside myself. I didn't know what I was doing. It felt more like a prayer than a calling, but seconds later my entire body was enveloped in blue flame.

I felt the hands holding me falter before the screaming started, and they dropped me.

Slumping against the wall, I opened my eyes. The men ran screaming for the cabin door, swatting at the cloud of tiny insects that pumped venom into their bloodstream.

The door flung open an instant later, and the men and bees poured out. As I collapsed to the ground, I caught a glimpse of Kai running toward me, barking directions to his men, demanding Rob and his companions be restrained.

I fell to the floor, pulling my knees to my chest. My body shook so violently I thought I might throw up.

Black boots stopped just in front of me, and Kai bent down slowly.

"Sol?" he said, his voice so soft and gentle I almost burst into tears at the sound. "Can I put this blanket around you?"

I nodded, without looking at him.

He gently wrapped me in a blanket and sat down on the floor next to me. He wasn't touching me but was close enough to feel his warmth.

"You're shaking, too," I observed.

"I'm trying not to kill him," he replied through gritted teeth.

"Oh."

I felt Kai's eyes shift to me, but I still couldn't bring myself to look at him.

"I should've been here," he whispered.

I didn't know how to respond. I didn't blame him. I wasn't even mad. But I couldn't say the words. My body was frozen in shock.

"How can I help you?" he asked, angling his body toward me.

"I'm cold."

Instead of going to my bag to find clothes, he went to his. He pulled out a large hand knitted sweater and trousers. "This is highland wool. The warmest there is."

I tried to smile as he handed me the clothes.

"Do you want me to go while you change?"

I shook my head. "Stay."

Finally looking into his eyes, I found them full of emotion—devastation, guilt, and something else that I couldn't name. For once, I could read everything in him. It poured out in a flood that almost stopped my heart.

He held my stare for a moment longer, and then dutifully turned away.

When I was done changing, I crawled under the covers, pulling them up to my chin and staring at the low wooden ceiling of the small, enclosed space we shared.

"Will you sleep up here with me tonight?" I asked without looking at him. I didn't think I could take rejection.

There was a long pause; All I could hear was the creaking of the wooden ship on the waves.

"Are you sure?" His voice was unsteady. It was alarming to hear anything other than steadfastness in his tone.

"Please." I didn't want to feel alone. I didn't want to be alone with my own thoughts. I was afraid of my dreams. The moment Rob had ripped off my dress, was the moment I realized just how sheltered I'd been, and I was unprepared for what was out there.

I was unprepared to be the person everyone expected me to be. I was unprepared to do it alone.

He nodded, likely sensing my thoughts that were quickly spinning out of control, and then climbed over me, putting his back up against the wall. The bed was so small that even against the wall, his chest was still pressed fully against my back, but he didn't touch me, instead, resting one arm above his head, and the other on his leg. His firm body was warm, and I wanted to snuggle closer to him, but remained where I was.

"He'll never touch you again. And I'll never let my anger get the best of me ever again. That's a promise," he whispered into my hair.

I inhaled deeply, the scent of jasmine and the sea washing over me.

⚜

"There is more to your attack than meets the eye," Captain Frasier said to the two of us from across his desk the next morning. It was covered in maps of all kinds. From known continents to obscure islands, to maps of the stars. I found my eyes scouring the many constellations scattered across the breadth of the wooden tabletop.

"What do you mean?" Kai asked.

He looked between the two of us. "I was able to get a little more information out of Rob's companions. It seems that there's an insurgency mounting overseas that is specifically designed to take out people like you, Sol."

"First, you make it sound like there are more than just my family, and second, you make it sound like I'm not human."

The captain sighed. "Your family alone is near impossible to kill, Sol. It would take more than one army to do so. So, even if you're the only ones with magic, I don't doubt it would take a lot of people and organizing to eliminate your family. Second, to these people, you aren't human, and it'd be wise to remember that."

"They're actually organized? I thought those were just rumors?" Kai asked.

"Seems not. According to these men, they were on their way to join some organization."

"And what did Rob say?" I asked the captain.

"Nothing. He's said nothing."

"And does his father know what his son is doing?" I asked.

"Unlikely, but that's also unknown."

"How big of an organization are we talking about? Do they have weapons? Plans? Is it just Sol's family they are targeting? What does destroying the forest have to do with all this?" I could hear Kai's anger rising.

"All unknown," his father responded sadly.

"That's what I'm supposed to find out. Lily should already have some information when we make landfall."

They stared at me, blinking.

"My father didn't tell you?"

Captain Frasier sighed, running a hand down the front of his coat. It was black and fitted, with silver buttons, and stitched with silver thread. There was no denying who he was when he wore it. He looked straight out of a pirate storybook. "No, he didn't mention that part."

"I was supposed to meet Lily and gather intel. I wasn't supposed to be in any imminent danger or even get close to that danger. Most of what we knew was hypothetical. We thought my brother had wiped out most of the threat," I explained.

The captain shook his head. "It's what we all thought."

"We should turn the ship around. Take Sol home," Kai said, and I immediately protested, but the captain held up his hand.

"We are two days from port. We'll dock, assess the situation, and then decide."

I let out a relieved breath, though I understood Kai's concern. But there was no harm in finding Lily before we made any big decisions.

"Listen, I knew Rob was a creep and that he didn't like me or my family. I didn't know he would take it this far, though. His dad is loyal to my family. But let me see if I can get more information from him."

"You're actually going to go talk to him?" Kai asked incredulously.

"No. I won't go within a thousand feet of him. But I have my ways of gaining information." I tapped the side of my head, and Kai's eyes widened.

The captain watched us, but didn't comment on my plan. "The other thing we need to discuss is their punishment. As it was on this ship, I have sole jurisdiction over what happens to them. All men know that there is no tolerance for that kind of behavior."

I shook my head. "It didn't get that far. I don't want his death on my hands. Can you ship him home in chains?"

"Your father will have him killed if he goes home," the captain replied.

"My father is a sensible man. He has dealt with far worse men."

"That I know to be true, but, Solana, it's *you* we're talking about."

"I'll send a message to my father. Death might be a more desired punishment for Rob." I shrugged. The captain was correct, I was my father's only daughter, and I could already see my father's glowing eyes and rising power as he was told of what happened.

"Very well. Is there anything you need from me?" the captain asked.

I shook my head.

Kai looked as though he wanted to say something. To protest. To stop me. But he kept his mouth shut.

Perhaps he was as afraid for me as I was for myself.

Chapter Fourteen

"We find out what Rob knows. I don't have to get close to him. I just need one of you to provoke him into thinking about his plans and motives," I said to both Kai and Mouse, sitting on the bed in our cabin.

Mouse tilted his head.

"She can read people's thoughts, Mouse," Kai explained.

"Oh, shit." Mouse turned toward me, his cheeks reddening.

I laughed.

"Don't worry, Mouse, I'm sure the second she heard all your dirty thoughts, she shut them out and hasn't had the nerve to listen to them since."

I laughed even harder, but Mouse looked like he was about to vomit.

"I've *never* listened to your thoughts. I wouldn't, not without your consent. I only listen to people's thoughts when it's absolutely necessary, or if it slips through. Believe me, before I could control it, I was in agony. You *don't* want to know what people are thinking all the time. It drives you crazy, not to mention the headache it causes."

I could tell Mouse wasn't wholly convinced that I hadn't invaded his thoughts. When I looked over at Kai he was looking at me thoughtfully.

"What?" I asked him.

He shook his head slightly, as if still surprised every time I talked to him mind-to-mind. "You still can't read my thoughts?"

I shook my head. "You're the only person whose thoughts I've never been able to hear."

Mouse was looking between the two of us, his mouth hanging open. "Why does it not surprise me that Kai's are the only thoughts you can't read?"

"Enough about me, let's make a plan," Kai said.

"You always do that," Mouse complained.

"Do what?"

"Change the subject or walk away when people start talking about you."

"I'm allergic to talking about myself," Kai deadpanned.

I burst out laughing. Mouse gave Kai a stern look. Kai simply smiled back at him sweetly.

"Well, I think Mouse has to be our baiter. Rob won't give Kai the time of day, and I'm not going anywhere near him," I said to the two of them once we all settled.

"Great," Mouse replied sarcastically, "throw me directly to the wolves."

Kai clapped Mouse on the shoulder. "Sol will be talking to you the entire time. Plus, they're locked up, they can't hurt you."

"I'm not worried about Rob. I'm worried I won't be able to stop myself from killing the bastard."

Kai laughed. "He's ten times your size."

"He's behind bars, smartass. I think that gives me the advantage."

"Enough, you two. You sound like my brothers." I huffed out a short laugh. "Let's get this done."

We made the walk below deck in silence. Anticipation and anxiety were thick in the air. I followed Mouse and Kai, but when I heard Rob's voice through the darkness of the cargo hull, I froze. Breathing suddenly felt difficult.

"You don't have to do this." Kai had walked back to me, whispering.

"Yes, I do," I replied, my voice shaky and hoarse. "If not for me, then for my family."

Kai nodded but continued to watch me. I was becoming used to his eyes on me, even though I still had no idea what they meant or what he was thinking. I came to expect it, though.

"Ready, Mouse?" I asked, still trying to take control of my breathing.

"Yes, Lady, I'm ready," Mouse replied, with a bit more confidence and determination than I expected.

I nodded at Kai who took his place next to me. Close enough that I could smell his scent of jasmine and the sea, but not close enough to touch.

Inhaling deeply, I told Mouse, *"Let's do this."*

Opening the channels, the thoughts of Rob and his companions came flooding in.

Bracing myself against the wall of the ship, I was bombarded with disjointed streams of thoughts. It threw me—the sudden onslaught. Kai must have sensed my distress because he grabbed my hand and squeezed.

I let him.

Narrowing my focus to just Rob's thoughts, Mouse's words suddenly became audible above the drum of my rapid heartbeat.

"Well, well, well. How the mighty have fallen," Mouse drawled.

"They must be all out of options if they sent you of all people." Rob's voice sounded far from defeat, and that alone had me trembling.

"Guess so," Mouse replied, maintaining his air of confidence.

"What do you want?" Rob growled.

"Just wanted to pay you a little visit. Talk about why the hell you would even think of touching her," Mouse snarled.

"And what are you going to do about it?" His voice was low and predatory. His companions snickered.

"I don't have to do anything, dumbass. You're already locked up."

Rob's thoughts were not quiet. Despite having just met me, he had very strong opinions, and they flooded my head.

"The bitch hasn't earned a damn thing."

I tried to ignore them. They were the thoughts of a mad man, and yet, something struck a chord.

What had I earned?

"What right do any of them have?"

"Whatever your motive for this little visit, you won't get anything from me," Rob hissed at Mouse.

"Anything?" Kai whispered to me.

"Not yet," I responded.

As if Kai somehow understood the half-lie, (though how could he?) he inched closer, still holding tight to my hand. Determined, it seemed, to remind me he wasn't going to abandon his promise to stay by my side.

Mouse went on, "So, why target her?"

The thoughts of the others finally poured into my head. But Rob's were still the loudest.

"She's not human."

"She's dangerous."

"She's an abomination. It's not right. No one should hold that kind of power. Her family has blinded the world to their evil. To their sickness. That sickness will spread if not stopped."

"We don't answer to people like you," one of Rob's companions snapped at Mouse.

Mouse ignored the comment, and continued, "What were your plans after we docked?"

They were good at keeping their mouths shut, but they were still thinking, and they had no idea someone could hear it all.

"You will never find them, because we have something you will never see coming. Because it's invisible." An internal chuckle followed the thought.

I stiffened, and Kai felt it. His concerned eyes met my wide ones. The information wasn't surprising, but it triggered a memory—Mason. No one saw that coming, and I was suddenly terrified of it happening again. I was terrified I wouldn't be able to find the information I needed before they struck again. Before they took someone else from me.

What were they hiding? What was invisible?

Kai held my gaze, and his face wasn't blank this time. It was full of question. But, it was full of something else. Something resembling desperation.

"So, you weren't going to meet anyone?" Mouse continued, unaware of my internal struggle.

More silence. Nothing but silence.

"If only you knew what was coming, you little rat."

"I'll enjoy watching them all burn."

"Power belongs to human men, not these . . . creatures. Certainly not women."

I wondered where the hate was coming from. He'd been hurt by someone, or something. That seemed obvious now. Women? Creatures? What had they stolen from him?

"Where were you going then, to check out the local brothels perhaps? Seems like your kind of thing," Mouse continued, and though it was meant to be a dig, it felt too real.

"You fucker!" Rob said as he violently slammed against the bars.

Kai shifted beside me, itching to move. From the new look on his face, he was ready to rip Rob to shreds. I placed a hand on his shoulder, holding him back.

He reluctantly released the tension in his stance, falling back against the wall next to me. Now, we were plastered to each other, our sides fitting together.

"They'll never find us. We're invisible."

There was that word again. What did it mean? How was it possible?

"OK, so that's a no, or maybe a yes? Where then?" Mouse continued.

Not a trickle of sound met our ears. Rob had calmed his anger, and everyone seemed to hold a collective breath.

"Did they ever think to check the forest they so desperately wanted to save? What morons. Right in front of their faces."

"Oh, shit," I whispered and clapped my hand over my mouth.

Kai raised a brow.

"We have a location," I told him.

He nodded. *"Should we get Mouse out of there?"*

"Not yet."

Even if I desperately wanted to get out of the heads of these men, I needed more.

"OK, so you won't tell me where or who, so maybe you could tell me if there are more bastards like you out there?" Mouse emphasized the last part, disdain dripping from his words now.

Rob laughed, but it wasn't a genuine laugh, it was one that fore-shadowed what he believed was to come. "Before long, you will be bowing at the feet of us *bastards.*"

I cringed at the promise in his voice.

"How many bastards are we talking about? Five? Ten?"

I snorted at Mouse's retort.

Rob didn't respond, but he didn't have to.

"Thousands and counting. Just because her mother 'saved' the world, doesn't mean she gets to control it. Time for a new order."

I swore under my breath. His hatred went deeper than I expected. But who started this war? Who was really in control here? Did Rob really have that much influence?

I racked my brain for any information I had on his father, and nothing immediately came to mind.

How I wished, in that moment, my parents were with me.

"Mouse, get out of there. I have what we need," I said, releasing Kai's hand, a bit reluctantly, and walking back toward the stairs that led to the deck.

I felt, more than saw, Kai follow me out, but he didn't say a word as we both emerged into the sunlight.

A few seconds later, Mouse came stumbling onto the deck behind us. Sighing, I walked over to the railing, looking out over the vast ocean. The day was calm and sunny. There was barely a breath of wind, though the ship still moved smoothly through the deep blue water. I naively thought no one would be able to touch me here, floating in the middle of the vast ocean.

There wasn't a moment I didn't think about what it might be like to be normal. To not have all this weight placed on my shoulders. To not be so different.

But then I thought of my family. Didn't they deserve a life of peace just like everyone else? When would we be able to stop fighting all the time? Fixing problems that weren't even ours?

These thoughts felt selfish, and I couldn't just sit idle and not help where I could. But that didn't mean I didn't hate that I didn't really have a choice. I was born into this life. I was expected to be the hero, but I didn't feel like one. I felt weak. Alone.

A single tear slipped down my cheek, and I could only think of Mason. Of what he'd say. What he'd do. And my heart *ached*.

Mouse and Kai didn't say anything but walked up and stood beside me. Silent support. I sensed they both knew what was going through my head.

"Thank you, Mouse. It can't be easy to talk to them," I said, my gaze still fixed on the shimmering ocean in front of me.

"Lady?" Mouse responded hesitantly. "They have something big planned, don't they? I could see it in their faces, and how confidently they held themselves, even though they were locked up."

Nodding, I swiped at the tear on my cheek. "Seems they've re-doubled their efforts. What my brother took out seems to be only a small fraction of what they have. Thousands of sympathetic supporters, and who knows how many resources. These supporters seem to be hidden somewhere in the forest they were trying to destroy."

Mouse's mouth dropped open.

"That doesn't make sense," Kai interjected.

I shook my head. "No, it doesn't. But it's a large forest. Easy to hide in."

"But why destroy a forest they're using to hide in?" Mouse asked.

I shrugged. "That's what we have to figure out."

There was a long silence.

"You OK?" Kai's voice was soft and hesitant.

I finally looked at them both. "No, but I will be."

"What now?" Mouse asked after a few more tense seconds, while Kai's eyes searched me, looking for some invisible crack that wasn't apparent on the surface. A crack right through my center. One that was tearing down the very fabric of what I knew—of who I was.

"We find Lily, see what she knows, and send word back to my parents as soon as possible."

"I'll go talk to my dad," Kai said, moving away from the railing.

I grabbed his arm, and his gaze met mine. There was a look I couldn't read on his face. Was it sympathy? Was it fear? Was it sadness? And why was his face now such an open book?

"No one else can know about this. I have no idea how many people on this ship are supportive of Rob's ideas, and they, no doubt, have already convinced others to join them."

Kai nodded solemnly.

Quickly dropping his arm, I realized I had been holding on to it far longer than necessary.

He glanced down where my hand had been, squeezing his fist, before he turned and headed toward his father's cabin.

Chapter Fifteen

"We only have two days until we come to port. What do we need to do until then?" Mouse asked me as the three of us ate our dinner in my small cabin later that night. We'd decided keeping me away from the mess hall and the people on the ship was best. For my safety, but also for the safety of Eric and the other crew members. I didn't want to put anyone else in danger as I had Mouse. Though, I had to admit, I missed Eric's mischief.

Once again, I was hidden away from the world.

"I listen. To everyone. See if I can get any more helpful information," I replied, my legs crossed as I sat on the floor stuffing mouthful upon mouthful of food past my lips.

Mouse smirked at my abhorrent manners.

"Is that a good idea?" Kai asked, a hint of concern in his voice.

I raised a brow, still in the middle of chewing my food.

"Don't you think you've been through enough in one day?" he continued.

I swore my heart stopped for a beat as I finished chewing and swallowed. "What choice do I have?"

"I could ask around." He looked at our incredulous faces before adding, "Discreetly, of course."

I shook my head. "I appreciate the concern, but my method is far less dangerous, even if it gives me a headache, and makes me lose even more faith in the human race."

Mouse nodded along in agreement. "Oh, we've always been a doomed species, Lady, and yet somehow we all find reasons to continue fighting."

Kai stared at Mouse.

"What's your reason to keep fighting, Mouse?" I asked, not really expecting an answer.

After a few moments of silence, he responded. "I thought that was obvious, Lady?"

Kai snorted, and I shot him stern look, before nodding at Mouse to continue.

"Well, I fight for people like you, Sol. The world doesn't deserve you, of course, but the world needs you." I think it was the first time Mouse had used my real name.

I shook my head. "No, Archer, the world needs more people like you. I'm no superhero. I was born with these abilities, but it doesn't mean I deserve them."

They both stared at me. Mouse's face hung with sadness. Kai's was, as usual, unreadable.

"There's always a reason, Lady. I believe that with my whole heart. You were given those abilities for a reason, you met us for a reason . . ." Mouse looked at Kai, for back up.

Kai glanced down at his plate and remained silent.

"The two of you are insufferable," he huffed, standing up and grabbing Kai's empty plate.

Kai raised his brows. "What did I do?"

Mouse glared at him. "Nothing. You did nothing. That's the problem!" Before either of us could respond, he was out the door.

Kai stared after him.

I smirked. Kai looked at me skeptically, knowing there was something brewing in my head.

"So, you have a lady friend, Kai?" I asked, as I tried to keep a straight face, waggling my eyebrows.

He laughed. "Really? That's what you want to know?"

I shrugged. "Seems like a reasonable question considering we've been sleeping together."

"First, you and I have very different definitions of sleeping together. Second, are you and Mouse in cahoots with each other? Trying to pry personal information out of me at all costs?" If he weren't smiling, I'm not sure I would have known if those were serious questions.

"Ha! Like we could, anyway. Also, I'm suddenly very interested in your definition of sleeping together." I stuffed more food in my mouth, looking at him suggestively.

Kai shook his head, but he was still smiling. "To answer your original question, no. This lifestyle doesn't exactly lend itself to any sort of long-term relationships. Everyone comes and goes, but not many stay."

"That why your dad never remarried?" I instantly regretted the question the second it slipped out.

Kai's face became serious again. "I guess."

"You think you'll ever do anything different?"

"Don't know what else I would do," he replied without looking at me.

"No thoughts on the matter? No interests? Hobbies? Dreams? If you say nothing, I'm going to assume you love ship chores and sleeping with random women who come and go. I mean, no judgment here, but . . ." I shrugged.

Kai smirked. A playful sort of smile that had my stomach flipping. "Sure, but none of them are realistic."

"And they are?" I coaxed him.

"I like art."

My mouth dropped open, and he chuckled, the sound doing nothing to help my stomach flips.

"What? I don't seem the type?" he asked, amused.

"To be honest, no. But then again, I've led a sheltered life . . ." I trailed off, and when he didn't say anything, I added, "Do you paint? Draw? Sculpt?"

"Draw."

"May I see?" I asked him a little hesitantly, expecting him to say no.

Kai shrugged and grabbed a bag he had stuffed into the corner of the cabin. He rifled through it, before pulling out a small sketchbook and holding it out to me.

"You really trust me with this?" I asked seriously, but I was smiling. I couldn't help it. His smile, his laugh and his playfulness had me feeling far too giddy.

"No." He laughed. "But nevertheless . . ."

I took the sketchbook from his hands, still looking at his face.

He nodded in encouragement, and instead of an unreadable mask, his eyes were alight.

Looking down at the book in my hands, I hesitated.

"I don't mind, you know," he encouraged.

I met his gaze. "I know. It just seems so personal. I know what it feels like to show people your art. It's a little like giving them a window into your soul. It feels so vulnerable. So raw."

Kai's smile faded slowly, his brow furrowing. "Well, when you put it that way, now I'm terrified." But he laughed as he said it.

I smacked his arm, and he let out an exaggerated humph.

I flipped the book open to the first page.

As I looked through the sketchbook, I was pretty sure my mouth was hanging open the entire time. He sketched the things he saw. The things that were most important to him. That was obvious. He drew everything with such care and detail that I found myself tearing up at times. I could feel the emotions on the faces of the people he sketched. I could see the light as it hit the objects he drew. His sketches of the ocean were my favorite. How someone could sketch an endless ocean and do it in a way that held my attention and made me feel something, was beyond me.

I was so lost in his sketches that I didn't even register Mouse opening the door and sitting down beside me.

"Glad he finally showed you," Mouse said, nudging my arm.

Looking up, I saw Kai roll his eyes.

I put my hand on my chest, exaggerating the movement. "I am honored. Truly," and though I said it sarcastically, I meant every word.

"So, what'd you think?" Mouse asked.

I addressed Kai. "These are really good, you know? The detail is incredible. The way you see the world . . ."

"He's deeply sentimental," Mouse said sarcastically.

I smacked Mouse's arm. "No wonder he doesn't want to say anything, when you give him such a hard time."

"It's one of Mouse's more loveable attributes, to be honest."

I shook my head. "I'll never understand this." I motioned to the two of them.

They both looked at each other and shrugged. "Us either, Lady."

I couldn't help but laugh at their antics. It felt easy with them—this sudden joy.

"Well, Kai, I suppose it's my turn," I said, grabbing my own bag and pulling out a folder of a few small paintings I had been working on.

Holding them out to him, he went to grab them from me, before stopping and asking, "You sure? You don't have to, just because I did."

I nodded. "I'm sure."

He smiled and took the folder out of my hands.

Everyone was silent for a while as he flipped through them. Leaning my back against Mouse, I felt the exhaustion setting in.

"These are incredible. They are fantasy, and yet, they seem so realistic, as if they are places that exist." I could hear the disbelief in his voice.

With my eyes half-closed, I replied. "Yeah. My mom describes the places she visits, and I paint them. I add a hint of fantasy along the way."

After a few moments of silence, Kai sighed and stood up. I opened my eyes wider to find him standing over me, his hand reaching for mine. "I think it's about time we get some sleep."

I groaned, and Mouse groaned behind me. Mouse had clearly fallen asleep against the wall.

Kai grabbed my hand and pulled me to my feet, then reached for Mouse next. I found the exhaustion to be so great that I just collapsed onto the bed. I didn't hear Mouse leave, and I didn't feel Kai cover me with a blanket, as sleep took me.

Chapter Sixteen

The next day was filled with other people's thoughts. They ranged from joyful and optimistic, with thoughts about being reunited with loved ones, to fearful and pessimistic with thoughts of something brewing on the horizon.

I didn't really learn anything new, though it became much easier to recognize who were allies and who to watch out for. Rob had clearly done some work while he was on the ship, and the once friendly hellos from some people turned outright hostile at times.

"I don't think it's a good idea for you to be spending so much time lounging on the deck," Kai said, glaring at anyone who came too close.

The crew stayed well away, and even the visitors sensed his malice and didn't dare look at me. How someone could emit such force without a word did something to me I didn't want to think about.

I waved him off. "They're harmless. Just scared and being manipulated."

"Oh, is that all?" he scoffed, sitting down next to me.

I had been painting, while keeping my mind open to the passing thoughts of people going about their tasks on the deck. Kai strained his neck to peek at my work.

I pulled it away. "It's not finished!"

"Why can't I look?" he practically whined.

The sound pulled me from the haze of being in other people's heads for so long, and I finally focused on Kai. I really looked at him and he stared back at me. As with the last time we shared our art, his face wasn't blank, it was full of anticipation and . . . was that hope?

"Because it's not done, and plus, why don't you show me yours first?" I pointed to the sketchbook he had tucked under his arm.

There was a newfound ease between the two of us, and even if I didn't want to admit it to myself, I liked the feeling of it.

He sighed. "Fine. At the same time?"

"Fine," I replied, putting down my paintbrush.

He reached under his arm and pulled out his sketchbook, holding it out to me.

I hesitated a moment before presenting my painting. He grabbed it at the same time I grabbed his.

I flipped to the last page of his sketchbook, and he stared down at the, still wet, painting. As he studied it, his brow pinched, and I almost opened my mouth to defend myself, but I shut it, wanting to see what he drew.

Peeling my eyes from him, I studied the half-drawn image on the page and couldn't help the gasp that escaped my lips.

He had drawn Mouse and I on the night of the full moon. I was wearing the only dress I liked and was laughing at Mouse who beamed back at me, as we danced around each other. He had drawn the two of us with such detail, it was easy to bring myself back to that moment. How he could possibly have remembered that exact moment, down to the slightest detail, seemed impossible.

I found him staring at me. "Do you like it?" he asked a bit hesitantly.

"I thought you weren't watching us?"

"I'm always watching." The words were gravel, and I ignored the thumping of my heart.

He waited for me, but I couldn't stop staring at the drawing.

"It's incredible." There were no other words to describe it. If his art was a window into his soul, I wanted to climb through it and discover what else was hidden there. For a man that wore almost no expression, he certainly knew how to capture the emotions of those around him.

I shivered, wondering what else he saw when he looked at me.

"So, mine?" I asked, shaking away my thoughts.

His smile faded. "It's beautiful."

With that, he handed back my painting and turned his head, staring across the deck of the ship.

The hope was gone. It was so fleeting I wondered if I'd imagined it.

I stared at the painting that had poured out of me and onto the paper. It was a painting of the selkies and the ocean. It showed the transformation from seal to human and back again. I had painted Kai's mother, because it was the only frame of reference I had of the selkies. I silently wondered if I had offended him by doing so.

Pulling me out of my own thoughts, Kai reached out his hand.

"Oh, sorry," I said, as I clumsily handed him his sketchbook. He took it from me and then stood up.

With his back to me, I asked, "Is that really how you see me?"

He stopped, but didn't turn. "I draw everything exactly as I see it," and before I could respond, he walked off across the deck.

"You don't have to do this," I said for the millionth time, circling Kai on the deck of the ship later in the day, sword in hand. He finally decided he wanted to fight me. I didn't know if it was because he wanted to or just wanted to remind the crew what I was made of so they'd stay away from me. Either way, I wasn't complaining. I needed to release some pent-up emotion, and nothing did that better than a good sparring session.

I ignored the sudden wave of memory of my sparring sessions with Mason, stuffing them so far down, I hoped they'd never return. Instead, I focused on Kai.

The warm afternoon sun beat down harshly and sweat already rolled down my chest. My fighting leathers didn't help with the heat.

Most of the crew was at lunch, so the deck was almost clear of people. The few left had all stopped to watch us. I caught a few of them exchanging bets, Eric included.

"I agreed."

It was the same answer he gave me all the other times I asked if he was sure. The answer did nothing to ease my worry that this was about more than proving he could hold his own in a fight.

"You're hesitating," I commented, both of us still circling each other, waiting for someone to make the first move.

"*You're* hesitating," he shot back.

It was true. I couldn't read his thoughts and that had me doubting I could beat him, especially given his reputation on the ship. I had to remind myself that I'd been fighting just as long, and I'd fought my brothers who had more than just steel to fight with.

"You're right," I answered and with my response, his movement faltered for just a split second. That's when I moved.

He was taller and stronger, so I had to rely on my speed. I swung across his body, aiming for his neck. He blocked and batted away my sword as though it were nothing but air. I recovered quickly, easily blocking his answering hit aiming for my own neck.

I backed up a step and smirked. "Don't hold back, now," I baited him.

"Now why would I do that?" His eyes held a hint of challenge, and that's all it took for me to strike.

We danced around each other, quickly learning how the other moved. I always found it kind of intimate, knowing how someone fought. Perhaps that's why I was so drawn to Mason. I knew every move he'd make, every shift of his feet. I knew his tells, and when he knew he'd already lost. I knew that the light in his eyes afterward was only for me. It was awe. It was pride. It was love.

This fight pulled me into a similar kind of trance. I found despite the physical effort, my breathing evened out and my mind calmed until nothing existed except Kai.

He didn't falter. He didn't make a single mistake, always correctly anticipating my next move. He made it look too easy.

Without hearing his thoughts, I had no advantage. It appeared that whoever made the first mistake would likely be the one to lose. I didn't want it to be me, but after a while my muscles tired and I was losing any chance I had.

Kai knew it too. I saw it in his eyes as he watched my movements with an unnerving intensity. His eyes shifted from my center, which he'd been watching to anticipate my moves, and settled for a moment on my face. The corner of his mouth kicked up for a split second and then he struck.

This time, he used his strength and my exhaustion to his advantage, pushing me from the center of the deck, toward the cabin doors.

It was all I could do to block him and stay on my feet.

I had to admit, despite my impending loss, his movements were beautiful, and I was in awe watching him.

Kai made one more push and my back collided with the wood of the cabin door behind me. I grunted at the impact, and his sword was instantly on my neck. The cold steel bit into my skin but I didn't feel it as I stared into his deep ocean eyes.

I expected him to look smug, or at least triumphant; instead all I saw was joy. His stoic facade crumbled more and more.

It took me so much by surprise that I froze, his body pressed against mine. I could feel every hard inch of him through my fighting leathers and suddenly wished I was wearing something thinner. I was glad I was already flushed and breathing hard from the fight, otherwise it would have given away what his proximity was doing to me.

Kai smiled ever so slightly before lowering his lips to my ear. "I'm not afraid to touch you, Chaos," he whispered in a deep, rumbling voice. His breath was hot and fast against my ear as his chest rose and fell with his breathing, brushing my own chest. "But I'm not sure what it will do to me if I do."

With that, he abruptly dropped the sword from my neck and stepped back. He turned on his heel and strode across the deck, depositing his sword back on the rack of weapons pushed into the far corner.

I stared after him, not sure what to do. Not sure of anything. How had he remembered my comment from all those days ago in the mess hall? Why was he calling me chaos? Why was my body so hot?

I was still breathless minutes later.

"That was quite the fight," Mouse commented, coming to stand next to me and pulling me out of whatever trance Kai had put me in.

Kai made his way back to the two of us, his eyes never leaving me. I snorted.

"I'm serious. I've never seen the equal of the two of you."

"He's better."

"He's not. In any given fight, on any given day, you'd have an equal shot at beating him." Mouse turned to Kai. "Isn't that right?"

"Oh, so you're actually including me in this conversation?" Kai sounded amused.

Mouse huffed. "Don't be a smartass."

Kai's eyes turned on me and without hesitation he said, "He's correct. It could easily have been me to make the first mistake, and you'd have won if I had."

"If I could hear your thoughts, I'd have beaten you in less than a minute," I grumbled.

Mouse laughed, but I couldn't keep my eyes off Kai as he watched me. For a moment he let his wall down.

"Better if she doesn't know . . ."

My eyes widened, and Kai must have realized the slip, building up whatever wall he'd built around his mind.

"Let's go," he mumbled, suddenly leaving Mouse and I staring after him.

"What was that all about?" Mouse asked.

"I have no idea."

Our last night on the ship was spent mostly in silence. I'm not sure any of us knew what to say, as we drew closer to land and the conflict waiting there. This was bigger than us, and it felt utterly daunting. The not knowing what we were about to face was the worst.

When Mouse slipped silently out of the room after dinner, Kai set up his bed on the floor. He completed his task in silence, while I chewed on my bottom lip.

"Is this what you want, Kai?" I asked, and he halted, turning to face me. "To follow me around, doing whatever crazy plan I have in mind?"

"Yes, Sol. I do." Without elaborating, he went back to setting up his bed, ending the conversation before it even started.

I fell back onto my pillow and sighed.

Why did I want to shake this man so badly, so he'd just tell me what was in that head of his?

We both settled into our beds, but sleep was elusive. I heard him rolling around in the dark, as though he couldn't get comfortable. My bed was small, but at least it was soft. The planks on the floor must have felt like torture.

"You should sleep up here with me," I said into the darkness. "You're too young for back pain."

There was a long silence, but Kai had utterly stopped moving.

"Don't be a stubborn ass. I told you, I don't bite."

"You snore, though."

I scoffed. "I do not."

Kai chuckled, and I heard the movement of his body as he rose from the floor.

"Wait, do I?" I asked as he stood over me.

"No, Sol. I was giving you shit. Move over, I don't want to be behind you and end up pushing you onto the floor."

"So considerate."

He shook his head and then crawled under the covers, lying on his back. He placed his hands behind his head and stared up at the wooden ceiling.

Turned on my side, it was still impossible not to touch him. The bed seemed made for a toddler, not two grown adults.

I jolted when my arm brushed bare skin. "Please tell me you aren't fully naked."

His chest rumbled with deep laughter. "I have pants on."

I let out an exaggerated breath of relief, but inside, my heart was hammering in my chest. I had the strangest urge to light a lantern and spend the night studying the various tattoos etched across his torso. Those thoughts led me to thinking about the muscles they covered . .
.

"What are you thinking about?" Kai asked, which pulled me from my almost inappropriate thoughts. "You tensed."

I quickly relaxed against him, and I didn't answer his question, too afraid the truth would slip through. The truth I hadn't even admitted to myself yet.

He didn't push me, instead he slid his pinky finger over mine, and wound them together. I shut my eyes. It was such a small touch, but it had my breath halting.

When I opened my eyes, I was too afraid to look at him. Too afraid of what I'd find. Too afraid that all of this was something that would disappear the moment we stepped on dry land. The moment it was no longer just the two of us.

He was like the sea breeze. A force one moment and still the next. You never knew what you'd get.

Kai had fallen back into deep thought. The urge to pry myself into his head to help me unscramble the confusing thoughts and emotions of my own head was almost unbearable. But I didn't want to push him, even if I had a million questions. About his mom, his tattoos, and the absolute respect of every crew member and how he'd earned that respect.

"Sol, I should have been here when Rob attacked you. I don't think I can live with it . . ."

That was not what I was expecting to come out of his mouth after long minutes of silence.

"Fuck, Kai, it wasn't your fault."

"But I knew," he whispered, "because I've caught him before."

"Shit. That's why you hated him so much?" It wasn't really a question.

"He should've been locked up long ago, but my words hold no weight against his status." Kai sounded defeated.

I wanted to grab him and shake him. *Carrying that weight around will only drown you.*

Kai remained silent and utterly still. He'd closed himself up again, but he still held fast to my finger. I let him, lying next to him in the silence he needed.

"Your mother is beautiful. You look a lot like her," I said after a while.

"You saw her? Her human form?" Kai sounded surprised.

"Yes. You have her eyes."

Maybe he wasn't ready to tell me about her, but I wanted him to know I would listen when he was ready to tell his story.

As silence once again embraced us, I finally fell asleep curled up in the warmth of him. Perhaps we needed each other more than we both realized.

Chapter Seventeen

I jerked upright when I felt the ship come to an abrupt halt and stretched my arms above my head.

Kai had already been up for a while, given the state of the cabin. Everything was fully packed and tidied up, and our bags were sitting neatly by the door. He was sitting against the wall, focused on the sketchbook in front of him. A small lantern was his only light to draw by.

"How long have you been up?" I asked, trying to rub the sleep from my eyes.

He didn't look up from his sketch. "An hour maybe?"

As I pulled back the covers and stood up, making my way toward my bag of clothes that already desperately needed to be washed, Kai added, "We just docked, though."

"Mmmhmmm," I sleepily responded, pulling out my standard training outfit. Without a second thought, I peeled off my T-shirt and shorts that I had worn to sleep, grabbing some thick leather pants and a tight-fitting cotton T-shirt.

When I caught Kai's gaze, I realized my mistake. My face instantly heated, but not from embarrassment. I suddenly felt hot all over because his eyes burned both brighter and darker than I'd ever seen before.

Kai let his eyes roam for another beat before he reluctantly tore them away, and quicker than the breeze, spun toward the wall.

My skin felt like it was on fire.

Shaking my head, I tried to get control of my fluttering heart. What the hell was that? I wasn't completely naked. I had underwear on. But damn, if it didn't feel like I'd been completely exposed. And not just physically.

Pulling the shirt over my head and buttoning my pants, I finished with a pair of leather boots.

"Finished," I said, the sound coming out more breathless than I intended.

Kai didn't say anything, he just stared at me as if he were trying to figure me out. What I wouldn't have given to know what he was thinking during those moments when it felt like he had a million things to say, and yet nothing came out.

"Why can't I hear your thoughts?" I finally asked him.

Before he could answer, there was a loud knock on our door, and I almost jumped out of my skin. A second later, Mouse came barreling through the door, a huge grin on his face.

"Ready you two?" he asked. "Did I miss something?" he added a second later when both of us remained silent.

I let out a short laugh and clapped him on the shoulder. "No, Mouse, you didn't miss a thing."

"Oh," he replied, though I could tell he wasn't wholly convinced.

"Let's go," I said, grabbing my two bags and heading out toward the deck. Mouse and Kai followed me.

The deck was bustling with activity as I went over to the railing of the ship and looked out over the docks and the city beyond it. The sheer amount of people and buildings was almost overwhelming. I had never been to such a large city before, and I stood there observing the movement of people for a long while.

"You'll keep me informed?" The captain's voice came from over my shoulder.

I turned to him. "As long as your ship is close to the shore, I can reach you at any time."

He nodded, but there was something sad behind his eyes.

"Once I find Lily, I'll let you know what information to send back to my father."

Captain Fraiser nodded again. "Be careful. Keep your mind open."

He addressed Kai and Mouse next, who had been silently observing the activity on the deck. "You two be careful too. Keep an eye out for each other."

We had decided Kai and Mouse would escort me until I found Lily and made a plan. After that, they were to go back to the ship to await directions from my parents.

Kai and Mouse nodded, and then the captain abruptly turned and walked toward the causeway, barking directions, the sadness in his gaze morphing into one of stoic authority.

Kai sighed deeply, staring after his father. Mouse's brow furrowed as he watched Kai.

"He loves you, you know," I said to Kai.

His eyes drifted to mine. There was sadness there. A deep sadness, trapped in eyes I couldn't stop staring at.

"I can hear what he can't say. I'm sorry if that's overstepping a boundary," I said when he still didn't reply.

"Come on you two, time to go," Mouse said, grabbing Kai's arm and practically dragging him toward the causeway. Kai remained silent in my head and outside it.

I sighed and followed.

As we made our way slowly down the ramp, I kept my eyes peeled for Lily and opened my mind to see if I could find her. I was met with nothing, as my feet hit the wooden dock.

"What's wrong, Sol?" Mouse asked, noticing the worry etched on my face.

"Something just doesn't feel right." Before I could finish my thought, a series of explosions went off around the ship.

The causeway we had just stepped off was blown to pieces, throwing people in all directions. The energy from the blast threw me a few feet into the air. I landed in the ice-cold water. A burning sensation erupted on my skin and spanned almost the entire left side of my body. My ears rang, and I felt completely lost as I desperately tried to find the surface.

With no sense of which way was up, I thrashed around blindly, the panic beginning to set in. I didn't know how long I was down, before I began to feel lightheaded. When thrashing got me nowhere, I let my body still.

After a few more moments of drifting, my vision began to black out.

Right before I lost consciousness, I felt a pair of hands on me.

Chapter Eighteen

When I finally regained consciousness, I was floating on my back, being dragged through the water beneath the docks. The sun tried to make its way through the cracks in the wooden planks, as I floated through the maze of wood and columns that rose from the icy sea.

After a few moments, I finally regained enough of my wits to turn my head just enough to see who was pulling me through the water.

Kai had one arm hooked under my arms and across my chest. His other was helping him swim. He had a gash starting at his hairline, leading down his cheek, all the way to his jaw, but otherwise he seemed unhurt.

"Where's Mouse?" I barely choked out.

Kai stopped and put his finger to his lips, so I asked silently in his head, *"Where's Mouse?"*

Kai began swimming again, pulling my aching body behind him. *"Ahead of us. Scoping out our route."*

"Is he hurt?"

"No more than I am."

"I can swim."

Kai hesitantly released me, and I found myself awkwardly treading water. He assessed me, then nodded in approval before continuing, leading me through the maze of docks.

"We have to keep moving or we'll freeze to death," he said

What had just happened began to sink in.

"Your dad? The ship?" I said in a panic.

"They're both fine. The ship, which looked to have only minor damage, pushed off the dock shortly after the blast. They're searching for survivors in the water."

"They need to get far away from here!"

Kai stopped and whirled around. He moved in close and gently grabbed my chin, forcing me to look at him.

"My dad knows what he's doing. We need to focus on getting to dry land, getting warm, and staying out of sight." His voice was dangerously low in my head—commanding.

"Those blasts were meant for me, weren't they?"

Kai didn't say anything, but he didn't have to. Leaning into his touch, he allowed me to silently process our current situation.

"Are you ready?" Kai asked after a few moments of treading water.

I nodded, and he dropped his hand. The warmth of it left me instantly, and I shivered.

It felt like we had swum for hours, but it was likely only a few minutes. The cold water cut deep into my bones, and my joints ached. It took all my stubborn will to make my limbs continue moving.

Kai moved through the water with ease and grace. It didn't surprise me that he seemed at home here, but I hadn't noticed the last time we were in the water together. His sudden anger was all I saw that night. Now, I couldn't help but admire his movement and the shirt that clung to his back, revealing every ripple of muscle. I focused all my attention on him, unwilling to let my mind wander back to my panic.

As we neared the shore, Kai held up his hand and we halted. The pounding of feet walking on the dock above us had my heart rate increasing and the blood pounding in my ears. So far, Mouse had led us in a direction that avoided the most crowded docks, but now it seemed unavoidable.

A rough, male voice flitted through the cracks in the dock. "We couldn't find her body among the dead."

"Then we need to sweep the entire area. She isn't on the docks, so she must be in the water. Post people up by the shore, she'll have to come out eventually." It was Rob.

I trembled involuntarily at the sound of it. How'd he get free? At the same time, it didn't surprise me one bit.

The men began moving again, and their voices soon drifted out of earshot.

I finally let out the breath I'd been holding. Kai watched me, his brow wrinkled with concern.

"We can't just walk out of the water. We need to find a way to swim north toward the forest that meets the sea. There's more protection there," he said.

"How will we make it that far? I'm frozen," I replied.

Kai took in my ghostly skin and blue lips. *"Tell Mouse to swim back and meet us. I have a plan."*

I nodded, and a few moments later, Mouse was next to me. He didn't look much better than I did, but he was more used to the cold water.

"That small boat over there," Kai said pointing toward a rowboat anchored just off the docks. *"There are empty grain sacks in there. Sol, you are going to hide under them. Mouse, you're going to row the boat."*

"And you?" I asked.

"I'll pull up the anchor and swim alongside the boat. There's no room for all three of us without being spotted."

I frowned, not understanding, or agreeing, with his ridiculous suggestion.

"I don't think I feel the cold like you both do," was all Kai said, then he continued. *"We need to swim under water as far under as we can and come up on the opposite side of the boat."*

"I don't think I can make it that far," I replied, the exhaustion and cold beginning to fog my mind.

"I'll help you."

Before I could argue, he grabbed my hand and pulled me under.

We came up on the opposite side of the boat, and moments later, as I tried desperately to suck air into my lungs, Mouse surfaced next to us, panting heavily. Kai's breathing had only slightly increased.

"Mouse first," Kai instructed, looking around in all directions to make sure we weren't spotted.

I tried to nod, but my head felt heavy, and all I could manage was letting it fall to my chest. Beyond the cold and numbness, I began to feel giddy.

"Shit. Change of plan. Mouse, when Sol gets in the boat, help her undress immediately and use your body heat to warm her. Hypothermia is setting in."

Mouse nodded, hoisting himself over the side of the boat.

I let out an involuntary giggle at the absurdity of the situation, and Kai eyed me with concern.

When Mouse tapped on the side of the boat, and before I could wrap my head around what was happening, Kai grabbed me by the waist and hoisted me into the boat.

I fell unceremoniously on top of Mouse. He grunted at the dead weight that was my cold body. I wasn't shaking anymore. All I felt was numb. Like I wasn't even in my body anymore.

"I need to help you get the wet clothes off, Sol. I won't look, I promise."

When I didn't respond, and I didn't move, Mouse shimmied around toward my head and began pulling my jacket off. At the same time, the boat began to move away from the docks, but I was oblivious to almost everything.

My shirt came next, and Mouse quickly covered me with some empty grain sacks. After that, he moved to my pants and proceeded to cover my lower half with more grain sacks, leaving on my underwear at least. Next, he removed his own wet clothes; I was so tired, my eyes closed involuntarily.

"Oh, no you don't," Mouse whispered as he crawled on top of me. "Don't close your eyes. Stay with me."

My only response was a groan, but I reluctantly opened them to find him staring down at me.

Despite the situation, he grinned. "Not exactly how I imagined I'd get you naked . . . but . . ."

I only sort of registered what he had just said, as the boat came to an abrupt stop. Mouse held his finger to his mouth and glanced around nervously.

There was a light tap on the side of the boat. Mouse quietly asked if I could talk to Kai for him. I inclined my head and opened communication with Kai, Mouse, and myself.

I started by mumbling something incoherent, but Kai responded, *"We aren't as far as I wanted, but I think we've been spotted. We must pull up to shore and lose ourselves in the forest. Can you move, Sol?"*

"She's still pretty out of it, and her feet and hands don't look so good, Kai." The panic was obvious in his voice, but to me everything seemed to be happening far away, as though I was stuck in a glass bottle and nothing, but muffled sounds could reach me.

"Shit."

"We might have to carry her," Mouse responded.

"That'll slow us down."

"Do we have a choice?"

Kai didn't reply right away, as if he was searching for a better option. *"No."*

The boat suddenly changed direction, and if it was even possible, it started to move with even greater speed. It didn't take long before the bottom of the boat scraped against the sand. I moaned at the impact. With my body warming slightly from Mouse's body heat, pain flooded my joints, especially in my hands and feet.

Mouse moved off me, grabbing our wet clothes as he climbed out.

"Can you move at all?" Kai whispered to me over the side of the small boat.

"I think so." My voice was hoarse and too quiet. I shook my head, trying to get rid of the fogginess.

Kai reached out, gently wrapping his hands around my wrists and pulling me to standing. The grain bags fell away, but I didn't care. I couldn't think. All I could focus on was staying awake and ignoring the pain. My legs shook, and my toes hurt so badly, I felt like I might topple over.

"I can carry you," Kai said, guiding me toward the edge of the boat.

I didn't question or hesitate. I let myself fall into his arms. His clothes were soaked and cold, but his skin was warm underneath. He made nothing of my nakedness, as he quietly instructed Mouse to grab the empty grain sacks and cover me.

"Cold," I choked out between chattering teeth.

"Hold her," he instructed Mouse, who took me, shifting his weight onto his good leg, and held me against his chest. He was gentle, his brow creased with worry.

Kai stripped off his shirt, dropped it on the ground, and took me back, pulling me gently from Mouse's arms. We didn't have more than a moment before a boat rounded the corner.

"Run," Kai shouted to Mouse, as he took off toward the thick forest ahead of us.

Mouse grabbed our soaking wet clothes and followed close behind. Both of us were slow, too slow. Kai from carrying me, and Mouse from his limp.

The jolting from the running was excruciating on my joints, but I gritted my teeth and focused on the rhythm of Kai's breath and thundering heartbeat as I held my head against his chest.

"Where are we going?" I managed to ask him.

"The village at the edge of the forest." He paused, as if even speaking mind-to-mind made breathing more difficult. *"I have a friend there who will hide us."*

"How far?"

"Few miles."

"You can't carry me that far."

"I have no choice."

"You could—"

He cut me off. *"Not an option."*

"Kai!" Mouse shouted from behind us.

Kai didn't have to turn around to know that whoever was following us was gaining ground, and fast.

Mouse halted, and doubled over, in pain or because he was out of breath, I couldn't tell.

"Leave me," he wheezed. "I am only going to slow you down further, and I can act as a distraction."

"Never," Kai growled, using the same tone he'd used with me when I tried to suggest the same thing.

"There," I said, inclining my head ever so slightly toward a thick stand of trees just north of us.

"Can't fit through there."

"No choice. We can hide. I can crawl."

Kai swore under his breath and then changed direction, headed for a stand of trees that were so densely packed together that no light reached the forest floor. It looked like a solid black wall. Fog crawled out of the openings between trees and disappeared when it hit rays of sunlight. Mouse followed close behind, the leaves under his feet crunching with every step and his breath growing heavier with each second.

Kai slowed just before the trees. *"I'll carry you as far as I can."*

"Just out of eyesight."

We passed the first stand of trees, and once inside, the temperature dropped ten degrees. I began shivering again. After a few more feet, Kai slowed to a walk, tucking me closer, dodging branches and underbrush.

I stretched my neck up to glance behind us. You could no longer see where we had just been. The fog closed us in, concealing almost everything beyond a ten-foot radius.

Kai stopped, and it was obvious why. We weren't going to make it through the next stand of trees. They were too densely packed, with branches low to the ground.

"So, we break branches?"

Kai shook his head. *"Too loud."*

"You think they would really follow us in here?" Mouse asked, his breathing still heavy.

"Wouldn't you?" was all Kai asked.

"So, we crawl," I said, and they both looked at me.

"Can you?" Kai asked.

"No choice," I replied, still gritting my teeth to hold back the severe pain in my hands and feet.

"Your hands," Kai observed, glancing down at them.

I followed his gaze and instantly wanted to cry. The cells at the end of my fingers were starting to die and were turning a dark shade of gray.

"I'll make it," I replied, though I wasn't sure I really believed those words.

He looked like he might try to argue with me, but must have thought better of it, placing me gently on the ground that was soft and littered with leaf debris.

The first step was excruciating as I slowly put weight on my hands, but I willed them to move, despite the pain. Before long, we lost sight of where we had entered. All sounds of anyone following were gobbled up by the trees.

The silence, now, was so all encompassing, that I wondered if anything could live here. The only thing I heard was the sound of our breathing, and the soft crunch of leaves beneath us.

I was so focused on making my hands and legs move, that I didn't notice the clearing ahead.

"Sol, stop," Kai whispered fervently to the left of me.

I halted. Ahead of us were rays of sunlight that penetrated just the edges of the trees. I couldn't see beyond the opening but craved the warmth of the sun.

"I'll go first. They could have somehow gone around, and might be waiting on the other side," Kai whispered.

He kept his pace slow, and his focus on the clearing. Just before the opening, he motioned for us to stop, and he crept forward slowly, glancing in all directions.

When he deemed it safe, he waved us forward, and I watched him disappear into the sunlight. Moments later, my head emerged from the trees, and then the rest of my body. I collapsed on the grass, and it took a few more moments for my eyes to adjust to the light.

When they finally did, I saw a brilliant field of wildflowers.

I spent a few more moments looking at the flowers and the sun dancing off their bright colors. Something was oddly familiar about this field.

I slowly sat up, and Mouse jumped over a few feet to help me.

"Thanks," I mumbled as I looked out across the field toward another grove of trees.

"Holy shit," I said, much clearer, my heart rate picking up.

"What's wrong?" Mouse asked.

I pointed forward, toward an ancient stone archway. The same archway I had painted back home. And this was the same field that led to it.

That's why it looked so familiar.

"I don't see anything," Mouse said, following the direction of my finger.

"That archway. The stone one."

Mouse looked again, blinking several times, and then shook his head.

I huffed out a breath, exasperated, and started crawling toward the arch.

"Sol, what are you doing?" Mouse hissed.

I didn't answer him, I just kept going, the pain continuing to radiate from my damaged fingers and toes. As I neared, I realized it was exactly how I had painted it. Worn stone, soft green moss covering every crack, and bright green lichen decorated the arch. Carved swirling patterns peaked out from behind the moss, faded from time. Even the words, in a language I didn't know, were the same. Somehow, every detail was the same. I couldn't even comprehend what I was seeing with my own eyes.

"Sol?" Kai asked, standing beside me.

"Tell me I'm not going crazy, Kai," I said, still staring in awe at the archway.

"You're not crazy, Sol," he whispered, "but we need to get you warm."

Catching a glimmer out of the corner of my eye, I almost jumped out of my skin. There was a soldier standing next to the archway. At least, I thought he was a soldier. He looked like no other soldier I had ever seen, though. His figure was tall and slender, but nicely built, with long blond hair pulled back and piercing green eyes. Metal chain armor hugged him over his chest and arms. A tight-fitting green shirt, and matching pants peeked out from under the armor. He held a spear and had a sword dangling from his waist. His gaze was aimed forward, ignoring us completely.

"Hey, you!" I tried to yell, but my entire body wasn't functioning correctly.

He didn't respond. In fact, he didn't even flinch. He stood stoic as though he was also made of stone.

I inched closer and tried again. "Hey! I'm talking to you."

"Sol, I don't think this is a good idea," Kai whispered, his concern rising.

"Who the hell is she talking to?" Mouse asked, completely baffled.

"Sol..." Kai's voice was firmer this time.

A warning I ignored.

Before anyone could stop me, I grabbed a stick and threw it at the soldier. Instead of hitting him, the stick bounced off some invisible barrier.

Mouse gasped beside me. He might not have been able to see the person, but he certainly saw the stick bounce backward.

"Asshole," I whispered under my breath when the soldier didn't even so much as glance in our direction.

With no other way to get his attention, I tried the only other thing I could think of. I mustered all the strength I had and threw my bright blue flame at him. It was a mistake. I had no energy left. The cold had stolen it.

I saw the soldier's surprised face as his invisible barrier burned blue all around him, right before I collapsed. Kai grabbed for me, only able to slightly break my fall.

My vision went in and out, everything blurring around me, but I saw the soldier draw his sword and step toward us.

Kai pulled me against him, covering me in his arms as if to protect me.

We had no weapons, and even though Kai was warm, he had also lost a significant amount of energy in our attempt to get to safety. If the soldier chose to harm us, we were defenseless.

We had escaped one threat, just to land in another.

The soldier stopped before us, raising Kai's chin with the point of his sword, as we both lay crumpled on the ground wrapped in each other.

My vision and mind were so muddled that I wasn't fully aware of what was happening. I believe I caught a slightly surprised look in the soldier's face as he stared at Kai, who still looked determined despite the precarious situation.

Mouse had inched closer to us, and I felt his body heat behind my limp head that was tucked in Kai's elbow.

The soldier said something in a language that sounded vaguely familiar. Kai tightened his grip on me, and when the soldier bent and appeared to want to take me from Kai, the air suddenly filled with loud buzzing. A second later, I lost the edges of things. Everything melted together in a blur of muted color.

Distantly, I knew the air was filled with bees, but their movement along with my fading senses, had the world disappearing.

That's when I gave in, and the world went black.

PART II

Chapter Nineteen

My first thought was that I was finally warm, and comfortable. Too comfortable.

Slowly opening my eyes to darkness, I saw a faint glow coming from somewhere I couldn't see. It illuminated the room enough for me to make out two human forms. One was asleep on a large chair near the corner of the room, and the other was asleep next to me.

The bed we were on was larger than any bed I had ever seen, and it was soft. I felt like I had melted completely into it. I turned slowly toward the figure next to me. His form was familiar now, even in the dark, and the scent of jasmine and the sea gave him away. Smiling to myself, something eased in my chest. Instinctively, I reached out and covered his hand with my own.

Kai stirred, and reluctantly opened his eyes, blinking several times. It took him a few moments to register that it had been me who had woken him.

"How are you feeling?" he asked, his voice gravely from sleep.

"Fine. Actually, better than fine. How is that possible?" I whispered, not wanting to wake Mouse.

Kai yawned before answering. "I'm still not sure how any of this is possible." His gaze dropped to my hand that was still holding on to him.

I abruptly let go and stuffed it under the covers. "Where are we?"

"Well, that's a bit hard to explain . . ."

"Try me."

"We're in an ancient kingdom run by magical people who call themselves the Tuatha Da Danann, or the Fair Folk," Kai replied very matter-of-factly.

"You're shitting me." I'd heard of the Fair Folk. My mother talked about them all the time, pouring through book after book that mentioned them. She'd had a weird obsession when I was young. I'd dismissed her research as fancy stories.

My mother, however, believed they were real, and spent much of her time searching for any hint of them.

Kai shook his head. "Wish I was, but, like I said before, nothing surprises me when it comes to you."

I narrowed my gaze. "How long was I out?"

"A couple of hours."

"Why do my hands and feet feel completely normal?"

"The Fair Folk have magic healers."

He was so serious, I couldn't help the laugh that escaped my lips. "OK, smartass. Instead of me asking you a million questions, and getting nowhere, why don't you just start by telling me what happened after I passed out?"

"That might take a while."

"Where the hell else do we need to be?"

Kai laughed quietly, the sound warming me. "When you called the bees, Cormac, some sort of prince, flung out an arm, repairing whatever shield you'd destroyed with your flame. He then just stood there in stunned silence until the bees gave up and flew off. The soldier spoke, then, and this time I could understand him. His first question was how a human had your abilities. I didn't know how to answer him. I told him you had many . . . eccentric abilities." Kai looked at me, the left side of his mouth kicking up as though he meant to rile me with that little detail.

"Go on." I didn't take the bait, though I wanted to.

"I explained that we were being chased, you had frostbite and likely hypothermia, and that you needed help. He still seemed very stuck on the fact that you had burned his shield, but he took us past the archway. It was like stepping into a completely different world. I won't describe the place, I'll let you see it with your own eyes." He stopped, his eyes drifting to the blankets that now covered my hands, and I clenched them together.

"He brought us to an infirmary. They healed your hands and warmed your body but told us it would take time for you to wake up, so they put you in this room. Naturally, Mouse had a million questions."

Laughing, I imagined Mouse's face, mouth hung open in disbelief, and his eyes alight with wonder.

I wish I had seen it.

"They wouldn't give us much information, and Cormac left after the healers had fixed you up. He hasn't returned."

A strand of dark hair fell across Kai's forehead, and I moved to brush it away, but stopped myself.

Kai watched me with a wry grin.

I sighed. "What the fuck?"

Kai shrugged but clearly didn't know what else to say.

"I like this bed, though," I said, pulling my hands out and running them along the soft blankets.

Kai shook his head.

"How long until dawn?" I asked him.

"An hour maybe?"

Sighing, I leaned back against the pillow, staring at the ceiling, if you could even call it that. It was open-air, branches twisting in and out of one another creating a beautiful, but unorganized, pattern of bark. Within, and coming from, the twisting branches were green leaves, each the size of my head.

"Are we in a treehouse?" I asked Kai as I continued to stare at the dimly lit branches above me.

"I guess you could call it that," he replied, following my gaze.

"This is about to get more complicated, isn't it?"

"It's way past complicated."

Mouse woke up just before dawn and joined us in the massive bed.

"Why the hell did you sleep in the chair? There's plenty of room in this thing." I asked, as he crawled under the covers.

"Didn't seem proper," he replied, pointedly glaring at Kai.

Kai grunted, ignoring the barb.

"I think we're way past proper," I said to Mouse, laughing. "Pretty sure you stared at my naked body for a few hours yesterday."

Mouse shook his head, but he was smiling. "Wouldn't want to get in the middle of you two."

I frowned, but didn't have time to respond, as a loud knock sounded on the wooden door made of braided bark in the form of interwoven Celtic knots. Symbols I'd seen my mom studying over the years. Symbols that were carved throughout our house.

Kai rose to answer it, and I stood up, pulling off the soft covers. I stared at my outfit for a moment before the door opened, and the soldier, or prince, Cormac, walked through. His eyes landed on Kai first and lingered there for a moment with a look I couldn't read, before he directed his attention to me.

Kai shut the door behind him, seemingly annoyed at Cormac's presence.

Cormac stopped at the foot of the bed, his eyes roaming down my face to my silk lavender nightgown that hid almost nothing.

Rude. It's not like I chose the outfit.

I glared back at him, also blatantly trailing my eyes down his body and pointedly stopping at his crotch, tilting my head to the side, and raising my brows.

He cleared his throat, and my gaze went back to his as I tried to hide my mirth. He clearly wasn't impressed, but Mouse couldn't help the squeak that escaped as he tried to hold back a laugh.

Cormac ignored him, and my little stunt. "How are you feeling?" he asked with a slight clip to his tone.

"Better."

He nodded once and looked around the room.

"Why didn't you help us in the forest?" I blurted, not sure why that was my first question.

Cormac cocked his head to the side, eyes narrowing. He seemed annoyed at our presence. "I'm Cormac, soldier, and prince of Tir Na Eabha." He started, as if I was rude not to start with an introduction when he started with a completely inappropriate perusal of my body. "To answer your question, most humans cannot see us. I didn't think you were talking to me, and even if I knew you were, I'm forbidden to have any contact with humans."

"Why?"

"That's a complicated question."

"Then give me the complicated answer," I countered, straightening myself, as he took a step closer, narrowing his gaze even further.

"Your kind drove my kind to near extinction. Our powers, and lives, are tied to the Earth, which you almost destroyed."

"Which my mother restored," I interjected.

A brief wave of surprise passed over Cormac's features before returning to a hardened glare. "Your mother is Willow?"

Now it was my turn to be surprised. "You've met her?"

"My mother has."

"Well, fuck." That was news to me. My mother had never mentioned coming this deep into the forest, let alone stumbling upon a whole different world full of mythical beings.

"Get dressed. I'll take you to my mother. She'll have the answers we're both looking for." Without waiting for a response, Cormac turned and walked out of the room, shutting the door behind him.

This man was used to giving commands and having them obeyed.

I hated him.

But I also hated my mother in that moment. Why would she keep something this big from me?

"Couldn't tell if he liked us or wanted to kill us," Mouse said, pulling me from my thoughts.

"And for a cranky magical person, why does he have to be so attractive?"

Kai and Mouse were oddly silent as I reached for the sage green dress draped over an ivory couch at the end of the bed. I supposed this was what they wanted me to wear to meet the queen.

"Is he though?" Mouse asked, staring at the closed door Cormac had just exited through.

"It's objectively true."

Mouse shot Kai a quick glance, who stood, as usual, without a flicker of emotion on his face. His body was tense, though.

"I don't suppose they have anything other than dresses?" I asked, staring at the lavender nightgown I was wearing, and the sage green dress now in my hands. "Where am I supposed to put my weapons?"

Mouse chuckled. "You lost all your weapons. They're in a bag at the bottom of the sea."

"Shit. I forgot. Damn, I'll feel naked without them."

Mouse shook his head. "You need to get out more. Mingle with us commoners."

I blew out a long breath. "If only I had that luxury."

A long, awkward silence followed. I refused to meet either of their gazes. I didn't need to see whatever would be staring back at me. Instead, I made for the bathroom to change.

"We'll step outside. Wait for you there," Mouse said, and the door opened and shut.

I peeled off the soft nightgown and hastily pulled the dress over my curves. It fell to the floor and felt as though I was wearing nothing but air. It fit like it was made for me. The neckline plunged just below my breastbone, and the back hit at the soft curve of my back. So much skin was showing, but the dress felt completely secure.

Magic. It had to be magic.

The gown looked like something my mother would have worn. It was sage green, but the stitched details were darker green, giving depth to the dress. The patterns were more Celtic knots and symbols, woven perfectly along the seams. It looked as though it was made from the Earth, for the people of the Earth. Fitting for what I knew of the Tuatha De Danann.

"I know you hate dresses, Sol, but you don't look half-bad in them," Mouse said, his eyes traveling up and down my body as I stepped out of the room and into an open-air hallway that wound its way around an enormous tree trunk and ended with stairs that led to the forest floor.

Kai let out a low, disapproving sound. But Mouse only laughed him off, waving for me to follow.

I did, feeling Kai's eyes blazing a trail of fire over every inch of exposed skin.

Chapter Twenty

Kai was right, he could not have done this place justice if he tried. The kingdom, called Tir Na Eabha, or Land of Life, was built unlike anything I had seen or read about. It was built as though it was a part of the forest itself. As though its very existence depended on the life around it.

I didn't understand my mother's magic. She certainly didn't either, even though she'd been searching the world for answers. But somehow, I could feel her here. I could feel the energy of her. I could feel the energy of the forest and the people who lived here. The energy channels seemed more obvious—more powerful.

Buildings wrapped around trees, winding their way all the way to the canopy. Rooms and balconies hung out from the trunks in circular patterns mimicking the shape of the trunk itself. They were made of intricately carved wood, designed to blend into their surroundings, and yet, also created as a piece of art. The craftsmanship was unlike anything I had ever seen. My house, compared to this, was almost laughable, and people traveled from all corners of the Earth to see our house.

Of course, I wouldn't admit that little fact to our house. It would likely kick me out on my ass for even thinking it.

The interior of the forest was dark, but the place was lit by floating orbs of light that had a mind of their own. They were floating around like ghosts with no particular location in mind.

The further we walked, the larger the place appeared to get. We passed all manner of Fair Folk, who made no attempt to hide their alarm at our presence.

I ignored their stares. Oblivious, almost, to them. Too lost in the surroundings to bother with what they thought of us.

Kai said nothing as he led me down paths that wound their way between the trees. I wondered how he knew where to go, but figured he'd memorized the way while I was passed out and recovering.

Each time I glanced over at him, he was watching me. He almost looked like he belonged here. Almost as ethereal looking as the Fair Folk—slightly more attractive, slightly taller, slightly more muscular, and slightly too beautiful to be real. Too beautiful to be human.

Kai's brow rose and I realized I'd been staring.

Cringing, I turned away. We came to a halt next to a large spiral staircase that wound up the largest tree in the forest. The breadth of the tree was unlike any I had ever seen. Her trunk could easily have fit an entire house inside of it. Her canopy rose above the rest of the forest, and sitting right below the branches and leaves was a building unlike all the rest.

An audible gasp escaped my lips. The building was not only the largest, but the most intricately designed. The wood was bleached, unlike the other buildings, and etched on its facade were a myriad of Celtic symbols and scenes of magic, battles, births, deaths, and rituals. My mother could spend eternity studying these and never get bored.

It told the story of the Tuatha De Danann. The children of the gods.

"The palace," Kai explained, still watching my reaction.

"I'm going to murder my mother."

"Maybe she never actually made it here?" Mouse offered.

Peeling my eyes from the tree, I looked at him. "Maybe."

Still, it was unlikely. There must have been another reason for her secrecy. And that conversation was one I wouldn't hold back on. Not with everything that had happened. Not after I almost died. Not after what happened to Mason.

I deserved the truth. No matter how hard that truth might be to face.

Kai's hand brushed the bare skin on my low back, urging me up the stairs.

I shouldn't have noticed his touch. Not when it was so fleeting. But my breath didn't get the memo as it caught in my throat.

Forcing myself upward, I counted the steps until my breathing returned to normal.

It took twenty-five.

Halfway up, I stopped to look at the entirety of Tir Na Eabha. From above, it was almost impossible to see the buildings. It's as if they had melted into the trees. Perfect camouflage. Perfect symbiosis. Perfect art. I couldn't wait to paint this place.

"Magic?" Mouse asked behind me.

I shrugged. "Or just really well thought out design." I considered for a moment before adding, "They tread lightly on this Earth. We could take a few lessons from them."

When we reached the top, two guards flanked the impressively large double white doors carved with the tree of life, eerily similar to the tree on my mother's library door. The tree on this one, though, moved and changed, or appeared to, as though it were a living being just as the forest around it. Perhaps the magic of the Fair Folk also fed into their dwellings, just as my family's magic fed into our home.

I wondered if the palace was as ornery as our house.

"Excuse me, we're here to see the queen," Kai said, looking toward one of the guards.

The guard didn't so much as flinch.

Kai turned and looked at me. I shrugged.

"Hey!" I screamed in the head of the guard closest to me.

The guard flinched and shook his head before meeting my eyes. The look he gave me was somewhere between surprised and furious.

"Humans cannot enter," the guard growled back.

The other guard held his position, but his gaze shifted to me.

Snapping my fingers, I ignited my blue flame, stepping close to the guard who spoke.

His wide eyes darted to the flame in my hand. He stepped back, crashing into the door, a slight tremor in his hands.

My flame could barely burn, but this soldier's reaction was as though I could take out the entire forest.

Interesting.

The doors behind the guard suddenly opened, and a stunning woman wearing a beautifully embroidered emerald floor length dress came rushing out. The guard resumed his rigid stance and wiped any expression off his face. But the small tremor in his hands remained.

"You're right on time!" the woman said cheerily, reaching her hand out to introduce herself.

I stared, open-mouthed at her extended hand. It wasn't her beauty, though that was exquisite, it was the fact that I was staring back at the very first person I had ever met who had red hair.

"I'm Orlan," she said, looking between the three of us, clearly confused by my lack of response.

Mouse cleared his throat. At the same time, Cormac came up behind Orlan, looking annoyed. No surprise there. I'm pretty sure that was his only expression.

"Solana, but everyone calls me Sol," I said to Orlan, taking her hand, ignoring Cormac.

She smiled warmly. "Come in. Come in." She waved us forward.

Cormac followed us in, not saying a word, and the doors shut on their own behind us.

The palace ceilings were high, open to the canopy above, and sunlight streamed in through the leaves, creating a soft light that bounced off the walls. Growing out of the bark were all manner of exotic plants, blooming with an intoxicating smell.

A single red flower caught my attention, and I walked over to it. Drawn to it by some invisible force.

Before I could touch it, Cormac grabbed my arm and yanked it away.

I wheeled around to face him, but before I could say anything, he dropped my arm. "Be careful, a single drop of its nectar will kill you."

I raised my brows, looking back at the flower one more time. If he meant to deter me, he failed. I thrived off dangerous knowledge.

"Cormac likes to be dramatic. Touching it would do nothing to you," Orlan commented before continuing down the hallway.

Cormac glared at her back.

"Sister?" I asked him.

He turned his gaze on me, brows pinching.

He nodded.

"Younger sister?"

He nodded again, looking at me as though I was something to be studied. As though I was an oddity.

I *was* an oddity to most people. I'd always been.

Winking, I followed Orlan through another set of doors into a large circular room.

Everything in the room, table and chairs included, looked as though they were part of the tree itself.

I was so busy studying the details of the room that I failed to notice another person had entered, flanked by two guards.

Kai brushed my arm, getting my attention, and I studied the woman who walked toward us with purpose and authority emanating from her very pores.

She looked only slightly older than Cormac or Orlan, but the way she held herself made her seem much older. She had long blonde hair, and piercing green eyes similar to Cormac's, and I shivered at the power I felt in her.

I bowed my head in reverence, not sure what the proper thing was to do.

"Mother, this is Sol," Orlan said, her voice still cheery and bright. I wondered if that was her usual attitude. So at odds with her brothers. "And this is my mother, Queen Nessa."

The queen inclined her head. "Your mother has told me a lot about you, Solana," she said, walking over to the table and sitting down. The guards followed her like shadows.

"She wanted me to help you," she continued, waving us over to the table.

This was all news to me. My mother never said a word, and so far, this conversation was only adding to my anger. And something I'd never felt toward my parents—disappointment.

Sitting down across from her, she continued to stare at me as though assessing my intentions. Mouse and Kai flanked me, and Cormac and Orlan took seats on either side of their mother.

The silence stretched between us. I had no idea what the protocol was here. How I was supposed to act. What I was allowed to ask or not ask. I was so afraid I'd say something to anger them, that I said nothing at all. Instead, I bounced my leg up and down.

It wasn't until Kai put his hand there, that I finally stilled.

The act didn't go unnoticed by Cormac, who was staring at where Kai's hand would be even though it was hidden by the table.

"What did my mother want you to help me with?" I asked, unsure what questions to even ask.

"Determining what your powers are and how to control them," the queen answered.

That was no surprise.

"Why didn't you agree to help?"

The queen sighed, relaxing her shoulders, looking more exhausted than I registered when she first walked in. "We have had laws forbidding our contact with humans for two thousand years."

"Two thousand years?" That seemed like a long time to be living alongside humans and not having any contact with them. "Why?"

"Before these laws humans and Fair Folk lived alongside one another. Worked together to ensure a thriving planet. As our two species mixed, children of both worlds were born. These children of mixed blood were seen as less powerful than the Fair Folk, and the council of Elders worried our diluted God-blood would weaken our magic and destroy our home."

"Except, that's not what happened. You disappeared and kept your *pure* blood, and the earth perished anyway," I commented.

The thought of never being good enough flitted into my brain. I wasn't of their world. I didn't have *pure* God-blood, but I didn't have pure human blood either. I was likely somewhere in between.

"Yes," the queen admitted without further explanation.

My head bounced between the three Fair Folk in front of me. "Why did it perish?"

Cormac answered, his tone so harsh it sent a shiver down my spine. "Because humans are ill-equipped to care for the Earth."

Orlan's easy smile turned sour. "And why are they so ill-equipped, *brother*?"

Cormac didn't even acknowledge the question.

"Because when we abandoned the humans, we took our magic. But it wasn't just our magic we took with us, was it?" she continued, her words a sharp barb aimed at her brother. "We took our knowledge of the Earth and how to care for it with us. And how long did it take, brother, for the humans to forget with their short lifespans?"

This time, he answered. "Seven human generations."

"Seven hundred years, and all knowledge was lost. We left them with *nothing*." Orlan's voice cracked with emotion.

Cormac's lips held their firm line, but he didn't try to contradict her.

"The source of our power comes from the Earth, and as she began to die, so did our powers. We had forgotten our own stories, and instead blamed humans. When the Earth perished, we faded into the Otherworld, afraid we'd never return to our home," the queen continued, solemnly.

"And when my mother restored the planet, you were able to return?" I guessed.

The queen nodded. "We are not sure how, or why, but the path to this place was reopened and the council decided we should return."

"But you still haven't changed your laws?" Mouse asked next to me.

The queen shook her head. "There are many among us, and among the council, that would start a war to eliminate the humans."

"You are parasites," Cormac hissed.

The queen shot Cormac a look that silenced whatever he was about to add to that statement.

When she returned her gaze to me, her eyes were softer. "At the moment, my hands are tied. I do not have the majority of the council vote to eliminate our human laws, as outdated and ridiculous I may think they are. I cannot risk the crown, standing against the council."

"So, what now? We just walk out of here? Forget you exist?"

The queen shook her head, looking as though she didn't know what to say.

"Excuse what seems to me to be an obvious question," Mouse interjected, "but is Sol really just human?" He shot me a quick, apologetic look.

"She clearly has God-blood, but without knowing her bloodline, she will be categorized as a human, despite her powers. Just as her mother was," the queen answered.

"What about testing her?" Orlan asked.

I perked up at that. I wasn't sure how I felt about being tested, but I was also curious to know what was hidden in my veins and where it might have come from.

The queen considered Orlan's question before addressing Cormac. "What do you think?"

Orlan rolled her eyes at the clear dismissal.

"What's the ultimate goal here?" he responded.

"I guess we cannot know how she will be received, even if we know her bloodline. All we can do is proceed one step at a time." The queen looked at me as if struggling with something.

"Bloodlines and testing aside, we have a more immediate problem," I said.

All three royals looked as though I were speaking a different language.

"We were attacked as our boat docked. An explosion meant to take me out. There is a mounting threat aimed at people like me. Which means—"

Orlan finished for me. "They're after us too."

"That's impossible," Cormac interjected. "Humans can't see the Fair Folk."

"And how do you know some of your own people aren't sympathetic to their cause?" I shot back.

"We'd know."

"Just like you knew I was nothing but a helpless human, before I dissolved your weak ass magical shield?"

Orlan almost spit across the table, reigning in her laugh.

Kai placed his hand back on my knee as a warning. Cormac noticed the movement, acutely aware of the two of us.

The queen held up her hand. "Enough. We will investigate your theories, Solana." She turned her attention to Cormac. "As a precaution."

With my mounting frustration, my blue flame sparked between my fingers. I wanted to shove the spark so far up Cormac's ass that he'd fry from the inside out.

"Keep that thought to yourself, Chaos."

Oh, shit. I didn't know I'd opened our communication channel. *"Don't act like you don't want me to."*

Kai's mouth kicked up into a mischievous grin.

Cormac didn't miss our silent communication, his eyes narrowing even further. He knew something was going on between us, even if he couldn't guess we were speaking to one another.

My smile turned sweet and innocent. A forced sweet, as I directed it at Cormac.

The queen addressed me next. "I will send word when we are ready to have you tested."

I nodded. I didn't really have a choice. It's not as though I could walk out of this place and forget everything I'd just learned. The Fair Folk made the mission I was sent here for much more complicated, and I was guessing they played a much larger role in it than any of us expected. It would explain a lot if, somehow, they were involved.

The queen stood, motioning for her children to do the same.

Kai, Mouse, and I stood after them.

"For now, stay in your room. Until you're tested, and I make a formal announcement of your presence, you will not be safe."

That statement made my stomach turn.

"Cormac and Orlan will be in contact with you," the queen continued.

That was code for keeping an eye on us to make sure we didn't leave our room.

The queen then turned on her heel and marched out of the room. Her guards and children followed.

It was an abrupt dismissal that left me with burning questions swimming in my head as we silently made our way back to our room.

On any other day, if my mind weren't occupied by everything I'd just learned, I may have noticed the dark eyes. I may have noticed we were being followed. And, as we closed the door to our room, those eyes climbed the tree, disappearing behind the foliage above.

Chapter Twenty-One

"You two were oddly silent during that whole thing," I commented, closing the door to our room.

"No offense, Lady, but this is all way over our heads," Mouse replied.

Falling onto the soft bed behind me, I stared up at the branches above. "It's more than I can comprehend too."

"What's our next move?" Mouse asked tentatively.

I sighed. "I need to find Lily."

"What about your test?" Kai asked.

Something caught my eye in the canopy above. A dark blur of movement, but when I tried to find it, I was met with nothing but a breeze blowing the leaves in a soothing dance. "Out of morbid curiosity I'll do their test. Lily's our priority, though. And we need to somehow send a message to my parents."

"You think the queen will help?" Mouse asked, sounding skeptical.

"Unlikely."

"Then what are you going to do?" Mouse asked, though the look on his face made me believe he already knew my answer, and he didn't like it one bit.

As I went to open my mouth, Kai interrupted. "Absolutely not."

I frowned. "You have no idea what I was going to say."

Kai stepped closer to me, eyes blazing. "I don't have to know to already know it isn't a good idea."

I shook my head at the words he'd said to me so many times. In this case, though, there was no light tone or hint of mischief. This time, there was worry behind those words.

"I'm not going to do anything stupid. I'm going to hide out by the palace and see if I can get any information from the thoughts of the Fair Folk that pass by," I said, stripping my dress, leaving me standing in sage green undergarments.

I didn't think about it. I'd gotten way too comfortable with these men.

"We don't know anything about the Fair Folk." Kai said, his voice a deep baritone.

"We'd already be dead if they wanted us to be," I shot back, grabbing my cleaned and repaired fighting leathers off the couch at the end of the bed.

Kai raked a hand through his hair. "I'm coming with you."

Pulling on my pants, I responded with a simple, "No."

He didn't listen, pulling off his formal coat and shirt, and tugging down a simple T-shirt and black pants.

Mouse's eyes volleyed between us, but he seemed determined to stay out of the argument.

"We have no weapons," Kai murmured, with a shake of his head, "and they have magic."

I waved a hand in his direction, finishing with my outfit. "No need."

Kai scoffed but didn't say anything as he opened the door and ushered me out, following as I exited.

"You're going to be the death of me, Chaos." His words were barely a whisper.

We stayed off the main path, slinking between trees and bushes out of sight of the buildings that wrapped around every large tree.

"What if the Fair Folk have superhuman hearing?" I asked Kai, trying to ease my anxiety and not knowing what to think of the situation we found ourselves in. Let alone the fact that humans were somehow illegal here.

Kai grumbled. *"Which is why I didn't like this idea."*

To make matters worse, it seemed every honeybee within a ten-mile radius decided it was time to follow me.

Kai kept glancing up nervously at the trees, and the buzzing that continued to grow louder the further we walked.

"Can you call them off?" he asked, halting my movement with a hand on my shoulder.

"They don't speak English," I deadpanned.

He didn't take the bait, but eyed me with something that would, no doubt, go unsaid. *"They're going to get us caught."*

I threw my hands up in frustration. *"No shit."*

I pushed forward, ripping his hand from my shoulder and ignoring his warning. There wasn't anything I could do about the bees. They'd always followed me.

Instead, I opened the channels around me, hoping to catch a threatening thought before we ended up with a sword through our heart, or a vine wrapped around our necks. The irony that I could be killed with the same magic my mother possessed, didn't go unnoticed.

Thoughts poured in, but so far, none were threatening. Surprisingly, their thoughts were a lot like humans—mostly mundane ones about what to make for dinner, or what time they needed to pick up their kids. Some included the odd thought about magic use, but with my family, those didn't seem strange either.

This time, we ended up on the other side of the palace. It was designed identical to the front, but the symbols and pictures were darker and more menacing. This side faced north, appearing to rarely receive any sunlight, giving the pictures an eerie quality.

I shivered involuntarily, staring up at the gruesome images before us. The entirety of the wood was carved with images of war and death. Blood red ink stained the bleached wood, making the tree appear as though it were bleeding too.

We crouched behind a bush, far from any foot traffic but close enough for me to hear thoughts clearly.

Both of us sat in silence as I filtered through the ordinary thoughts, waiting for anything important.

"Human? Here?"

I sat up straighter, and Kai glanced over.

"Humans cannot be trusted."

"Parasites, the lot of them."

"I don't understand why the queen doesn't wipe them off the earth."

I furrowed my brow.

"Sol?" Kai whispered, trying not to disturb my eavesdropping, but clearly concerned.

Holding up a finger, I concentrated on the few streams of thoughts that mentioned humans.

"Powerless creatures."

"While we're at it, we should get rid of the Old Ones too. Vermin, the lot of them."

"I've never met a human! How exciting! I hope the rumors are true."

"Humans don't have magic, why are we so afraid of them?"

I chucked at that one. Why, indeed?

"Traitors."

That one word caught my attention, and I tried to drown out every other thought.

"Siding with humans, disgraceful."

That's all I got from that stream of thought, as their channel drifted too far. I cursed under my breath.

"We'd be so much better off working with humans, instead of hiding out here like powerless cowards."

I raised a brow at that one.

"There will come a time when we need humans, and they will abandon us as we have abandoned them."

"The queen will go against the council, I'll make sure of it, and then we will take her down."

Kai must have noticed my tense body and rapid breathing, because he nudged my knee, stealing my attention.

I looked at him through wide eyes. *"I think someone is planning to take the crown."*

"But why?"

"I have no idea," I replied, frustrated I couldn't hear more.

I sighed. All I wanted was to find Lily and protect my family. This felt like a major detour that I didn't need to get myself wrapped up in.

"They just let that human wraith get captured. Disgraceful."

"What?" I choked, willing the person to keep thinking. Knowing, without knowing, that they were thinking about Lily.

Kai tensed, ready for an invisible threat, his eyes scanning the forest around us, but always landing back on me.

"She could have helped us."

With that last thought, whoever it was that was thinking them drifted out of range.

"Fuck," I muttered out loud, startling Kai.

It was a dumb lapse in judgment, because a moment later, a man came out of the thick brush, sword pointed at me. Vines wrapped around our limbs, immobilizing us, and I had the strangest urge to laugh.

Kai struggled against the hold, but the vines just wound tighter around him.

"Don't struggle," I muttered, knowing my mother's magic and how it worked.

Kai stilled, his eyes drifting to the soldier in front of me, his sword now against my throat.

"This is awkward," I decided to start with.

I could feel Kai rolling his eyes. Not only at my dumb statement, but at the fact that he knew this would happen and he let me do it anyway.

The soldier studied me, cocking his head to the side.

I cocked my head to the side, mirroring his. Apparently, I had a death wish, but mocking was my self-preservation strategy. A shit one, though.

"You're under arrest," the soldier finally gritted out through clenched teeth. "Humans are not allowed to trespass on this land."

"We weren't trespassing, but I can see how you might think we were," I replied, sounding less terrified than I felt.

The soldier raised a brow.

"I was brought here against my will."

The soldier now looked completely confused.

Get in line, I thought to myself.

It was Kai's turn to raise a brow. *"And what are we getting in line for?"*

"Shit. How did your channel open?" I asked, as if he'd know the answer.

Kai shook his head, and the soldier's head swiveled between us, clearly sensing something.

"If you have issue with our presence," I continued to the soldier, "you need to bring it up with your queen."

The soldier's eyes widened. "The queen?"

Now he looked downright lost.

I sighed. I didn't want to start more trouble, but trouble seemed to be my middle name these days.

"I am under her protection, and only here by her request. I'll be gone soon." I didn't know if any of that was true. Were we under her protection? She did say to stay in our rooms, which I immediately ignored.

The guilt seeped in, making me feel foolish.

"What's he thinking?" Kai pulled me out of my unhelpful thoughts.

"I should kill them. But if they are here at the queen's request? Are they lying?"

There was a pause in his thought process as we stared at each other. The killing part didn't bode well, but the queen made him question himself.

"Maybe they are handing over these humans too."

I saw the moment the soldier made his decision, and though I knew it wouldn't be death, the glint in his eye and his step forward made my gut twist.

Kai must have seen it, too, and he lunged for the soldier in front of me, but the vines pulled tighter and began to circle his neck. He choked as his airway began to close.

It took me another moment to realize a vine was also snaking around my throat. I opened my mouth to shout, but all that came out was . . .

Scorpions? Were those scorpions?

A whole army of scorpions poured from my mouth and ran for the soldier.

His eyes grew comically wide as he scrambled backward, tripping on the underbrush and falling on his ass. The magic he held around us slipped, and Kai sucked in a deep, gasping breath.

"Did—" Kai began, but I pushed the vines away, grabbing his arm, not letting him finish that question. We took off through the forest.

Oddly enough, most people didn't give us a second glance. We were a crashing blur of bodies tearing through the lush forest, and I assumed they thought we were one of them.

When we reached our room, we raced up the stairs, not stopping until the door was locked behind us.

Kai collapsed against the door, heaving breaths moving his chest up and down. I fell on the bed, trying to suck in enough air.

Mouse looked up from a table in the corner of the room, mouth half-full of food.

He didn't look surprised at our entrance and swallowed casually.

"I'd ask what happened, but I can already guess," he said, nonchalantly, taking another bite of food.

"Scorpions," I huffed out between breaths, still in shock over what happened. Or, *how* it happened.

"Excuse me?" Mouse straightened in his chair, food hovering just in front of his mouth.

Kai, his breath back to normal, pushed off the wall. "A soldier wanted to harm her, and scorpions came out of her mouth," he explained with so little emotion that even my mouth fell open.

He finally noticed our attention and shrugged as though all of this was perfectly normal.

"Well," Mouse began, "I did *not* expect that."

I groaned, my head falling into my hands. "I wish that was the worst of it."

When both men remained silent, I pulled my face from my fingers and was met with confused stares.

"I can't confirm it, but I think some of the Fair Folk are planning a coup, and I think the Fair Folk are responsible for Lily's disappearance." My voice sounded far more defeated than I intended.

There was a long pause where both men glanced at each other with a look I couldn't read.

"So, even more complicated than we anticipated?" Mouse asked.

I dropped my head back into my hands. "Way past complicated."

Chapter Twenty-Two

When I woke, Kai and Mouse were both gone, but something warm was touching my head.

Moving away from it, I found a ball of brown hair curled up on my pillow.

I let out a small scream, and the creature jumped up, the brown hair falling around its face and body. Large black eyes stared back at me. Through the long hair, the color of bark, I made out green skin, and a long, thin body, though the creature couldn't have been more than three feet tall. It had feet that looked like hands, and hands that had many more fingers than the usual five.

"I didn't mean to scare you," a voice drifted into my head. It didn't sound human, though I could understand every word.

The creature inched closer, fixing its black eyes on me, studying me intently. It took all of me not to run or scream again.

"I'm Ardil. You're Sol. And we have waited millennia for you."

My eyes widened.

"It has been thousands of years since there has been someone that can communicate with ALL Folk."

I had no idea what to make of this creature. It looked as if he were taken straight from the books my parents read.

"Who, or what, are you?" I asked, unsure of where to start. Unsure if that question was offensive.

"The Fair Folk call us tree spirits, or the Old Ones, but we are Crann Bethadh, The Feeding Tree, and we have been around far longer than they have, and we will be around long after they are gone. Though they believe us to be powerless, we possess magic far older than theirs. They have forgotten."

Shaking my head, I only became more confused. *"What do you want from me?"*

"To restore the old ways."

"Old ways? And how do you propose I do that? I know nothing."

"Oh, but you know more than you think you do. If you listen closely, the answers are there."

I shook my head again. *"You're speaking in riddles."*

Just then, the door opened, and before Mouse walked through, Ardil disappeared into the branches above. I stared after him, but he was already gone, blending effortlessly into the canopy. I felt his eyes, though. Always watching. Or perhaps, it was his magic probing my own.

"Sol?" Mouse asked. He carried a tray of food, and had frozen in the doorway, staring at me with a wrinkle between his eyes.

I waved him off. "I'll explain later."

Mouse moved to the opposite side of the room, setting down the tray of food on a small table by the window.

"Where's Kai?" I asked, shaking the sleep from my limbs, feeling a bit odd without him.

Mouse eyed my sympathetically. "I think he just needed a little space."

I pouted, and Mouse shook his head and chuckled. "Be careful, Sol. You could fool me with those looks."

"Fool you how?"

"Fool me into believing there's something there."

"Something where?"

Mouse eyed me suspiciously, and then the lines of his face softened as he spoke, "You honestly don't know?"

I let out an exasperated sigh. "Haven't we established that already?"

He chuckled. "Fool me into believing there is more there between the two of you."

"Ohhh . . ." I dragged out the word and then ran a hand through my hair.

Mouse raised his brows at my reaction and then snorted. "You two are impossible."

I narrowed my eyes. "Excuse me if there has been a lot going on. And I'm sorry, but Kai doesn't exactly make it easy."

Mouse snorted. "That's an understatement."

"Perhaps you should talk to him," Mouse added, when I didn't respond, in between spooning eggs into his mouth.

I took another deep breath and let it out slowly. It's not that I didn't want to talk to him. It was that I was afraid. Afraid of what it meant if it was anything more than attraction. I hadn't let myself think too hard about it, and I hadn't planned on thinking about it—well—*ever*.

Before I could speak, the door opened, and Kai strolled in. He was shirtless and wet, like he had just gone for a swim. I stared at him as he threw his shirt on the chair and stalked toward the bathroom without saying a word or even glancing in our direction.

"I think you're drooling," Mouse laughed through a mouthful of food.

Shutting my mouth, I glared at him. "I'm *not* drooling. And even if I was drooling, it would be entirely your fault."

"Mine?" Mouse acted surprised.

"Yes, yours," I growled, standing up and throwing open the dresser drawers to find some clothes. "If it weren't for your little comment, I would still be blissfully unaware of his shirtless form."

Mouse snorted. "Right."

When Kai emerged from the bathroom, only a towel wrapped around his waist, I couldn't help the heat that flooded my cheeks, unable to look away.

Mouse laughed so loudly that Kai finally snapped his attention away from his task of getting dressed.

"What?" Kai's eyes darted between the two of us.

"Nothing," I mumbled, my eyes downcast as I continued to fumble with my clothing.

"What'd you do to her, Mouse?"

"Me?" Mouse asked incredulously.

"I've never seen her so—so flustered before." His brow was creased, and the lines of his mouth were pinched.

"Oh, for the love of the Gods, can we just drop it?" I practically shouted, standing up and shoving the chair away, before I stalked to the door.

"I'm definitely missing something," Kai stated.

"No shit." Mouse laughed harder as he watched me walk to the bathroom and slam the door behind me.

"And why the hell did you leave the room?" I shouted at them from the safety of the bathroom.

"The queen sent an escort," Mouse shouted. "Though I'm pretty sure Kai ditched his."

"I didn't ditch him; he chose not to follow me into the lake."

Behind the doors I rolled my eyes and willed my heart to slow.

"What did I do?" Kai whispered to me later.

I shot him a questioning look, before it dawned on me what he was asking. "You did nothing."

"Then why do I feel like there is something I should know, but somehow don't?"

"I'm surprised Mouse didn't say anything after I trapped myself in the bathroom." I spoke into his mind, because I didn't want anyone to overhear us as Orlan, Cormac, and the queen walked across the great hall in the palace to meet with us.

We were meeting to discuss my test, and I hoped, to also discuss what I'd eavesdropped on.

"He said to ask you."

"Of course he did." I rolled my eyes.

"So, you're both going to leave me in the dark?"

"Appears that way."

"Since when were you too afraid to say what was on your mind?" he challenged me with a grin.

My eyes darted to his lips, and then back to his eyes. *"I'm not afraid."*

"No? Then why don't you just tell me?"

"Because it's more fun this way."

Now it was his turn to look at my lips as I curled them into a challenging grin, and then without realizing, I bit down.

I heard his intake of breath right before he turned away from me, switching his focus back to the room.

Orlan greeted us cheerily, and I was beginning to think she didn't have any other emotion besides elation.

Cormac and the queen sat at the large table in the center of the room, motioning for us to join them.

Queen Nessa had a beautiful silver gown on, that sparkled as if it were made of light. It hugged her tightly until her waist, then fell gracefully from her waist to the floor. The sleeves were long and embroidered in silver thread with trees that appeared to move in a phantom wind as she moved her arms.

"Cormac will take you to your test," the queen got straight to the point. No greetings or idle chit chat.

Orlan went to protest, but her mother held up her hand, and Orlan simply sighed.

"Ariella will conduct your test and will bring you both back to the palace to report on the results," the queen continued.

Nodding, I looked to Kai who was staring at Cormac. There was a warning in that glare.

Cormac appeared bored, but it was clear that he noticed Kai's attention.

"It's OK, I'll be fine," I said to Kai who finally tore his eyes away from Cormac.

"It's not you I'm worried about."

I laughed out loud, unable to hold it in, and Cormac volleyed between Kai and me, knowing something was going on but he was at a loss for what was happening.

Deciding it wasn't worth it to keep my power from them, as they'd come to light after my test anyway, I explained, "I can speak mind-to-mind."

The three Fair Folk royals looked at each other with a hint of shock.

It was the queen who spoke first. "All Fair Folk used to have that ability."

I sat up straighter in my chair. "Used to?"

She sighed. "As the Earth died, our power waned. We've lost a lot."

The weight of those words hung heavy in the air between us. I suspected it wasn't just a loss of magic she was talking about.

"Any other powers we should know about," Cormac snapped.

Orlan looked enraged by her brother's tone.

"I can read your hateful thoughts," I said without a hint of emotion.

Cormac's eyes widened, but Orlan clapped with delight, and I had to admit, I was curious about their relationship. They seemed the opposite in every way.

"You're a channel jumper," Orlan exclaimed.

"A what?" I asked.

"Your mother explained the channels of energy she can feel right?"

I nodded.

"You can not only feel those channels, but you can also communicate and hear through them. Hence being able to read thoughts. But people with both abilities often could jump through the channels and use them as a mode of transport. Of course, this is only in theory. Folk with those abilities haven't existed for a very long time, if at all."

My eyes widened, and Mouse let out a little gasp.

Orlan looked between the three of us, understanding dawning. "You've jumped before, haven't you?"

"Once. But it wasn't from one place to another. It was from one *world* to another."

Orlan looked at her mother and brother, who were studying me, brows wrinkled.

"Do you know what this means?" Orlan said, awe filling her voice.

"Yes. It means we have a much bigger problem," Cormac said, not taking his eyes off me.

Before anyone could say anything else, though, the doors abruptly swung open, and two guards dragged a man into the room.

In the commotion, I didn't notice the man, but as the queen ordered the guards to stand down, and they stepped back, I gasped, and before I knew what I was doing I closed the distance between us and punched Marcus right in his eye.

He instinctively grabbed his face, backed away, and wheeled toward me, eyes widening as he realized who had just hit him.

The room was eerily silent, and no one dared to move. Not even the guards.

"How could you?" I whispered through gritted teeth, shaking with anger.

"Sol . . ." he whispered back.

"How could you?" I said, louder this time, hating the anger I couldn't quell.

Marcus hung his head, still holding his eye. "I'm sorry, Sol," he whispered, sounding as though he was begging for mercy.

"You left us without saying goodbye. You let us believe you were dead. I was a *child*, Marcus. I *needed* you," I seethed.

Marcus shook his head, tears spilling down his face. "I'm so, so sorry, Sol. I have no excuse. I was broken. I knew you wouldn't understand."

"You never even tried to explain it. And I knew why. We all knew. But I really needed to hear it from you. You were like a *father* to me."

More tears spilled from his eyes, as he finally pulled his hand away from the eye that was quickly swelling and took a step closer to me.

"I would spend a lifetime making it up to you, if I could just make that look on your face go away. Everything I've done since I've left has been for you."

Putting my head in my hands, I let out a sob, and Marcus closed the rest of the distance between us and wrapped me in a hug. A hug that felt so much like home, even though it had been fifteen years since I'd felt his comforting arms.

"You have to know that I'd do anything for you, kiddo," he whispered into my hair, as I shook in his arms, desperately trying to stuff the emotion back into my body.

After what seemed like a few minutes where no one even moved, he finally pulled away, his stare serious again.

He stepped back reluctantly, keeping an eye on my face. "Apologies for the dramatic entrance, but we have a problem." He looked around the room and addressed everyone. "I found Lily, but I couldn't get to her, it was too dangerous." He looked back at the queen and added, "They're advancing quickly, we have very little time."

"What?" I stuttered. His presence had shocked me, but knowing he was looking for Lily almost knocked me over; Kai caught me just before I did.

"I've been a human contact for Ness, here, for the last few years," Marcus explained.

My eyes widened, and the queen added, "In secret, of course."

Marcus nodded at her but quickly returned his attention to me. "I have only been reporting on what's happening with the humans around these parts, but it came to my attention about a week ago that Lily was here. I went searching for her, hoping to speak to her, but found her missing. Half of her contacts were also missing. The remaining group that had been working with her had scattered. I tracked down one of them, and he explained that they'd been taken by the very same group who has been destroying the forest and attacking your family."

Kai squeezed my arm, sensing my distress. But he didn't know why the knot in my stomach tightened. The queen seemed uninvolved in her disappearance, which meant this whole thing was far more twisted than I expected. It meant that the thoughts I'd heard didn't make any sense, and this web everyone was weaving was becoming more tangled the further we dug.

"You—" I couldn't finish the statement.

"I've been using my tech to gather intel for Ness, in attempt to get the council to trust humans again."

I opened my mouth, and then closed it again, unable to form a coherent thought.

"Sol, Ariella will be waiting for you. The timing is not ideal, but the test will help our cause." Nessa turned to Cormac who was watching me with a pinched face, as though he was worried about me.

That couldn't be right.

"We'll talk when you're done, kiddo," Marcus whispered, taking a hesitant step toward me.

Instinctively, I stepped away from him, crashing back into Kai's solid chest.

Marcus flinched, and my heart sank. I hadn't meant to hurt him with my reaction, I just didn't know how to process everything.

Mouse pulled me from the torrent of emotions. "Well, it's always an honor to meet another of Sol's family," he said, reaching a hand out to Marcus.

Marcus stared at him with an odd look on his face, before composing himself and taking Mouse's outstretched arm.

That seemed to break the tension in the room, and the queen ushered everyone to the table.

Mouse winked at me, before following the others.

I was left with Kai, who I was still, somehow, plastered to. And Cormac.

The former finally separated himself from me, taking a large step backward, and the latter watched us with an unreadable expression.

I shook my head. *"Cormac might be a total ass, but I'm beginning to think the two of you have more in common than you think,"* I said to Kai.

A deep growl filled my head. *"If you ever . . ."*

I laughed. *"You just proved my point. Broody, the both of you."*

Cormac's face pinched, and color rose to his cheeks. He hated that we were talking about him, but I was absolutely thrilled at his reaction.

Cormac begrudgingly offered me his outstretched arm. I stared at it for a moment, then looked back at Kai, who winked. It was enough to get me to take Cormac's arm.

"I'll most definitely set the bees on him if he so much as says the wrong thing," I said to Kai, feeling the urge to reassure him that I wouldn't take any shit from Cormac.

Somehow, I felt his smile through our channel. It felt like pure sunlight.

Chapter Twenty-Three

We walked the entire way in silence. Cormac had dropped my arm after we exited the queen's palace, but stuck close to my side, a hand on the sword at his waist the entire time.

Cormac kept his eyes straight ahead, ignoring the stares and whispers from his people, but he was tense beside me, and it suddenly hit me what he was risking being seen with me.

"Thank you," I said to him.

His eyes softened the hard lines that appeared to be permanently etched on the sharp angles of his face, and he nodded almost imperceptibly.

I let my gaze wander to the diversity of the homes that existed here, along with the diversity of plant and animal life that seemed to thrive here in Tir Na Eabha. Suddenly, I felt proud of my mother. Despite her secrecy, she had done this. She had restored more than just our world. She had restored Tir Na Eabha.

She had restored magic.

When we reached the outskirts of the kingdom, Cormac stopped in front of a modest building that was located halfway up the tree. We climbed the stairs that wound around the trunk and emerged into a small, sparsely decorated space.

Ariella's workspace consisted of only one large room. It was open to the forest above, like all the other buildings, but it wrapped around a large tree in a circle and its sides were open to the forest as well. There was only a modest vining railing that kept you from falling off the side onto the forest floor.

It looked like every child's treehouse dream, and I smiled at the familiarity I felt toward my treehouse back home.

Ariella wasn't what I expected. She was very clearly one of the Fair Folk, but she had silver hair and deep wrinkles. Up until this point, I hadn't met any Fair Folk that didn't look like they were in their twenties or thirties.

She was also the only other woman here I had seen that wasn't draped in a long, colorful dress. Instead, she wore loose linen pants, the color of leaves, and a clean white linen shirt that was fitted, but not tight.

Despite looking old, she walked gracefully and easily, as the other Fair Folk did. Almost as if they were floating.

"I've been waiting for this day," she said to me, holding out her hand. Her voice was soft, but sounded ancient, as though she saw both the past and future.

I silently wondered if she could.

"It's an honor to meet you," I said, stepping forward and taking her hand.

She stared at me with light blue eyes that seemed concealed behind a mysterious fog. It was an uncomfortably long stare that was only broken when a honeybee landed on my shoulder.

A moment later, a hundred more bees descended on her workspace, landing in various places around the room, humming lightly.

"They're singing," I said, their sound filling my heart with warmth and familiarity. A reminder that no matter how far I traveled, or how strange things got, there would always be a piece of home with me.

Ariella looked at me thoughtfully, and I added as way of explanation, "They usually only come to me like this when I'm in danger. This a nice surprise."

Ariella continued to look at me as though I were a puzzle that was impossible to solve.

Cormac, who had found a chair, was eyeing the bees, wary of them.

"Shall we begin?" Ariella finally asked, choosing not to comment on the bees.

Nodding, I followed her to the opposite side of the room, where two easels waited with blank canvases.

I must have looked confused, because Ariella explained. "I've heard enough about you to have a pretty good idea of what your skills are. Don't worry, these tests are easy and won't hurt."

She walked over to the first canvas, picking up and holding out a pallet of paint and beckoning me forward.

Hesitantly grabbing the paint, I waited for her instructions.

"I want you to paint a *place* you love on one, and a *thing* you love on the other."

"OK," I said a bit hesitantly, stepping in front of the first canvas and freezing.

"Whatever comes to mind first. And don't worry about quality. Just do your best to make it look like the place and the thing, so your magic doesn't get confused." She chuckled as though she knew something I didn't, before walking away and sitting down next to Cormac to wait.

I sighed. I had painted hundreds of times, but somehow this seemed different.

"First place that comes to mind," Ariella said to my back, sensing my hesitation.

Taking a deep breath, I closed my eyes, completely unaware of a pair of black eyes watching me intently from above. When I opened them, I spent the next hour painting my mom's library in extraordinary detail.

When I put my paintbrush down, Ariella let out a surprised whistle. "You have talent girl. And I don't just mean your magic."

The color rose to my cheeks; Cormac studied the painting intently.

"Now the other," Ariella said, pointing to the other blank canvas. "No background details. Don't put the thing in any sort of space. Just paint the thing."

I nodded, knowing exactly what I was going to paint.

This time it took me only twenty minutes or so, but I used what Kai had taught me to paint a very detailed honeybee.

"Well, if all else fails, you can definitely have a job teaching art class, wouldn't you say, Cormac?"

Cormac wasn't looking at the painting this time. He was watching me.

"Do I have paint in my hair?" I asked him, awkwardly brushing my hair with my paint-stained hands. "I always get paint in my hair."

He laughed then. It took me so much by surprise that I froze, staring.

"Never mind the paint, dear," Ariella said, motioning to my first painting. "I've heard about your blue flame," she waved her hand toward Cormac, confirming who she'd heard it from, before adding, "I want you to touch the painting with your blue flame."

I sucked in a substantial amount of air. I had only done that once before, and it ended with me in some other world with someone I desperately wanted to be here with.

Ariella gave me a knowing look. "You've done this before."

I nodded.

"Show me," she said softly. "I won't let anything happen to you."

My hands shook as I reached out, calling my blue flame and lightly touching it to the first painting.

A familiar feeling took over my body, like I was being sucked through a tube. I closed my eyes, afraid I'd be sick, but it was over quicker this time. I fell, ungracefully, onto the floor of my mother's library, my hip slamming into the stone floor.

When I opened my eyes, she was there on the couch, a book in her lap, staring at me wide-eyed.

"Mom!" I shouted from the floor.

After only a fleeting moment, before I had a chance to rise, I felt the, now familiar, pull and knew I didn't have time.

"I need you!" I shouted, as the room quickly began to fade, and the falling sensation began again.

Before I lost sight of the room, Alieus, Aiden, and our father rushed in. I saw them only for a moment before I was surrounded by darkness, with a feeling like I was careening faster and faster.

A few seconds later, I fell back onto the floor of Ariella's workplace, and had to hold my hand over my mouth, afraid I was going to throw up.

The tears gathered, unbidden, in my eyes, and I swiped at them. I didn't realize how much I needed my family until that moment. How much I wanted to stay in that library. How much I wanted to run away from everything that seemed far too large for a girl who had spent her life hidden away from a world that seemed intent on destroying her. On destroying her family.

Ariella held out a hand. I took it and stood to face her. She stared at me for a long while, as if she knew where I had gone and what I was feeling. I felt exposed but oddly comforted by her. She felt a lot like my mother.

"We've only read of Folk with your abilities. It was fabled that long ago, we possessed powers like yours, but most Fair Folk have reasoned that these powers were just made-up bedtime stories and had never been true. We have forgotten . . ."

Shifting uncomfortably on my feet, I willed my stomach to stop rising in my throat and my tears to stay put.

Suddenly, out of nowhere, Cormac walked over handing me a sandwich.

With a shaky hand, I took it from him and studied it. It appeared to be a regular sandwich.

"It's not poisonous," he said, so seriously I couldn't tell if it was a joke.

I huffed but took a bite. The food settled my stomach, and I mumbled my thanks to Cormac as Ariella nodded toward my second painting. "This one should be an easier test. Less nausea producing, I suspect."

"Same as before, touch the bee with your blue flame," she added.

"What's supposed to happen?" I asked her, not wanting any surprises.

She shrugged. "Guess we will find out together." She chuckled as she walked back to Cormac, whose face was scrunched in concern. Perhaps he did have more than just two looks and two feelings.

"You scared of me? For me? Or because this bee might come right out of the painting and attack you?" I asked Cormac, my back to him.

"All of the above?"

I snorted, then touched the bee with my blue flame, less hesitantly this time, and the bee instantly came floating out of the painting and circled my head. It's joyous humming filled my ears.

Ariella squealed in delight.

When the bee landed on my open palm, Ariella and Cormac came over to study it.

"Can you talk to it?" Ariella asked.

"I don't know," I replied. I had told Kai I couldn't, but I suspected I was wrong, considering I could talk to Ardil, and considering the bees seemed to respond to my emotions when I was in danger.

I reached out with my mind. *"Hello, it's nice to meet you."* It was all I could think of to say.

The bee vibrated in response, and Ariella let out another ecstatic noise. "Can you ask it to do something?"

"Can you fly to that branch and back?"

The bee immediately flew to the nearest tree branch, then wheeled around and came back to my outstretched hand.

This time Ariella clapped, pure euphoria lighting up her every feature.

"OK, now send it back," she instructed me.

"How?"

"The same way you brought it here."

Touching it lightly with my flame, the bee instantly disappeared back into the painting.

Ariella clapped again, as she looked between my hand and the painting.

When she went to open her mouth to speak, Kai's voice drifted toward us from the other side of the treehouse. "We have a problem."

Chapter Twenty-Four

Kai filled us in briefly as we ran back to the palace. People jumped out of our way, their curious gazes following our path.

The council had caught wind of humans in Tir Na Eabha, and one of the council members came to detain us. All hell broke loose when they arrived, and Kai was able to slip out undetected.

I couldn't gauge how Cormac was taking the information, so I opened his channel.

"The council is overstepping."

It was the only confirmation I needed that he wouldn't hand us over, so I shut the channel, focusing on keeping up with the two men whose legs were far longer than mine.

We raced up the hundreds of steps, and by the time we reached the doors, I was struggling to suck air into my lungs.

Kai eyed me, and despite the situation, the corner of his mouth tipped up.

"I'm surprised you made it this far without falling," he said as the three of us caught our breath before throwing ourselves into the mayhem.

I rolled my eyes but didn't further engage him. But his smile didn't go unnoticed.

"Let's go," Cormac grumbled, finally pushing the doors open. He straightened his shoulders, his body tense. He went from seeming almost human to a true prince in a blink.

We walked calmly down the hallway even though shouts echoed from the main hall.

My gaze drifted to the living wall and landed on the red flower. Without stopping, I plucked a flower and stuffed it in my pocket.

Kai raised a brow next to me.

"Just in case," I said.

Kai shook his head but didn't say a word.

Cormac paused at the door to the main hall. A door that was covered in carvings of various Celtic symbols. His hand lay motionless on the door, as if he didn't want to enter. As if he didn't want to be in the middle of all of this.

It was only a moment, but it was enough to have me questioning the burden leadership caused. What sacrifices Cormac may have made in the past and what sacrifices he might be about to make.

And I knew nothing of his people or his life. I knew nothing of the motivation behind his words and actions. I knew nothing of the Fair Folk. Hell, I knew nothing about myself.

When Cormac pushed open the door, the space was filled with soldiers surrounding the perimeter, not allowing anyone in or out. At the center, the queen was arguing with someone I didn't recognize, though he was clearly one of the Fair Folk.

Marcus and Mouse were pressed up against the chests of two soldiers, their hands, feet, and mouths bound with vines, unable to move or speak.

Orlan was pale, listening to the conversation between the queen and the mysterious man.

I wanted to run to Mouse and Marcus, but Kai grabbed my arm, holding me back.

"Wait. Listen. Observe," he said, and I relaxed, sticking close to him.

Cormac strode forward to join his mother, and my hand drifted to the flower in my pocket. I stroked its petals, doing as Kai asked—watching, waiting.

"We can no longer stay separate, Councilman," she pleaded. "We are already involved whether we want to be or not."

"You know the law," was his only response. "We cannot allow them to leave and inform the humans of our location."

"They already know our location! And you know it!" the queen shouted, losing her composure.

"You know the laws," he seethed, and then he turned to the soldiers holding Mouse and Marcus, one of which I recognized. The soldier that tried to kill us in the forest. The one I set scorpions on.

Suddenly I realized exactly what had happened, and the guilt churned in my stomach.

I had done this.

I had put everyone in danger because of my selfishness. If I had obeyed the queen, we wouldn't have ended up here.

"Kill them," the councilman ordered.

At the same moment Kai whispered, "Now."

And, somehow, I knew exactly what he meant.

The bees descended on the great hall in numbers I couldn't even fathom. The hum of a million wings drowned out the yelling, and their swirling force created a gust of wind.

Everyone stopped at the spectacle, watching in horror as they were surrounded by the sheer power of the unity of a tiny insect. A super-organism that together could pump enough venom into our bloodstream that there would be no surviving it.

Wide eyes looked around in panic, but no one moved. A few vines shot out of nowhere, swatting at the tornado of bees, and a clump of them fell to the ground.

I tensed, wanting to protect them. Kai held me back. "Wait," he whispered.

The bees reformed their tornado, instantly filling in the space the dead bees had created.

"What are they waiting for?" someone asked with a shaky voice.

That's when Kai let me go, and I stepped forward into the swirling mass. They parted for me.

"Me," I said.

Everyone stared, unsure what to do.

I caught the eye of the councilman, and where confusion and terror should have been, there was something else—curiosity.

That's when everything got even more confusing. Ardil dropped from the branches above, landing at my feet. Along with him, a dozen more creatures dropped, forming a circle around me.

"What the?" a soldier stammered.

"She is not fully human, but nor do I believe she is one of us."

The voice came from the doorway to the great hall, and everyone's attention shifted to that voice.

Ariella addressed the queen next as we all stood there in stunned silence. "She's a channel jumper. She can move herself from channel to channel, but she can also pull things through the channel to her.

Her flame appears to activate the channels, but I suspect that is only coincidence. I believe her blue flame has a different sort of magic. One that has *never* been seen in our people."

I had no idea what she meant by that, and from the looks on everyone's faces, no one else did either.

"Impossible," the queen said.

That seemed to be everyone's favorite word lately.

"That doesn't excuse the presence of the other humans," the councilman cut in.

Ariella chuckled, stepping to my side, unafraid of the bees or the Old Ones surrounding me. In fact, the Old Ones parted to let her through. "No, but I doubt you want to know what these bees will do if you harm any of them. It only takes one thought, or one desperate emotion, and you will incite the wrath of a million venomous insects intent on destroying the threat." Ariella waved her hand as if that didn't even matter. "Besides, we cannot afford to fight right now, which is something you're aware of, councilman."

She said councilman as if she knew something we didn't, and the man paled.

"Call off your dogs," Ariella said, glaring at the councilman.

There was a long stretch of silence, while the councilman stared down Ariella, who stood statue-still next to me.

Finally relenting, he waved his hand, and the soldiers released Marcus and Mouse, and together they all exited the hall, not giving us a second glance.

Once the doors slammed shut, the bees dispersed, and all but Ardil remained next to me, the other Old Ones disappearing into the trees.

"Well, that was fun," Ariella said, smiling.

I shook my head, as did the queen.

"You have traitors among your people, Ness. They wouldn't have been able to hide themselves, and their resources, without the help of the Fair Folk. They're shielded, somehow. We can only see what we want to see." Marcus picked up their conversation as if nothing had just happened.

"Impossible," she mumbled, turning away from Marcus.

"Is it, Mother?" Cormac said, stepping toward her.

Wasn't he always the skeptical one? What was happening here?

She looked up at him, worry wrinkling her brow.

"There are only a handful of Fair Folk that can shield on such a large scale," Cormac continued.

"But that's impossible," the queen repeated.

"I know it seems that way. All those Folk are from powerful families. To risk that . . ." He inched closer to his mother.

The queen was silent for a few moments, and Orlan looked white as a ghost behind her.

"We need to get Lily out. She will know everything," Marcus said, carefully.

The queen shook her head. "It's too risky, and too dangerous."

"Do we have a choice?"

She looked at him, and I couldn't read her face.

"You have the ability to wipe them out, Ness. To keep your people safe. Why not do it?" he asked, but his voice was still careful and quiet, as though he were walking some fine line.

"Because I have no support! Did you not just see what happened here?" she shouted.

Kai broke the long silence that followed the queen's declaration. "We'll get Lily," he said, nodding toward Mouse.

Mouse's eyes widened but he made no move to contradict him, only mumbled, "Sure, pick the man with a limp. That'll end well."

Kai pretended not to hear him.

The queen appeared shocked by the notion that two humans would just walk right into an enemy camp. I didn't blame her, in fact, I went to open my mouth when Cormac cut me off.

"As will I." He stepped next to Kai, who went rigid but kept his mouth shut.

I wasn't sure where Cormac stood on any of this. He was cold and cryptic at the best of times and appeared to switch opinions quite easily and often.

The queen appeared shocked by his sudden willingness. "You'd risk your life for this? And your crown?"

Cormac nodded. "It's not just for them, it's for us too. We can't sit by and watch the humans destroy our home again."

Of course, this was about humans to him.

"You'd put the entire blame on us?" I couldn't help the tumble of words.

Cormac's gaze shifted to mine, his eyes nothing but narrow slits. "What have humans proven over the last five hundred years?"

"And what have you proven? That you only care about your own interests? That you refuse to fight for the literal source of your magic? You don't get to tell us how to do things when you abandoned us, and this very Earth! No wonder your magic is fading. No wonder the Earth refuses to give it back. This isn't about diluting bloodlines. This is about abandoning common decency."

Kai stepped closer to me until our shoulders were touching. I had crossed a line, and everyone knew it. Cormac's face contorted into pure rage, color rising to his perfect cheekbones.

Ardil stepped in front of Cormac, drawing his attention.

I cleared my throat. "This is Ardil."

Once again, everyone paled, though I didn't understand why.

"Channel jumpers can also communicate through channels, allowing them to communicate with almost all living things," Ariella explained as though she knew the questions swirling around in their heads.

Ardil nodded in confirmation.

"What? How?" The queen's voice was nothing but a whisper.

"Ardil says the Old One's will help me get Lily back," I relayed to them, my mouth turning down in confusion.

"We will help you, if you help us in return."

I relayed that information too.

"What is it that you want?" the queen asked Ardil.

"Freedom."

My lips parted, about to ask the obvious question, but Ardil answered before I had a chance to ask. *"Many of our kind are enslaved by the Fair Folk."*

My face must have turned from curiosity to appall, because the queen whispered, "He's asking for freedom, isn't he?"

I nodded slowly.

The queen sighed, shaking her head.

"Mom." Orlan's voice drifted softly from behind her. "You know it's the right thing to do."

"The right thing, yes, but they will have my crown for it. And what kind of monster would they have take my position?"

"Ness?" Marcus whispered.

She turned her attention to him, and I swore there was a tear in her eye.

"Let us take a small group to get Lily out. There is no need to make these big decisions yet. We don't even know what we're really up against."

The queen looked at him for a long time, before slowly resigning herself with a nod.

She addressed Ardil, next. "I cannot promise you freedom, but I do promise to try."

"A very diplomatic answer," Ardil replied, and I couldn't tell if he was being sarcastic or if he was serious.

I didn't relay that statement and waited for his answer.

"You have a deal, Queen, but I expect real action, not just empty promises."

I relayed the information to the queen, and she nodded in agreement. "You have a deal."

Then she turned to the entire group, "Marcus, Cormac, Kai, Mouse, Ardil, two of my most trusted guards, and a group of Ardil's people will leave at dawn and retrieve the human."

Marcus cleared his throat, and the queen corrected herself. "Lily. Excuse me. I would appreciate everyone's discretion at this time. Now is not the time to drop this bomb on our people."

"I want to go too," I interjected, and everyone turned to stare at me.

"You are too valuable to risk," the queen said.

Where had I heard that before?

"Sol . . ." Marcus whispered.

I turned and glared at him.

"If I may?" Ariella interrupted. "Sol, one day, I believe you would be able to channel yourself into their camp, grab Lily, and channel you both out of there, and they wouldn't even know what hit them. But you can't do that now, and we need to work on getting there."

I gave her a skeptical look but was resigned to my fate. A fate that was so common, I barely gave it a second thought.

As if understanding my many different emotions, I felt Kai step next to me, almost close enough to touch.

I opened our communication channel. He felt it the instant I did.

"I don't like what you're thinking."

I almost smiled, his words already having their desired effect.

"I always like what I'm thinking."

I felt the warmth of his smile as though it were mine. As though we were connected in a way that I hadn't felt before.

"If you're going to do something no one else is going to like, could you at least warn me ahead of time?" he asked.

"Unlikely."

Kai shook his head, but he was smiling. Genuinely smiling.

I remained a silent spectator as everyone prepared for what seemed like an impossible mission. The tension hung thick in the air. Thoughts drifted in and out of my consciousness as I opened and closed channels. Thoughts that weren't surprising.

This mission wouldn't be successful.

And it was my fault Lily was in this situation in the first place. It'd be my fault, too, if they failed.

That thought haunted me, and likely would for eternity.

Unless I did something about it.

Chapter Twenty-Five

"So, Sol, Cormac mentioned you have some pretty impressive powers," Mouse said, once we had reached our room again after hours of planning.

I snorted. "Cormac did not say that. He's incapable of complimenting anyone."

"He does seem to have a stick up his ass half the time. Not unlike someone else I know." Mouse stared pointedly at Kai as he said it.

Puffing out air, I tried to stifle my chuckle. "Kai doesn't have a stick up his ass, he's just shy."

"Can you two stop talking about me like I'm not even here." Kai sat on the edge of the bed.

I crossed my arms over my chest. "We wouldn't if you actually engaged in our conversations every once in a while."

Mouse held back a laugh.

"A little hard to get a word in edgewise with you two."

Now it was Mouse's turn to snort. "Hard not to get a word in if you never even try."

I laughed and then pressed my palm to my lips.

Kai glared at me, but his eyes were alight.

Taking in his joy, I held onto his gaze for a moment too long, before answering Mouse. "Yes, I've discovered there is much more to my power than bees and a pathetic blue spark. But I have a long way to go in being able to use it for anything useful."

"I'd say those bees have been very useful and also impressive," Kai commented.

I narrowed my gaze. "I'm not my mother, brothers, or even father, to be honest. Power like that . . . well, it seems rare even here among the Fair Folk."

"Don't do that," Kai said, standing up.

"Do what?"

"Dismiss your ability. Belittle yourself."

"I'm not," I snapped at him, and he stepped closer, leaning over me.

"You are, and you do it all the time."

"And what if I do? Why should you care?"

"Because you are so much more than you give yourself credit for."

There was a fire in his eyes I hadn't noticed before. He leaned even closer, until his breath skated along my lips. "Stop diminishing yourself," he practically growled at me.

"You stop shutting yourself away, and then maybe I'll stop being so hard on myself." If he wanted to play with fire, I was all for it.

I was born of fire.

"What do you want to know?" He held his ground and held his stare. His voice was deep and rough and full of challenge.

"Oh, shit," Mouse whispered loud enough for us to hear, but neither of us broke our stare.

"Why haven't you told your father about seeing your mother?"

He didn't hesitate with his answer. "Because he'd forbid me from seeing her."

"Why have you followed my family into danger twice now?"

"Because you're my friends, and it's what friends do."

Mouse snorted again, but we still held our gazes, never wavering.

"Do you pity me for what happened to Mason, and that's why you're risking your life now?"

I heard Mouse's sharp intake of breath, and Kai's eyes widened a bit. "I don't pity you."

"So, what is it then?"

"I don't know." He suddenly looked uncomfortable.

"That's not an answer."

"It's the only one I have." I could tell he was telling the truth. At least partially.

"What's someone with your artistic talent doing on a ship?" My voice suddenly lost some of its fire, though I didn't know why.

"What's someone with amazing power and talents doing hiding away from the world? Playing small?" he was whispering now, and he was so close I could smell the sweet scent of jasmine and the saltiness of the sea.

"You can't answer a question with a question," I whispered back, suddenly feeling too hot.

"Can't I?" His mouth curled up in a challenging grin.

We both fell silent, just staring at each other. Mouse was the one to break the tension when he cleared his throat. Kai instantly backed up and dropped his gaze.

"As fun as this was, we have a challenging few days ahead of us and could all use a little rest," Mouse said as his eyes darted between the two of us.

I nodded, not sure where my words had gone.

A knock on the door interrupted our bedtime routine. When Mouse opened it, he shot Kai a look and both snuck out of the room without a word, leaving Marcus standing in the doorway.

He hesitated, nervously running a hand through his hair.

I waited, wanting to run to him, but also unsure of everything between us.

Marcus cleared his throat. "May I come in?"

I nodded, and he took a few careful steps inside the room, pretending to look around.

"I'm sorry for punching you," I said, a little unsteadily.

He stopped his perusal of the room, his eyes landing on me. His features melted, tears pooling. "You had every right."

Shaking my head, I took a step closer to him. "I was so angry."

"I know, kiddo. And I did that to you. I won't beg for your forgiveness, or make any excuses, but I will offer an explanation if you want one."

Sitting on the edge of the bed, I nodded again. I didn't want to hear the explanation, but I also didn't want to lose him again, right after I'd just found him. Not without telling him what he meant to me. Not without hearing the same from him. I wasn't blind. I knew his feelings hadn't changed. He was, and forever would be, part of our family.

Marcus sat next to me, our arms separated by only inches. He didn't look at me as he spoke, and his voice shook with emotion. "I couldn't stay. Not because of you or your brothers or your father or the community we built. All of that was perfect. But I couldn't help but feel like I was trying to live someone else's life."

Reaching out, I covered Marcus' hand with mine. He continued, "Your father had the life I wanted, and as much as I tried to ignore the feelings I had for your mother, the stronger they seemed to get. I finally broke one day, needing to get away. Needing to make my own life."

"But why did you leave us without saying goodbye?" It took all my will to keep the tears from spilling.

Marcus squeezed my hand, finally turning to me. "Because I thought if I said goodbye, I wouldn't have the courage to go."

Squeezing my eyes shut, I felt a single tear escape. "It felt like losing my father."

Marcus choked. "I fucked up. I've spent the last fifteen years regretting it but not able to come back. I have been a coward."

There was too much pain. I didn't know how to let go of the anger and feelings of betrayal.

We sat in silence, both grieving in our own way.

"How'd you come to be here?" I asked after a while.

He took a deep breath. "I traveled to many different places, hoping I'd find somewhere to land that felt like home. I got odd jobs along the way, mostly fixing broken tech equipment. When I landed here, something felt different. I couldn't explain it. One day, sitting on a bench overlooking the sea, Ness sat down next to me."

Marcus must have caught the surprise on my face, because he chuckled. "It seems she also felt the need to get away. I didn't know who she was for a long time. We met often on that bench, mostly in companionable silence. She finally explained who she was, and I think she expected me to either laugh or run away. I did neither. Because little did she know, I already knew an amazing family full of magical people."

I smiled at that.

Marcus continued, "After that, she hired me. Sort of. Mostly, we just continued to meet on the bench, and I would give her information about what was happening in the human world. Eventually, she gave me the key to entering her kingdom, but I never did. Not until today, that is. The key was only for emergency use, as she knew the guards would capture me the second I stepped through the arch."

It all made a little more sense now. The informality at which he addressed her, and his role here.

Marcus fidgeted with his hands in the uncomfortable silence that followed. I didn't know what to say to him. I knew he had questions for me about our family. It had been so long, and there was so much to say but I finally landed on, "Mason died."

Marcus knew, as everyone else did, that even at the age of ten, Mason was the person I wanted to spend the rest of my life with.

Marcus didn't say anything, instead he pulled me into his lap, wrapping his arms around me. Silent and steady support. What he had always been.

That's when I let the tears fall again. I had lost Mason, but somehow, I'd found Marcus.

In that moment, I'd already forgiven him.

Lying awake in the darkness, I listened to Mouse snore on the floor
next to the bed. I was wrung out from talking to Marcus, but a peace
had settled over me.

Kai wasn't sleeping, but I didn't have the nerve to say anything.

A few more tentative breaths, and the mattress moved. Without
warning, Kai's fingers wrapped around mine.

"You don't have to do this. Neither does Mouse. This isn't your fight,"
I said.

"I have to, Sol." He stroked my thumb with his as we lay silently on
the bed, facing each other in the dark.

*"Why, though? You're a sailor, not a spy or a soldier, though you have
the body of one."*

I couldn't see his face, but his thumb stopped sliding over mine,
and it was almost as if I could feel his smirk.

"I'm surprised you noticed."

I frowned into the darkness and wondered if he could feel it because
he chuckled.

"You didn't answer my question," I said.

He was quiet long enough I didn't think he'd answer.

"I have to do it for Mason and you," he finally said.

"You don't have to do a damn thing for me, Kai. You owe me nothing. And Mason wouldn't want you risking your life."

"I owe you everything, Sol."

"I don't understand."

He stopped again and didn't say anything for a long while. I wanted to scream and shake him. I wanted him to tell me what this really was all about, but he didn't. True to his nature, he locked it all away. I felt a deep sense of disappointment, and maybe a little grief, as I shifted on the bed, suddenly wanting to pull away.

He held fast to my hand and inched closer to me.

"If I don't do this, Sol, I'll never be able to live with myself," he whispered, his breath tickling my ear.

"But I still don't understand why." My voice was pleading.

"Don't you, though?"

Maybe I did understand and was a coward. Too afraid to admit it to myself. Too afraid to say it out loud. Maybe I wasn't ready for him to say it, either, and he somehow understood that.

The loss of Mason was still raw. For him too.

My thoughts swirled in my head like a thousand racehorses, and through it all, he held my hand.

Kai finally brought my fingers to his lips, his mouth lightly grazing my knuckles, and I shivered at the contact. It was his way of saying goodnight, but the feeling of him seemed to do the opposite of making me want to sleep. My entire body came awake, and I found myself wanting *more*.

He must have felt the change in me, because he tensed, still holding my hand.

"Kai?" I whispered, not sure what I was asking. Not sure what I wanted.

A finger came up and pressed against my lips, silencing me.

Kai's finger lingered on my mouth long enough for heat to build in my core, and I squeezed my eyes shut.

"Kai," I said again.

"Yes?" Damn, even in my head his voice was deep, raspy, and alluring. How he could affect me with just one damn word was concerning.

"Kiss me."

Kai stilled, pulling his finger from my mouth. Suddenly, I was glad I couldn't see his face in the dark.

"Fuck it," he said a second before his lips crashed into mine. My mouth parted easily, letting him devour me.

I'd felt our mutual attraction from the moment we met. I'd felt the heat between us, and the tension. But I thought the feeling was purely instinctual. Simply lust. And maybe since Mason passed, a little bit of loneliness fueled it too.

How wrong I was.

I was starved before him, and there would be no going back from here. No way I could stop myself from tasting him again and again and again. No way I could ever let him sail away when this was all over.

He'd snuck his way into every inch of my being, and I hadn't even noticed.

Something clicked between us, and I felt it in him, too, as our lips and tongues tangled, my body crushed against his.

I let out a strangled whimper that had Kai making a deep rumbling sound from deep in his chest—more fuel added to our collective fire, as our lips became almost desperate.

He kept his hands at my hips. The only sign he wanted more, just as I did, was the increase in pressure of his grip, and the hardness I felt low against my stomach.

If we didn't stop now, I didn't think we'd be able to.

Pulling back, I separated our bodies. Needing space but also desperate to fuse my body to his.

Kai let go of my hips, both of our breaths rough and loud in the silence of the night that filled the space around us.

"Fuck, Sol, the things I want to do to you." Heat built at his words. *"The second we're alone, I'm doing all of them."*

My body shivered at his promise.

"And I cannot wait to hear all those sounds I know you were holding back. I could almost hear them in my head."

I chuckled. *"What about the things I want to do to you too?"*

He shook his head, and I felt him smile into the darkness, but he didn't respond.

Right before sleep took me, I heard his soft, deep voice echo in my head.

"Chaos."

Chapter Twenty-Six

Kai and Mouse were gone just before dawn, and I didn't even hear them leave. I felt their absence as I got up and dressed for the day, pulling on a pair of linen pants and shirt.

No jokes with Mouse, no brooding and silent Kai.

Even the energy of the room felt different. As if the tree felt their loss too.

On top of that, was the feeling in my chest. A familiar feeling. A feeling that I might lose something before I even had a chance to figure out what it was.

That history would repeat itself.

But there was one difference this time around—there was no way in hell I'd let it happen.

Kai had every right to be wary of my thoughts. They would get me in trouble, but I didn't give a damn. The two of them were worth the risk. Marcus and Lily were worth it too.

After pulling back my hair, I finally left the empty room, neglecting my breakfast, and made my way to Ariella's treehouse.

Even with an escort, a soldier Cormac had assigned to me, the Fair Folk were bolder, openly staring and gawking as we passed. Their thoughts flitted into my head, similar to the sailors on the ship. Many seemed curious, some angry.

Living longer didn't seem to make a difference. They were no different from humans.

When I reached the treehouse, I found Ariella lounging by the fireplace at the trunk of the tree, despite the muggy heat of the approaching summer, sipping on tea. The chair she sat in was large, padded with big green pillows. She looked half asleep.

She gestured to me to take the seat across from her.

"Has your mother taught you how to see the channels?" Ariella asked me.

"She tried once. I wasn't a very good student."

Ariella chuckled at my admission. "That's where we should start."

She dove right into instruction. There was no time for idle talk. "Close your eyes. Visualize me. Can you see my energy surrounding me?"

I nodded.

"Now can you see any of that energy traveling away from me?"

I nodded once again.

"Can you follow a trail of it?"

"It seems to be going in every direction, and it's moving." I scrunched my brow in concentration.

"Visualize the energy traveling outward from my chest."

I tried to do as she asked, but anytime I followed the channel of energy from her heart toward me, I lost it.

"Maybe you should use energy that's familiar to you. Try calling to the bees."

I did as she instructed, and a small swarm of them descended from above, settling on the branches all around us. A few landed on the coffee table at our knees.

"Pick one of them and see if you can find its channel."

I tried again, closing my eyes and focusing on the bee's energy. It wasn't hard to find, and this time, its channel was evident—steady and unchanging.

"Now see if you can transport the bee to you, using its channel. No flame."

"How?" I'd never done that without my blue flame. Even though Ariella believed it had nothing to do with my flame, I was skeptical.

"Pull."

She made it sound so easy.

Wary, I took in a deep breath, focusing on the invisible channel of energy, and then I pulled with my mind. To my surprise, the bee landed in my hand.

I opened my eyes, delighted by my success.

Ariella gave a little whooping cheer and clapped her hands.

"Hmmm, I think we should master this with familiar energy channels, but perhaps we should also work on seeing the channels that are everywhere around us. Your mother would be a much better help with that, but, alas, we are without her," Ariella said.

"Now let's see if you can transport a bee somewhere out of sight. To do this, you must have a very detailed visual of the place you're sending it to, or it will get lost in between the worlds and die."

"Oh," I said, alarmed by that.

"That's why I had you paint the place in detail. I needed to know that you wouldn't get lost. Paintings help, but you should be able to do it by simply visualizing where you're going."

Taking a deep breath, I released it slowly in a steady stream.

"You won't have any problem. You have a very detailed imagination, which is why you are so good at painting!" she said cheerily.

I couldn't help but smile at her enthusiasm and confidence.

"Orlan is back at the palace, correct?" she asked me.

I nodded.

"Perhaps you could send her a bee, and contact her through your communication channel to see if she received it?" Ariella offered.

I laughed. "Maybe I should warn her first?"

"Oh, very good idea."

"You OK with me sending you a bee for my training? I'll send it right back," I asked Orlan.

She squealed with delight, causing me to flinch. *"Yes!"*

Concentrating on the bee, I visualized Orlan. Not knowing exactly where she was, I felt it was safer to just visualize her. A moment later, I pushed. It was the best explanation for what I did—pushing the bee through energy channels to Orlan.

An instant later Orlan let out a surprised laugh, and I knew it had reached her.

Another moment later and the bee was back on the table.

Ariella gave me another huge grin and an ecstatic clap.

The rest of the morning was spent doing similar drills, and afterward I was completely exhausted and drained.

Ariella finally released me into Orlan's care around lunch. All I wanted to do was nap, but Orlan insisted on feeding me.

"I know just the place!" Orlan said cheerily, as she picked up her pace, and instead of taking the path to the palace, she veered off on another path that turned north through the forest.

We passed all manner of smaller, more modest homes, tucked between large tree trunks on the ground, but also smaller dwellings that wove in and out of branches higher up. The Fair Folk were much more packed in this part of the forest.

The looks from the Fair Folk here were generally more friendly. Some of them smiled at us, and others greeted Orlan, who responded enthusiastically, stopping to ask about their families or their jobs or their lives.

As we continued to walk, I asked the obvious question. *"Come here often?"*

"Oh, yes! This is my favorite part of the Kingdom. You won't find kinder people, or more talented ones!"

"They don't treat you like a princess here."

"Oh no. None of that nonsense. The council got tired of governing this part of Tir Na Eabha, and I offered to oversee it."

We passed a few shops where the people were creating some decorations for the upcoming summer solstice celebration. They wove together real objects, but animated them with their magic, making a simple art piece come to life. I stopped to stare, as a young child blew bubbles and filled them with light.

Orlan observed my reaction.

That's when I caught sight of an Old One, they were the color and texture of bark, with a few leaves sprouting from their arms, legs, and head. The Old One was teaching a child to weave bark into a beautiful basket. The child laughed when he made a mistake, and an unmistakable smile lit up the Old One's face.

"Here, everyone is equal. Here, there are no borders, boundaries, or outdated prejudices," Orlan explained.

When I met her eyes, they were shining. "It's incredible, Orlan."

"Perhaps a model for the future, if the council will get their heads out of their asses. They won't even visit to see what we've created."

That didn't surprise me. From what I'd heard of the council, they didn't like change, or any threat to their absolute power.

They were no different from humans. No different from Rob.

"Cormac has helped with this place too." I raised a brow, and Orlan laughed. "He may be grumpy, a bore, a pessimist, and a skeptic, but he has a heart, and this place proves that."

"Oh, that's all?" I asked, nudging her shoulder.

She smiled. "I give him a hard time, but he will make a great leader one day."

Not knowing how to respond to that, I let my gaze drift back to the small village that was bursting with light, love, and laughter. It felt a lot like home, and my chest squeezed at the feeling.

"Most people here have very little magic, but the magic they have is truly exquisite. This is where all the best art comes from."

Looking around me, I understood the truth in that. A small girl, who appeared to be around the age of eight, created large, colorful fabric butterflies, animating and lighting them up. They created a trail of sparks behind them as they flew through the trees.

Stopping, I bent down next to the girl, watching her work her magic. When she spotted me, she didn't flinch. She didn't even look surprised by my presence. She simply smiled, holding out the fabric butterfly—a silent invitation.

Not knowing how to animate the butterfly I held out my hand and channeled a bee. The bee hummed, and the girl squealed, her face alight, staring in awe at the little creature.

"May the bees dance with your butterflies?" I asked.

The girl's eyes widened, and she nodded vigorously.

Smiling, I channeled more until the air was humming with the sound of ten thousand wings.

Everyone had stopped to watch the spectacle.

The bees waited for my command hovering in place, dancing in a synchronous figure eight movement.

Tearing her eyes from the bees, the girl concentrated on her butterflies. A dozen of them lit up with glowing blue light and then, slowly, they lifted into the air, filling the spaces between the bees.

The girl looked at me expectantly, and I nodded, directing my attention to the spectacle.

And then they danced together, filling the forest with the sound of elated humming, and everyone watched, their eyes wide and full of wonder.

"You can call the bees." It wasn't a question, not really. When I turned to the mysterious voice, I found an older woman, looking around the same age as Ariella, but with the Fair Folk and their long lifespans, it was impossible to tell how old she was.

"The bees are shepherds of death. It is said they take souls from this world and help them pass into the Otherworld," she continued, her eyes still watching the bees and butterflies.

"But they're also said to be tears of the Sun God, associated with life and nourishment," Orlan interjected.

"Yes, but they have the unique ability of existing in both worlds," the woman replied.

I had no idea what that meant, or why she was telling me this. Bees had always followed and protected me since birth, but they had never been associated with death. At least, not that I knew of.

The woman turned her gaze on me. Her eyes were golden, the color of honey, glowing in the same way most of the Fair Folks did. "Be wary of that blue flame."

With that, she disappeared in a puff of smoke. I jumped in surprise, and Orlan chuckled. "She's not one of us. She's from the Fire Kingdom. They don't channel like you but can make themselves invisible for a time. Usually no more than a minute or so."

There was so much I didn't know, and so much I wanted to ask the woman, but she was gone, and the little girl was grabbing at my sleeve trying to get my attention.

She pointed at the sky, and the butterflies formed a helix, spiraling back down to the earth. When they landed gracefully, the girl released her magic, and they collapsed on the soft ground. She scooped them up and placed them back into a wooden box.

When she stood, it was my turn to point to the sky. The bees clumped together and then disappeared in an instant as I channeled them home.

The spectators clapped, including the girl. "You should be part of the solstice show!"

"Oh, I don't know—"

"That's a great idea!" Orlan cut in.

"I'll think about it. Thank you for letting your butterflies dance with my bees," I said to girl.

"It was great fun!" She squealed and bowed her head to me and Orlan, before rushing off to join her friends who had clumped together by a tree to watch the mini show we had created.

Orlan ushered me forward, and we continued further into the heart of the village. We watched the various solstice preparations as we passed.

"Kai would love this place," I commented.

When Orlan didn't answer right away, I glanced at her. She had a grin on her face.

"It's not what you think."

"Sure," she said in a knowing voice.

I laughed. "We share a love of art."

"That's all?" she asked, winking.

I gave her a sideways glance, and she slowly came to a stop in front of a café that was entwined by the most fragrant roses I had ever smelled. The vines twisted in and out of one another, forming a living roof above the tables. The flowers poked through the vines, spilling their scent, and their lovely petals, all over the tables and ground below.

"How lovely," I said, as a very handsome man came up to us. He had long, dark hair, pulled back, broad, muscular shoulders, and light blue eyes fixed only on Orlan.

She blushed as she greeted him and introduced us. "Dorian, this is Sol."

Extending my hand, I smiled at him.

He took it and gave it a soft kiss, bowing his head with reverence I wasn't expecting. "Always an honor to meet one of Orlan's friends."

I eyed Orlan over his shoulder, smirking as she had when asking about Kai.

She scoffed.

Dorian led us to a table next to the walking path that had an unobstructed view of the town and its bustling activity.

After he seated us, and left, I asked, "You come here for the food, or the guy?"

Color rose to her cheeks again. "Both?"

I chuckled, and we ate and chatted about life here. I told her about Mason, and she told me about Dorian.

"Your brother?" I asked, as we were finishing up the most delectable chocolate rose cake I had ever tasted. "What's his deal?"

She sighed. "I suppose I don't give him enough credit for the things he's done. I have the privilege of being second born, so the pressure is off me. I can't imagine what he has to deal with."

"I know a little about that."

She raised a brow.

"We have nothing of the history and formalities that you have, but being first born in an extraordinary family, in a world full of humans, comes with high expectations, and *a lot* of judgment."

Orlan looked at me thoughtfully. "Well, Cormac is a good guy. He's also secretly funny. He doesn't show it to many people."

Now, that was something I couldn't believe.

Orlan laughed. "Maybe he'll show his true colors on the solstice."

"Mmmhmm" I said skeptically.

Orlan laughed again, as Dorian came up to our table and smiled down at her. "All finished?" he asked.

She nodded, the color permanently painting her cheeks, as he took the plate from in front of her.

"Will you be at the solstice party?" I asked Dorian.

Orlan's eyes widened at my question.

He looked at me and said, "I will be there."

"Will you come find us?" I asked him.

Orlan's mouth practically dropped into her lap.

Dorian turned to her, as if asking her permission.

She smiled at him, and he turned back to me. "I'd be honored to."

"Good." I said, standing up.

Orlan stood too, and I grabbed her arm and turned her toward the bustling forest paths.

"See you there!" I said over my shoulder, as we disappeared into the crowd.

Orlan didn't say anything at first, but as we ventured further from the café, she finally spoke, "We don't do that. We usually stick with the royal bloodlines."

I stole a glance at Orlan; she was staring straight ahead of us, brow wrinkled as if trying to figure something out.

"What would happen if you did?"

She stopped walking. "I don't know."

"Seems to me, it's worth a shot. What's the worst that could happen?"

Orlan laughed. "Cormac won't be happy."

"Good." I said without hesitation, and laughed right back at her, as we continued on, making our way through the bustling village, and back to the forest paths leading to the palace.

Her delighted smile was all the response I needed.

Halfway back, Orlan surprised me with a question. "Did you enjoy growing up in the human world?"

There was a long moment of silence where I contemplated what she asked. "Yes, but I was different." Another pause in my words had us both halting. I met her eyes. "No matter who you are or where you come from, if you don't fit the narrow expectations of the society you're in, you are treated differently. Subtle discrimination at best, and violent oppression at worst."

Orlan silently studied me, searching for something in my face. For the first time since I'd met her, her brows were pinched.

"The constant barrage of assumptions about us," I continued again, as emotion I didn't expect rose, "it's exhausting. Soul crushing. It fundamentally changes you."

"That's why you care so much. About us and the Old Ones." It wasn't really a question.

I nodded. "I think everyone just wants to be seen. To be heard. To live and love without fear. And it should be simple—"

"But somehow it's not." She finished my sentence with a sigh, turning and continuing along the path.

We didn't speak the rest of the way.

Chapter Twenty-Seven

I woke two days later to Mouse screaming in my head. I was up instantly, my ears ringing at the pained sounds.

I didn't know what to do.

"Kai!" I shouted but got no response.

I tried to reach Mouse but also got nothing. Even his pained screams had suddenly gone silent.

Racing around the room, I threw on my fighting leathers, and then I did the most idiotic thing I'd ever done, I attempted to channel myself to them without knowing if I'd be lost forever in the in-between.

I didn't care. I didn't think I'd want to live in a world without them anyway.

Latching on to Kai, every muscle in my body responding to the memory of him, I closed my eyes and the familiar feeling of falling came over me.

I didn't know how long it took before I collapsed onto wet grass. It could have been seconds or minutes. I instantly heaved up the contents of my stomach, shuddering in the process.

I should have been more alert, but my vision was blurry, and it took a second to clear.

Registering shouts and the sound of boots falling on wet earth, I willed my brain to focus on my surroundings.

One voice rose above the others, and I latched onto it.

"Run!" Kai's voice came from behind me, and I didn't allow myself to look as I pushed off the ground and sprinted toward the trees.

The rain fell relentlessly, blurring the world around us. It took all my concentration to stay on my feet as my boots slipped on the ground.

Not stopping until I reached the safety of the densely packed trees, I finally regained my breath and cleared the dizziness of the channeling and consequent run I wasn't expecting.

I studied everyone as they crashed through the trees and caught up to me.

Mouse had a gash on his forehead that was dripping blood down his face. He wiped at it to keep the blood out of his eyes. Kai held onto Mouse's elbow, keeping him from collapsing, his limp seeming even more severe. Marcus struggled to catch his breath but looked unharmed.

Cormac was last, using vines to trip their assailants, who looked human and carried only swords. Ardil and his people were with him, coming in and out of sight, blending so perfectly into the landscape you had to strain your eyes to catch them.

When the initial threat had eased, and everyone had a moment to rest, all eyes turned on me.

"Surprise?" I managed with a half-smile.

Mouse snorted, but no one else looked impressed.

"What now?" Kai asked, addressing the question to Marcus, ignoring my presence. Or, ignoring his anger that I put myself in the middle of danger without a plan—again.

"We take them out, so they don't go snitching on us to the rest of the camp," Cormac explained, sounding like it was easy to take a life.

The sound of our pursuers suddenly stopped, utter silence descending on the forest except for the patter of raindrops on the leaves. Cormac had choked the men with his vines without so much as blinking. All before anyone could utter a word.

Ardil dropped in front of me, his big black eyes assessing. I couldn't tell if it was judgment or something else entirely.

"I'm sorry?" I tried.

Mouse snorted again. "You don't sound sorry."

"You shouldn't have come. This is what he wanted," Kai sounded as though he was on the verge of losing control.

I swung around to face him, relieved to see him alive. My first instinct was to scan him for injuries, but his tone had me staring him down instead.

"I know, asshole. But you didn't respond. What did you expect me to do?" I couldn't help the defensiveness as I stepped closer to him.

I wanted to go back to before he came into my life. Before he decided I was worth more than his own life.

The same as Mason had.

"You could have gotten yourself killed!" I had never heard Kai yell, and it rendered me speechless.

"This isn't the time or place for this argument," I said.

Kai held my glare as Marcus cut in. "What's done is done. We need a plan."

"What happened?" I asked, tearing my eyes away from Kai.

"Ardil found Lily, but the human scouts caught us when we tried to reach her. We barely made it into their camp." Marcus sounded exhausted.

"They have way more people than we expected, and not just humans. They have an army of Folk." I couldn't gauge Cormac's feelings about the information he just revealed, but it had me reeling.

We suspected that was the case, but to hear it was true left me baffled for one very specific reason. "These humans want to wipe all magical people off the planet. Why would the Folk ally with them?"

"Either they don't know the human's true plans, or they were offered something," Cormac answered.

"You can get to Lily." Ardil's voice filled my head, and even he sounded tired.

I glanced down at him. *"Kai's right, it's what they want."*

"We saw where she was being held. My people scouted the area and the guards stationed there. If we time it correctly, you shouldn't run into any trouble."

I shook my head out of pure instinct. I wasn't capable of that.

Marcus interrupted. "What did Ardil say?"

Marcus paced back and forth, listening as I explained Ardil's plan. He didn't speak right away. None of them did.

"Look, I'm sorry I barged in and ruined your plan," I began.

Mouse cut me off. "It was a shit plan."

No one contradicted him, and it was Cormac who explained what they'd found. There was a large camp with thousands of people. Most of it was hidden by Fair Folk shields. They didn't have the exact number of Fair Folk or what families they belonged to. Cormac didn't know any of them, but mentioned their shielding meant they were from powerful bloodlines.

That didn't bode well for any of us.

Lily was being held with other captives in a prisoner's tent near the center of their camp. It was guarded by two soldiers who rotated every two hours. So, if I was going to spring her out, I'd need to go in during their change and hope they decided to chat and distract themselves long enough for me to get her out.

"There's one problem," I interrupted Cormac. "I've never channeled anyone *with* me. I don't even know if it's possible."

"It's possible." Ardil looked thoughtful. *"Channel jumpers used to jump with others. I remember them doing it all the time."*

My mouth dropped open. "You *knew* channel jumpers?"

"Knew of *them."*

Even Cormac looked surprised at Ardil's revelation, as I translated for them.

"What else aren't you telling me?" I asked Ardil.

"You know everything you need to know."

"That's a bullshit answer," I shot back, and I swore Ardil smiled.

"This is a lot of speculation and not a lot of evidence," Kai cut in.

"Why don't you practice?" Ardil said.

"Here? Now?"

Ardil nodded.

"How?"

Ardil pointed his thumb at Kai. *"Take him somewhere. He could use a cooldown."* Ardil chuckled. At least, I thought it was a chuckle.

"He wants me to be the test subject, doesn't he?" Kai didn't miss a thing.

"He's the least likely to get caught in the in-between," Ardil added.

I raised my eyebrows.

"You got here using him, didn't you?"

"How did you know that?"

Ardil chuckled again, not answering my question.

"Fine," I grumbled, grabbing Kai's arm.

Kai jolted, not expecting it. "What are you doing?"

"Taking you somewhere to cool down?"

Kai narrowed his gaze but didn't try to stop me.

I pulled him a few feet away from the others. "Where do I take him?"

"Somewhere familiar."

I grumbled something incoherent. Then I took him to the only place that truly felt like home.

My art studio.

The fall was longer this time, and the nausea started before we crashed to the floor.

Kai was instantly retching. "That feels awful."

I groaned. "Let's hope I don't have to make traveling that way a regular thing."

Kai helped me to my feet and paused, finally registering where we were. "This is your art studio?" he whispered, like it might disappear if he spoke too loudly.

I pulled back my hand. "It is." I watched him marvel at the space.

"It's not usually this clean," I commented, almost laughing to myself.

Without warning, a hundred red roses sprouted from the vines around the room and petals drifted down around Kai, landing softly and filling the space with an intoxicating smell.

Kai turned to me in question, and I rolled my eyes, talking to the ceiling. "Still in love with him, I see. And yet, you live with me for twenty-five years, and I still get shit on?"

A moment later a white flower turned its head in my direction and spit water all over me. The water, combined with yellow pollen, made it look suspiciously like urine.

"Did you just piss on me?" I shouted.

Kai's laugh pulled me out of my momentary feud with the house. The sound echoed around the room, and I wanted nothing more than to stay in this moment. To forget why we were here. To forget what we had to go back to.

Kai stepped into me, brushing the water off my shirt, smiling down at the yellow stain I would never be able to get out. When he met my eyes, his smile disappeared as if he could read my mind.

"When this is all over, I'll get you home. I promise," he said.

"I'm afraid when this is all over, this will no longer feel like home." It was my biggest fear. That all of this would change me so profoundly that I'd no longer feel like I fit here. That I wouldn't feel as though I deserved this, when so many others were suffering all around me.

How could I come back?

Kai took a deep breath, his chest rising and falling in a steady motion. "The ship no longer feels like home to me, either."

His confession had my breath halting.

"Where will you go?" I asked, afraid of his confession and what it meant for him—for us.

Kai didn't answer, instead turning and taking a hesitant step toward the paintings sprawled around the room. No one had touched them. They were precisely where I'd left them.

"These are incredible, Sol."

I sighed. "Thanks."

I was so caught up in my thoughts, that it took me far too long to realize the house was completely silent.

Our house was never silent.

Starting for the door, I poked my head out. There was no movement, no voices.

"Sol?" Kai must have noticed the silence, too, because he suddenly sounded worried.

"They must be out." Even coming out of my mouth, it sounded wrong. There was always someone home.

"I know you want to stay, but we should get back. Lily doesn't have much time."

I finally met Kai's eyes. His anger had cooled to sadness.

"You're right." I walked back to him and held out my hand.

Kai didn't grab it right away. "We'll get you home," he repeated.

His voice was so soft tears filled my eyes.

I nodded, and he grabbed my hand, squeezing it lightly.

Stepping into him, I wrapped my free hand around his waist, and it startled him so much that he tensed.

Not giving him a chance to pull away, I thought of the forest we'd just come from, and then we were both falling through time and space.

I didn't want to open my eyes when I smelled the pine of the forest floor underneath me, but Ardil's voice filled my head.

"At least you didn't vomit this time."

"Thanks, very reassuring." I stood up, dusting myself off.

"I take it, it worked?" Marcus asked, looking between Kai and me. Kai was still puking on the pine needles.

"It worked," I mumbled. "When do I get Lily out?"

"You have thirty minutes until the guards change posts," Cormac replied, sounding unsure of the plan.

"You don't think I can do it?"

"I have no strong opinion either way. You continue to surprise me, so who's to say." It wasn't exactly a compliment.

"You really have a way with words, no wonder the ladies are lined up."

Mouse snorted, covering his laugh.

Cormac ignored both of us.

"She's shackled to iron posts," Kai interrupted. "Do the chains need to be cut for you to channel her?" He addressed the question to Ardil.

"I am not sure," Ardil said, and I translated.

"You'll need these, then." Kai rummaged through his bag, pulling out a pair of bolt cutters.

I groaned. "And where am I supposed to put that?"

He scanned my body, his gaze moving slowly, and I felt my cheeks turn pink.

"They'll fit on your belt," he said, walking over and stuffing the handle through the top of my belt, letting it dangle from my hip.

I wrinkled my nose. Kai was close enough to flick it, and I smacked his hand away, earning a chuckle from him.

Marcus stood from the fallen log he was sitting on. I saw how the years wore on him. "Never in a million years would I have thought I'd agree to let you go into an enemy camp with thousands, without backup."

"She'd do it for me," I whispered, knowing Lily wouldn't hesitate if our roles were reversed.

Marcus nodded. "I know she would. We all would."

I stepped forward and hugged him, and we stayed that way for a long time.

"My people will stay hidden, but they will be with you. You will not be alone."

I pulled away from Marcus. *"Thank you, Ardil."*

Ardil sketched a bow and then turned to his people. Once again, I hadn't even noticed they were there. They clung to branches, looking like leaves. Other's looked like wisps of grass blowing in the breeze. Some had hands that looked like flowers. Each one blending in so perfectly, that unless you knew what to look for, you'd never spot them.

"If it doesn't go well—" Kai began.

"It will." I almost broke down when he looked at me with those depthless ocean eyes.

Mouse came over and clapped me on the shoulder. "You better make it back, otherwise, I'll be stuck with this grump for eternity." He nodded in Kai's direction.

Kai frowned.

"Can't have that, can we?" I laughed.

"It's time," Cormac's deep voice broke our conversation.

Not hesitating, I latched onto Lily's familiar channel, and then I was gone.

I didn't know what to expect, but luckily, I landed on my feet, and nothing came out of my stomach.

A win was a win.

There were a few gasps, and I swung around, my eyes still adjusting to the dim light inside what appeared to be a sparsely furnished tent. Five people were chained to iron bars embedded in the ground around the periphery. Lily was one of them, though she wasn't conscious. Her whole body was covered in wounds, and her face so swollen I didn't think she could see through her eyes, even if she could open them.

Noticing a few missing fingers, I tensed, clenching my fists.

The prisoners started mumbling. It was enough to snap me out of my horror.

Racing to her, I pulled out the bolt cutters and snapped her chains.

"Take me! Take me!" someone yelled.

"You cannot leave us here!" another shouted.

"Shh!!" I whispered, assessing them.

Lily's body was limp in my arms, though I could feel her chest rising and falling. I looked down at her and sighed. I knew what I had to do. I just didn't think I could.

"I'll be back for you," I whispered, then I was gone.

Not waiting, I placed Lily in the grass at Marcus' feet and was gone before anyone could stop me.

Landing gracefully back in the prisoner's tent, I barely felt dizzy or nauseous, but I didn't have time to think about it.

Creeping closer to the tent's opening, I listened to the guard's chat as they changed positions.

We still had time.

I cut the chains of the prisoner closest to me. She was tall and muscular. Her hair and clothes were caked with mud, and she had a severe black eye but otherwise seemed unhurt. Her gaze met mine as I freed her, and it was full of resolve. She was a warrior.

"Why are you here? Who are these people," I asked her.

The intrusion on her mind, had her staring blankly at me, eyes wide.

"Quickly," I said, snapping the first chain.

"We're all prisoners."

I had gathered that much, but nodded, urging her to go on.

"We've all been tortured for information."

"What kind of information?" I said, snapping a second chain.

"Defenses, strength, numbers, and resources in Tir Na Eabha. And what we know about the others."

"Others?" I asked, freeing the last chain.

The woman rubbed her wrists and stretched out her legs. *"Location of the Fire Folk, Air Folk, and Water Folk."*

"So, they are real too?" It wasn't really a question, and I didn't intend for that to slip out.

The woman didn't answer, just stared at me.

"You're one of them," she said.

"The Fair Folk?" I laughed, waving my hand. *"No. Well, not really,"* I added awkwardly.

"No. Not the Fair Folk." She shook her head, looking at me as though she'd seen a ghost. *"You're a daughter of the . . ."*

Her sentence was cut off by the sound of a guard outside the tent.

I grabbed the woman's arm.

"I'll be back for the rest of you," I whispered to the shocked faces in the dark, and then I was gone.

Placing the woman in the grass at Mouse's feet, I knew they'd be waiting to talk me out of going back, so I channeled as fast as I could, ignoring their protests.

My luck held. The soldiers were still yacking away outside, totally oblivious to their prisoners disappearing.

I cut the chains of a boy next. He couldn't have been more than fifteen. He reminded me so much of Aelius that I let out a pathetic choking sound as tears gathered in my eyes. He gave me a concerned look but didn't have a chance to speak before he was lying on the grass next to the warrior woman, and I was suddenly back in the prisoner's tent.

Two prisoners were left, both silently begging me to take them next.

That's when I heard the guards.

"I better go check on the scum. The unconscious one dies tonight." The guard's voice sounded closer, and fingers curled on the fabric of the opening.

I didn't know what to do. My vision was getting fuzzy around the edges, and I swayed on my feet. The channeling was obviously affecting me.

There were only two options: Channel myself with my remaining strength, leaving the prisoners to their fate, or stay until I regained enough strength to take them with me.

The answer was an easy one—I refused to leave them.

The two guards ducked through the tent opening and froze at what they found.

"Hi," I waved at them, giving them a cheeky smile as my legs gave out.

Chapter Twenty-Eight

I woke with a splitting headache, groaning as I tried to sit up. Chains shackled around my wrists stopped me, and I finally looked around. It was dark. The interior of the tent was pitch black. I could only make out a few shadows I suspected were a table, some chairs, and the other two prisoners chained on the opposite side of the tent.

Shit. I couldn't channel the prisoners out if I couldn't reach them.

I assessed my body. Nothing was broken or bruised. The only pain I felt was my throbbing head. It wasn't surprising that they hadn't hurt me. They likely wanted me conscious before torturing me.

They'd also stripped me of all my weapons, including the bolt cutters.

I wondered if I could channel without cutting the chains. I had forgotten to try earlier but now didn't feel like the right moment to experiment. I was still weak and dizzy.

I needed more time that I didn't have.

Opening the channels, thoughts invaded my head. I rubbed at my temples, my headache getting worse.

"The one they've been looking for..."

"We need more shielder's on the front line..."

"The ammo delivery is delayed . . ."

"The heir of the blue flame. Could the rumors be true?"

"Hypocrites for using the Fair Folk . . ."

"The key to their undoing . . ."

"Unless she knows what she is, there will be no escaping them . . ."

"The council is late . . ."

Closing the channels, the last thought had my heart rate picking up. The Fair Folk Council? Were they involved in this somehow?

I didn't have a chance to find out more.

"She's awake," one of the guards sneered, opening the tent flap, allowing light from a torch outside to come spilling in.

I blinked at the sudden assault on my senses.

One guard entered, carrying a lantern, while the other remained stationed outside. The guards appeared human, and the one in front of me appeared far too smug.

"The boss has been looking for you."

"I'm that popular, huh?" I shot back, and I could see the other prisoners staring at me, their bodies tense as they listened.

"I don't think you'll be as smug once the boss shows up."

Acting bored, I lifted my hand to check the dirt beneath my nails.

One of the prisoners snorted, and the guard shifted his gaze, glaring at him. He bent down, his face inches from mine. His hot breath brushed my cheek and I tried not to recoil from it.

"When he gets his hands on you, you'll be carved up worse than your friend."

I didn't glance down, but I knew there was a dagger strapped to his hip. I'd spotted it when he first entered. All I had to do was keep him close.

Smiling, I held back my anger and revulsion. "Looking forward to it."

The guard looked like he wanted to punch me, annoyed that I wasn't showing any fear. He inched even closer, and that's when I moved. I dragged my hand to his waist while he was caught up in his growing anger. He didn't feel a thing.

"How about I carve a piece out of you right now?"

Giving him the middle finger, I slipped the dagger from its sheath and slid it under my thigh.

"I can see why he wants you dead."

"I'll take that as a compliment," I smiled sweetly back at him.

He raised his arm to hit me, but I disappeared. Or rather, tried to. His hand collided with my face, and the force of it threw my head sideways.

I felt the heat blooming where he'd hit me, but what worried me more than my face, was that I couldn't channel.

The guard must have noticed my surprise, because a slow smirk grew on his horridly chapped and cracked lips. "The boss had some magical chains made just for you. It renders your magic useless."

Well, fuck.

They knew my magic, and worse than that, they knew how to stop me. They had more information than we expected. But who was the rat?

Kai was right. I had walked right into their trap.

The guard moved closer, reaching for my shirt. His motives were crystal clear, but I waited until he was close enough, before grabbing the stolen dagger from under my thigh and punching it through his neck. He fell onto my lap, his blood soaking my pants, gurgling noises coming from his mouth as blood poured from it.

Grimacing, I rolled him off me. A few moments later he was still, no longer twitching, and his eyes stared blankly at the ceiling of the tent.

Both remaining prisoners were wide-eyed, staring at the dead guard.

"Perks of growing up with two brothers and a dad who's a soldier," I said, trying to lighten the mood.

They blinked.

I started to shove the bloody knife into the lock of the magical chain, trying to break it open before more guards caught on to what I'd done.

The knife didn't work. It didn't even leave a scratch on the enchanted metal.

Growling in frustration, I stashed the dagger in the holster at my thigh.

"I heard them talking about that chain," one of the prisoners whispered, his young voice trembling.

My eyes shot to him. "What did you hear?"

He stared at me, visibly shaking. "It prevents any magic that involves the energy channels. I don't know your magic, but I'm guessing it was meant to imprison you and your family. If you are, in fact, who everyone is talking about."

"Fuck," I mumbled.

"But there was another prisoner among us. They executed her a day ago. She kept mumbling about another power that wouldn't hold you. Another power you already had."

I didn't know what question to ask first. There was so many swimming through my head. I settled on, "What power?"

The prisoner didn't have a chance to reply as the flap of the tent was thrown open, and none other than Rob stood there, silhouetted by the light behind him.

"Great," I grumbled, even though my body betrayed my fear.

Rob stood triumphantly, as though he'd already won, even though his guard lay dead next to me. His usual self-satisfied smile graced his slippery lips. "Not so powerful now."

"Where have I heard that before? Oh, that's right, the last time I kicked your ass and made you scream like a little girl."

The young prisoner who had given me all the information snickered, and Rob turned his attention to him.

Shit.

Rob walked over to the boy, and I struggled against the chains that held me. I saw the knife before the prisoner did.

"Stop!" I yelled.

Rob swiveled his head in my direction, but made no move to change his mind.

"You're all pathetic," Rob drawled, turning back to the boy who was trembling. A bead of sweat slid down his face.

Rob placed the knife on the boy's forearm and drug it slowly to his hand. Small droplets of blood fell from the wound, but it wasn't a deep gash.

"You picked the wrong side, kid," he said to the boy, who flashed me a panicked look.

I struggled against the chains even more, but Rob only laughed.

"You see, Solana, there are many people who know more about you than you do. It wasn't hard to convince them to share that information."

"Torture, you mean."

Rob shrugged and then dragged his knife down the boy's other forearm, giving him matching lacerations. The boy didn't make a sound, but his clenched jaw gave away his pain.

"You have me, why torture the boy?" I asked in a last-ditch attempt to save him.

"This isn't torture for the boy. It's torture for you. Knowing that you have the power to save him but can't."

"Fuck you," I spat.

"Oh, but that's right, how silly of me," Rob moved the knife to the boy's cheek, and the boy shut his eyes, tensing. "Power isn't some fancy magic trick. Power is the influence you have over people. And, as you can see, my influence has grown." He stretched his free arm wide, emphasizing his point.

I shook my head, my magic itching to teach this man a lesson, but I couldn't. In his eyes, I was powerless. But he was wrong. I was wrong too. I'd been wrong all along about the power that ran through my veins.

"You're right," I said. "Power isn't some grand gesture or fancy magic trick, but you're also wrong. It's not the influence you have *over* people, it's the ability to show people what a better life could look like. And then giving them the resources and ability to *choose* the life they want."

Rob scoffed, leaning so close he was practically spitting in my face. "People cannot handle that choice. They are practically begging to be controlled."

I almost laughed. "No. They are begging to feel *safe*, and you are exploiting their fear, doubling down on a lie you convinced yourself is truth because you are so afraid to lose any semblance of control. But control is a lie, too, and you fell for it."

There was a flicker of something in his eyes, and this time, Rob dug in the knife in further, and at the first sound of the boys scream, I combusted.

Literally.

My body ignited in blue flame, and to my absolute shock, the flames engulfed the chains holding me and burned them into nothing.

No ash. No burnt metal. Just gone, as if they'd never existed.

Everyone froze as if they didn't know what to do, but I didn't hesitate. I channeled to the boy, grabbing hold of his arm, and then to the final prisoner who was going in and out of consciousness.

It answered a question too: Freeing them from the chains before channeling wasn't necessary.

But one question remained: Could I channel two of them with me, especially in the state I was in? But I had no choice.

Rob reacted too slowly.

Smiling in triumph, I whisked the three of us to safety.

And then I was falling, exhaustion taking over as I struggled to keep consciousness.

The last vision I had was Kai catching me before I hit the ground.

Chapter Twenty-Nine

I didn't know what I was expecting when I woke, but I certainly wasn't expecting Ariella.

She was sitting next to my bed, glasses falling down her nose, as she read an old book. So old it looked like the pages would turn to dust with a single touch. Magic was probably the only thing holding it together.

"Where's Lily?" I croaked, my mouth feeling dry.

Ariella looked up from her book and gave me a smile way too wide for the current circumstance we found ourselves in.

"She's recovering with the healers."

Groaning, I tried to sit up, but Ariella held out her hand and pressed me back into the mattress. "You almost completely burned yourself out. Give yourself time."

"What does that mean?"

"Means you used strong magic too fast and too long. Magic you weren't used to or had never done before. You could've died." She said it so matter-of-factly I didn't know if she was serious or not.

"I didn't know that was possible."

"Most Fair Folk learn the limits of their magic before they can even walk."

I pursed my lips, and Ariella laughed, patting my knee. "You'll learn."

"How?"

"You need to be more efficient with manipulating the energy channels. Right now, you use too much energy to travel. That's why you get nauseous."

I sighed loudly, and Ariella chuckled again. "Like I said, you'll get it." She grappled with what to say next. "I suppose it's about time I let those boys know you're awake. They've been fussing over you for days."

"Days!?" I shouted, sitting up.

"Two days." Ariella said it as though it were normal.

"It's the solstice?"

Ariella nodded. "We'll work on your magic starting tomorrow. Go have fun today."

"We're on the brink of war and the queen decided to still hold the celebration?"

Ariella didn't say anything for a few moments, studying me thoughtfully. "The queen doesn't want panic. She's trying to manage the council, the people, the threat against us, and *you*."

"Me?"

Ariella smiled, but she didn't answer my question. "Tell me what you discovered."

When I narrowed my gaze, she elaborated. "Don't tell me you were in the middle of the enemy camp and didn't open your channels and *listen*. I picked you for being smarter than that."

She was trying to bait me, but I didn't bite. Instead, I asked the question that had been haunting me. "What does 'heir of the blue flame' mean?"

Ariella blew out a long breath, her milky eyes meeting mine once more. "I've had my theories about you and your mother, but that's all they are—theories. Seems the enemy also has their own ideas, which doesn't bode well."

"Why?"

"If they know the true source of your magic, then they might know how to render your magic useless against them."

"They had magic chains that wouldn't allow me to channel any-where," I mused, staring at the familiar canopy above the bed.

"How did you free yourself?"

"My flame." I didn't know why it worked. My flame was harmless, but maybe I was missing something. It clearly burned past whatever magical wards were imbued into those chains.

"It's beyond the magic of the Fair Folk."

"Beyond ours too." Ardil suddenly dropped from above, landing in front of me on the bed. I jumped, startled.

"What does that mean?" I asked them both.

Ariella shook her head, silver curls bouncing. Her eyes drifted, deep in thought.

Ardil studied me, his magic brushing against my skin, trying to make its way in.

"Stop that!" I shouted, shivering.

Ardil chuckled. *"My magic won't harm you."*

"What is your magic?"

"We are guardians of the forest. Our magic can see beyond the surface of things."

I resisted rolling my eyes. He always spoke vaguely. Always in riddles that made no sense.

"Your mother's Earth magic. It's different from the Fair Folks. The Fair Folk can only draw from life that already exists. Your mother can draw from . . ." Ariella's next words were almost a whisper. "Nothing."

I didn't know how to respond to that.

"And your blue flame was associated with the Morrigan in myths soldiers hardly remember anymore . . ."

Her words drifted off into the breeze again, and the silence was so deafening, I was tempted to interrupt the awkwardness with some dumb comment.

Even Ardil stilled—listening.

"It's almost as if Danu and the Morrigan . . ."

She didn't finish that statement. Her eyes instantly cleared, and she turned her hardened gaze on me. "There are secrets we have forgotten. They must be uncovered."

"By whom?"

"You." She said it so definitively, I felt as though I'd asked a dumb question. It probably was. I was just becoming more and more confused as I learned more about the world of magic and of the Fair Folk and Old Ones. There were too many secrets to count. Too many secrets that had been buried and forgotten, and a part of me wondered if there was a reason they had been.

Maybe they should stay that way.

"There is a reason your family was given these gifts," Ariella continued.

I'd heard those words too often. They certainly felt more like a curse than a gift, but I didn't dare say any of that to her.

"You *must* learn the source of your power. I fear the entire balance of the world rests on that information."

"Great," I replied sarcastically. I'd thought I already carried the weight of the world. That weight appeared to still be growing. A weight that could easily crush me. A weight that might even crush the entire Earth along with me.

Ariella gave me a sympathetic smile, standing and heading for the door. She paused at the threshold. "Child, there's no reason to pretend to be ordinary, when you're already extraordinary."

With that, she poked her head out the door and said, "You can come in now." Her voice held a hint of mischief.

Ardil jumped back into the branches without so much as a good-bye. I shook my head.

Ariella slipped out the door next, and a familiar form took her place. Relief instantly washed over me. I hadn't realized how much he made me feel like the world was right until this moment.

"You fell on your face."

I had to admit, that wasn't the first thing I expected to come out of his mouth, though the last thing I remembered before passing out, aside from Kai, was falling on my face.

"And you're surprised?" I smirked.

Kai approached the bed cautiously, sitting down on the edge. I pushed myself further up, the strap of my nightgown falling down my shoulder.

Kai tracked the movement, and I felt the heat of his stare.

"You look worse than me," I commented. It was true. He looked as though he hadn't slept in days. Dark circles deepened the color of his eyes.

He snorted but otherwise ignored my comment. "You almost killed yourself."

"But I didn't."

He opened his mouth and then closed it again.

"You can't keep putting yourself in danger like that." Instead of anger, he suddenly looked afraid, and I wanted to reassure him that I'd never do it again, but I couldn't, because it wasn't true.

"I have to," I whispered, brushing a fallen strand of hair off his brow.

"You don't."

"I do because"—I choked a bit on my words—"because I have the power to make lives better. I have the power to make people feel safe. I have the power to make the world better."

I finally understood what power was. It had clicked in the prisoner tent, and my conversation with Rob, and now I couldn't run from that power. No matter what outcome, I was here to see this through. I was here to help. I was not going to back down.

Kai must have seen it in my eyes because he sighed, his forehead coming to rest on mine. The same strand of hair I'd pushed back, fell on my forehead this time.

"Fuck," was all he said, but within that one word was a promise.

A promise to stick by my side, no matter the consequences.

Kai reached out and slowly dragged the strap of my nightgown up my arm, lingering on the soft part of my shoulder. Shutting my eyes at the feeling of him, I took a deep breath, willing my heart to slow down.

"I—" Kai didn't finish what he was going to say as Mouse came barreling through the door, out of breath. Kai dropped his hand as though my skin was on fire and put space between us.

Mouse bent over, putting his hands on his knees, breathing heavily. "Ariella just told me you woke up. Came as fast as I could."

I smiled. "You didn't have to kill yourself getting here. I wasn't going anywhere."

"Lily is anxious to talk to you before she meets with the queen in an hour," Mouse explained.

At that, I jumped out of the bed, steadying myself against the bed frame when a bout of dizziness caught me. Kai reached out, putting a hand on my elbow.

"It'd be unfortunate to kill yourself getting out of bed too quickly," Mouse chuckled.

Flipping him off, I let them watch me struggle into more appropriate clothing. I threw a linen shirt over my head, and struggled into a pair of linen pants, ignoring the fact that I hadn't showered in days.

"Don't trip on your way there!" Kai shouted, his teasing tone returning, as I raced out the door.

"Asshole."

Kai laughed, but then I actually tripped on the stairs, falling into the railing and catching myself before tumbling down.

"Fuck."

"You tripped, didn't you?" I barely understood the words as his deep laughter filled my head.

I didn't dare answer him.

Chapter Thirty

As I made my way down the steps, a child's laugh echoed through the forest, slipping around branches and leaves. An innocent laugh. A laugh that was unaware of the strange woman in their magical kingdom. Unaware there was danger on her doorstep.

I wanted to melt into the ground and disappear. Instead, I kept going. It was all I could do.

Freezing at the bottom of the steps, I was shocked to see Cormac pacing back and forth across the path, wearing down the soil beneath his feet.

When he finally noticed me, he froze. His eyes scanned my body, but not like the first time we met. This time he was likely looking for lingering wounds.

He cleared his throat. "I came to escort you to your friend. And—and to see how you were doing."

"I'm feeling much better. Ariella told me I almost burned myself out."

Cormac nodded as though he already knew that. "There was a lot of blood."

"It wasn't mine."

"Who's?"

"A guard. I put a knife through his neck."

He looked as though he wanted to ask more questions, but thought better of it, gesturing for me to follow.

We didn't have to walk far. Cormac stopped in front of another building similar to the one I was staying in, only a minute down the path.

When he went to climb the stairs, I stopped him with a hand on his arm. "With all due respect, Cormac, I believe I should see her alone."

"But . . ." He looked as though he wanted to argue with me. Something in his eyes made it seem as though it wasn't just curiosity that drove him to accompany me, but something like concern.

"No one's first sight after a traumatic event should be a mythical, grumpy prince she doesn't know." I smirked. "No offense, of course."

Cormac didn't say anything, but conceded, letting me enter without him, and dutifully standing guard outside the door.

Something had shifted in him, and I was curious to find out what had happened in the last two days that would have brought about such a change, but right now, Lily was my priority.

I didn't know what to expect as I walked through the door. Ariella didn't say anything about Lily's condition, just that she was awake. I trembled with the thought that the person I'd find would not be the same person I promised to sail across the world to help.

The healers opened the door and ushered me inside. The curtains were drawn, and it took a moment for my eyes to adjust.

There was nothing but silence as I crossed the threshold, but then I saw her.

Her head snapped in my direction, and before I knew it Lily was out of bed, flinging herself into my arms.

I grabbed her small body and held it against my own. A sob racked me, and I slowly slumped to the ground, taking her with me.

"I was so scared, Lil."

"I'm here," she whispered into my hair.

I pulled her away from me, studying her face. Lines of red marred her perfect skin. A particularly large one cut across her sharp cheekbone, ending at her jaw.

Evidence of the pain she'd endured. For me. For my family.

"The healers say the red scars will fade," she said, noticing my stare. She reached up and put her finger between my brows.

I must have been scowling.

"Lil, this is my fault . . ."

She grabbed my chin, squeezing hard and pulling my gaze to hers. "Stop."

I tried to shake my head as more tears spilled down my cheeks, slipping between her fingers.

"I've always known the risks in what I've *chosen* to do with my life, just as my mother did. I am not the person to stand by as the world tries to destroy what our parents fought so hard for. *None* of my choices are yours, and they certainly aren't your fault."

Lily was ten years older than me, but she always felt older. Likely because she was born into the same world my parents were. Her life was a constant struggle for survival. But now, she chose that life, and even if I didn't understand why, I respected her choices.

"There are things we need to discuss with Marcus and the queen. We need to move quickly. We are standing on a bomb that has run out of time. But, all things considered, you should still participate in the solstice celebration. Kai needs you."

My nose must have scrunched, because she flicked it. I had no idea what she meant by that.

"We talk to the queen, hash out a plan, and then we spend one fucking night enjoying ourselves. I think we can do that. Otherwise, what are we fighting for?" she added.

"My mother has always fought for the Earth."

"She fought for your father, Olivia, and Kat first. Because an Earth without the ones we love isn't an Earth worth saving."

"It's all connected."

Lily bopped my nose one more time, scrambling off my lap. "As your mother has always known."

I nodded, staring up at her from the floor.

"I don't know what will come of all of this, but I do know this is bigger than us. There is a fight coming, and you need to be ready for it. We all do." She sighed, running a hand through her dark hair. "When this is over, I'm going to take a long ass bath and lie on a beach somewhere no one can find me."

She didn't spare me another glance as she marched out the door calling Marcus' name. Already back to work.

Typical Lily.

I sighed, finally pushing myself off the ground and following Lily into the adjacent room—Marcus' room.

Cormac was already there, talking to Marcus. "The enemy is on our doorstep for a reason."

I interrupted them. "Because of me."

They both turned to see Lily and me standing shoulder to shoulder.

Cormac shook his head violently. "No. If you were the sole reason, they'd be only on your doorstep across the sea. They knew when we returned. This operation is so much bigger than we thought, which means they've been planning this for years. And we've been foolish and blind."

This was why he'd changed his opinion of me seemingly out of the blue. He knew the truth now. He saw it at that camp. He finally understood the gravity of the situation. And, possibly, he knew I could help. Perhaps I didn't have his full trust, yet, but we were getting somewhere.

Putting a hesitant hand on his arm, I said, "Perhaps it's time to stir the pot a bit. What say you, Prince?"

The corner of Cormac's lips turned up just enough to be noticeable. "What do you have in mind?"

Pulling my hand away, I snapped my fingers, igniting my blue flame that I now expected had more power behind it than I ever thought. "We light 'em up."

I didn't have a plan, and studying Cormac, I knew he didn't either. But there was a bit more clarity that hadn't been there before. I could see the wheels turning in his head. I could feel the shift.

"With what army? With what support?" he asked seriously, though his lips twitched with the hint of a smile.

I shrugged. "Who needs armies when you have magical princes,"—I winked at him, then turned my head to Lily—"foolishly brave humans, and magical anomalies such as myself?"

Cormac shook his head, but his lips had finally turned into a full smile. "Clumsy, mouthy, magical anomaly, you mean."

I put my hands on my hips, feigning hurt. "Don't deny you like it." I held my fingers up. "Just a little."

He pinched my fingers closer together. "A little bit."

I huffed out a laugh. "I like it when you take that stick out of your ass."

"And there it is." But Cormac was still smiling.

Chapter Thirty-One

"You're quiet," Kai's voice was amused as we sat, eating lunch before we had to get ready for the solstice celebration. "I think that's a first."

I narrowed my gaze. "Don't get cheeky. I just . . . I just don't know what to say."

"Rendered speechless. It's my good looks." He winked.

My mouth fell open. "Who the hell are you and what did you do with Kai?"

We were sitting at the table in our room, waiting to meet the queen. I was pushing around the food on my plate. My appetite hadn't returned.

Kai didn't appear to have moved, but he'd somehow inched his body closer to mine. His pinky brushed against my fingers, and that's when the tears sprung, unbidden.

Kai didn't say a word, but let me cry, his touch my only anchor.

"I thought I lost her. I thought I was going to die. I thought I wasn't strong enough to save those prisoners," I sputtered the words, unable to look at him.

His fingers stopped, but he didn't move his hand. He didn't say anything for a long time, and when he spoke his question stunned me. "Can I take you to the place Mason died?"

When I didn't do anything but stare at him, open-mouthed, he said, "I want to show you something."

I nodded, unsure if I was ready. Unsure if I wanted to go, but somehow, I knew I needed to. Maybe Kai did too.

Kai held out a hand, and I took it. "You think if I think about the place in enough detail, you can channel us there?"

I shrugged, which he took as a yes. A moment later my brain was flooded with a detailed image of the spot.

It shouldn't have surprised me, given Kai's detailed artistic ability, but it did. I realized, then, that he thought differently than most people. Instead of thinking in words, he thought in images.

Perhaps that's why I could never hear his thoughts because there was never anything to hear, only see.

He must have guessed the conclusion I came to, because he smirked, like he already knew that was the answer.

Holding onto the image in my head, I closed my eyes, and we jumped together.

We landed on steady feet in a large open space. There were no trees, but the scorched earth was almost invisible now. So many small plants and bushes had grown since that day.

Small saplings sprouted among the bushes, coming up to my knees.

The earth was shockingly resilient when allowed to heal her wounds.

"Your mother didn't want to re-grow it," Kai explained. "I think she wanted to leave it as a reminder of what happened. As a memorial of those who were lost."

I looked away, nodding, tears forming.

Scanning the large area, my eyes landed on a group of people, no more than small figures in the distance on the other side. They were working together and appeared to be planting seeds.

"Well, I'll be damned," Kai said with a smile.

I squinted, trying to get a better view of the group. "It's not just humans."

Kai studied the group, brow furrowed. "You're right." He laughed. "Not so separate, are we?"

I shook my head, my eyes landing on charred ground that hadn't grown in. Walking toward it, Kai followed without a word.

"Why hasn't this grown back?" I asked, though I doubted Kai had an answer.

His silence had me halting and my eyes meeting his. They were glassy and the color had drained from his face.

"Kai?" I asked, cautiously.

"That's where he died."

That was not what I thought would come out of his mouth, and I looked between him, and the spot on the ground.

We both stepped closer, and I fell to my knees on the border of the charred, dead land and the green grass filling in around it.

I splayed a hand over the black earth, letting my tears fall. The earth soaked them up.

At some point, Kai walked away. I didn't know how long I stayed like that—hand on the earth, tears spilling into the soil.

When Kai joined me again, he announced his presence only by lowering a fisted hand. "Here."

Removing my hand from the ground, I turned my palm upward.

He dropped seeds onto my dirt-streaked skin.

I looked up through bleary eyes, and he nodded toward the dirt. "I think they will grow if you plant them."

There was no way he knew that, but I felt the truth in his words. Like Mason was waiting for me to finally let go. Like he was giving me permission to.

"Here," I said back, shoveling half the seeds into Kai's hands. "We do it together."

Kai didn't respond, but he knelt beside me, and we both spread our seeds, covering them with a thin layer of rich soil.

When we were finished, I wiped my hands on my pants and stood, but Kai didn't follow.

His words were barely a whisper as he stared at the spot he witnessed Mason's death over a year ago. "I saw you that day."

I swung my head to him, and for the first time, his eyes were full of tears. A whole ocean of them. "The moment they told you Mason was gone." He stopped, taking a deep breath, his eyes finding mine. "It was like all the air was sucked out of me as I stood on the deck and watched you scream. As I watched you fall to the ground. It was like time stopped. Frozen in a moment I can't seem to get out of my head. Something broke in here," he said, tapping his chest. "Something I didn't know was even capable of cracking any further. I don't know how to explain it. I don't always have the right words. Hell, I don't usually have *any* words."

I snorted at that, trying desperately to keep the tears from spilling again.

"I knew there was nothing I wouldn't do to see you smile again. I didn't know you at all. Only stories I'd heard from Mason and your brothers. But at that moment, I felt like I was really *seeing* you for the first time."

"Seeing all the broken pieces. That's what did it for you?" I tried to joke.

"We're all just a little broken. A little lost. Just looking for someone to reach out a hand. To make us feel like we belong somewhere."

"Is that what you're doing? Reaching out to me?"

He didn't speak right away. He just stared into my eyes. "I've been reaching since the moment I met you. I just didn't know it."

"I think I've been reaching too."

A long silence stretched between us. It wasn't awkward, it was freeing.

Something had shifted between us. Something had shifted *within* us.

"Will you tell me about your mother?"

Kai stiffened, but I noticed the moment he realized that maybe it was time he let his story free. "I haven't talked about her in twenty years."

I sputtered. "Twenty years?"

"She left when I was seven years old, and my father forbade me from talking about her since." He said it as if it were a perfectly suitable explanation, even though we both knew it wasn't.

"That's fucked up," I said before I could stop myself.

He nodded. "I don't remember much about her, but the thing that I remember most was her love of the sea. She often spoke about the sea as if she knew every secret it held. She would tell great tales of the places and creatures that lurked below the surface."

Kai paused for a moment as if trying to recall something. "Every full moon she would disappear after I fell asleep and would always come back as dawn rose. She never told me where she went, but I always knew. Deep down, I knew."

"And your father? Did he know?"

"Yes."

I waited for him to continue his story.

"We were happy, at least, I thought we were. One night, shortly before she left, I heard my parents arguing in the kitchen. They were arguing about her going home. My father couldn't understand how she could abandon her family, and my mother couldn't understand how he could keep her in a world she didn't belong. The next full moon, she didn't come back at dawn, and my father's grief soon morphed into anger. The father I should have had to help me grieve was suddenly gone too." Kai sucked in a shaky breath. "To this day, he won't talk about it. He wanted to forget it ever happened. Forget she ever existed."

"And you?" I whispered hesitantly.

He didn't respond for some time. "I want to remember her. I want to know her. I want to understand why she left. I want to understand why my father wants to forget her so badly."

"Have you asked him?"

"He won't talk about it."

After that we were both silent for a long time.

"Sol?"

"Mmm?"

"How could she choose the sea over her own family?" There was so much anguish in that one sentence.

"Maybe she felt like if she stayed, she'd be only a shell of herself, and in that process she'd lose you both anyway?"

Kai didn't respond.

"Kai?"

"Mmm?"

"She wouldn't go to great lengths to visit you every full moon if she didn't love you."

He didn't say anything, and my heart broke even more for him. He'd been grieving her for twenty years. An endless cycle.

There were no words to comfort him, but I did know something about grief. Even if my grief was still new. Still raw. "Grief isn't linear. There is no finish line. It comes back over and over again, when you least expect it. And it holds on, squeezing so tightly it feels as though you can't breathe. You cannot control it. There is only surrender," I whispered, my own grief rising again, trying to make its way to the surface and pour out of me.

"Surrender," he repeated.

There wasn't anything else I could say to him. All I could do was *stay.*

I saw the moment he let go of his story. It took several minutes of silent contemplation before his eyes turned from dull to bright. Like some invisible weight had been lifted.

"I don't like what you're thinking," I said, suspicious of the change.

"It was pretty badass that I stepped in to try to save Lily," he commented, changing the subject.

I rolled my eyes. "First, I saved Lily. And second, the ego of men will be the death of me."

"It's sexy, though. Admit it."

"Signing yourself up to die is not sexy, idiot."

"Shit. Thought that was something that might get me laid. Really misread that."

I sat up straighter. "Holy fuck. Seriously, who are you?"

He snickered. "Still me."

"Well then quiet the fuck down. You're freaking me out."

He laughed. A full belly laugh that had a smile lighting my face. I forgot how much I loved the sound of it.

"We're alone. Finally." He waggled his eyebrows.

I sighed. "We're actually not. Have you forgotten where you got those seeds?"

"Damn," was his only reply, and it was laced with humor.

Chapter Thirty-Two

I expected to wear one of the many dresses left for me in the wardrobe in our room, but as Kai and Mouse headed out to give me space to get ready for the solstice, Kai handed me a garment bag. He didn't give me a chance to open it before he was out the door.

Unzipping the bag, I admired the embroidery. It was akin to the pattern of ivory flowers from my dress Rob ruined on the ship. The only dress I'd ever loved.

Opening the bag further, revealed a similar dress, but with a few obvious differences. This one was floor length—more formal. The neckline was cut low in the front with sheer fabric spanning between both sides of my chest. The back was also cut low, the same sheer fabric spanning the breadth of exposed skin. And even though it was simple, the detail was extraordinary, and it was imbued with magic too.

After slipping on the dress, and taming my wild red hair, I stared at the reflection in the mirror and didn't recognize myself. Shrouded in fine fabric that glowed with the same magic that made my eyes light up, I looked as if I belonged here. As if I were one of the Fair Folk.

But was I? I looked the part, but I certainly didn't feel like one of them. Deep down, I still felt human. I still felt like the little girl who ran wild with her brothers, besting invisible foes, and laughing until my belly hurt. The girl who couldn't even light a candle with her flame and knew far too much about others because she couldn't control the thoughts that invaded her head.

Who was the girl looking back at me now?

A soft knock on the bathroom door had me shaking away the uncomfortable thoughts.

"Come in."

Orlan poked her head through the door and froze. She stared at my reflection, and a slow smile crept up her face. "You look . . . Kai was right. No one will be able to keep their eyes off you."

Heat rushed to my cheeks and I hid the fact that those words affected me more than they should have. That man noticed far more than he ought to, all while making you think he didn't notice a damn thing. And knowing now what he saw when he looked at me, only made me realize I was beginning to see him the same way.

"I'm ready," I said, turning from the mirror and looping my arm through Orlan's.

When we left the room, Kai and Mouse were nowhere to be found, but Cormac was waiting. He leaned against the base of the tree, watching the floating lights pass between the branches, lighting up the whole forest so that it glowed with a thousand stars.

Cormac was decked in what I assumed was the royal colors—green and gold. His jacket fit him impeccably. Celtic symbols and trees were carefully sewn into the jacket. Just enough detail to accentuate Cormac's otherworldly beauty, but not enough to feel gaudy.

Orlan's gown was similar, except the colors were switched. The gown was shimmery gold, and the details were green.

Magical butterflies flitted among the lights, adding an array of beautiful color to the greens and browns of the forest. The sight was something beyond anything I could have imagined. Even my paintings didn't come close to the magic that enlivened this place.

My chest constricted as I thought of my mother and what she'd think of all of this. How I wished she were here.

It was only when Orlan spoke that I finally tore my eyes away from the trees. "You can pick your mouth off the floor."

My gaze shot to Cormac, who averted his eyes at the same moment.

Orlan snickered, pulling me along the path toward the palace.

Cormac followed silently behind us.

I was quiet as we walked along the paths, taking in the beauty all around. The Fair Folk had decorated with more than just lights and butterflies. Flowers wove themselves in and out of branches and bushes, coloring the world around us. And the scent—it was intoxicating.

All of it was so much to take in, and when Orlan stopped, I felt the tug on my arm a second too late. Her arm slipped out from my elbow, and I went plowing into a solid wall of a man.

He grabbed my waist, steadying me, and held on until my feet were solidly planted on the ground holding me upright.

My eyes traveled up the deep blue pants that hugged his muscular thighs, and then to the white shirt peeking out from the pant line, form-fitting around his torso, and leading to the top few buttons that had been purposely left undone, revealing the black ink I had become so used to seeing. A blue jacket hugged his strong arms, and when I met his eyes, they matched the color of his suit.

I stared into those eyes that held me captive from the moment I met him. The eyes that taught me how to drown out all the noise in my head. That saw me in a way no one else ever had.

"You don't look half-bad."

"I clean up nice."

I scoffed, and his eyes roamed down my dress. *"The dress is beautiful, Sol. Maybe try to stay out of bodies of water this time?"*

I smirked. *"No promises."*

"Don't worry, I know by now to always expect the unexpected."

"I hope that's a compliment."

Kai didn't get a chance to reply as Cormac cleared his throat, and I became acutely aware that we looked as though we were just staring at one another.

Stepping back, Kai dropped his hands from my waist, even though I wanted nothing more than to stay wrapped up in him.

"Cormac is to escort you," Orlan said.

I shook my head. "But, but I'm human."

Orlan winked. "Exactly."

"I don't understand."

"My mother wants to make a statement to the council and the people," Cormac explained.

"Gotta love being used as a political pawn." I meant it as a joke, but when silence followed, I realized the implications of that joke too late.

"You're not . . ." Cormac stumbled over his words. "You really think that's what you are to us?"

I shook my head, not wanting to stir the pot, not wanting to make this harder for anyone. Not wanting to make it harder for *me*. "It's the nature of who I am. That's what I've always been, and I suspect you know a little of what that's like."

"You can say no," he said.

"Can I?" Could I? Could I walk out of here and no one would stop me? Could I leave this mess for others to fix?

The answer was no. I couldn't walk away. Not without consequences I wasn't prepared to live with.

I was stuck, and everyone knew it. I had unintentionally walked into a complicated mess and somehow ended up at the center of it all.

"We wouldn't stop you," Cormac replied, a hint of unease laced his words.

"I know you wouldn't." We all knew the consequences of me walking out of here, though. I was too involved, and I suspected I wasn't only a pawn being used by the crown. I was a pawn being used by Rob, and possibly even the council.

I was stuck somewhere in the middle.

"You are so much more . . ."

That thought. It wasn't Cormac or Orlan. It wasn't the Fair Folk around us.

It was Kai.

"Careful there. Your thoughts are betraying you."

Kai cocked his head to the side, narrowing his gaze. *"And what if that was on purpose?"*

"Was it?"

When he didn't respond, I said, *"Didn't think so."*

"You are, though."

Kai didn't get a chance to clarify as Cormac reached out his arm, lowering his lips to my ear. "I won't let them hurt you."

Our reception went as expected. Gasps echoed through the clearing as Cormac stepped in front of his people. I didn't have to open the channels of thought to know that the majority were appalled that someone like me was on the arm of their prince.

But it was the group toward the back that caught my attention. One person had a smile a mile wide.

Dorian.

I angled my head toward Orlan, who followed my gaze to the same group. The same man. The man she wasn't supposed to love. The man she loved regardless. And the man who loved her back.

I drowned out everyone else's thoughts and focused on this one small thing—this one piece of hope in a sea of uncertainty.

The queen and the prince made no mention of me in their welcoming speech. They acted as if my presence was normal. As if I was supposed to be standing at their sides. As if I'd always been standing at their sides. I was relieved, in a way, that that's what they chose to do. I was uncomfortable enough.

I'd lost sight of Kai when the queen joined us before her speech, and now my eyes frantically sought him out.

"Don't worry, Chaos, I haven't left you." The dark amusement in his voice made my stomach flip.

I saw his eyes before I saw the rest of him. Something about the way he was looking at me.

A golden cup being shoved in my face, drew my attention back to Cormac and the queen. I stared at the cup before realizing he wanted me to take it. As I peeled it out of his hands he lowered his mouth to my ear. "This is faerie wine. It's more powerful than you're used to. Careful with how much you drink."

I arched a brow, suddenly far too curious about the red liquid in my cup. It smelled like flowers and honey.

The queen raised her glass to indicate the start of the celebration, and everyone followed her lead. Collectively, everyone took a sip of the wine, and then the Fair Folk spread out, leaving a stage in the center of the clearing.

The wine felt warm and tingly as it slid down my throat. Tinged with something that felt eerily similar to Ardil's magic.

I scrunched my nose, looking at the liquid.

"It won't bite," Cormac's voice echoed with mirth.

"What magic is in this?" I asked, meeting his gaze.

"None."

"You don't feel the magic?"

Cormac's mouth formed a firm line as he stared at his own cup. "It's just fermented grapes."

"Then what makes it stronger?"

Cormac brows pinched.

I took another sip, feeling the same magic brush against me as I swallowed. "There's magic in this, and I'm almost certain the Old Ones know it."

"How would they know?"

"Because this feels like their magic."

"You can feel their magic?"

I nodded as if it were a common occurrence, but Cormac's reaction had me thinking maybe I was imagining things.

"Come on you two!" Orlan shouted. "It's time for the show!"

Cormac eyed me, still skeptical, but ushered me to our seats beside the queen. At the same table were two men and two women, who I assumed were their wives. They were all finely dressed with an air of arrogance and privilege surrounding them.

I already didn't like them.

I must have been scowling, because Orlan elbowed me, winking.

Putting on a fake smile I took my seat.

"The halfling..."

"She doesn't deserve the privilege..."

"She has their magic. Why does no one see that?"

"She will ruin everything..."

"Not long now..."

"Sol?" Cormac's concerned voice had me snapping out of the flowing thoughts of those around us.

"I'm OK," I answered automatically.

Cormac re-filled my glass.

"Careful, Sol, you'll be stripping and dancing naked if you have too much of that," Orlan giggled.

Cormac glared at his sister, and the other Fair Folk at our table looked like someone had slapped them.

Orlan didn't even acknowledge them.

For a group known in mythology for their sexual promiscuity and flaunting their god-like bodies, these four clearly didn't fit that description. But when I looked around, the diversity of dress was large. From flowing gowns to bodies covered in fur or feathers or draped with plants, many of the Fair Folk had close to nothing covering themselves.

It was beautiful.

"Perhaps the wine will inspire." Ariella's voice came from behind me, and when I whirled around, I found silver curls falling elegantly down a dress the color of a sunset. Bright and colorful enough to steal your breath. The dress was made for the woman who wore it so well.

"Inspire what?" I asked, taking another large gulp, still shivering at the brush of magic burning down my throat.

"A performance." Ariella swept her arm to the large clearing, now being prepped for the entertainment.

I shook my head. "Can't. I'm not on the list."

Orlan jumped out of her seat. "I'll go add you!"

I sprang out of my chair, trying to grab her arm, but was too slow.

Ariella chuckled, watching her race to the Fair Folk in charge of the show.

"Thanks," I mumbled miserably as I slumped back into my chair.

Ariella took Orlan's empty seat beside me. "Look at it as a way to practice your channeling. And as an outlet for your creativity."

When I didn't say anything, Ariella continued. "It's been a while since you've painted. I know there's something in there that needs to crawl its way out of you. And you may not be able to make things grow, but you have the world at your fingertips. Anything you need, you can channel."

I hadn't thought of it that way. Magic, just like talents, were usually only thought of in ways they could be useful to you or someone else. Even though I was an artist, that mindset still dominated my thinking. I didn't realize that perhaps my magic could be used to create something beautiful or inspiring—art, just for the sake of art.

Nothing more.

I sighed. "Fine. I'll try."

"That's the spirit!" Ariella clapped my back as Orlan returned to our table and Ariella turned to leave. "Enjoy the show!"

Orlan beamed at me as she sat, and I sipped more wine from my glass.

"I'm getting you back for this, you know," I said.

"Oh, I'm counting on it."

I shook my head, but a smile split my lips as we watched family after family take the stage.

I had to rewrite everything I thought I knew about magic and art. Everything from the simplest act of growing a flower, to creating beautiful architecture using only the materials from the forest and then letting the Earth reclaim it at the end. Some families were skilled with animals, others with plants, and some were simply Earth artists, creating what only imagination could. The whole thing was unlike anything I had ever experienced, and I couldn't peel my eyes away for a moment.

"You're next," Orlan whispered, shaking me out of the trance I was in.

I gulped. "Next?"

Orlan nodded, taking the cup of faerie wine from my hands and helping me stand.

I swayed on my feet, oblivious until now, at how much the wine was affecting me. My hand shot out and grabbed the chair. I waited until the world stopped spinning before letting go.

A low chuckle caught my attention.

"She's going to topple over in the middle of her act."

"Would you like to take my place, Prince?"

Cormac shook his head dramatically. "Not a chance."

"Then I suggest you keep those thoughts to yourself."

Cormac's eyes widened.

I patted his shoulder. "If I were a betting woman, I'd be betting on me falling on my face too. No hard feelings."

I sauntered toward the clearing, most of the Fair Folk eyeing me suspiciously and giving me a wide berth.

I ignored it all. The looks, the thoughts, the fear, the curiosity—all of it. Though my palms were sweaty and my heart rate climbed, I didn't stop. Not until I reached the clearing and the whole forest stilled. Watching. Waiting.

I had absolutely no clue what I would do, and at that moment, I wished I had at least thought a little about it. But then I caught Kai's eye.

The world disappeared around us. It felt like a strange magic had stolen us away from everyone, and when the music started, I suddenly didn't feel so afraid.

Without thinking, I released my magic. I didn't have to find it. I didn't have to ask. It flowed out of me as if it had been waiting for me to release it this way.

Blue sparks leapt from my fingertips, creating light of all different colors, a bit like fireworks, but without the sound.

The bees came next, humming with the music, dancing between the sparks. And then, not knowing how, I channeled all sorts of things, starting with blue butterflies.

They listened to my choreography, dancing along with me, and then all manner of creatures followed, spilling out of me and surrounding me in a beautiful dance of life.

At one point, I channeled a few monkeys who decided it was their job to start pouring wine for everyone. The crowd burst into laughter, and then everyone began dancing along. Before I knew it, I was surrounded by Fair Folk of all ages, dancing and laughing among the creatures, both big and small.

The fear that was present just moments ago melted away in an instant.

And then he was there, standing across from me.

"I had wine."

"I see that," he replied, absolutely beaming at me.

"I winged this whole thing," I said, sweeping my hands around the forest clearing.

"Like I said, expect the unexpected."

"My dress is still dry." I swept my hands down the soft fabric.

"For now." The glint in his eye felt like a challenge.

"Dance with me," I said to him. It wasn't a question.

He stepped forward, no hesitation, but before he reached me another form blocked his path.

"Dance with me?" Cormac asked.

My eyes shot over his shoulder to Kai who had stopped a few paces behind Cormac, waiting for my answer.

When my eyes returned to Cormac, I knew I couldn't say no to the prince. Not with everyone else having stopped to wait for my answer.

Resigned, I nodded, taking Cormac's outstretched hand as he led me to the center of the Fair Folk dancing to the music, even though my heart sank.

I caught Kai retreating into the crowd surrounding those dancing, but before I could reach out to him with my mind, Cormac spun me into a lively dance that had me concentrating so hard just so I wouldn't trip over my own feet.

When I stumbled and stepped on Cormac's toes, he hissed through his teeth but pulled me closer to steady me. The move didn't go unnoticed by those around us.

"She's after power…"

"She's manipulating him…"

"Maybe this is the start of something better…"

I clung to the last thought, letting it fuel me as I forced myself to finish the dance without making a fool of myself.

It was clear that this little move of Cormac's was having the desired effect, but the thought that it was only driving a larger wedge between the people of Tir Na Eabha lingered. I didn't think we were changing minds; we were only solidifying them. And that terrified me.

"Where are the Old Ones?" I asked Cormac as the music slowed enough for me to relax.

Cormac angled his head so he could look at my face. "They have never celebrated with us."

"They aren't invited?"

Cormac looked perplexed, his brow furrowing. "It's not that they aren't invited."

"Then why aren't they here?"

Cormac shook his head. "I don't know. It's just the way it's always been."

"Do they have their own celebration?"

I hadn't realized we'd stopped dancing until Cormac dropped his hand from my waist, running a hand through his hair. "I don't know."

Cormac froze, staring over my shoulder. When I turned, I found Orlan dancing with Dorian. Her head lay on his chest, her eyes closed, as they swayed back and forth together. But it wasn't their dancing, or their closeness that made my heart swell. It was the smile on her face.

When I turned back to Cormac, I found a man who looked as though he was truly seeing for the first time in his life. As if his whole world had just opened up.

I placed my hand on his shoulder. "We're better together."

When he met my eyes, there was a sadness in them that I didn't truly understand, but I let him keep his thoughts. I didn't want to intrude.

"Stronger, too, I suspect," he said.

I nodded, and then pulled my hand away, remembering I owed Kai a dance. Looking around the edge of the clearing, I frantically searched for him.

"Go," Cormac whispered in my ear, his breath skating along my ear.

He knew what I was looking for. He'd always known, since the day we met.

I smiled, pushing up to my toes and planting a soft kiss on his cheek. "Thank you for the dance."

"Thank you for opening my eyes and my world."

I found Lily, Mouse, and Marcus at a table on the outskirts of the clearing. Kai was suspiciously missing.

"Nice act." Mouse winked as I sat down beside them.

Mouse was sitting suspiciously close to Lily, with a hand on her elbow.

I raised a brow.

"Archer has been very helpful," Lily explained as she noticed my gaze.

"Helpful, huh?" I waggled my brows, and Mouse turned an adorable shade of pink.

"Where's Kai?" Marcus asked, looking more relaxed than I'd seen him in a while.

"I thought maybe you all would know."

They all collectively shook their heads. "He hasn't been to our table," Mouse explained, suddenly sounding concerned.

"You can find him, you know." Ardil dropped down from the branches above, landing next to me.

I sighed. *"I know, but what if he doesn't want to be found?"*

Ardil snickered, staring at me with his eerie black eyes. *"That boy could use a slap to the face if you ask me."*

"What's that supposed to mean?"

"Are you really so blind?"

I huffed. *"Perhaps if you stopped talking in riddles all the time! And why aren't your people at this celebration?"*

"We're not welcome."

"There's more to it that you aren't telling me."

Ardil remained silent, unwilling to explain further.

"Fine, but I feel your magic in the wine even if the Fair Folk can't."

Ardil made a sound that I interpreted as a gasp. *"You feel it?"*

"Are you admitting it?"

Ardil nodded slowly.

"Why won't you tell me?"

"I don't have the authority to tell our secrets."

"Who does?"

Ardil didn't answer right away. *"The One who is no longer with us."*

I sighed, shaking my head at his half-explanations.

"I came to tell you to go find Kai," Ardil said, changing the subject.

It appeared our conversation came full circle without ever answering any questions. It left me feeling even more confused.

"I'm going to find Kai," I explained to everyone at the table, and then I latched on to Kai's familiar channel and whisked myself away.

Chapter Thirty-Three

Kai almost jumped out of his skin when I appeared right in front of him.

Clamping my hand over my mouth, I held back my laugh. The wine still flowed freely through my veins. "Sorry for the dramatic entrance. I couldn't find you any other way."

Kai loosed a long breath, taking a small step back. "And what if I didn't want to be found?"

"Tough shit," I shot back, which made the corner of his lips curl.

Suddenly noticing where he had run off to, I turned toward the sound of falling water. Here, the forest sloped upward, and the water fell from the top of a cliff. It wasn't a torrent of water, nor was it a steep waterfall. Instead, it fell gently against the rocks as it tumbled into a small pool at the bottom. The water rippled outward toward the edges, and a small stream meandered through the forest behind Kai, then disappeared into the night.

"How'd you find this place?" I watched the moonlight reflect off the water.

Kai moved closer to me, coming so close I could smell jasmine and the salty tang of the sea. I inhaled deeply without realizing I was doing so. The scent was more comforting and alluring than I ever let myself admit. Not until this moment when all my senses seemed heightened. When his proximity made me shiver and the desire to reach out and touch him became almost unbearable.

"I found it the first day we were here, when you were still unconscious." He sounded almost sad.

"It's beautiful. Why didn't you tell me about it?"

"I don't know, Sol." He was looking at me now, but I couldn't even guess at what he was thinking.

"And why didn't you stay and dance with me?" It came out whiny, and I furrowed my brow, still annoyed at the effects of the wine.

His mouth twitched slightly at my expression. "I don't know."

"You say that a lot," I whined again, turning back to gaze at the falling water.

When he didn't say anything further, I whirled around to face him and with an anger I didn't know was there, I practically shouted at him. "No! You don't get to do this to me, Kai. You don't get to shut me out. You don't get to be all silent and brooding, even if I find it somewhat . . .alluring." I paused, forgetting my anger for a moment, and then picked it back up. "I want to know what you're thinking! And not just because I can't read your thoughts. I want to know because you *never* tell me. And that's not fair, because I'm an open book, and I always ask you and you just . . ." I trailed off again, forgetting myself.

I suddenly hated the wine. I hated what he did to me every time he was close. I hated the lingering feeling of his lips that I thought about far too often. I hated that we hadn't had another chance to figure out what was going on between us. And I hated that he still didn't feel as though he could tell me what was going through his head.

Most of all, I hated that he still didn't trust me.

"You want to know what I'm thinking, Sol!?" he shouted back, his eyes narrowed, full of more emotion than I'd ever seen. "I'm thinking I can't breathe when you're around. That you take up every thought in my brain, and it's excruciating. I can't stop thinking about touching you, or how your lips felt against mine. That I hate and love that feisty mouth of yours. That I don't know what to do with all of this *want* and this *need*. That I'm so afraid I'll lose you, and that I'm powerless to protect you. I'm thinking that I'm *scared*, Sol. I'm so very scared." His last words were nothing but a whisper.

He had stepped closer until we were almost touching, and his gaze held mine. Suddenly, I was drowning in the vast ocean of his eyes.

"Fuuuck," I dragged out the word, unsure what else to say. My brain was foggy, but my body was alight.

And then I couldn't hold back anymore as I stepped into him and pulled his mouth to mine.

Kai's breath hitched and then it was as if the whole world suddenly came crashing down, and all that mattered was the feel of him against me. I sighed against his mouth, finally satisfying the incessant thoughts of his lips.

I had the illusion the kiss would be gentle, but it wasn't. It was demanding, as our lips and tongues crashed against each other.

Crushing myself further against him, a soft moan escaped me as his hand trailed down my back and came to rest on my hip.

He pulled back, eyes ablaze, and breathing just as heavily as I was. "Are you sure this isn't the wine speaking?"

"The wine might make me less afraid. Foolish even. But it doesn't control what I want, Kai. What I've wanted for a while," I replied breathlessly.

It was his turn to swear as he grabbed the back of my neck with his free hand and then our lips were locked again. I couldn't get enough.

"So, you're giving me permission to do the things I wanted that night you asked me to kiss you?" he whispered against my lips.

"All of it. Destroy me, Kai."

When I looked up from his lips to his eyes, I found him gazing at me with a desire I had never seen before.

"Damn. I think I like this version of you."

"It's all your fault." His voice was deep and gravelly.

I shuddered as his hand trailed back up my dress and began to unbutton it. He held my gaze, steadfast in an intensity I craved. When he reached the last button, I stepped back, shrugging the dress off. He watched it fall from my shoulders and then off my hips onto the soft earth beneath my bare feet.

Trembling slightly, he directed his gaze to travel the entire length of my near-naked body.. He shut his ocean eyes for a moment, and when he opened them, I swear I saw the slight glistening of a tear.

I stepped into him and ran my fingers along his bottom lip, and his breath hitched as my fingers dipped to trace his neck. They stopped at the top button of his shirt, and then I began unbuttoning his shirt. As every inch of skin was revealed, my pulse increased, the tension in my body growing. I wanted to rip off his clothes, and yet, I wanted this to last.

Before I got to the last button, his mouth dropped to my ear, tracing circles around it with his lips and tongue. My hands halted as

I let out a breathy sound, and he chuckled deeply in my ear before his lips found my neck and dragged them along my skittering pulse.

I was barely able to free the last button, when his mouth stopped on the soft part of my breast.

"Don't stop. Please." It was a breathy plea.

"I want this to last. To go slowly. But fuck if I can't help but want all of you right this moment." His words were so gravelly and deep, and his eyes were so intense that I may have let out a slight whimper. His desires were a mirror of my own.

Finally able to pull his shirt down his shoulders, I let it fall to the ground. An instant later, he grabbed my ass and hoisted me up. I wrapped my legs around his waist as he kissed me breathless.

He knelt, lowering me onto a soft bed of pine needles, their heady scent wrapping around the two of us. When he pulled back again, allowing me to breathe, his eyes landed on face and held. Something like reverence gleamed in them..

I must have been quite the sight—red hair sprawled everywhere, cheeks flushed, freckles laying in stark contrast to my light skin, lips parted slightly, and my chest moving up and down as I desperately tried to control my breathing.

"Fuck, Sol. I want to memorize every inch of you this way. By watching, touching, tasting. Until your image—your entire being is etched for eternity into my very soul."

My heart nearly stopped in my chest. Because I wanted to do the same. To say the same about him, but the words caught in my throat.

He stole all thought as he bent forward and captured my nipple in his mouth. The sensation had me arching into him, and he hissed as I lifted my hips against his.

I ran my fingers through his hair; his mouth found my other breast and then trailed down my stomach, stopping just above my underwear line.

I wiggled my hips as he pulled away again, and he chuckled at my impatience.

His movement became even slower, and he pulled my underwear down my legs at an excruciatingly slow pace.

"I want to throttle you right now," I said through gritted teeth, as he threw them to the side and stopped. His gaze raked along my body, agonizingly slow.

"Good," he purred, a wicked grin on his face.

Pushing myself up to sitting, I grabbed at his pants, but he halted my hand.

"I want to touch you first." His words were a breathy plea.

Letting out a long breath through slightly parted lips, I fell back against the Earth, letting him take control.

He sensed my surrender, and the look on his face told me he'd take full advantage of the power he held over me.

The fire in my belly grew with the anticipation as he bent down and brushed his lips across mine. Barely a touch, and my mouth chased his, only to find he'd moved to place a light kiss across my closed eyelids.

I held my breath, not sure what he'd do next, and part of me didn't want to know. I relished giving up all control to this man.

He could have me, body and soul.

He trailed light kisses along my jaw, then down my neck, and when I reached out to pull him closer, he pulled away clicking his tongue.

"Not yet, Chaos."

I wanted to challenge him, push back, but he must have seen it in my face. He grabbed my hands and pinned them above my head.

I glared at him but didn't move to pull out of his grasp. If this is how he wanted to play, I'd let him.

He smirked and then his mouth found my skin again, this time brushing his lips across my collarbone and trailing down to my nipples, swirling over the already peaked bud.

He continued his slow trail down my body, devouring me with his mouth, tongue, and gaze. Learning every inch of my body. Seeing, as always, more than anyone else ever did.

My body felt as though it was on fire, but I was powerless to control my need. I squirmed, but Kai held me firmly. All I could do was take what he was giving me.

By the time his mouth was where I desperately wanted him, my whole body trembled. I'd never been so thoroughly explored. So thoroughly desired. So thoroughly exposed.

When his mouth finally found my center, his tongue circling slowly, I cried out. It was all too much and yet not enough. And then his fingers found my entrance, and he moaned against me, the sound vibrating through me, as they slid through the wetness pooled there.

He pushed one finger inside of me as his tongue pressed against me harder and faster. My hips arched, urging his fingers deeper, and the tension built to an almost unbearable level.

"Kai." I didn't know if it was a warning or a plea.

"Come for me, Chaos," he rasped, and then there was nothing I could do but obey.

Waves of pleasure crashed over me as I fell apart under his touch.

It took me a few seconds to regain my sense of self, and when I opened my eyes, Kai was watching me.

"Good girl," he purred, crawling over me.

My eyes widened and I sat bolt upright, scooting away from him. "What the fuck?" I stuttered, trying to catch my breath. "Why the hell did I find that so—so hot?"

Kai chuckled, looking far too smug, and then he slowly crawled to me. I watched him, desire stirring again.

When he reached me, he leaned in, his lips grazing my ear. "Because you haven't been told often enough how incredible you are. Now open your legs."

Fuck, this man was going to be my undoing. This quiet, mysterious, and secretly filthy man was my new addiction.

Lowering myself back to the ground, I let my legs fall open. His eyes fell to me, and his gaze darkened, and then he was on top of me, his mouth crashing into mine. I could taste myself on his lips as his hips ground against mine.

I reached for the button on his pants, and this time he didn't stop me.

He continued to move against my hand and hips, making me fumble the task.

When the button was finally free, he sat up, pulling his pants completely off in one quick motion, and I couldn't help but stare. His skin was dark and made darker by the sun. His muscles were honed from years of labor, and a few strands of his dark hair fell free, falling across his beautiful face. His tattoos covered most of his torso. Most of them depicted creatures of the sea. A few were symbols I didn't recognize. I could spend eternity learning about this man.

He grinned at my stare. "Like what you see?"

"You make it impossible for me to not like what I see," I replied, swallowing hard, staring at the length of him.

He chuckled as he slowly lowered himself between my legs and paused, his mouth just above mine. I whimpered, impatient as always, and to my delight he obliged me not a moment later. This time, his lips were gentle as he simultaneously pushed into me.

My head fell back, and when his pace picked up, the tension curled so tightly I thought I'd snap in two.

Wrapping my legs around his waist, I coaxed him deeper, and he groaned as his head fell into the crook of my neck. His movement was urgent now, and there was nothing that compared to this. Absolutely nothing.

"Sol . . ." My name on his lips broke the tension, and I didn't know if I was screaming as my whole body unraveled underneath him.

"Fuck," Kai whispered into my neck as he moved one last time and then collapsed on top of me.

I laughed, and I didn't know whether it was the wine or the after-effects of being completely destroyed and wrung out, but I patted his back. "Good boy."

He lifted himself enough to meet my gaze, and the look in his eyes set me to laughing so hard I couldn't breathe.

He shook his head, but his smile was wider than I'd ever seen it.

Once I calmed myself, and wiped the tears from my eyes, he pushed off me and fell next to me, pulling me close. He ran his hands through my hair.

"I think you've ruined me," I finally said to him.

"You have that backward."

I grinned like an idiot. "Remind me why we didn't do this earlier?"

"It was impossible to get you alone."

"I'm a very important person," I said sarcastically, but Kai tensed beneath me and when I met his eyes, they'd shifted into something far more serious.

He wanted to say something, but he was trying to find the words. I ran my fingers along his torso, tracing the outline of his tattoos.

"Do you have any idea how Mason talked about you?" he whispered hesitantly.

That threw me. I didn't expect him to bring Mason into this, but how could he not? He spent two years with him. He knew him better than he knew me. I just never allowed myself to acknowledge that.

"Fuck, Sol. Do you even know how much he loved you? And even if you only loved him half as much, I'd still feel guilty. I'd still feel less than."

"Less than?" I squeaked out. How could he think that after all everything we'd been through and everything we'd shared. But of course, deep down, I knew exactly how he could feel like that. And all that was made worse by the fact that his mother had abandoned him. That he felt like he wasn't worth staying for.

I just didn't know how to show him it wasn't true.

"Less than?" I asked again, louder this time. I sat up, staring down at him. "There is nothing less than about you. Nothing. You are so used to people leaving that I think you're more afraid of someone actually staying."

I cringed; I didn't know how he'd take my harsh words, but he needed to hear them. "I'm not fucking going anywhere. And if Mason had survived, I'm almost positive that wouldn't have changed a thing between you and me. He would just have had to join us. Or rather, you'd have joined us. And as crazy as that sounds, I know it's true."

Kai arched a brow, his lips twitching.

I rolled my eyes, laying my head back on his shoulder.

"You into that, Chaos?" he asked with amusement in his voice.

I shrugged. "If it was you and Mason, yes. Anyone else, fuck no."

Kai chuckled, hands resuming their movement through my hair. "So, not Cormac?"

I sputtered. "Absolutely not."

He laughed again, the sound sinking into my heart.

Silence between us followed, as we listened to the forest and waterfall around us. We didn't need to say anything else. We already knew things had changed between us. Something bound us together, and there'd be nothing that could separate us.

I realized, then, I had never needed to hear his thoughts. I just had to trust that what I felt whenever he was near was *real*.

Chapter Thirty-Four

We had fallen asleep, wrapped in each other, still completely naked, the softness of the forest floor cushioning us and wrapping us in its alluring scent.

Ardil's voice woke me. *"Sol, there's something I need to show you."*

Opening my tired eyes, I found him standing right next to me, his wide, black eyes, only inches from my face. I twitched, startled, and Kai groaned but didn't wake.

Ardil chuckled, and I found I was getting used to the odd sound.

"Don't say it," I said.

"Say what?"

"You know what," I grumbled, rolling out of Kai's arms, careful not to disturb his sleep.

"The Old Ones don't view mating the same way you do."

Grabbing my dress, I threw it over my head. I didn't bother with the buttons.

"How do you view it?" I asked, my curiosity getting the better of me, though I doubted Ardil would say anything that made any sense.

"The Old Ones view it as a way to increase the flow of magic through the forest."

I froze, staring at the odd creature. My mother's magic was enhanced in that way, too, and although what Ardil said made sense, it only increased my confusion about his people.

"What is your magic?" I asked for the hundredth time, hoping he'd finally answer.

"Follow me," he replied, jumping back into the trees and swinging from branch to branch without looking back.

Sighing, I glanced at Kai's sleeping form. He was so peaceful and content. I walked over and grabbed his clothes, placing them on top of him to keep him warm, and then I ran after Ardil.

Ardil kept his pace slow enough for me as I raced through the forest, the branches grabbing at my dress. The magic of the dress kept it from fraying, but it hindered my movement. After about ten minutes, Ardil stopped. Slowing to a walk, I steadied my breathing.

"We're here."

Ardil hopped through a small opening in the trees, and when I stepped through my breath stalled in my throat.

I stared at the sight in front of me. A pool the color of moonlight sat nestled among willow and hawthorne trees. Not a breath of wind rippled the surface, making the pool appear as though it was a mirror. But it wasn't just the pool, it was what surrounded it. Clinging to almost every branch of every tree was an Old One.

It was as if they were waiting for us.

"Ardil?" I asked, unsure what I should do or say.

"My people came to meet you."

Ardil peered up at me; he waited for the question he likely knew was coming. *"Are you their leader?"*

"In a sense."

Of course that was his answer.

I shook my head. *"What did you want to show me?"*

Ardil pointed toward the pool of water. *"This is the source of our power."*

"A pool of water?"

Ardil shook his head, stepping closer to the water. *"It's not just a pool of water. In your myths it has been referred to as the fountain of youth."*

I coughed, pounding my chest. *"Excuse me?"*

"Our magic is healing magic. This pool holds the essence of our power. A power that we can no longer access in its entirety."

"The pool doesn't work anymore?" Stepping closer to the water, I crouched down to inspect it. It was ethereal, glowing from within, not unlike the eyes of the Fair Folk—my eyes.

"The magic has faded over the years."

"And the Fair Folk don't know about this place?"

"They know, but they've forgotten its true power."

I sighed, running a hand through my hair. *"And why are you telling me this?"*

"Because I believe you can restore it."

Standing, I paced back and forth along the edge of the water. *"How, exactly, do you think I can do that?"*

Ardil didn't get a chance to answer, as the Old Ones suddenly moved, converging on us.

Words flitted into my head, all sounding as strange as Ardil's voice.

"She doesn't look like she holds the magic needed . . ."

"Should we really trust her?"

"Will she be the key to our freedom?"

"The magic is stirring . . ."

Closing off the thoughts, I rubbed my temples. Ardil grabbed my hand, redirecting my attention. When I looked up, a beautiful nymph approached me, a bundle in her hands. She had flowing green hair and skin, with golden eyes that glowed in the moonlight. Her body looked mostly human, but her movement was more graceful, and her hands were webbed. She wore no clothing.

Her voice slithered against my brain as she stopped in front of me, holding out what looked like her child, but her child was motionless in her arms. *"Please help."*

I looked to Ardil.

"Her babe is sick. We should be able to heal her, but our magic continues to fade. I believe you can help."

"How?"

"Hold the babe, take her into the waters, and simply ask them to heal her."

I narrowed my gaze. *"That's it?"*

"That's it."

"So why can't you do it?"

"Because the waters will not listen to me anymore."

I had no idea why he thought they'd listen to me, but I was willing to try. I wasn't going to leave this mother with a dying child without at least giving it a shot.

Nodding, I took the child from her mother. Her small body was warm, and I felt her breath, but the baby still didn't open her eyes or make a sound.

I stepped to the edge of the pool and the Old Ones gave me space, retreating backward to watch. The forest was silent all around us, as if it was also waiting to see what would happen.

Taking a deep breath, I placed one foot into the still pool. The cool water wrapped around my foot, and the ripples moved outward.

"The magic will seek balance," Ardil said as I walked further into the water.

"What does that mean?"

"To heal her, to give its magic, it will ask to take something in return."

"A bargain?"

"Yes."

"It will ask me to give something?"

"No." Ardil turned to the mother. *"It will take something from her or the child."*

My heart rate increased, and I wasn't sure I could go through with it.

A soft voice entered my head. *"Do not fret, child, I have already struck a bargain with the magic. I just need you to complete it."*

I still had no idea what that meant, but her words were reassuring, and I truly believed that if I didn't help, this child would die. I felt it. Her energy channel was barely there—a wisp, fading with every second.

Continuing into the pool until we were both submerged, I let the child float on her back and then I closed my eyes. Though I didn't know what the hell I was doing, I felt the magic surrounding us. It felt like Ardil's magic, but stronger. It felt like the pools of energy my mother felt beneath the surface of the earth. The magic she used to heal my father. The magic she used to bring back Olivia before I was born. A magic I had no idea I was capable of accessing.

Having nothing to lose, I took a deep breath and simply asked that great pool of energetic magic to heal the child.

Nothing happened at first, as I continued to let the child float in front of me, holding her gently. But then she squirmed, raising a small fist.

Her mother let out a choked sound, and then the child wailed. The screeching sound almost made me drop the child to cover my ears, but I pulled her closer, cradling her against my chest. Turning toward the shore, I waded into shallower water. The child calmed by the time I reached the edge, and she peered up at me, her eyes the same color as her mothers.

I smiled down at the child, who now pulsed with renewed energy and life force. I reached out to hand the child to her mother. The nymph clutched the child to her chest and golden tears spilled down her face.

She pinned those glowing eyes on me. *"Thank you."*

I nodded and stepped out of the water. Every eye in the forest was on me as the silver water dripped down my dress, soaking the soil with magic, new sprouts popping up all around me.

Ardil held my gaze, and a smile lit his face. It was an oddly terrifying sight, but I smiled back, aware that this was the first time I'd ever seen him smile.

"Thank you, daughter of the flame."

"You couldn't help but get yourself into trouble, could you?" Kai laughed as I walked through the door of our room, soaking wet.

I shrugged. "Thought the dress needed a good swim. Didn't want this one to feel left out."

Kai laughed deeply, and I thought there was no better sound in the world.

"Will you help me take it off?"

His eyebrows rose as he got up from the bed, already shirtless and in his usual sleeping attire. I couldn't help but stare at him as he approached.

He smirked as my eyes rose from his chest to his face.

Rolling my eyes, I turned around so he could help me peel the wet fabric off my skin.

"You worried about tomorrow?" he asked, carefully.

"Why should I be? It's not like we are on the edge of war, trying to convince the Fair Folk to fight for their own home, trying to unite the humans and the Fair Folk, trying to protect my family and keep them safe, trying to eliminate the Fair Folk hierarchy, changing social conditions for the Old Ones, learning about my own magic, and on top of all of that . . . there's you . . ." I sighed, turning to face him as the dress fell to the floor at my feet.

"That all?" he replied sarcastically, still grinning wildly at me.

"Could you focus please?" I said, as his eyes slid down my body, but I wasn't serious, and he knew it.

Before I could react, his lips were on mine.

Laughing into his mouth, I wrapped my arms around his neck and hoisted my legs around his waist.

He grunted a little at the sudden weight but carried me over to the bed and laid me down softly. As he did, he pulled away and looked down at me.

His smile made my heart skip a beat, before he said, "You'll be the death of me, Sol," and then his lips were on me again, and I could no longer think, only feel.

A loud knock on the door woke me, and Kai jumped out of bed to answer it, pulling on his pants.

Smiling at his bare back, I pulled the covers up around my neck.

It was Orlan, who entered looking much less cheery than normal, but when she noticed I hadn't moved from the bed she turned and looked between Kai and me. The color rose to my cheeks, and I cursed Kai for his cool and collected manner.

Orlan smirked.

"Don't say it," I said, reaching for a shirt and pants at the bottom of the bed.

"I wasn't going to say anything," she said, still smiling at me.

"To what do we owe the honor of your presence?" Kai interrupted, walking over and pulling a shirt over his head.

Orlan became serious again, "Mother is preparing everyone to evacuate."

"Shit. When?" I asked, hurriedly pulling on my clothes.

"Beginning tomorrow."

"Tomorrow?" I almost screamed at her. "I thought she was going to wait to make that decision."

"I did too, but then I woke up and the palace was already being packed up and . . ."

"What about Cormac?" I asked her.

"Don't know. Haven't seen him this morning."

"I'm going to talk to your mother. Right now," I replied, walking toward the door.

"Sol?" Orlan's voice stopped me. "You won't change her mind. The council has spoken. They won't allow her to interfere with the humans. Her crown will be taken if she refuses to comply."

"I have to try."

Cormac stepped away from his mother to greet us.

"Not going well?" I asked, even though it was obvious.

"No. Lily is accusing our council of betraying us."

I cocked my head to the side. "And you don't believe her?"

"The council would never go against the people they're supposed to protect."

Jamming my fists against my hips, I said, "And a group of men has never gone against its own people to gain more power."

"It isn't a dictatorship, if that's what you're implying. Our council makes decisions and laws," he said defensively.

"And your council is elected by the people?" I asked, already guessing at the answer.

"No, council positions are either inherited or passed down via apprenticeship."

I snorted. "That's worse than dictatorship. Instead of being ruled by one narcissist, you're ruled by a whole council of them."

"How dare y—" Cormac started, but I cut him off.

"How many women are on your council? How many Old Ones? How many Fair Folk of mixed blood? And I won't even mention humans. You wrote us off millennia ago."

Cormac gazed at me, confusion wrinkling his handsome features.

"Your council cannot possibly have the best interests of your people in mind if it doesn't even represent your people. You say you want to change things, but all I see is you're complicit in the obvious discrimination."

The rage in Cormac's eyes had me thinking I may have pushed him too far, going backward on all the progress we'd made with each other. I took a large step backward, bumping into Kai's strong chest.

Cormac clenched his jaw. "Our council has been around longer than the entire human race. You'd do well to remember that."

"You just proved my point. It's an archaic system that is no longer working. You said it yourself, the decision to hide away as the Earth died all around you, while you had the power to stop it, was wrong. It was an awful way to eliminate humans, and you know it."

"That's not what the council was doing!" Cormac screamed.

"No? Then what was their goal? If not to eliminate the one race that could wipe out your *pure bloodlines.*"

Cormac's mouth snapped shut. I'd gone too far. The room had gone completely silent, and I felt all eyes on us. But I couldn't sit there and say nothing. I was so tired of everyone thinking they were better than everyone else. I knew what it was like to feel small, to feel powerless compared to those around you, and I wasn't going to back down. I wasn't going to stop fighting for those who had no voice.

"She's right, and you know it, Cormac." Orlan's voice was quiet. Careful.

Some of the fight drained from Cormac's eyes as he faced his sister. I felt some of the tension melt out of Kai as he noticed it too.

"I know she's right," he practically growled. "But we don't have the power to change it."

"If anyone has the power, it's you," she replied.

Cormac shook his head. "I can't risk our mother's crown."

"It's your crown too," Orlan shot back.

Cormac didn't need to say anything because his mother finally broke her silence. "She's right, but we need to be careful in how we approach this issue with the council."

"Ness, we don't have the time to be careful, and with Lily's accusation . . ." Marcus trailed off.

My head shot to Lily who stood there, obviously frustrated.

"And it's not that we don't believe her, but we're barely hanging on since returning to this forest. Going against our own people just doesn't make sense," the queen explained.

If the council was involved and going against their own people, there had to be something in it for them. But what? Power? Control? Resources?

But why ally with someone intent on killing your own people?

She was right, it didn't add up.

"And if the council *is* involved?" I asked.

The three royals didn't say anything for a long time. When the queen finally spoke, it was full of deep-seated grief. "Then the very structure of our civilization will fall."

"And the threat marching on your kingdom? You'll just ignore it? Run from it? Just like you did with humans? Just ignore the fact that you're already involved whether you like it or not? You can't hide forever," I said with more confidence than I felt.

"What would you have me do, Sol? I agree with everything you said, but if I don't have the support of my people, I have nothing." The queen sighed.

"So then, we get the support of your people."

I must have said something ridiculous, because every gaze in the room landed on me and stared like I had three heads.

Just then, Ardil dropped from the branches above and landed softly beside me.

"You have our support," Ardil said to me and to the group.

I translated for the rest of them.

The queen's eyes widened.

"My people know what it's like to be forgotten. We have seen the rise and fall of many civilizations and witnessed many wars between all peoples. We have watched the Earth die because of humans and Fair Folk. We have watched all of it, and done nothing, out of fear. We will no longer sit idle while we watch as history is repeated. Solana is the first of the Fair Folk who can hear us. It has been thousands of years since we have been heard. My people have taken that as a sign that we are meant to help change the course of history. That we are meant to fight for what is right."

Ardil's words made my eyes tear, and I struggled to translate for everyone. As I finished, hundreds of other Old Ones dropped from the branches, some were holding swords, knives, or bows, and others simply came as they were.

Everyone stood motionless and silent watching the Old Ones surround me.

"It was foretold that there would be one that would come along that would restore our healing waters and the magic that powers it. That has already come to pass. So, we will fight alongside Solana, to whatever end."

That last bit of information seemed the most surprising to the queen. She appeared confused but tears misted her eyes. Something about what he said triggered something in her. Something I had a feeling I knew nothing about.

"I'm afraid," she finally whispered.

"Ness." Marcus' voice was careful. She tore her gaze from the Old Ones standing before her. "Perhaps it's time to stop hiding? Perhaps it's time to take a stand?"

The queen considered what Marcus said.

"How long do we have?" I asked, because no one had told me after Lily was rescued how long we had until their forces were upon us. All I knew was that it was worse than we thought.

"Less than a week," Marcus replied.

"So, what do we do?" I asked him, panic rising in the pit of my stomach. Kai held firmly to my hand.

"Organize whatever forces we have, and stand against them to protect the forest, and its people."

"But why would you risk everything for us? You could go home. Leave the forest to burn, while we hide away." The queen seemed confused by Marcus' willingness to help.

Marcus turned to her. "Don't you understand? They won't stop with one forest. One Fair Folk stronghold. They will make their way around the world, taking out the Fire Folk, Water Folk, and Wind Folk, and then they will target humans with Fair Folk abilities. No matter how peaceful you are, Ness. No matter if you attack or run. They'll keep coming until all magical Folk are eliminated. If you leave, you won't be able to ever come back."

The queen shook her head. "I just don't understand."

"I do," I said, my voice breaking.

Everyone turned and looked at me.

"I've seen it in the way humans look at us. Me and my family. They fear us. They fear our power will be used to harm them. They fear that unchecked power will bring destruction, just like the Elite did. They see us as another Elite force coming to oppress them. They cannot even imagine a world where people with power will not abuse that power. They have lived so long in their own fear, they cannot see a different future."

A long silence settled between the vast diversity of Folk filling the palace hall until there was barely any room to move.

"I think it's time, Queen Nessa, to take a stand. Show them a different way," Ardil said, absorbing every word.

I translated for Ardil, and the queen stared at him for a long time. "I can't, not without the support of my people."

"I will stand against them, and my soldiers will follow," Cormac said.

The surprise on my face made Cormac laugh. "Don't seem so surprised. I am a better person than I seem."

"Are you, though?" Orlan chimed in, smirking at her brother.

He went to grab her, but she slipped away from his grip, quick and graceful in her movement. All the while, the queen stared sadly at her two children.

The queen turned back to me. "Do we even stand a chance?"

It was Lily who answered. "You could obliterate their forces if you stay, Your Highness. They possess powerful Fair Folk, at least ten of them. They have technology and communications beyond anything I have seen in my lifetime, and a seemingly endless supply of weapons. They have been plotting this for a very long time. Probably since Sol was born. They have only remained hidden because of their Fair Folk allies."

Everyone remained silent, waiting for her response. Waiting for their fate.

"Orlan," she finally said, "can you ask around and see if we can get more volunteers to fight? We have little support from the pure bloodlines, but maybe there are others that are willing to help?"

Orlan nodded and smiled. She glanced at me and winked.

The queen turned to Cormac. "Work with Solana and Ardil to prepare your men. Any who don't want to defend have that choice. I'll deal with the council."

Cormac nodded once, and then his gaze turned to my hand that was still holding on tight to Kai's.

"We have three days to prepare. You all are dismissed," the queen said, waving her hand.

Orlan was the first to hurry off.

"I will gather my men, and send for you in an hour," Cormac said, his brows set in a firm line.

"Thank you," I replied. I would never be able to thank him for what he was risking. And maybe he wasn't risking it for me. Maybe he was risking it for his people. But, whatever the reason, I was hopeful.

He nodded, with a look I couldn't read, and then turned and left.

Mouse eyed Kai and me suspiciously, a smirk forming on his lips.

I held up my hand, trying to hide my smile as I did. "Don't say what you're about to say."

"Me? What on earth would I have to say to the two of you?" Mouse said sarcastically, beaming at us.

Chapter Thirty-Five

An hour later we were standing in a training ring designed for Fair Folk. The ring was in a large clearing. A wooden fence surrounded the circular area, and only dirt covered the ground inside. I felt the shimmer of a magical shield as we passed through the large gate, guessing it was used for keeping any magic used inside from escaping.

There were around fifty soldiers gathered in the ring, all were Cormac's men, and maybe a hundred Old Ones that Ardil had gathered. Racks of weapons were stored at regular intervals around the edge of the ring.

"This isn't enough fighters," I whispered under my breath to no one in particular.

We approached Cormac, who had his back to us, deep in conversation with a group of soldiers. Cormac was wearing his green pants and shirt with the bronze armor on top. He looked like he had the day I first saw him—a soldier.

All discussion ceased when the soldiers noticed me. Cormac turned, registering what made his men stop talking. I had no desire to listen to their thoughts. Afraid, maybe, that they had strong opinions about working with me.

"Communication with Ardil's men will be tough without you," Cormac commented, nodding in the Old Ones' direction.

"I doubt they will take orders, even from me, but I'll make sure they have a basic idea of what we have in mind."

Cormac nodded. "Let's begin, then."

We spent the next hour mainly hashing out a defensive plan. We still had very little information about our enemy, as most of their operation was still hidden, but we planned for most situations. We also planned for the real possibility that we'd be overrun in an hour or less.

To my surprise, Orlan showed up with Dorian and another fifty or so Fair Folk willing to join us.

Cormac paced, exasperated. "They don't know how to fight. They aren't soldiers."

"We'll show them. We need the numbers. If they can do anything, even just serve as communication runners, or get the injured away from the fight, it will help," I offered.

Cormac sighed, staring down at the plan we had hatched. "I'll start with Dorian's group. See if they have any experience with weapons."

"The better question is, how are you going to use your magic to aid you?" Ariella's voice floated toward us.

I smiled as she came up to my side and put her hand on my elbow. "I think it's about time I help you use your channel jumping abilities to aid you in this fight."

My eyebrows rose. "I thought they were more like cool party tricks?"

Ariella laughed. "Oh, child. Our best warriors of the past were channel jumpers. Just ask Cormac."

"Those are just bedtime stories," Cormac said.

Ariella laughed again. "Are they though?"

Cormac pointedly looked at me, and after a brief, uncomfortable moment, he turned and walked away without another word.

Ariella blew out a breath beside me. "That one's in need of a woman's company."

It turned out, Ariella was right. Channel jumping allowed me to be anywhere on the battlefield, along with channeling anything and everything I needed. What I enjoyed most, though, was channeling living animals to complete various tasks.

"You're having way too much fun with this," Kai commented, as I channeled another swarm of bees to chase Mouse around the training field.

Ariella giggled at the sight, and she let me play around for a while, which had the effect of lifting everyone's mood. Eventually though, she stopped me.

"Let's try hand-to-hand combat using channeling. No channeling bees to help. I want you to channel yourself to avoid your head being chopped off. You will know their move before they strike by listening to their thoughts, and then you can channel appropriately," Ariella explained.

I nodded and smiled. "Who's my opponent?"

"Well, there really is only one person who stands a chance," Ariella replied nodding toward Cormac.

I shook my head. "I don't think that's a good idea."

Ariella laughed. "And why not?"

I blew out an exasperated breath. "I feel like the answer to that is obvious."

Ariella chuckled but ignored my apprehension and went to fetch Cormac.

When he joined us, he had a sly smile on his face.

"There are no rules. Magic can be used. First to pin the other with a killing strike, wins," Ariella said.

Cormac and I both nodded, the smile still gracing his lips.

As we walked to the center of the training ring, everyone stopped to watch. Even the Old Ones gathered around.

I didn't mind the audience, I was used to it, but I wondered if it bothered Cormac. I also wondered if I actually could beat him, and whether he believed I could.

"Don't underestimate your opponent, soldier," I said, as I steadied my nerves.

He narrowed his eyes. "I would never underestimate you."

He sounded sincere, and his response surprised me, but I didn't let it show.

We took our positions across from each other, and everything stilled. Anticipation hung thick in the air. Even the magic of the forest seemed to stop—waiting, watching. As if this moment was some sort of turning point. Something bigger than it appeared to be. Something that might change everything.

I shivered as Ariella gave the signal to begin, and Cormac raised his sword, advancing on me.

Anticipating his first move, and right before he struck, I channeled behind him. Aiming to strike the back of his neck, I was met with his magic shield.

"Shit," I huffed, as he wheeled around, a glint in his eye.

Not waiting, he advanced on me again, this time opting to swipe my feet from under me. As I jumped to avoid his sword, I channeled to his left side, and the instant before my strike, it occurred to me—I had destroyed his shield before.

Cormac turned to his left faster than I anticipated, and forced me to channel again, this time to the opposite side, where I threw my blue flame at his shield. The flame created a small hole that I lunged for, but as I did, Cormac turned and went for my exposed middle.

I backed off in time to avoid his strike, and to my dismay, he magically repaired the shield before I could hit again.

Backing up, I created some space between us.

He smirked at me again, clearly enjoying himself. I had never seen him so carefree. I suppose fighting gave me the same joy. The freedom to move and lose the world for a moment. To lose expectations and responsibilities.

Vines suddenly sprouted from the ground, encircling my ankles, holding me in place. It was enough of a distraction to give him the advantage, and this time, he lunged for my ribs.

I barely had enough time to channel, and this time I was sloppy with my location, and ended up a hundred feet away.

He spun around and laughed, slowly walking toward me. "Give up, yet?"

"Faster, Sol. You have to channel faster," Ariella shouted.

"I'm a bit new to this!" I yelled back.

Cormac came within striking distance again.

"You said there were no rules," I shouted toward Ariella, backing slowly away from Cormac, "so why can't I channel bees, but he can use vines to slow me down?"

"Because you're smarter than that," Ariella said matter-of-factly.

I didn't have enough time to make a retort before Cormac struck with impressive speed. Barely avoiding the blade, I ducked under his sword.

I had no idea what Ariella was talking about. I wasn't sure I could channel any faster, and if I couldn't channel anything else to help me, I was stuck.

Cormac and I danced around each other for a while, both of us beginning to sweat and pant at the effort.

"She never said you couldn't channel more of your own fire," came Ardil's bored voice.

"Shit, Ardil! You're brilliant!" I said and his dark chuckle filled my head.

This time, when Cormac struck, I channeled behind him, and called my blue flame, this time channeling more energy into the flame, and setting it on Cormac's shield.

His eyes widened, as his shield began to burn all around him. It gave me just enough time to swipe his legs from under him and pin him to the ground, my knee on his chest, and my sword across his neck.

I smiled triumphantly, and he gazed at me with a look that resembled awe.

Ariella and Orlan let out triumphant whoops and cheers, clapping far more loudly than was necessary.

The Old Ones didn't appear to have any opinion on the outcome, though their expressions had shifted.

As for Cormac's soldiers, they didn't appear amused, but I caught one of them stifling a laugh.

Easing myself off Cormac, I held out my hand. He took it, pulling himself up. It took him a minute to let go.

"Very good! Very good!" Ariella clapped as she approached. "Looks like you've found your equal, General," she said to Cormac, clapping him on the shoulder.

"Seems that way," he said, still looking only at me.

Orlan came up to her brother and smacked him on the back. "You got your ass handed to you by a woman! A part human woman, at that!"

I smiled at the scowl that formed on Cormac's lips.

"Word travels fast around here," Kai commented, returning to our room with even more food in hand. "Most of the kingdom knows you beat Cormac."

Rushing out of bed to eat more, I mumbled through a bite of delightfully sweet watermelon, "Good."

"Your appetite knows no end," Kai laughed as I stuffed even more food into my mouth.

"Using magic makes me hungry."

Kai silently watched me eat for a while, a hint of a smirk plastered on his face.

"What is it?" I finally asked him, sensing something was bothering him, despite the happiness.

"He's in love with you, you know," he replied, looking away.

"Why does that matter?"

"If you two were to marry, it might make everything easier," he said, still not facing me, his gaze locked on the open window and the sound of soft chatter of the early summer forest.

When I didn't respond, he finally looked at me.

I was frowning. "I don't want to marry him."

Kai sighed. "I know you don't, and I wouldn't even mention it, but if it were something that would make the council change their allegiance . . ." He looked down at his hands, clearly feeling things he had no intention of revealing to me.

"How could you even think that?" I asked. It felt as though we had gone right back to the beginning. Back to when I couldn't read a single thing about him.

It took him many minutes to say anything, but I waited, wanting to give him the time to sort out his thoughts, despite my irritation.

"Sol, I don't want to watch you die." His voice trembled as he said it.

Swallowing my food, I stood up and walked around the table to where he was sitting. He looked up at me with fear and sadness in his eyes. Straddling his legs, I sat in his lap, pulling his lips to mine.

Pulling away, reluctantly, I said, "One, we only have three days. If he proposed an alliance through marriage right this second, it still wouldn't be enough time to change the council's mind, and two"—I took a deep breath—"two is, I love you, and there's no way in hell I'd marry Cormac."

Kai finally smiled. "Even if the fate of the world rested on that choice?"

"Let's hope it doesn't come to that. And if it does, maybe I could legally marry him, but keep you as my plaything," I said winking.

He laughed and kissed me again.

"Sol?"

"Hmm?"

"Promise me if you see no possible way to succeed that you'll get out of there."

I had no idea why he spoke as though he wouldn't be right by my side the whole time, but I nodded anyway, cupping his face gently with both hands. "I promise," I whispered, and kissed him again.

After a moment he shifted, separating our lips. "Wait, you love me?"

"Yes, now shut up and keep kissing me."

He smirked and did as I asked.

Chapter Thirty-Six

The next morning, I woke early, hastily put on my training outfit, stuffed food into my mouth, and left the room before Kai was even awake.

Racing for the palace, I hoped to catch Orlan before she started with her duties for the day.

The guards at the palace doors didn't even give me a second glance anymore, so I pulled open the main doors and headed toward the large meeting room in the center of the building.

Angry voices halted my steps as I approached the room, and I discreetly tucked myself behind the door to the room, hiding among the plants that lined the wall.

I hadn't caught the name of the councilman I already met, but I recognized his voice as he spoke in a low growl to the queen, who seemed angry, though she held her voice steady.

"We'll have your crown, Your Highness, you know the rules."

"This isn't in any of our laws," the queen replied with a slight clip in her tone.

"It's implied," he responded, just as shortly.

"Implied does not hold. If you want to change the law, then fine, change the law, but you cannot put your filthy hands on her."

"You know we cannot change the laws that quickly. It will be too late by that point."

"Then I suggest you and your entourage of scheming councilmen leave it alone and actually help me keep this kingdom safe."

The councilman didn't say anything to the queen, but I heard his exasperated sigh, as the queen stormed out of the meeting room seconds later, dressed like she was ready for a battle.

I didn't move from my spot, knowing full well that the councilman was still in the room.

"You can come out now," came his voice, but it was different from the way he spoke to the queen. It sounded low and menacing—he was out for blood.

Steeling my nerves, I held my head high, placing a hand over the dagger concealed on my thigh. I stepped out from behind the door to face him.

The councilman looked no older than thirty, but he was far older than I could fathom. He was tall, muscular, slender, and graceful as all the Fair Folk were, but there was something in the way he looked at me that made me think there was something far darker hidden in him.

"Seems you have some explaining to do," he said.

I batted my eyelashes at him. "And what would you like me to explain?"

I could almost feel his frustration. "You know what."

"I have no idea what you're talking about, but I would like to know what the hell that was all about, because it was very clearly about me." I didn't hide my derision.

"You're a smart girl. I'm sure you can figure that one out on your own."

At that moment, Ardil jumped down from the canopy above and landed next to me, a snarl escaping his mouth, teeth bared.

The councilman let out a twisted laugh and snarled back. "You have no power against me, *Old One*, so I'd suggest going back to whatever shithole you came from."

Ardil made to lunge at the councilman, but I channeled faster, blocking him from going for his throat.

Ardil growled at me but backed up, obeying my silent plea.

"What's this about?" I asked him.

"Ask him," Ardil replied, still glaring at the councilman.

"Ardil's keeping secrets from you, is he?" the councilman practically purred.

I swung around to face him. "What have you done?"

The councilman laughed. "I haven't done anything. His kind got what was coming to them all those years ago. My ancestors took away their power as punishment for their crimes."

I glanced over at Ardil who still had a snarl on his face. *"Is this true?"*

"They take away any power that is greater than theirs out of the fear of losing their absolute control."

"This is why you can't talk to them, and they can't talk to you? Because of something that was done thousands of years ago?" I addressed the question to the councilman.

"Their crimes cannot be forgiven," the councilman replied, glaring at Ardil.

I shook my head, not really comprehending this tangled mess I found myself in the middle of, and it's not as though Ardil had been forthcoming.

"What law do you want changed because of me?" I demanded, changing the subject for the moment.

The councilman turned his glare onto me, taking a step closer. "You and your family are quite the conundrum, Solana. Not pure of blood, but not purely human either, yet you possess a power older than any living Fair Folk. You cannot be one of us because you have broken our most fundamental law of interacting and influencing humans, and yet you cannot be left to exert your power on humans unchecked." He clucked his tongue, circling around me. I tightened my grip on my dagger, not letting him out of my sight. I didn't know what kind of power he possessed, but I guessed since he held a council position, he was both very old and had considerable power.

"It has been suggested that we allow you to become one of us, marrying into one of our pure bloodlines, and having you cease any contact with humans, but what to do with your family?" He clucked his tongue again; I ground my teeth to stop myself from ripping that tongue out of his mouth.

"Because you are not truly one of us, nor truly human, you are outside our laws." He smiled at me. "But if you are outside our laws, then no one can be punished for any actions toward you."

I backed up toward the exit, Ardil glued to my side. It was a clear warning, but one I had no idea what to do with.

When I reached the doors, the councilman let out another laugh. "It's your fault your friends are in danger. You should have left the second you got here."

My heart rate sped up, and though I looked calm, I was terrified. "What?" I stammered, though I already knew what he was going to say.

The councilman continued his slow steps toward us. "You got in the way—"

I didn't hear the rest of what he had to say as I grabbed Ardil's hand and channeled the two of us back to my room. We landed with a thump on the floor, and I was up in an instant, looking for Kai, but he wasn't there.

"Sol," came Ardil's shaky voice. *"It's all my fault."*

It was the first time the Old One sounded afraid, and it had the hair on my arms standing on end.

"What's your fault, Ardil?" I asked him, still looking around for any signs of conflict or of being followed or watched.

"We knew what was going on, and we did nothing."

"What are you talking about?"

He winced at my tone, before launching into his story. *"Thousands of years ago, one of the Royal Fair Folk fell in love with a lowly water spirit. It had never been heard of, a union between the Fair Folk and the Old Ones, and yet the Crown Prince was so head over heels that he had the law changed, and they were married the following year. Everything went smoothly until they had children. The crossing of bloodlines caused mayhem with the magic. The children were powerful beyond belief, to the point that no one had ever seen power on that level, but the children couldn't control their power and killed without warning. Many Fair Folk and Old Ones were lost in the pursuit of containing them, and the children were ultimately killed. The water spirit queen sought revenge on the Fair Folk for the murder of her children, and a war raged between the Fair Folk and the Old Ones. Ultimately, the Fair Folk were stronger, and we were forced to surrender. As a result of that war, an ancient curse was placed on us, rendering all magic except for healing magic unusable, and taking away our ability to communicate with the Fair Folk. As a result, we fell out of favor and were mostly forgotten. Some of us were later enslaved in Fair Folk households. We have forgotten the power we once possessed."*

"Why are you telling me this now?"

"We thought . . . we thought . . . because you could hear us that maybe you could help us break this ancient spell and return us to our former glory."

"What else aren't you telling me, Ardil." Ardil had just revealed more information than he ever had, but I could tell there was more to the story.

He looked at me tentatively. *"We see and hear everything. They are playing a dangerous game."*

"No riddles, Ardil!" I couldn't help the dread that was rising in the pit of my stomach.

"They are setting a trap for you. An impossible decision."

"What decision?" I tapped my foot on the ground, my impatience growing with each revelation. Time was running out.

"A choice between the humans, the Fair Folk, or your family."

A trap. He said a trap. That could only mean . . .*"Where's Kai?"* Fear took hold of my heart and turned it to stone.

"He's the bait." Ardil was trembling now.

"WHERE. IS. HE!?" I screamed, grabbing Ardil around the neck.

"They are taking him to the front lines."

I dropped Ardil and ran.

I found Cormac on the training field right where he was supposed to be. He registered the look on my face. "What's wrong?"

"Did you know they're trapping me?"

The look of pure confusion and shock on his face was enough of an answer. "The council has been planning this, likely since my mother came to visit. I wouldn't be surprised if they are the sole power behind the group that is now marching on this place."

"What are you talking about, Sol?" Cormac stiffened.

I shook my head. "I don't know, Cormac, I don't know what they want from me." Before I knew it my head was in my hands and my knees dropped to the ground.

He was next to me in an instant.

"They have Kai, and they likely have Lily, Mouse, and Marcus. They want me to choose between the humans, the Fair Folk, and my family," I continued, feeling defeated.

Everyone had stopped training and were slowly converging on us. I ignored the stares.

"Tell me *exactly* what happened," Cormac whispered next to me.

Looking up at him, I found a predator—or was it a king?—staring back at me. I told him everything I had overheard between the councilman and his mother, and then I told him of my own conversation with the councilman and what Ardil had revealed, and before I could stop him, he was racing toward the palace.

"Cormac!" I yelled after him, but it was useless, he was already gone.

Chapter Thirty-Seven

Channeling myself to Lily's room, I found it empty. I went to Marcus' room next and found only a half-eaten meal on the table by his bed.

Not knowing what else to do, I found Cormac's channel and dropped in right next to him. I expected him to be talking to his mother, but what I *didn't* expect was to be standing in the middle of the entire council.

They sat in a circular chamber surrounding a stone platform that felt eerily like a sacrificial stone from ancient stories. Cormac stood in the center, addressing the councilmen surrounding him. His mother sat next to an elaborately dressed man in robes that looked like those the pope used to wear in the history books my mother studied.

Stumbling backward, I watched as everyone became silent, their curious eyes locked on me. Cormac placed his hand on my lower back to steady me.

"So glad you could join us, Solana" said the cheery voice of the councilman in front of us. "Prince Cormac was just filling us in on some of the details of your earlier conversation."

My eyes shifted to the face of the familiar dark-haired councilman I had talked to earlier. His demeanor suggested I had fallen right into his trap, as planned.

My eyes darted back to the councilman in front of me, as Cormac's hand stiffened on my back.

"It seems we have all been deceiving one another," the councilman said.

Looking around at everyone surrounding us, I opened my mind to their thoughts.

They came flooding in, and I staggered by the force of them. It had been a while since I'd opened my mind to so many thoughts.

Cormac must have noticed the change, his eyes darting to my hand that had shot up to my temple. He watched me as he spoke to the council. "We have an immediate threat to our kingdom, councilman, the issues surrounding Solana and her friends and family are secondary. Those can wait."

"Quite right you are, Cormac. But you see"—the councilman took a step closer to us, and Cormac's gaze snapped to the threat, his hand drifting to the sword at his hip—"her staying and fighting with our people cannot be tolerated."

"Why not?" Cormac growled.

"Imagine how it would look to everyone else, having this abomination protecting *our* forest."

The queen abruptly stood, and I grabbed Cormac's arm to prevent him from plunging a sword through the man's chest, even though I had a similar inclination.

"Councilman," the queen boomed, "if the council will not hold to our agreement, then what do you propose we do?"

The councilman gave her a sadistic sort of grin. "Well, if she were one of us, the law would protect her, and she would have a say in this mess we're in."

"I will marry her," Cormac said, not looking at me. "It's what you all want, right? For her blood to be part of the bloodlines again?"

"Cormac . . ." I whispered, but he didn't acknowledge me, too caught up in trying to protect me.

"That is part of what we want."

"Cormac! It's a trap. This is what they want *us to do."*

Cormac furrowed his brow.

"Their thoughts—they want us to agree to be married. They want you to put up a fight against this invisible threat. But there is something else going on here. Something they aren't saying. Something they aren't even thinking about."

"What do you want me to do, Sol?" he practically pleaded with me, knowing we had to make a decision, and we needed to do it quickly. Time was running out, not just for me, but for the entire kingdom.

I wanted to get one step ahead of the council, but I feared they were already out of sight. Ultimately, I didn't think this was about my blood. I didn't even think it was about the battle on our doorstep. There was something bigger. Something that had been planned long before I showed up.

"Agree to their terms. We have no choice." My thoughts drifted to Kai and his suggestion I marry Cormac to satisfy the council. At the time, I thought it was paranoia, but now, I wasn't so sure. But if he knew, the question was how?

I shook off the thoughts, knowing Kai wouldn't have done that. He wouldn't have left out important information if he knew it. It had to be a coincidence.

Cormac grabbed my hand and gave it a light squeeze before raising his head to the councilman in front of us. "We will agree to be married, if you agree to help us defend our home and Sol's family."

The councilman smirked. "It's a deal, Prince."

Cormac walked me back to my room, and I couldn't even look at him. I caught him stealing glances my way, but I didn't want to know what he was thinking.

"What can I do?" Cormac pleaded.

"I need to find Kai, Lily, Mouse, and Marcus. I need to get them out of here."

"Channel to them."

Shaking my head, I finally met his gaze. "I can't. If they're somewhere unsafe, I could be putting them all in danger. I need to know where they are."

"I'll find them," Ardil's voice drifted into my head, just as he dropped down in front of us. *"It's the least I can do."*

I nodded, unsure of what to say to him. He looked at me sadly, before he jumped and vanished among the branches once more.

I couldn't read the look on Cormac's face. When he finally spoke, his voice was cracked and broken. "I know this isn't what you want. I know you don't want me, Sol. I suspected what they wanted, but I shut down any mention of it before it became anything tangible. But I also know they'd rather have you and your family killed rather than let you pass your blood onto humans."

The shock on my face must have been evident, because Cormac whispered, "We are no better. When your mother restored some semblance of balance, we returned, but not to restore our relationship with humans. We came back to find out why the Earth had gifted this ability to a human. Your mother saw right through us the moment she stepped foot in the council chamber, and stormed out, vowing to never help us."

"That's why she never told me about you. But why didn't she warn me?" I whispered to no one, looking away from him.

"Sol?" he asked so quietly I could barely hear him. He did nothing to hide the pain in his green eyes, the light already dimming from them. "We were so very wrong."

Perhaps it was the loneliness, or the feeling of being trapped, but I closed the distance between us and threw my arms around Cormac's waist, burying my head in his chest.

He hesitated for a moment, before he wrapped his arms around me and rested his head on the top of mine, inhaling deeply.

"If it's any consolation, I don't want to marry you, either," he confessed.

Cormac's words caught me so far off guard, that I jerked and stumbled backward. He grabbed onto the fabric of my shirt, preventing me from falling on my ass, and then laughed.

"Didn't expect that, did you?" he asked, amused.

I shook my head.

Cormac released me once he was satisfied I wouldn't topple over. "It's not exactly a secret, nor is it frowned upon. It may be the only thing our people aren't backward about."

I wrinkled my brow, not fully understanding where he was going with this.

Cormac chuckled, "I'm not good with words when it comes to my personal life."

"No shit."

Slight pink color painted his cheeks. "I think I'd rather marry Kai."

His confession didn't surprise me as much as I thought it would. Suddenly, every glance made sense.

I laughed at my stupidity, and for not realizing sooner. "Sorry, he's mine."

Cormac laughed back, rolling his eyes playfully. "No shit."

"They are in the dungeons," came Ardil's voice, making me jump from surprise at the sudden intrusion.

"Are the guards watching them?"

Ardil nodded. *"But we have a powder that will knock them out for a short while."*

"I'll meet you there."

Ardil nodded again and then disappeared.

"They're in the dungeons. Ardil is going to distract the guards while I slip in," I explained to Cormac.

"What are you going to do once you're in there?"

"Channel them out, one-by-one."

"Where?"

"The docks."

"Will they have allies there?"

"I sure as hell hope so. Kai's father was supposed to stay, but that was before the attack on our ship."

"Be careful, there are eyes everywhere." There was concern in Cormac's voice, but he made no move to stop me.

"What do we do when they find the cells empty?" I hadn't thought through the plan. All I cared about was getting them out, but what if getting them out meant I was putting myself in more danger.

"They'll know it was you." Cormac immediately caught onto my line of thinking.

"Please tell me this plan will work," I begged him.

"Get them out, Sol. I'll deal with whatever fallout there is."

"I'm your betrothed. The fallout could mean your crown."

Not breaking his gaze, he replied, "So be it."

Minutes later, I was in a dark cell in a location I couldn't place, staring into Kai's worried and tired eyes. The space was small. Stone walls enclosed it on three sides, and iron bars separated the cell from the damp stone hallway. The stench of rot filled the space, and I wanted to cover my nose at the assault.

"I'm getting you all out of here," I explained, grabbing for Kai's hand.

He pulled away, hesitant.

"I'll explain later, we don't have time . . ." I pleaded with him, still holding out my empty hand.

He let out a long breath, then reached out. An instant later we were standing at the edge of the forest as it touched the bright blue sea in front of us. Kai's fathers ship was anchored offshore in the bay. Waiting, as promised.

As I blew out a relieved breath, Kai turned to me, his eyes speaking more than his words ever could. His surprise at our location, his surprise at my presence. A million desperate questions swam through his ocean eyes, along with something much darker—fear.

"Kai . . . I can't . . ." I couldn't get the words out before I fell to the sand, tears streaming down my face.

"Sol?" he asked cautiously, bending down next to me, and placing his hand on my lower back.

Looking up at him as he stared into my eyes, I somehow knew that he knew exactly what had happened. "I'll go," he said, his voice close to breaking. "If that's what you want, Sol, I'll go."

I nodded, because I didn't think I could say anything to him. I didn't think I could truly say goodbye. How we had gotten here, I couldn't even guess. It had happened so fast. We were happy and joking about me marrying Cormac, and before I knew it we were standing here, saying goodbye.

"You knew," I whispered.

His eyes were full of sorrow, as he nodded his confirmation.

"How?"

"Sometimes I can see things before they happen," he explained, looking away from me toward the sea. Toward his father's ship.

"Why didn't you tell me?"

"Because I didn't know how. Because what I see doesn't always come true, and it's only a picture—a moment in time." He still wouldn't look at me.

A long silence followed, both of us unsure what to do or say to one another.

"So, that's it?" I finally asked.

"I see no other way out, Sol. The only other option if you deny them is everyone you love dies. I cannot let you choose any other way."

It took me until this moment to realize that what I felt every time I looked into his eyes was more than feeling, it was a *knowing*, a sight beyond sight, and as I stared into his deep blue eyes, tears streaming down his face, I suddenly saw his future. Our future.

Reaching for him, I pulled his lips to mine. He was hesitant at first, but then his hands were around my waist as he crushed me against his body and kissed me so deeply I thought I'd drown in it.

When we finally pulled away from each other, I whispered, "I love you," before I channeled away, leaving him alone, on the edge of the sea he loved so much, hoping it wasn't truly a last goodbye.

Hoping he was wrong.

Hoping there was another way.

❦

Channeling back to the dungeon, I followed Lily's familiar channel.

As I dropped in front of her, the first thing I noticed was her wide eyes, full of fear. Then the knife across her neck.

"Channel again, and I'll slit her throat," came the low voice of the dark-haired councilman.

"Hurt her, and I'll hunt you down and butcher you," I hissed back.

He laughed, but it wasn't a joyful laugh. "You hold no power here. You are under our rule. Channel anyone else out of here and I'll have your entire family murdered."

"I thought that was your plan, regardless," I replied, trying to sound bored instead of fearful, as the knot tightened further inside my stomach.

The councilman's eyebrow rose, but only slightly. It was the only inclination that I had hit some invisible mark.

"Let her go," I snarled. "I'll heed your warning."

The councilman lowered his knife slowly, and then pushed Lily forward, where Mouse caught her.

"I'll get you out," I said to both of them. *"If it costs me everything, I will get you out."*

"Sol . . ." Mouse's voice filled my head, but I didn't let him finish. Closing off communication with them, I turned and followed the councilman out of the cell and toward whatever fate awaited me.

The councilman dropped me in front of Cormac's room, if you could call it a room. It was a suite of rooms high above the forest floor, overlooking the entire kingdom. The suite had a bedroom, bathroom, office, and a large sitting room with an impressively large fireplace.

"Keep a leash on your future wife, Prince, or the deal is off," was all he said before he turned and left me standing there.

Cormac didn't say anything, as he led me into his office that had an impressive view, and a large balcony hanging over the trees below, motioning for me to sit.

I stopped and stared at him for a moment, teetering on the edge of total collapse, before I finally moved my legs, and fell into the chair.

"What happened?" he asked, carefully.

"I got Kai out, but the councilman was there when I returned, a knife on Lily's throat. He threatened to have her, and my entire family killed if I tried to channel anyone else."

Cormac sighed and ran a hand through his hair, looking out the floor-to-ceiling window. "They are human, I cannot free them. They have every right to hold them there according to our idiotic laws. As for your family, they don't fall into either category. The law says nothing about what they can or can't do."

"You think they're hunting them? You think they already have a plan?" I couldn't keep the panic from rising again.

He looked at me for a long time, and I tried not to think of what he had said earlier, as I held his gaze.

"I think they've been planning this since the day we returned to this forest, and they knew who had created it. I think this is bigger than you or me or the group that is marching into this kingdom. I think it's all connected, somehow, too. I can only guess, but my guess is that the council wants the same thing as that group—for humans and Fair Folk to stay separate, and you and your family are in the way of that. Not on purpose, of course, but simply being who you are. My mother and I are also in the way of that since we have been fighting the council for a change in the laws."

I raised my eyebrows at that bit of information. "If we can prove the council is working with the army that's at our doorstep, is that a breech in your laws? Can they be punished for it?"

"It would be treason, so yes, it is punishable."

"But how do we prove it?"

Cormac finally looked away and loosed a long breath. "The only way to find out is if we can either one, infiltrate their camp, and have you pull the evidence from the thoughts of the people in charge, or two, walk right into the trap they are setting for us, where it will likely reveal itself."

"And if we walk into it, what chance do we have?"

Cormac shook his head sadly. "Very little. They will either kill us, or we will continue to be their pawns in this game they are playing."

"Cormac?"

He finally met my gaze.

"You could give me up to them. You could get out of this. Your mom could remain queen, and you, heir to her throne. You don't need to do any of this."

Eyes hard, he shook his head. "I do."

I felt the truth in his words, even if I didn't fully understand. "What do we do now?"

"Prepare for the fight of our lives."

Chapter Thirty-Eight

I was woken later that night by Ardil's tentative voice in my head. *"Sol? Sol?"*

"What?" I murmured, reluctantly opening my eyes to find his black eyes staring back at me.

"I think we've found something that may help."

Sitting up, I stretched my arms above my head, instinctively reaching for Kai, before realizing my mistake and pulling my hand away, clutching it close to my body.

The cold sheets lingered on my skin, and I took a deep breath, willing away the ache.

"We've been looking for a long time for a spell to counter the curse that's been placed on us. We've scoured the entire Fair Folk library, without much hope, until today." Ardil looked at me expectantly.

"And?" I replied, unable to keep the yawn from escaping my mouth.

"We found an old list of books that are supposed to be in the Fair Folk archives, and on that list is the title of a book that may restore our powers. Problem is, we've scoured every shelf in their extensive library and found no evidence of it anywhere. But we also found a picture of the Fair Folk Library and noticed something odd. The picture shows the library rooms

as they are today, except one room. That room is nowhere in the actual library." Ardil paused, and I sat up a little straighter.

"*You think it's a hidden room? Or somewhere else entirely?*"

"*I don't know, but, Sol, if you memorize that picture, you can channel into it! You can get that book!*"

"*How do you know it's not a trap?*"

I wanted to help, if I could, but this was a really big risk for something that may or may not exist.

"*We don't know. But, the book of spells is well-known, even if it hasn't been seen in millennia. It does exist. It's just been lost. I also believe that you are the only one who can access it, and that was by design.*"

Squeezing my eyes shut, and running my hand down my exhausted face, I contemplated the information. There were too many unanswered questions to count. Too many unknowns. But if we were going to change things, we needed every advantage we could get. Ardil and his people with fully restored powers might tip the scales.

"*I'll do it.*"

Ardil's face lit up for the first time, well, ever. He slammed the list on the bed.

"*This one,*" he said, pointing to a title that was written in the Ogham language, the ancient language of the Fair Folk.

"*Magic Spells, and their Counterspells,*" Ardil explained.

"*Subtle and creative title,*" I commented dryly.

Ardil let out a short chuckle, before he flipped to the end of the book and we both stared at the picture of the hidden library room.

It was nothing special. In fact, it looked far more ordinary than my mother's library and even Cormac's small office whose walls were covered in books. It had shelves lining the walls, no windows, and the shelves were square and ordinary, no special markings on them whatsoever. The carpet inside the room was bright red, which was the only odd thing about it, and there were wooden, round tables scattered around the center of it.

"This could be any old library. You sure I'm not going to end up in someone else's library?"

Ardil shrugged, or at least, I think he did. *"We have to try."*

Nodding and resolute in my decision to help, I quickly changed into my fighting gear and strapped a few daggers into the straps on my legs, trying to prepare for anything.

Ardil watched me. *"If anything feels wrong, channel back immediately. The room itself might be a trap or enchanted. If it's enchanted, you'll feel the magic. Before it latches onto you, channel out. Do you understand?"*

"You think that's possible?"

"This one room contains more powerful information than the whole of the Fair Folk archives combined. And I include the Air, Fire, and Water Folk in that statement."

I shuddered at the thought. *"You don't think anyone else knows about this place?"*

"I think if they did, we'd be in a heap of trouble. Likely already dead, or our magic stripped completely."

"So, even the Fair Folk have forgotten this knowledge?"

Ardil nodded.

I took a deep breath. My mother should have been here. This was her territory—what she'd been looking for since my birth. Hunting knowledge wasn't my strength.

Closing my eyes, and chasing away my thoughts, I flung myself into the unknown.

⚜

When I opened my eyes, all I could see was blackness. There wasn't a speck of light, but I could smell the books. Their scent was a familiar tickle in my nose from spending hours upon hours in my mother's library.

Igniting my finger, my blue flame cast eerie shadows around the room.

Looking down at my feet, I found the familiar red carpet from the picture, and to the right of me was one of the wooden tables. It was an exact replica of the pictures, not a table or bookshelf out of place.

"How the hell am I supposed to find this book in the pitch black" I grumbled to myself as I started walking over to the shelf closest to me. There must have been a hundred bookshelves. And to think I thought getting here would be the challenge.

The books were covered in inches of dust, as if they hadn't been touched in thousands of years. They were all written in the Ogham language—the ancient language of the Fair Folk, so I had no idea what information was held beneath my fingertips.

"If my mother could see this place," I whistled, as I continued to dust off the bindings of the books and scan them for the title I was looking for.

As I was scouring the second shelf, a breath of wind swept past my neck, so slight, I'd have thought it was just a draft, except there were no doors or windows in the room.

Whirling around, I held out my blue flame but saw nothing. Turning back, I shivered, every inch of hair on my arms standing on end. I ignored the feeling, and picked up my pace, scanning the titles of the books. The faster I found it, the faster I could get out of there.

A book binding caught my eye, and I bent down to inspect one of the volumes more closely. I didn't notice them, at first, but as I went to put the large volume back on the shelf, two red, glowing eyes stared back at me. And then I saw the white teeth, as the creature snarled at me. They were sharp and jagged, nothing like any animal I had ever seen.

Dropping the volume, I reached for my dagger hidden in a band around my thigh, simultaneously backing up and keeping my blue flame lit before me.

I grunted as I hit the wooden table behind me. It wasn't just one pair of eyes staring at me, it was dozens.

"What are you?" I asked, not really expecting an answer.

"*You are not supposed to be here.*" The ancient voice filled my head. It didn't sound human or like any of the Old Ones I had conversed with. This was something far darker and older.

"*I just came to find a single book. I mean no harm,*" I replied, turning in a circle, as the eyes inched closer, closing me in.

A rumble of noise filled my head, as the voice answered, "*A single book from this place could cause a millennium of harm.*"

"A single spell, then." I tried to keep my voice steady, but my trembling hands gave me away, as one of the creatures stepped fully into my light.

The thing looked somewhat like a wolf, but as though it had been twisted, and morphed into something resembling a demon or monster. Though it was thin, and looked starving, it had powerful muscles beneath its midnight black fur.

It laughed again. Or at least, I think that's what the low rumbling noise was. *"A single spell has more power than you have in your entire body."*

"I assume you are here to protect these books?"

"Smart girl."

"So, who has access to these, then?"

"No one in this world," the thing barked into my head, and now I was so close to them that all they had to do was extend their necks and I'd be dead in an instant.

I tried to stall the inevitable, as my brain raced for a solution. *"Then why have this place at all? If no one can access this information?"*

"They will return."

"Who?"

"Not you," the thing said, an instant before it lunged.

Not thinking, I simply reacted, plunging my dagger into the neck of the creature closest to me. The creature shrieked, and black blood squirted all over me, at the same moment they all moved toward me with inhuman speed.

I tried to channel back to Ardil, but all that did was slam me into the bookshelf across the room. I grunted as sharp pain vibrated through my shoulder.

I was stuck here.

The creature laughed again, inching its way toward me, not rushing, knowing it had me trapped. The others fell into formation behind their leader.

"Pathetic attempt."

"Your manners leave something to be desired." Attempting to stall the creature, I glanced around in the room. *"Seeing as I'm your first guest in millennia, I expected better."*

The creature cocked its head to the side, stalking closer. *"Entertaining guests isn't our job."*

"Torture and death it is, then."

They seemed intent on drawing out my fear, closing the distance with slow, calculating steps, never taking their eyes off me. Everything felt as though it was happening in slow motion. Like they wanted to drag out the inevitable. Like they wanted to see me tremble.

Whatever they were doing was working. I was terrified, trembling as I watched them. I had no other weapon. Channeling was my only way out, and if I couldn't do that, I was stuck. Even if I was able to kill every one of them, I still wouldn't get out alive.

"I'm confused, though. How do you even know who the one person allowed here is? They could be dead right?" I asked, using the only weapon I had left—information that may or may not be useful in saving my ass.

"We will know them by smell."

Lifting my arm, I smelled my armpit. *"Yuck. Definitely not me."*

Did the creature just roll its eyes?

"The smell of their magic, halfling." It said it as though that were obvious.

"What does magic smell like? I've only every been able to feel it."

The creature paused, the others halting behind it. *"You feel magic?"*

I didn't know how to answer. I was pretty sure that's what I felt when Ardil was around. What I felt from the creatures in front of me, now. It felt electric. Like a bomb ready to explode. A well of never-ending energy crackling from their black fur. It was different from Ardil's magic which felt soothing. This magic felt twisted—wrong.

"You feel like lightning; I can feel it on my skin." I shivered, not entirely on purpose. The feeling was intense.

The creature looked back at its companions, as if contemplating something.

"You should not exist," it answered, pinning its attention back on me, and inching ever closer.

"If I had a dagger for every time someone's said that to me."

The creature halted at my retort, considering me with its glowing red eyes.

When it resumed its forward march, I knew there was no changing this creature's mind. It wasn't going to give me any useful information, either. This was it.

Sneering, I crouched into a defensive stance, anticipating their attack. It only took a moment before it lunged at me, colliding with my chest and pushing me to the floor, knocking the wind out of me.

I sucked in a pained breath as the thing went for my neck. I rolled my body to the side just a fraction and pushed. The thing barely missed my neck and instead dug its fangs into my shoulder.

Letting out a blood curdling scream, I plunged my dagger into its eye. It scrambled off me, whimpering and screeching. The sound was so twisted and shrill I wanted to cover my ears, but instead I clutched at my shoulder which was now soaking my shirt with blood.

I only had a moment left before the rest of them were on me.

Scrambling to my feet, I backed against the shelves, still somehow clutching my dagger.

"Nobel attempt." The voice drifted into my head.

All I could manage was a pained whimper. There must have been magic or poison in their saliva. Whatever it was was draining me fast.

"The Fair Folk have become weak," the thing said, stalking toward me.

"Didn't we just determine I'm not one of them?" I growled, trying to stay on my feet as my head began to spin.

The thing cocked its head to the side slightly, sniffing the air in front of me.

"You smell something else in my blood, don't you?" My legs wobbled beneath me, threatening to give out completely.

"You smell . . . wrong . . ."

I laughed, though it was a laugh of desperation.

The thing began inching closer again. *"An abomination."*

"That's one way to look at it."

I had stalled the thing as long as I could. I had a decision to make. I could fight with everything I had left, or I could let the thing end me quickly. I had always been a fighter, but for the first time in my life, I was without hope, and utterly alone. No one could get here but me.

There would be no walking away from this, and all I could think of was what would happen to those I loved if I wasn't there to make things right.

When the creature made its move, leaping to close its fangs on my neck, I was expecting pain and darkness, but instead all I could see was blinding blue light.

Had someone come to rescue me?

It took me a second to realize the light was coming from me. I was covered in my blue flame, glowing like a beacon in the dark.

The creatures hissed and backed away.

"What are you?" it asked.

A moment before I struck, I replied, *"A child of the flame,"* and then I erupted.

Everything happened so fast, I didn't register what was going on around me until the library became deathly silent and still, and all that remained of the creatures was the one that had been talking to me. The others had disappeared, leaving nothing behind, not even ash.

Taking a few steps toward the creature, I noticed it was alive but struggling to breathe.

"Child of the Morrigan. Child of the blue flame. The fated one," It wheezed.

"What does that mean?" I asked, bending to hear its fading voice.

"We were wrong. The prophecy will come to be. Our job is complete."

Having no idea what the creature meant, I decided to use the last of its energy to ask the most important question, *"Where's the book?"*

"The consequences could be catastrophic," it struggled to get out through pained breaths.

"What creature deserves to be enslaved, it's powers stripped from them, for millennia?"

It didn't say anything for a few moments, before it sucked in one last lungful of air. *"The bookshelf in the very back. Bottom shelf. Purple binding."* It paused, trying to save its last breath. *"We are free."* And then the creature went limp.

Staring at the body, I almost expected some strange magic to revive it. When nothing happened, I looked at my shoulder and found the blood had soaked through my fighting gear and was dripping off my fingertips onto the red carpet.

I watched the dripping for a while before I remembered my task and stumbled toward the back shelf. Falling in front of it, I braced my good arm against the bottom row and scanned the books.

My breath came in shallow bursts now, my vision blurry. A burning started in my shoulder and spread into every vein in my body, but the book was where the creature said it would be. Grabbing it, I pulled it tightly against my chest. Then, I turned and sagged against the bookshelf.

How the hell am I going to get home? I thought to myself, struggling to keep conscious.

As a last-ditch effort I thought of the channel that was most familiar to me, and I smiled as the familiar feeling of falling took over, and everything went black.

Chapter Thirty-Nine

I groaned as my burning body hit the floor. I heard hurried footsteps and then a panicked voice, but not the one I expected.

"Sol!" Cormac shouted frantically, picking up my body which felt useless now. I couldn't even lift my head, but somehow, I held onto the book.

There was a blur of movement above me, before padded feet landed silently next to Cormac.

"Help her!" he pleaded with Ardil.

Ardil motioned for Cormac to kneel. As he did, I finally released my death grip on the book and let it fall to the floor. Ardil gave it a quick glance before his eyes widened, and I let the darkness take me.

I woke up feeling much better than I expected. Besides a gnawing hunger, and a slight twinge of pain where the creature bit me, I felt normal. Strong even.

Hesitantly, I reached up and touched my aching shoulder. Two raised scars ran from the top of it, to my chest.

"I didn't think you were going to survive that." His voice was soft and shaky, like he had been up all night.

"I didn't think I was going to either," I replied, slowly pushing myself up to a sitting position and bracing myself against the bed post as my vision blurred and the world spun around me.

"Take it easy," Cormac said, moving closer.

We weren't the only two people in the room. Apparently, all the Old Ones decided they wanted to wait for me to wake up.

My eyebrows rose, and Cormac explained. "I think they were worried about you. I get the feeling they didn't think their healing waters would work this time."

Now I was even more confused, as I turned toward Cormac, who must have sensed my questions, because he continued. "When we saw your wound, Ardil immediately brought you to his people. They put you into the healing waters and nothing happened. I couldn't talk to Ardil or his people, but with the way they were watching you, I could sense that something was wrong." Cormac ran a hand through his hair.

"We were afraid it was too late," Ardil said.

Cormac seemed unaware that Ardil was speaking, because he resumed his explanation. "And then, without warning, you suddenly jerked awake, but you weren't truly awake. Once we had you on dry land, we could tell you were alive and breathing, but you didn't open your eyes or respond to us."

I didn't have a single memory of the events he spoke of. I didn't even dream about anything. It was as if I wasn't even in my own body. That thought terrified me even more than their explanation.

"Sol," Ardil's voice held a warning in it. *"The cost . . ."* He shook his head before continuing. *"The cost would have had to have been great."*

"But how? I wasn't conscious. I couldn't have agreed to any of it." I spoke out loud so Cormac could follow the conversation.

"Sometimes, fate takes over these decisions. You are still needed for something, but I fear the cost for bringing you back will be too great."

"What do you mean?" I couldn't help the panic that began to rise in my throat.

"You were dead. Or almost. I fear the cost is a life for a life." Ardil sounded tired all of a sudden, and I wondered if he regretted asking me to retrieve that book, though he wouldn't have known what I was going to face in that library.

"Whose life?"

"Without you being conscious, I doubt we will discover it until it's too late. But I fear it will be someone close to you."

Cormac must have sensed the type of conversation I was having with Ardil, because he came and sat next to me, putting a comforting hand on top of my own.

"The creatures that attacked me. Do you know what they were?" I asked Ardil. Though I hadn't described them, I had a feeling they knew what I had faced based on my wound.

"We've heard of the guardians, but we thought they were long extinct."

"Well, I think they are now," I said with a sigh.

"What do you mean?" Ardil sounded both shocked and curious.

"I killed them all."

Ardil didn't say anything for a long time, and there was a restless shuffle of feet, paws, hands, and claws all around the room from the rest of the Old Ones who had listened to the whole conversation.

"How?" Ardil's voice sounded shaky.

"The moment I realized I was going to die my whole body became engulfed in my blue flame, like it was trying to protect me. And I'm not sure what happened exactly, but it felt like a thousand flames exploded from my body, and the next thing I knew *all* the guardians were gone except for their leader. It spoke to me then, but I didn't understand what he was saying." I sucked in air, trying not to relive the moment when I knew I would die.

"What did it say?" Ardil asked, but he sounded like he already knew the answer. Ardil's body trembled, which was something I had never seen him do.

"He said I was the 'fated one.' The one they'd been waiting for, and that they had completed their task, and they were now free."

Ardil didn't say anything, neither did the other Old Ones, but it was obvious something had just happened. The other Old Ones, one-by-one, began to lower to one knee, or bow.

"Ardil," I said, cautiously, "what is going on?"

"Our people had a prophecy. It was told that there would be one who would come along and change the course of history. Someone who would break the barriers between the worlds. Someone with a blue flame who could sever the bonds that tie every life to this Earth."

"Wait, what?" I'm pretty sure my mouth was in my lap.

"Sol?" Cormac's voice sounded concerned.

I waved him off again. "Ardil, that's not what I did." My voice sounded as panicked as I felt. Is that what I'd done? Completely destroyed the energy channels of the guardians? Is that why there was nothing left?

Ardil shook his head. *"That is not what my people believe, Sol. Look around you. It makes sense, now. All of it. Why we can speak to you. Why your flame is blue. Why the waters healed you even though you were already lost to us. Why you were able to defeat every guardian with a single blow, even though the only ones who can kill them are the missing Gods. Why you are hunted by the Fair Folk and the humans. I know you don't want to hear this, Sol, but someone suspected what we do. Or, worse, someone already knew what you were. This whole thing is about taking you out, so that the prophecy can't come true. There have always been forces that do not want the change that the prophecy speaks of. They do not want the borders and barriers to be broken, because that means that the power they hold will slip. It has always been about power. You threaten that."*

I shook my head probably harder than I should have. The dizziness returned with a vengeance, and I had to steady myself. "Rob hinted as much. I know you speak the truth, but I still don't believe it."

"I do," Cormac cut in, and I wasn't sure how he picked up on enough of our conversation to understand. "The abilities you have are a myth. And in those stories, those people were always the fated ones, or the chosen ones. They were always the hero."

"I don't want to be a hero, Cormac. I just want to see everyone safe, and I want to go home."

Cormac surprised me, by reaching over and pulling me into his lap, holding me close. "I know you don't want to be here. I know this is a lot. I know you don't know my people well enough to put you and your loved ones at risk for us. But Sol?"

I looked up at him, and his eyes were bright. I could see golden specks in them that I hadn't noticed before. "You've already changed so much. My sister is now openly in a relationship with someone who would have been forbidden before you. The Old Ones are coming out of hiding. And the majority of the Fair Folk now recognize that the Old Ones shouldn't be enslaved. My people have already accepted you too. They will follow you. The council knows that. That is why they are forcing us to marry. To do what they know you don't want, just to keep you leashed and under our archaic laws. They are desperate to keep their grip on their power." The gold in his eyes grew brighter. "You have no idea what you've already done. It is clear to everyone in this room, hell, in this whole kingdom, that you are fated. I just wish you could see that."

I wanted to deny what he was saying, but I also somehow felt the truth in his words.

"Did my mother know?" I asked, because the question had been burning a hole in my heart this whole time.

"No, and if she had any suspicions, she didn't voice them. Her intentions were pure. She only wanted to help you." The queen's voice came from the doorway, now ajar, and I wondered how long she and Orlan had been standing there. Dorian was just behind them, as were some of Cormac's soldiers.

"Is it time?" Cormac asked his mother.

I hadn't noticed the armor at first, but now, as I looked at them, I realized everyone was dressed for battle. The whole room stilled, as the air seemed to be sucked out.

The queen nodded. "We are out of time. We must move now." She directed her attention to me. The air in the room stilled as she contemplated her next words. "They will follow you, Sol. As will I."

Chapter Forty

S till exhausted, I dressed for battle, pushing away the fatigue, fear, and uncertainty, along with thoughts of Kai. When I was ready, I followed the three Fair Folk royals, not knowing what to expect. On our walk through the forest, only the wind spoke, whispering through the trees, setting an ominous tone.

I'm not sure what I was expecting when we reached the archway to Tir Na Eabha, but I sure as hell wasn't expecting to come face-to-face with the council members.

"Shouldn't someone have locked them up by now," I mumbled, as Cormac and I walked toward the head of the rather large army that had gathered. The wildflower field I had painted was now trampled with all manner of Fair Folk. From Cormac's soldiers who were outfitted for a battle, to Fair Folk of all ages and abilities. Some were dressed in armor, but many were not. Some came prepared with swords or bows, but many were only armed with their magic.

I spotted Ariella among everyone gathered.

"You shouldn't be here for this," I said to her, as I stuck close to Cormac, making our way toward the front of the group.

"And miss all the fun?"

I rolled my eyes, but a smile found its way to my lips.

"I heard what you did with the guardians. You have the ability to sever the bonds that keep us on this Earth. It isn't to be used without severe caution."

"It's so unlike you to be so serious."

She chuckled in my head. *"I'm not worried about you, Solana. I'm just glad to witness this. I'm not sure how much longer I'll be here, but I'd happily spend these days watching you break down every barrier all our species created to keep each other small."*

"I'm not ready," I replied, frowning.

Ariella laughed, and the sound felt like a summer breeze caressing my skin. *"You're ready. If you can take on the guardians, and Cormac, and come out of it alive, you're ready."*

I sighed. *"What if I fail?"*

"Then, at least you opened a door, and opened eyes, for those to step in your place and continue. Everything that's happened has led to this. From the moment your mother was gifted her abilities from the Earth herself, it was always going to lead to this. It's time to stop hiding. All of us. It's time to create the Earth your mother dreamed of. The Earth we all dreamed of."

I had been so wrapped up in my conversation with Ariella that I hadn't realized that we were approaching the council members, and everyone was silent and staring at us. I let out an involuntary shiver as I felt every gaze tracking me.

"It looks like they are going to rip my head right off my shoulders," I said to Cormac.

"I won't let them get anywhere near you."

"And I won't let them hurt your fragile feelings." I couldn't help the sarcastic smirk as I looked up at Cormac.

He paused, and a half-smile appeared before he replied. *"I'd expect nothing less. I'm fully expecting a fantastic display of your abilities that will make every one of them scream like little children."*

"I have a few ideas . . ."

I realized then that we had both stopped and were staring at each other as everyone else was still waiting.

Taking a deep breath, I strolled up to where Queen Nessa was standing with the head councilman. Her face was twisted in rage, and I could only imagine what he had said to make her look that way.

Not waiting for formalities, I jumped right into my demands I already knew they would scoff at. "I'm going to make this simple for you. I want Lily, Mouse, and Marcus freed, I want to ensure that Queen Nessa keeps her crown, and I want every one of you to step down. If you follow those requests, I'll let you live. And before you tell me I have no authority to make those demands, I'll just put this here for you."

With that, I channeled an army of some of the most ferocious and poisonous species on the planet. The spiders came first, and the crowd took a large step back as the tarantulas poured from me. Thousands of them.

Next came the snakes, and I was particularly proud of the amount of cobras that were not afraid to show their fangs. After that, all manner of predators came through. From lions, tigers, jaguars, bears, and last, the wolves. Two of which took up guard next to my side. The rest circled the group of council members as if they were herding their prey. Everyone else decided to create an even larger gap between them and the animals that were all focused on the council.

The council had powers beyond what I could imagine, but even they couldn't deny the power of hundreds of some of the most vicious predators on the planet, now caging them in.

They watched, eyes darting between the animals as some of them prowled closer.

"If you strike first, they will descend on you all at once," I warned.

"This is not how things are done!" one of the councilmen yelled, eyeing a black jaguar that had pinned him with its green eyes and was stalking toward him.

"You're so concerned with old ass rules that you've forgotten that humans and Fair Folk and Old Ones and even animals and plants are *not* things; we are living, breathing, thinking beings with *power* and autonomy. Your pure bloodlines don't exist and never have. It was an illusion that you fell for, and I will not rest until I've broken down every wall, literally and figuratively, that you've built."

"You bitch," one of them snapped, trying desperately to bat away the cobra that had come within striking distance.

"I really wish men could come up with a more creative term," I responded, sounding bored.

Someone in the crowd chuckled, which made me realize that I had forgotten I had an audience.

"Shit," I said to no one in particular, but Cormac laughed and answered, *"Keep going."*

"Where are Lily, Mouse, and Marcus?" I asked the council.

"Why would we tell you that?" one of the council members spat at me

"Might I remind you, that you are seconds away from a blood-bath?"

"Your animals will never get past our shields," another snarled at me.

Cormac laughed, because he knew what I could do to their shields.

Winking at Cormac, I sent a stream of blue flame at the group of council members, and everyone watched as their shields were devoured by the flame.

Their wide eyes told me that they were unaware of what I could do, and as the shields dissolved, the tarantulas crawled toward them, climbing their legs.

One of the council members screeched like a small child, and I swore I heard Orlan giggle; Cormac let out a huff of air before clamping his hand over his mouth.

"Where are they?" I asked again.

"They—They are with—"

The councilman was cut off by shouts from the scouts. "They're here!"

Everyone stilled and turned toward the edge of the clearing, expecting soldiers to spill through the trees right then and there.

"Positions!" the queen shouted, and everyone snapped to attention, quickly forming ranks behind us.

"How many, Cormac?" I asked, as we hurried to the front of the lines, leaving the councilmen in their cage of prowling animals behind us.

"What about us!" one of them shouted. "You can't leave us here! We're defenseless!"

I didn't bother with a response.

"The scouts said a few hundred," Cormac replied.

"That's it?"

Cormac shrugged.

"Lily said there were *thousands*."

"Maybe they decided to not risk everyone? Maybe they thought they could take us out with a few hundred, thinking most Fair Folk would go into hiding."

I considered his reasoning, but something didn't feel right about it. It felt like we were missing something. It felt like the day Mason died. That we were about to repeat my parents mistake, and the enemy knew it.

"I'm going to try to make them a deal. I want to avoid bloodshed, but we're ready if they attack," the queen explained.

No one responded. We all turned and watched the edge of the forest, waiting for them to spill into the clearing. Even though I could protect myself, and that I'd been trained for this my whole life, I could still feel my heart pick up its pace.

There were still so many unknowns.

I didn't know what I was expecting, but I certainly wasn't expecting Rob and three of his cronies from the boat to come into the clearing alone, with knives held to the throats of Lily, Marcus, and Mouse.

Wheeling toward the councilmen, who were still wary of the animals, I found looks of triumph.

Turning back, I snarled to no one in particular, "Well, I guess that confirms what side they're on. No surprise there."

"Backstabbing sons of bitches," Orlan ground out through clenched teeth.

I stepped forward. "I must deal with this alone," I said to all of them, and when Cormac went to protest, I added, "Please."

He nodded and reluctantly stepped back to his mother's side.

"Why am I not surprised to see you, Rob?" I tried not to focus on the death grip they had on Marcus, Lily, and Mouse, whose eyes were all wide with fear.

"It was always going to end this way," he sneered, a vicious smiling forming on his twisted lips.

"I suppose this is the part where I ask what you want so I can get my friends back in one piece?" Through my racing heart, and shallow breaths, it came out dripping with sarcasm.

Rob's jaw ticked slightly before he responded. "There's no deal between you and me. The deal we made was with the council."

"Well, as you can see, the council is in no condition to make a deal right now," I said, motioning to the men still caged in by the animals.

Rob raised an eyebrow before returning his gaze to mine. "Then, the deal is off, and everyone dies."

"You won't make a deal with me, then?" I asked, trying to keep my panic at bay.

"Not you. Never with you," he snapped, his knife digging further into Lily's throat, causing a stream of blood to run down her chest. She remained silent, jaw clenched.

I almost lunged for her, but held back as I noticed, too late, that one of Rob's companions had signaled, and a storm of arrows descended on us.

"Shields!" I heard Cormac yell, and an instant later, the arrows bounced off the Fair Folks shields, burying themselves in the grass.

"You'll die, Rob." I shouted at him.

"You underestimate me. Everyone always has, including my own father," he spit, backing up, Lily still pressed against his chest, the knife cutting in further.

"Sol!" Cormac yelled, as hundreds of soldiers suddenly burst through the trees, sprinting toward us.

"Archers!" the queen yelled.

Everything happened so fast, I didn't really know where to look, or even what to do.

"Get them back!" Cormac yelled at me, his eyes pleading.

Channeling to Mouse first, I landed behind the man holding him and easily took him down. Before Mouse could mutter a word, I grabbed his arm and channeled him to the back of the Fair Folk army, farthest from the front line.

"Stay here," I demanded, before turning to get Lily and Marcus.

"Sol!" he shouted.

I turned my head toward him. His eyes were sad. "We were wrong. They don't have a dozen Folk. They have *hundreds*. We're completely outmatched."

"Where are they? The scouts only saw a few hundred men." I was so confused and running out of time to save Marcus and Lily.

"They're shielded. As they were when they attacked your family. They're right beyond the trees. They have weapons I've never seen. They can take us all out in one sweep. Sol, we must retreat."

"Shit."

Not wasting time, I channeled to Cormac next.

He was taking the brunt of the foot soldiers who had descended on our front lines. They were mortal and easily taken out by the Fair Folk soldiers. The Fair Folk fought with sword and shield, but ripples of Earth magic came from everywhere. Vines and roots tripped the mortal soldiers allowing the Fair Folk to take them out, while the ground shook in other places, felling even more of the mortals. Some of the Fair Folk were able to split the ground under the feet of the mortal soldiers, and they fell into the dark earth below.

I repeated what Mouse had told me, unable to hide the desperation and fear in my words.

"Take down the shield, Sol. We'll make a call once we know what we're dealing with. And take out the weapons, if you can. We'll handle the Fair Folk and the foot soldiers. Get Marcus and Lily back." His words left no room for negotiation, and I was secretly glad I didn't have to make any of those decisions. I was in way over my head.

Disappearing again, I ended up behind the man holding Marcus. He was slowly backing up toward the line of soldiers on his side of the field.

He never saw me coming as I slit his throat, grabbed Marcus' stunned face, and channeled him back to where I left Mouse.

"Sol," he stopped me before I channeled to Lily. "Rob is expecting you to channel to him. Be careful."

I nodded, and then, instead of channeling to Lily and Rob, I channeled to where I thought the shield was. Unsheathing my sword from my back, I cut down the foot soldiers in front of me.

Walking forward, I sent out blue sparks, in search of their shield.

Hearing Rob's laugh over the sounds of fighting, I swiveled my head in his direction. "You think you can beat us with a few sparks?" he barked at me.

I ignored his taunt, while keeping an eye on his every movement. Lily seemed almost relaxed now, and I caught her smirk as I continued throwing out sparks. I wondered why she was smirking, but I didn't get much of a chance to think about it as one of my sparks hit the shield and bounced along its border.

Channeling as much of my flame as I could, I sent it in a constant stream toward the shield that was hiding most of their army and weapons. As the shield dissolved, I caught Rob's reaction. It had its desired effect, and Lily was able to wrench herself free, flattening Rob to the ground in an instant.

Lily swiftly turned and bent down, grabbing his dagger, and as she went to plunge it in his chest, I channeled to her and stopped her arm mere inches from his heart.

She looked up at me, her eyes wide, a question forming on her lips.

"Wait," I said to her, still holding her arm above his chest. His body was unmoving, resigned to his fate.

When his eyes met mine, I asked the one question that had been burning inside me. "Why?"

His venom was gone, and he looked away as he responded. "Because my mother was killed by your parents."

My eyes widened, my breath catching. I'd heard the story. It was an accident that happened ten years ago. Even Rob's father admitted it was an accident. He'd accepted it. We all had.

Or I thought we all had. But now it all made sense—some of his thoughts and actions, and his hatred for my family.

"She followed them. Believed in them. Fought for them. And they lead her to her death." He said the words with such pain.

I knew where he was coming from, and what he was feeling. It didn't make it right, but at least I understood.

Lily looked at me, a silent question in her eyes.

I turned to Rob and said the last words I'd ever say to the man. "Your mother fought for what she believed in. That is noble. That is brave. You are fighting from a place of anger, fear, and pain, and others are getting caught in the crossfire of your sadistic rage. To numb your pain, you are creating that same pain for others. You are repeating a vicious cycle. But I won't let you. This ends now."

Without giving him a chance to reply, I nodded at Lily, and she struck him over the head with the blunt end of her knife, knocking him out.

Shouts, and everyone running in the opposite direction had me glancing toward where I had taken the shield out. Two large wooden catapults wheeled forward, and a line of hundreds of Fair Folk soldiers stepped out in front of us.

"Shit!" I said, grabbing hold of both Lily and Rob, and was gone in an instant.

We landed outside the circle of animals still holding the council hostage, and Lily helped me drag Rob.

"So, you're just going to leave us here to die?" one of the council members asked, watching us.

Without looking at the man, still focused on hauling a now unconscious Rob who was almost twice my size, I answered, "Yes."

The animals parted just enough to let us through, and we dumped Rob in the center.

"You probably have much to discuss once he wakes up, but as much as I'd love to hear that conversation, I have to protect what you failed to." Without waiting for an answer, I channeled Lily to where Mouse was at the back of the line of soldiers trying to press forward.

"I have to help," I said to them all. "Please stay safe." Knowing I'd probably break down if I allowed any of them to speak, I channeled back to where Cormac was fighting in the front, taking down soldiers like they were blades of grass. His shield held, as arrows bounced off it, and his vines tripped others, choking the life out of them as they fell to the Earth.

"What are we facing?" I asked, also cutting down a few soldiers who came at me.

Cormac turned his head only briefly, before he resumed slicing into the mortal soldiers. "I don't know. Those catapults are moving into position. I don't know what they carry. The Fair Folk soldiers haven't moved. I'm not sure what they're waiting for. I don't know what bloodline they're from. I don't recognize them, so I can't even predict what powers they have."

"You sound very unfazed by all this," I commented, taking out another soldier with a single swipe of my sword.

"This is the easy part," he said, cutting down another mortal. "I don't know what to think about what's coming."

"I'll take out the catapults," I replied, about to channel, but Cormac grabbed my arm.

"You can't do it alone." His grip slipped from my arm as two soldiers charged us at once.

"Then come with me."

"I can't leave my mother."

I turned toward where his mother was fighting a few feet away from us.

"She seems just fine without you," I commented, almost laughing at his protectiveness of her, when she seemed perfectly capable, dancing around the soldiers and taking them out as easily as her son. She clearly had strong Earth powers. Tremors in the Earth rippled from her, and vines tore limbs off countless soldiers.

He studied his mother for a moment, before sighing.

I went to grab his arm, to channel us both, when shouts erupted from ahead of us, and it was suddenly raining bullets, flaming arrows, and bombs? I had never seen a bomb, but my father warned me about them. I didn't think there were any left, and I didn't think we had the resources to make more.

Apparently, I was wrong.

As they landed around us, Cormac threw himself over me, protecting both of us with his shield.

I felt the shield shudder at the onslaught, and when I peeked through his arms, I saw dozens of Fair Folk soldiers fall. Blood sprayed everywhere, and there were shouts of pain that drowned out the noise of fighting. I lost sight of his mother and Orlan.

My heart beat faster as another round of bullets and bombs descended on us.

Without thinking, I pushed Cormac off me and rose to standing.

"What are you doing!?" Cormac shouted. I heard the panic in his voice but didn't have time to respond.

I lifted my arms, desperately hoping my idea would work.

As the bullets came within inches of me, they suddenly disappeared. I channeled them away and spread the area of channeling outward all around me. Throwing a net of safety around everyone. The bullets, bombs, and arrows disappeared as quickly as they had appeared.

Shouts of surprise filled the air around us, but I focused all my energy at the endless stream of deadly weapons coming at us.

"I can't hold this for very long!" I shouted at Cormac who, in shock, watched the bullets disappear out of thin air.

My voice must have shaken him out of his stupor, because he yelled a bunch of directions shortly after, and the Fair Folk advanced on the army in front of us.

Walking with the advancing soldiers, I struggled with the effort it took to channel it all away. It wasn't perfect, and a few bullets made it to the ground, but I was able to hold most of it off, preventing countless casualties.

Approaching the catapults, the Fair Folk line of soldiers on the other side finally moved, and I couldn't process what was happening as bolts of lightning suddenly erupted from them, flinging around and under my net, striking our Fair Folk soldiers and stopping their hearts. Their bodies fell to the ground, and a collective thump reverberated through the ground and into my bones.

"Cormac!" I yelled, frantically searching for him, still channeling what I could.

"They're Fire Folk!" he yelled back. "Hold your shields!"

Some of the Fair Folk retreated, concentrating on fortifying their shields against the lightning I couldn't seem to channel away. The lighting was too fast for me to catch.

Just when I thought I couldn't take any more of the onslaught, more mortal soldiers streamed out from between the Fire Folk, swiping at the Fair Folk's shields. It distracted the Fair Folk enough that their shields slipped, allowing a few streaks of lighting to pass through.

Cormac's eyes widened as he focused on the overwhelming onslaught of soldiers and Fire Folk. We were not going to win this fight. Combined with the bullets, bombs, and their numbers, there was no way we were getting out of this alive.

Panic rushed through me. I had only seconds before they over-whelmed the Fair Folk. I had to drop the net. I had to let the bullets through. It was the only way I could use my flame to sever their connection to this Earth and take them out before they destroyed us.

I hesitated only a moment, when a familiar flash passed my peripheral vision and landed, taking out a few of the soldiers and Fire Folk closest to the front line.

It was a fireball.

Turning, I saw an onslaught of fireballs coming from behind us, and alongside the fireballs were liquid streams of fire, slicing through the lines of soldiers. An instant later, a wall of thick vines appeared in front of us, and built up so quickly, stopping all movement on both sides.

And then I saw them.

My family.

Chapter Forty-One

Releasing my hold on my channeling power, I fell to my knees. The living wall my mother was constructing built taller and taller, halting the bullets. The bombs tore holes in the wall, but she quickly rebuilt the damage.

For a moment, we were safe.

Cormac let out a low whistle at what my mother was doing, and my heart swelled.

"Sol!" Her voice was like a balm to my weary soul.

"Mom!" I choked out, a sob threatening to spill out of me.

Aiden and Aelius reached me first, and I don't know why but I punched them both. Hard.

"I hate you assholes so much," I said, my voice trembling, as I reached for them and pulled them into a hug a second later.

"That hurt, by the way," Aelius whined, and I let out a choked laugh.

"Sol," my father said, as he reached us. I could see his eyes glowing blue. The same flame I carried in my own eyes.

And then the tears sprung free.

My mom squeezed her way between my brothers. There were tears in her eyes too. "I'm so sorry, Solana. I'm so sorry." She repeated it several times.

"I couldn't do it, Mom. I couldn't do it by myself." I barely got the words out.

"You're not alone. You've never been alone." Her voice was just as shaky as mine.

"And when were you going to tell us you could literally make bullets and bombs disappear? And I'm guessing that circle of very scary animals has something to do with you too?" Aiden said, looking over my shoulder.

"Well, I would have told you, but I was a little busy getting the shit beat out of me for the last month. I'm sorry I didn't have the time to write," I spat back through my tears, but I was beaming at him.

"Perhaps we should do some of the ass kicking, now?" Aiden answered, smirking like he had a secret.

"Mom's wall won't hold for long, kids," my dad cut in, and I could see his gaze assessing the situation beyond us.

"We're sorely outnumbered; they have catapults, bombs, bullets, flaming arrows, and hundreds of lighting wielding Fire Folk. The lightning appears to be able to get around my channeling," I quickly explained to them.

"So, harder than it looks?" Aelius chimed in.

"Yes, asswipe. I was about to die."

Mom cut me a stern look.

"We need to take out the catapults," Cormac's voice came from over my shoulder. I hadn't noticed his presence.

"Cormac," my mother said, inclining her head, though I could tell by the tone of her voice she wasn't exactly happy to see him.

"Willow," Cormac replied, inclining his head as well. "Thank you for coming."

My mother looked as if she was about to say something that wouldn't be helpful, so I cut her off, "I'll channel to the catapults and take them out, who's coming with me?"

"Oh, I wouldn't miss that," Aiden announced, coming to stand next to me.

"How do we take out the Fire Folk?" I asked, turning to Cormac.

"Leave that to us. If you can keep the mortals away, and the bullets and bombs, we can take them out."

I turned to my parents. "Take care of the mortals. I'll channel as much away as I can. Aiden and Aelius will take out their weapons."

"What about us?" In the commotion and distraction my family provided, I hadn't noticed the large presence making their way toward us.

And that voice. My heart skipped at the sound, and my breath halted. Wheeling around, I found myself face-to-face with Kai.

I caught the broad smile of Aiden out of the corner of my eye, as my mouth fell open.

Kai's thoughts spilled into my head.

"How is it possible that she's even more beautiful? Even covered in gore . . ."

"I'll never leave her again . . ."

Having heard more than enough, I launched myself at him, almost knocking him off his feet. He caught me, though, and before I let any more tears fall, I covered his mouth with my own.

He smiled into my lips before he let me shamelessly kiss him in front of everyone.

Someone cleared their throat, and I was sure it was Aelius.

I reluctantly pulled away. "You came back."

He leaned in and rested his forehead against mine. "Of course I came back. I'll always come for you."

It was then that I suddenly noticed the hushed whispers from the Fair Folk. Their attention had drifted beyond us.

I pulled away from Kai. A large group of Folk that were clearly not Fair Folk walked toward us.

Kai turned to them, and there was a familiar face among the approaching Folk. It was Kai's face. The same, and yet her hair was blonde, and her skin was light, and she was several inches shorter than him, but their eyes were identical.

Kai smiled as she stopped a few feet from us, and he turned back to me. "I went to my mother, and she went to the Water Folk and asked for their help."

"They were reluctant, at first," his mother cut in, stepping in front of me. Her smile was warm, as she continued, "If they weren't, we'd have been here sooner. I brought what help I could."

"Your help is much appreciated," Queen Nessa said from over my shoulder, but the rest of what she was about to say was cut short as my mother yelled.

"I can't hold it much longer! They're breaking through!"

I found her frantically patching up the holes in the wall, my father right beside her, and then there was a flurry of motion, as the Fair Folk fell back into their ranks, commanded by Cormac, and the Water Folk fell into ranks between them. The Water Folk appeared to be commanded by a striking female with fish-scale armor, and more than four limbs.

Aiden grabbed my arm, stealing my attention. "Ready, Sol? Mom's going to let us through the wall."

"No need for that, I'll channel us," I explained, sheathing my sword on my back, turning back around to try to find Kai.

"Channel?" Aiden asked, and I had forgotten that they didn't know.

"Yes. It's how I went into my painting, and how I ended up in the library for a quick minute. But there's no time to explain." I stalked over to Aelius, still searching for Kai who had disappeared into the sea of Folk preparing for the onslaught of weapons and lightning.

"I'm not going to vomit, am I?" Aelius asked, sounding very concerned.

"Really? That's what you're most concerned about?" I huffed, grabbing them both, and an instant later, the three of us were at the base of the catapult, in the heart of enemy ranks.

Everything seemed to pause for a moment, as the surprised faces of the soldiers focused on us. The Fire Folk had started advancing on our soldiers, as mom's wall began to crumble. We were left with the mortal soldiers manning the weapons.

"I'll cover you!" I shouted to Aiden and Aelius, as the soldiers slowly realized what was happening and who we were.

As the bullets started coming, I channeled them away, and my brothers set fire to the first catapult. It exploded, flaming pieces of wood raining down all around us.

"You could have killed us," I snapped at them, channeling away the wood that threatened to hit us.

"I knew you had it," Aelius retorted.

I ignored his comment, as we raced forward, further into their ranks. My brothers cleared a path of fire ahead of us, while I continued to channel away bullets and bombs. The second catapult wasn't far ahead, but it was surrounded by hundreds of fresh soldiers.

"How many do they have?" Aiden asked, spewing liquid fire at oncoming soldiers, melting them before they even had a chance to scream.

"Lily said thousands," I grunted as a new onslaught of bullets from automatic weapons began to pelt us.

Aelius whistled next to me.

"A little help," I ground out.

"Sure thing." Aelius angled his body to where the bullets were coming from, and with stunning accuracy, hurled fire balls. An instant later, the air was free of bullets.

The reprieve didn't last long, as new soldiers and new weapons took their place.

"It's never-ending," Aiden exclaimed next to me. I could sense the unease in him.

We were so focused on what was ahead, that a group of human soldiers had snuck up behind us.

"Sol!" Aiden shouted.

Heeding his warning, I whirled around, sword in hand, and cut down a few of them.

"Either of you know how to make a Fair Folk shield, by chance?" I asked, as I swung my sword and took out a few more soldiers. Aiden and Aelius were taking out the rest of them using a combination of swords and fire.

"No," Aiden grunted as a soldier hit him in the back with the butt of a sword. A second later, that same soldier was on fire, his bones melting into the Earth.

"Shit, you two are worthless," I said, taking out a few more soldiers. With the split second of space, I channeled some help. All manner of predator came. Large jungle cats sprouted from thin air and leapt at the soldiers. Screams guttered as their throats were ripped out. After the cats came the wolves, and then the grizzly bears, to pick off anyone left standing. And much to my delight, the bees joined the madness, swarming in the hundreds of thousands, blinding and distracting the soldiers.

"Damn, it's the bees that scare me the most," Aelius commented. "There are so many, and they are so small. At least with a bear, it's a large target."

Aiden snorted. "Let's take out the catapult and get rid of the bombs."

The three of us raced forward among the chaos, and my brothers easily took out the second catapult. Soon after that, we found the major supply of bombs, which I easily channeled away, as my brothers held off the soldiers.

"Grab onto me," I shouted at them after completing our task. "We're going back to help the others."

I transported us back to the front lines.

As before, I didn't have much time to register what was going on, but what stood out was the streams of water jetting out from the Water Folk, capturing the electricity of the lightning from the Fire Folk, and directing it back at them. Their shields glimmered with the electricity, and some of the shields fell, electrocuting the Fire Folk beneath them.

The tides had turned, but the battle was still far from over.

"Sol!" Cormac yelled, and I snapped my attention to him. "We need to take out their shields!"

Nodding, I fought my way toward the closest Fire Folk soldier. I could see, and feel, my mom's influence as wind threatened to topple me, and I had to dodge roots and vines to get to where I was needed. Trying to ignore the chaos around me, I focused on reaching my target.

When I was close enough, I sent my flame, taking out two of their shields, and as their shields fell, Cormac took them out with both sword and vine. They never saw it coming.

We continued that way for some time. The minutes bled together as I fought my way down their line, taking out their shields one-by-one. I didn't think about where my brothers were, though their constant stream of fire told me they were still standing. My mothers earth, air, fire, and water abilities were hard to miss, and my father was likely fighting by her side.

But the soldiers kept coming. They were an endless stream of bodies. Even without the weapons we had just taken out, they were a force not easily broken.

As I caught my breath, I surveyed the area. There were so many casualties on both sides.

This had to end.

At the very same moment I had those thoughts, my gaze found Kai's, and my heart stopped.

He was surrounded by Fire Folk. A mortal among near Gods. Gods who could wield lightning.

As he locked eyes with me, the world seemed to pause. I knew that look. It was defeat. It was acceptance. And for a moment, he just smiled at me. Like there was no one else around.

And then a single thought made its way through the walls in my mind.

"I love y . . ."

Chapter Forty-Two

The thought was interrupted by a bright flash. A bolt of lightning sent straight to his heart.

All I could think, repeatedly, was *not again. Not again. Not again* . . . as I fought mindlessly, pushing my way toward his lifeless body, desperate to reach him.

And then I felt it. This burning sensation, that no amount of water or magic could stop. I was burning, but I couldn't put it out. I couldn't stop the fire, even as my tears began to fall.

My world stopped, and now everyone around me had also stopped.

The Fair Folk backed away from me, revealing his body on the ground. Unmoving. His mother rushed to his side, her face etched with panic. And something in me snapped.

Screaming, I fell to my knees. A pulse of energy released from me as I did. I didn't care what the consequences were. I was too broken. Staring at the trampled field under my hands, I felt the soft dirt, watching the colors of the trampled and bruised flowers. I didn't know how long I knelt there. It could have been a minute or an eternity.

The silence was the first thing that hit me. It was too quiet.

I looked up, the tears still streaming down my face, and my family rushed toward me. Everything seemed to be happening in slow motion.

The rest of the world seemed stunned—frozen. Their eyes were watching me. Afraid.

I didn't care.

"Sol?" It was my father's voice. He knelt beside me and placed his hand on my back.

The lines of his face were fuzzy through my tears.

"It's over," he said.

He was referring to the battle, but I couldn't help but feel his words like a vise on my heart.

"Your mother is going to try to help," he explained, and now I could hear the worry in his voice.

As he spoke, a line of trees appeared to be moving closer. I couldn't focus my eyes, as another large group approached. The world was suddenly not as silent as it had been a moment ago.

My father turned his head and stood up, like he was going to defend me.

The bodies approached, but I didn't care.

"Sol?" A familiar voice. One I had heard many times in my head. But this wasn't a voice in my head any longer.

I snapped my attention up, and standing in front of me was Ardil. Behind him were what looked like thousands of Old Ones of all shapes and sizes.

"You spoke out loud," I said, my voice broken.

Ardil nodded, a sad smile forming on his dark lips. "Because of you."

"I don't understand."

"The book. We broke the curse." He looked around. "I apologize we couldn't be here sooner. We wanted to help but knew we would be stronger without the curse. It seems we are too late."

I heard his words, but they were hard to process. My brain felt too slow. My body hurt. My lungs burned.

"You can bring him back. You and your mother have that power. But you must hurry," Ardil said, now looking at where my mother knelt beside Kai's body.

"What?" I wasn't sure I heard him correctly.

"Ardil's right," Ariella came up beside me. Her hair was a tangled mess, and she had blood all over her, but she looked unharmed. "You have the ability to sever the bonds that keep us here, but your mother has the ability to rebuild them. But she can't do it without you."

I jumped up. "How?"

Ariella looked over at my mother and gave her a single nod, before turning to me. "Your mother knows how. She can show you."

"We will help, too," Ardil said, and as I walked over to where Kai lay on the ground next to my mother, the Old Ones moved, forming a circle around us. The Fair Folk and Water Folk moved out of the way and watched the whole thing in stunned silence.

"Reach out to him. Search for his energy," my mother said, in an eerily calm voice.

"It's not there." My voice was shaky and cracked as I spoke.

"His channel is gone, but his energy is still there. Where do you think it would go, Solana?"

I looked at her then, searching her face, trying to understand what she meant.

She tried again. "Energy is returned to the Earth. Where do you think his energy would travel to?"

I didn't have to think. I knew. "The sea."

Kai's mother gasped, as she sat next to him, holding his limp hand in her own. Tears streaked down her face.

"Find it then, Sol," my mother said, a little louder now.

I shook my head. "How?"

"You're a channel jumper. Jump to it," Ariella cut in.

"You don't have to jump, physically, you can jump energetically." It was Ardil's voice this time.

I put my head in my hands, the tears threatening again. All of it felt right, I just didn't know how to do what they wanted.

It was my mother's voice next. She spoke quietly. "Close your eyes. *Feel* for him. Follow the feeling of him, until you find his very essence. His very life force. Call him home, Solana."

I didn't know what she was saying, but I yearned to feel him again. That oh-so-familiar feeling that allowed me to channel jump to him with alarming accuracy.

Closing my eyes, I stretched out my senses. I knew where he'd be. And instead of my body traveling to the edge where the forest met the sea, my essence, or life force, did.

The image formed in my brain, though it wasn't real.

He was standing on the edge of the sea, his back to me, staring out at the endless blue. He held a sketchbook in his hand.

I found myself smiling despite everything.

"Come back with me?" I asked, my voice shaky. I was unsure of everything.

He turned slowly, and a half-smile formed on his lips.

"I thought you'd never come," he replied.

"I'll always come for you," I repeated his words to me.

He smiled brighter, then, and I reached out my hand. As he went to grab it, he said, "I want to live by the sea."

I smiled, the tears falling down my face once again. "We will."

"Promise?" he said, and his voice sounded so hopeful, I almost wept harder.

"I promise."

"Then let's go home," he said, grabbing onto my hand.

And then the image faded.

Snapping my eyes open, I realized my mother was in the middle of explaining something, but I only caught the end of it. "Weave it together . . ."

"What?" I mumbled, suddenly feeling nauseous.

"We must rebuild the channel. Connect it back to the Earth," my mother explained, grabbing my hand.

When I turned back to Kai, his body was still lifeless, but I could feel the energy now. I could feel *him*. Closing my eyes again, I opened my senses.

I gasped as I finally saw what my mother had tried to explain to me all these years. The web of life, connecting everyone and everything. Pulsing energy channels alive and moving.

It was beautiful.

As I watched, I saw the circle of energy around us. The Old Ones. It was as if they were also channeling energy, because the energy began to fuse together and creep toward Kai.

"Grab it, Solana. Grab it and link it to him." My mothers voice pierced through the energy channels all around me.

Reaching out, I did as she said, pulling the channel the Old Ones somehow created toward Kai. I added my own energy to it, until it was glowing so brightly, I thought it'd blind me.

A sharp inhale was the only sound as I opened my eyes.

Kai's mother was staring wide-eyed at her son, and as I watched him, his chest began rising and falling.

I let out a sudden sob, unable to stop myself.

"You know, I was perfectly happy by the sea."

My eyes shot to Kai's. They were open and staring at me.

"I hate you so much," I said in response, and then I launched myself at him, pulling him into an awkward embrace.

He chuckled into my hair, as his arms encircled me.

A soft whistle interrupted us, as a male's voice spoke. "I never thought I'd see the day . . ."

His voice snapped everyone out of the trance they seemed to be in, and Cormac jumped between the man and us, raising his sword.

The man chuckled. "I mean you no harm. I'm aware I'm the leader of the Fire Folk, and you have every right to be suspicious. But those soldiers acted on their own volition. It wasn't sanctioned by our people."

Cormac relaxed, but only slightly. The man continued. "We caught wind of the situation." He turned his head, as another man laughed behind him. "The pun is intended there, Avel," he said, turning back toward us, "and we came as fast as we could."

I stared between the two men. The second one, Avel, was clearly one of the Air Folk, because he looked nothing like the other Folk. Avel had golden-brown skin, dark brown hair, onyx eyes, and was wearing simple armor with a crest of a dragon in his breast plate. His helmet, that he held in the crook of his arm, was adorned with feathers from a bird I had never seen.

"Avel is the leader of the Air Folk, I am Azar, leader of the Fire Folk," Azar explained.

"It's been a long time," Queen Nessa's voice sounded from behind the two men, and they both broke out into smiles as they turned to face her.

"It's been too long," Avel said, moving to kiss her on both cheeks. The queen let him, and she smiled as he pulled away.

"You've all traveled far, and we're all weary," she said to them, ushering them away from us.

I stared, dumbfounded, at them, not even realizing I was still lying awkwardly on top of Kai, who hadn't budged or spoken a word. His arms were wound tightly around me, as if he were afraid to let me go.

Cormac looked down at the two of us, breaking into a smile, and then a deep laugh. "I was a little boy the last time all the Folk were together."

"How long ago was that?" I asked because I had never thought to ask him that question.

"Two hundred years ago."

My mouth must have been in my lap, because Cormac laughed even harder. "Come on. Let's get cleaned up and rested. I'm afraid we all have a lot of talking to do."

I groaned and reluctantly peeled myself off Kai.

He grunted as he tried to sit up.

When I turned my attention to our surroundings, my breath halted in my lungs.

There was nothing left.

The only evidence a battle had occurred on the side of the enemy was weapons scattered among the bloodstained dirt. No bodies remained. Not even ash. No evidence the soldier's had ever existed at all.

I'd erased them from the world.

Cormac watched my gaze. "You don't have to feel guilty. You saved us."

"But . . . but I killed *all* of them. What if they had wanted to surrender? I didn't even give them that choice." I couldn't help the crack in my voice—the crack in my heart.

Leaping up, I ran for the empty side of the battlefield, searching. Searching for some scrap of life. Any scrap of a life force I could pull back to this world. Searching for any way to fix what I had done. To bring back what I'd taken. What I had no right to take. What I had no desire to take.

I wanted to keep my family safe, keep the Fair Folk safe, but I never wanted *this*.

"Not like this," I whispered as I fell on top of the trampled flowers. "Not like this."

A hand on my shoulder had my tear-streaked face finding the familiar lines of my mother's features staring down at me. Her face had tracks of the tears, mirroring my own, though I'm not sure our tears were for the same reasons.

She knelt beside me, her hand never leaving my shoulder. "You cannot bring them back."

I knew I couldn't. It wasn't just the lack of bodies to tie the energy to, it was the lack of energy.

"Where did it go?" I asked, my voice cracked.

It was Ariella's voice that spoke from somewhere behind us. "It is final death."

She paused, coming around to face us, sitting on the trampled earth. Her eyes volleyed between the two of us. "Your flame not only kills, it destroys the energy channel. Energy usually travels back into the Earth waiting for rebirth, but there is a point in time when death is truly final, and the energy never returns."

I didn't know how to respond to that. I didn't know what it meant. I didn't know how it was possible. I didn't know what to do with that information.

"You are life," Ariella continued, looking at my mother, "and you are death," she said, her eyes landing on me. "And there is only one who possessed the power of both."

"Danu," my mother whispered.

The name of the goddess rang in my memory. She was the creator—the original goddess in the stories of the Celts. But there were other stories from around the world that were almost identical. The goddess had a different name in each of those cultures, but the story was the same. She was the creator of life, and she could also take that life away.

"But how?" I asked in a rasp, my voice raw from emotion and exhaustion.

Ariella shook her head sadly. "I cannot answer that. All I can tell you is one day the reason for the reemergence of this magic will come to pass, and it's imperative you figure out the answer to that question."

My mother nodded, squeezing my shoulder. We both felt the weight of her words and the weight of what we carried in our veins. The weight threatened to crush me, as the horror of what I'd done to thousands of soldiers burned inside me. An act I couldn't fix. An act I couldn't erase.

My mother sensed my emotion, because of course she did. She pulled her hand from my shoulder and pulled me into her chest. We both crashed to the soil, clinging to one another.

"I know the guilt you carry." Her words were broken. "I know I cannot erase that guilt, but I can tell you that you are not alone. We will carry this together."

Sobs racked my body, and tears fell in an endless well into the Earth beneath us. My mother's tears, too, spilled into my fire hair.

I didn't know how long we lay there, and I had squeezed my eyes shut, wanting the world to disappear for just a moment. Wanting to regain my breath.

I had almost lost Kai in the same way I'd lost Mason, and in the process, I'd discovered a horrible truth about myself. A horrible magic that had no right to exist. And it was mine to carry.

My mother's fingers running through my hair finally woke me from my trance. "Everyone's gone to rest," she whispered.

Opening my eyes, the world came back into blurry focus through my wet eyes.

I registered the rain, which didn't surprise me, given my mother's tears usually created rain, but what caught my attention was the sea of color surrounding us.

I sat up, my head spinning in every direction—flowers as far as the eye could see, painting the world in color as the gray skies poured their own tears all around us.

"We did that," she said, her hand finding mine and squeezing.

My eyes met hers, and I smiled.

Chapter Forty-Three

As we walked back to my room, we didn't talk. I didn't even look around me. I was so overwhelmed and exhausted that all I could manage was putting one step in front of the other as we made our way back through the archway and into the forest.

When we stopped in front of our room, my dad and brothers were there. So was Kai and his mom.

My mother stepped in front of me, raising her arms, and then dropping them. For the first time in my life, she was uncertain. Vulnerable. Perfectly imperfect. Perfectly her.

We all had made mistakes, and we would continue to. It wasn't about the mistakes we made, but what we did to make up for those mistakes.

"You didn't tell me you'd been here," I said, trying to start the conversation we still needed to have.

Squeezing her eyes shut, she let out a deep breath. When she opened them again, they were full of regret. "I have no excuse. I should have told you, even though I believed they were going into hiding again, and you'd never get the opportunity to stumble across them. It was a mistake I will never be able to amend."

"No more secrets."

Her sad eyes met mine. "No more secrets."

Stepping into her, I wrapped her in one more tight embrace. We both stayed that way for a while, letting all the regret melt.

Her eyes darted behind me, and then she stepped back, joining my father who had watched our interaction in silence.

"We'll meet you two later. Rest," my mother said. She sounded like she understood more than her words revealed. She turned away, my father's hand in hers, and I watched them walk toward the palace.

Kai's mother nodded at him. Her smile was bright on her face, and then she, too, turned and followed my parents.

I didn't know what they had discussed, but I didn't need to. I was just glad Kai had a chance to know his mother again.

I didn't really know what to say to him as we made our way up the steps to our room.

He had died. I, somehow, had brought him back to life. I didn't know what to do with that information.

"I suppose I should thank you," Kai finally said, as we both stood there staring at each other.

"You think, because I brought you back to life, that something might go wrong? Like you might grow an extra head or something?" I asked; it was a ridiculous question, but I did worry that bringing him back meant something might go wrong.

Kai laughed, finally stepping toward me. He grabbed my hand and pulled me into him. "No extra head's, Sol. It's just me."

"Hmmm," I mumbled thoughtfully.

"Will you kiss me, Sol?" The question was soft and hesitant.

I pulled back from him, so I could see his face. "What's wrong, Kai?"

He took a deep breath and looked away from me for a moment. I wasn't sure he'd answer. "I knew I had died. I felt the sudden detachment from my body. I wasn't scared, but I was sad because I wouldn't get to kiss you again. And for some reason, that knowledge hurt the most."

Reaching up, I turned his gaze back to mine, running my fingers along his jaw. "You can touch me whenever you want, for as long as you want."

Before he could respond, I pulled his mouth to mine.

I thought my exhaustion would make the kiss lighter, somehow—less intense.

I was wrong.

We kissed each other like we were starved. As if we only had this one moment. This one chance.

I was so wrapped up in the way his mouth felt against mine, his tongue matching mine, that we crashed into a wall.

I yelped, and Kai smiled before he swept me into his arms.

"Where are you taking me?" I asked, a little disappointed our mouths weren't still smashed together.

"The shower," he commented, walking into the bathroom. "We both look and smell like death."

He set me down gently on the bench that stood against the far wall and turned on the water. I wasn't sure you could call it a shower, because it didn't look like any shower I had ever seen. The water fell like rain from the tree branches above onto smooth stones below. Moss grew along the trunk of the tree that acted as the far wall of the shower. It smelled like the forest, and the scent alone was intoxicating.

Kai pulled his shirt over his head and dumped it on the floor. "I'm building you a shower like this in whatever home we make for ourselves."

I turned and found myself staring at his naked body.

When I realized he wasn't saying anything, and that I was still just staring at him, I looked up at his face to find him smirking at me. I felt the heat rush to my cheeks.

"Our home? You and me?" I asked, a bit dazed.

"Yes, Sol. Who else?" he asked, and I could feel the laughter behind his words as he stepped in front of me and bent down, his lips brushing mine, as he reached for the bottom of my shirt.

"I didn't think you liked me all that much," I murmured into his lips, as he tugged it off.

He smiled, and it reached his eyes. "You're right, Sol, I don't like you very much." He reached for my bra next. "I love you. My heart is yours. It always has been. And nothing can keep us apart. Not even death. I will always come for you. I will never leave you." He leaned closer, and then whispered into my lips, "And maybe instead of growing another head, I'll grow another cock for you to play with."

I snorted and pulled away. "Seriously, where did you come from? I don't know what you did with Kai, but I want him back."

Kai smirked, and my stomach dropped, heat pooling in the very core of me. "Well, if I'm going to play with fire, I better bring some heat too."

"That was ridiculously cheesy, and completely illogical," I replied but I couldn't help my chuckle.

When he had taken off all my clothes, and was staring down at me, I had a slight moment of panic.

"You OK, Sol?"

"Yes. A bit intimidated, I think."

"Intimidated? Of me?"

"Yes, you," I said, standing up and working up the nerve to look him in the eye.

Kai scoffed. "You are quite possibly the most powerful and intimidating person on this entire planet. You just took out an entire army, and you could kill me in less than a second and I wouldn't even have a chance to defend myself, and you're intimidated by *me*?"

"Yes, Kai," I responded, sounding angry, though I wasn't, "because I don't know what to do with all these feelings. I don't know what to do with the *wanting* or *needing*. I feel like I'll burn up if I don't touch you. And the last time, I didn't feel so intimidated because I still had some of that stupid fairy wine in me." I didn't know why, but I was out of breath as I finished.

Kai held back a laugh. "That's what you're afraid of? Shit, Sol, I don't think you could do anything wrong even if you tried." He took a step closer to me, and I had to angle my head up to look at him. "Believe it or not, I just want to touch you, too. If I could spend every day getting to touch you, that's all I'd ever need."

He reached for me, then, and I let him. He pulled me against him, crushing me to his chest. Reaching for my chin, he angled it up before his lips crashed into mine.

I was lost again, as he led me into the shower, the warm water spilling over the two of us.

He pulled away, and I almost grabbed him to hold his mouth against mine, but he smiled wickedly and reached for the soap behind me. It smelled like citrus and pine, and he turned me around, which

I reluctantly let him do, and washed all the blood and dirt out of my hair, massaging my scalp as he did.

I moaned involuntarily and heard a deep chuckle behind me as he rinsed the soap from my hair.

And then he took the soap and slid it across every inch of me, his other hand following the trail, pressing lightly against my skin. He went so slowly I almost complained, but before I could, he guided me back under the water, letting the suds wash away.

He spun me around making sure every inch of me was soap free, and then he pushed me up against the moss tree trunk, and the look in his eyes was molten.

"What are you planning to do?" I asked him, a little shakily.

He dragged his gaze from my body up to my eyes. "You did say I could touch you whenever I wanted for as long as I wanted, and I was just going to make good on that promise." His voice was lower than I expected, and I felt it in every part of me.

"Well, fuck," I practically groaned.

"That is the idea, isn't it?" The smirk on his lips made my legs weak.

Before I could respond, his mouth was on mine, and then tracing along my ear, and down to my jaw and neck. He held my hips firmly, as his mouth trailed further down to my collar bone.

I grabbed his waist, and tried to pull him against me, wanting to fuse our bodies together, but he denied me, pulling back for a split second to grin.

"I hate you," I ground out.

"I highly doubt that." He chuckled against my skin, as his mouth found my nipple.

I couldn't help the moan that escaped my lips, as I arched my back into his touch.

His hands moved, then, one reaching around and cupping my ass, the other rising up my torso to massage my breast and other nipple.

Though it felt divine, I needed more. I was burning and thought I'd burst into flame if he didn't move faster. It was torture, but such a good kind of torture.

"Kai," I was able to get out through my shallow breaths. It was a plea, or a demand, or both.

He pulled back only to drop to his knees.

"God's, you're beautiful," he said a moment before his mouth found my center.

I jerked slightly at the brush of his mouth on me, but then I melted into the feel of his tongue circling around the most sensitive part of me.

And now I felt like I was really going to burn alive.

"Kai," it was a warning, but from what, I had no idea.

He mumbled something incoherent, as his fingers slid inside of me, and I gasped.

Now he was moving both his tongue and his fingers in a steady rhythm, and the tension just kept building.

I felt it before I saw it. I really was burning, and my skin glowed blue.

Kai gasped, and he pulled away, looking up at the flames licking my skin.

"Shit," I said, breathlessly.

"I'm not about to be attacked by bees, or killed again, am I?" Kai asked, but I could tell he wasn't serious.

"I honestly don't know." I was completely overwhelmed and felt like I might explode. Quite literally.

"Fuck it," he growled suddenly, standing and hoisting me up against the soft moss.

I wrapped my legs around his waist, as his lips crashed into mine again, and he groaned against my mouth.

"Kai," I pleaded against his mouth, "I don't want to hurt you."

"You won't," he whispered against my neck, and then he added, "hold on tight."

My fingers dug into his shoulders as he pushed into me, and I might have been screaming his name as he began to move. His rhythm was faster and stronger than it was before, as if there was nothing that could hold him back. As if he was burning just as much as I was.

"It's getting worse," I croaked out between breathless moans. My body was straight up radiant now, and I didn't know what would happen, but the flames didn't seem to hurt Kai.

"It's incredible. *You're* incredible." His movement became more desperate, as the tension grew to an almost unbearable level, and then he released one arm from under my ass and planted it next to my head, leaning in close. "Come for me, Sol," he whispered into my ear, and then I cracked, or burst into flame. I wasn't sure which it was.

"Fuck!" he yelled, and I could feel this wave of energy coming from me, or him, or maybe both of us, and I snapped my eyes open, as Kai grabbed me with both hands again, and sank to his knees, still clutching my shaking body, and then he began laughing.

"Why are you laughing?" I asked, pretty sure my mind and body had just been shattered.

"Because I was scared shitless bees would attack me, but instead your flame created that," he said, pointing behind me toward the trunk of the tree.

I turned my head around, still clutching him, and couldn't help the little yelp that escaped my lips.

"Are they glowing?" I asked, still a little breathless.

"That's what it looks like," Kai replied, his eyes darting between me and the bright blue flowers that now covered the tree trunk, and branches above. The flowers had a white center and glowed brightly as if they were enchanted by some sort of magic.

"Well, maybe my magic is more like my mother's than I thought," I commented, staring up at the branches.

When Kai didn't respond, I turned back to him, he was studying me closely. "Do I want to know what that means?"

"Probably not, but I'll tell you anyway," I said with a sly grin. "My mother discovered her magic after sleeping with my dad for the first time."

"Yup. Didn't want to know that."

I laughed, burying my head in the crook of his neck.

"Sol?" he asked hesitantly, turning my hand over.

"Yes?" I pulled myself back and stared down at my hand in his.

He ran his thumb gently over the inside of my wrist. "Why do you have a jasmine flower on your wrist? It's a very sacred flower in my grandmother's culture."

I sucked in a surprised breath. "I knew you smelled like jasmine, but I didn't know it had anything to do with your family."

"I smell like jasmine?"

"And the sea."

He didn't respond, and I shifted on his lap.

"You didn't answer my question," he finally said.

"Remember when I told you about finding myself inside my painting, and I talked to Mason?"

"Yes . . ."

"Before I left the Otherworld, Mason touched my wrist and told me it was a gift. A reminder of him but also hope for the future. I didn't know what he meant by that"—I let out a short laugh as the tears gathered in my eyes—"but now I do. I know he was leading me to you."

Kai didn't say anything, he just tangled his hand in my hair and kissed me. Softly, this time.

Pulling back, reluctantly, I asked the question I'd been wanting to know since I left him standing on the shore of the sea, convinced I'd been saving him. Convinced I'd never see him again. "What happened after I left you on the shore?"

Kai took a deep breath, pushing my unruly wet hair out of my eyes. "I went to find my father. I explained everything, including that my mother would visit me on full moons. He agreed to help me find her. If I could get the help of the Water Folk it would make a difference."

"How'd you know that? How'd you know you could accomplish that in such a short period of time?"

Kai ran his fingers through his long hair. "I knew because I saw it. I saw the Water Folk in the battle. I only get glimpses of the future—tiny moments. They don't happen often. Sometimes they turn out to be true, and other times they don't. I thought it was a useless gift, but ever since I met you . . ." He trailed off for a moment, clearly fumbling with his words. "I've been seeing more, and it's all come to pass. I—I should have told you. I should have told you everything."

Grabbing his hand, I pressed my lips to his fingers. "I don't blame you. Not for any of it. The agreement with Cormac to try to get us out of any sort of bloodshed, the battle, your death. None of that was your fault. None of it could have been prevented, even if you had told me. And you *did* tell me about your visions."

His voice cracked a little. "I don't know what's important to say or not. I don't know if telling someone changes the outcome. I don't know—well, I don't know much of anything."

I smiled sympathetically, still holding onto his hand.

He looked at me for a long while, and I ran my finger along his thumb.

"You want to know what I see most often?" he asked.

I nodded, unable to stop touching him.

The corner of his mouth curled up into a half-smile. "I see you painting. A whole house full of paint. Your fingers permanently stained with color. And your smile. You're always smiling."

I grinned back at him. "Are you just trying to get me to kiss you again?"

He pulled his hand from mine and gently curled his fingers around the back of my neck and urged me closer. "Perhaps," he whispered into my mouth, and then he leaned in and pressed his lips against mine.

Chapter Forty-Four

I didn't know what to expect when we entered the main hall of the palace, but I sure as hell wasn't expecting to see my mother sobbing in Marcus' arms.

I caught my dad's eye. He smiled and gave me a thumbs up. I had to hold back my laugh at his awkwardness. Gods, I missed them, but I resisted the urge to interrupt. My mother and Marcus had so much to catch up on, and they needed closure.

I found Lily and Mouse right away. His hand was on the small of her back as she talked to someone I didn't recognize.

She politely dismissed the person as I approached, and her bright smile melted some of the tension I'd been holding since they were taken.

"So, are you going to find that beach you spoke of?" I asked her.

She nodded, quickly glancing at Mouse beside her.

"Alone, or?" My eyes shot to Mouse's hand that hadn't moved from her.

Mouse winked but let Lily speak. "Perhaps not completely alone."

Her tone was confirmation enough.

I didn't want to admit that I was remiss to let them out of my sight, but they needed to get away. They needed to rediscover who they were—both individually and together.

"Will you go back to the ship?" I directed the question to Mouse.

"I think I'll try something new," he said, his gaze locked on Lily.

Lily remained silent, not elaborating on Mouse's statement.

"OK, I can take a hint." I laughed, I wasn't going to get any more information out of them. "But the two of you"—I pointed between them—"are going to spill the tea when you get back."

Mouse grinned. "Deal."

"You ready?" I whipped around to find Cormac standing right behind me, while Mouse and Lily excused themselves.

I hmphed. "Is that a serious question?"

A half-smile formed on his lips. "Come. I'm sure you will capture all the Fair Folk hearts with your polite and respectful communication style." I had never heard him use such sarcasm, and it threw me off.

"It captured all your hearts," I mumbled, starting to walk to the great hall.

Cormac chuckled beside me.

"I'll be sure to put on my best performance."

"Looking forward to it," he said, turning to walk around the table to the other side.

"Oh, Gods, I'm going to fuck this up," I said to Kai.

"No, you won't."

"How do you know that?"

"Because I know what it means to you. To see the world you dream of become a reality. Peace. Prosperity. Sharing of resources. No borders. Art. Joy. Love. All of it. It's all possible now."

I wrinkled my nose, and Kai laughed, flicking it.

"I can't do all that." I'm pretty sure I was whining like a child.

Kai chuckled again. *"You already have. Look around you."*

I did as he asked and found a sight that almost brought me to tears. Humans, Fair Folk (and not just the pure bloodlines) from all kingdoms, Old Ones of all kinds, people of mixed blood, children, and even animals.

"Animals?" I asked Kai.

He shrugged. *"I'm guessing they came because of Ardil, and because you can communicate with them. They want a place at the table."*

This was all so much bigger than I expected. So much bigger than me. So much bigger than Rob and his attempt at erasing my family—erasing all magical people. This was the start of something new.

"We're going to start in a minute," Queen Nessa's voice came from my left. "We'd love for you to sit with us."

Ardil stood next to the queen and winked. At least, that's what it appeared to be.

I nodded, a bit baffled by everything, and followed them into the great hall, now overflowing with all manner of creatures.

"If you all would join us," Queen Nessa boomed over the chatter, and everyone began to make their way to the seats around the massive table.

The Fair Folk kings and queens took their seats next to each other, and a small boy crawled onto the Air Folk king's lap. Avel was the name of the king, if I remembered correctly. I watched the boy for a moment, as his dark locks fell over his beautiful face. His eyes were the color of the darkest night.

When I turned my gaze back to the rest of the room, I caught Kai's face as he also stared at the boy.

"What do you see?" Somehow, I knew he saw something, just as I felt something as he stared at the boy.

Kai turned slowly toward me from across the table and shook his head slightly, as if he was coming out of a daze, and when his gaze found mine, he looked almost sad. *"I don't know what I saw. The boy was grown, at least, I think it was the boy. He's important somehow. My visions are so random and don't reveal much."*

"I felt something when I looked at him. I can't describe it."

Kai didn't have a chance to respond as Queen Nessa began introducing everyone, and I had to focus on memorizing everyone's names and faces.

"I hope you're listening. I won't remember all these names," I said to Kai.

All I heard was a slight vibration in my head that I thought might be a soft chuckle.

The name that I wasn't going to forget, however, was the name of the boy—Alizeh. Heir to the throne of the Air Folk kingdom.

The rest of the day passed in a haze.

Initial talks began between everyone at the table. Not all communication was peaceful, and the beginning would be rough, but we couldn't expect change overnight. All we could do was move forward one step at a time. It took a willingness to change things, and leaders willing to fight for that change. And we had that. We had leaders around the world that were willing to listen and were willing to *try*. And that's all it took.

Hope.

That's what we'd created.

"You OK?" Kai's voice was quiet next to me.

I smiled. "More than OK."

He smiled back at me and leaned in to kiss me.

"Gross. I don't think I'll ever get used to that," Aelius said.

I rolled my eyes, pulling away from Kai, as Aelius walked over to us. The rest of my family was in tow.

"Oh, grow up Aelius," Aiden chimed in. "It's not like we don't have to watch your tongue in Rose's mouth all the time."

Aelius crossed his arms, opening his mouth to say something, but then shut it quickly at our mother's look.

I couldn't help my chuckle.

"I wanted to tell you three something very important and serious, but I can never seem to do that. It's constant bickering and noise with you all." My mother sounded exasperated, but she was smiling.

"What is it you wanted to say, Mom?" I asked her, reigning in my snarky comments.

"I wanted to say that I'm so very proud of you. All three of you. You accomplished something, Solana, that I never dreamed was possible."

"I had a lot of help," I replied, looking around at all the people around me.

"Regardless, I'm so very proud."

I stood, and wrapped her in a hug, my family joining a moment later.

When we pulled away, there was a tiny sapling growing out of the floor in front of us.

"Mom!" I yelped.

"I don't think that was me," she responded, cocking her head to the side, staring down at the tiny tree.

"It was probably Sol—" Aelius started, and I smacked his arm before he could continue what was about to come out of his mouth.

"Ouch! What was that for!?" he yelped.

I just glared at him.

My mother gave me a half-smile, but luckily, she didn't press me further.

"Come, kids, let's join the others," my father said, grabbing my mother's hand and leading her into the ballroom where everyone had gathered for a celebration.

I stared ahead at the people gathering in the main hall. There were Fair Folk, Old Ones, humans, and animals of all kinds chatting and laughing. All of them were at ease and acting as though they were meeting a long-lost friend.

"For a person who wanted to do nothing but paint and become invisible, you've made a hell of a name for yourself," Aiden said, coming up behind me and scanning the room around us.

I elbowed him, and he flinched, finally turning his gaze on me. "It wasn't my choice, really, but I can't say I'm disappointed. I wouldn't have been able to paint and become invisible in a world constantly at war. Now, maybe I'll get that chance."

Aiden smiled warmly. "As will the rest of us because of you. You and Mom."

"And you."

Aiden huffed. "Aelius, Dad, and I were always going to be the muscle."

I narrowed my eyes, and Aiden's eyes lit up in amusement. "It's not a bad thing, Sol. We're proud to be your brothers. We're proud to help you out." A sly smirk spread across his lips. "And proud to give you endless shit just because we can."

Punching his arm, he laughed, rubbing his hand over the spot. "We'll always be here for you, Sol, and we love you even though we have odd ways of showing it."

I exhaled long and slow. "I love you both, too, and I am so proud to be your big sister. And—and I'm glad we get to do this crazy life together."

Aiden wrapped an arm around my shoulder and tucked me into his side, kissing me on the top of my head. "Someone's waiting for you," he said, angling his head toward the refreshment table.

Kai was casually leaning against the table, watching the two of us.

"I'll go put him out of his misery."

"He does seem to hate big groups of people, doesn't he?" he asked, trying not to laugh, as he watched Kai awkwardly try to talk to someone that came up to where he was standing.

"Hates it," I replied, still watching Kai as I pulled out of Aiden's embrace.

"Well, go on then. You two deserve some privacy. You don't need to be here, you know."

"I know."

"Just channel yourselves away. You can go anywhere now . . ."

I winked at Aiden. "Oh, I have many ideas." I stepped into the room, Kai's eyes trailing me the entire way.

And together, we forged ahead into a new world.

448

Chapter Forty-Five

The next few years were a blur of activity. Kai built us a house at the edge of the forest where the trees met the sea, just as he promised. It was a small, modest, stone cottage, and it was ours. We filled it with love and lots of art.

We also got married, and though I wanted a very small ceremony, none of the Fair Folk or Old Ones would hear of it. So, we had the biggest wedding celebration by the sea, and all manner of Fair Folk, Old Ones, humans, and others came from all over the world to celebrate with us. It was a party that rivaled the summer solstice, and I danced until I couldn't stand anymore.

As promised, representatives from all races and bloodlines around the world met twice a year to discuss all manner of issues and worked peacefully to find solutions. It took a while for everyone to fully trust each other, but by the fifth year, things were running smoothly, and violence had decreased everywhere. The Earth was still healing, but it was damn close to a paradise again. My mother and father came often to Tir Na Eabha to help, and with my channel jumping, it was easy to go home to visit family and friends.

My brothers eventually got married too and blessed me with two nieces and a nephew. How Aelius convinced anyone to procreate with him was beyond me, but I digress. The little ones had strong fire in them, just like their fathers, and I thoroughly enjoyed watching them burn things around the house, much to their parents' dismay. My mother simply chuckled. I'm sure she was thinking it was payback for all the things my brothers burned when we were little.

We had found the peace I'd been craving since I was little, and we both took advantage of it, spending as much time as we could doing all the things we loved.

One afternoon in early summer, we sat on a blanket on the sand watching the waves roll in and out, while painting and drawing. It was our daily routine when the pressures of who we were wasn't consuming our time.

Kai wore his happiness well. It transformed him, making it almost impossible to look away. He had always made it hard for me to peel my eyes off him, but now, there was something even more alluring. The joy made his eyes crinkle in the corner in a way they never had before, and I held on tight to the image; we had created this joy together.

It was easy to get lost in watching him draw. I was often the subject, and today was no different. He caught every detail of me as I sat, painting the ocean as I saw it—a mysterious world full of mysterious creatures I had only begun to know.

His drawing, however, would include something both of us had wanted for a while. A round belly full of the most precious being we'd ever know.

A little girl.

Everything was so perfect it felt almost like a dream.

It's funny, though, how life can change so quickly. How easily you forget that life is fleeting. That life cannot exist without death. That creation and destruction are lovers. It was something I learned over the years. Something my flame taught me—the flame of the Morrigan. The flame of death.

"Kai," I said, nervously, setting my paintbrush on the paint pallet.

"What's wrong?" he asked, setting down his sketchbook beside me.

"I think I'm in labor."

"It's too early." Panic rose in his voice.

"I know," I whispered, as a second contraction came hard and fast, startling me with its intensity.

"What do you need me to do?" His voice was steady, but his body tensed.

I met his gaze. His ocean eyes held a fear greater than any I'd known, and with the increase in my heartbeat, I knew my eyes mirrored that same fear.

"I—I don't know."

"Call for Ariella, or your mother?" Kai asked, his voice so soft it scared me more. I wanted him to shout. I wanted him to be angry, because I was. I was so angry. This was not how this was supposed to happen.

I shook my head as another contraction came on. They were already too fast and too close together. "My mother is home, and I cannot risk channeling to her. Ariella might not make it in time."

Kai grabbed my already sweaty palm, stroking his thumb across my palm, as if he wanted to both soothe me and keep me tethered to him.

"She's the cost," I said through clenched teeth, squeezing Kai's hand, as another contraction hit.

"What are you saying, Sol?" he asked even though he already knew. Perhaps he didn't want to admit it to himself.

"Her life is the cost for mine being saved after the guardians tried to kill me. This time, it can only be her life or mine. There is no saving both of us. Not even with my magic, or my mothers."

Kai fell back on his heels, dropping my hand, and ran a hand through his hair. I reached back for him. I didn't want to let go. I couldn't.

"When you saw her, when she was older, was I there?" I already knew the answer, but I had to ask it anyway.

A few more tears fell down Kai's face. "No."

"Kai?"

He looked from our joined hands to my face. There were tears now in his beautiful ocean blue eyes.

"You've seen this, haven't you?" I barely choked out the question, my breathing heavy with raw emotion and the pain of labor that shouldn't have started for three more months.

He hung his head, "I didn't—I didn't want it to be true."

I didn't know what to do with that information. "When?"

"On the ship. The night of the full moon."

My eyes widened. Everything suddenly clicked into place. His anger—it wasn't just about his mother or my recklessness. And his reluctance with me wasn't just about Mason. It was about this moment. A moment he knew was coming, and it terrified him.

"I saw this moment, and knew I had to stay away from you. I thought"—he choked on his words—"I thought if I stayed away it wouldn't come to pass. I thought I was strong enough . . ."

His words made my chest hurt. He believed all this was his fault.

"Kai," I started, as another contraction hit and stole my words. He held my hand through it, still stroking the skin lightly. Still trying to protect me. He was always trying to protect me, from the moment he laid eyes on me.

"I tried to stay away, but no matter how hard I tried"—his words were barely a whisper—"I couldn't. It was selfish."

"Stop," I gritted out through clenched teeth. "You cannot know what could have been if you had stayed away. And, I wouldn't have let you stay away. I *couldn't*. I needed you like I need the very air we breathe."

His eyes swirled, like the churning ocean. I swore images flashed across them, telling a story I couldn't quite catch. My heart clenched, wanting to ask him a million more questions. Wanting him to tell me all the stories he saw that no one else could. Wanting the time for him to do so.

It was always about time. There never seemed to be enough of it.

I sucked back a sudden sob. "But you also saw her? Grown?"

He met my eyes, his tears falling now, streaking his cheeks as they fell from his chin, all but confirming.

I didn't say anything as another contraction hit me, the pain doubling with every one. The realization that this was happening too fast, hit me. I had a decision to make, though it was no decision at all. I knew what I had to do.

What I *needed* to do.

"I know what you're thinking, Sol, and I won't let you do it!" he suddenly screamed at me, desperation filling his voice.

"You *know* her life is important. I know you've seen it. I cannot let her be the price." Though I tried to keep my voice strong, it was beginning to crack. My breathing was too fast, stealing all the words I wanted to say to him before I no longer could.

That's what I hated most. That I didn't have more time to tell him. More time to be with him in this beautiful life we created. More time to know the beautiful child we created together. It was what I regretted most with Mason, and even though I had more time with Kai than Mason, it would never feel like enough.

Kai shook his head several times. "I won't let you do it."

"Look at me, Kai." I was crying now.

He raised his eyes to mine, and I saw all the things we shared and all the things we could have shared as we grew old together. I saw it all in his eyes. Eyes that had always held stories and secrets and futures. Eyes that saw me, body and soul.

"You have given me the life I always dreamed of. The love I always dreamed of. Every second with you has been the greatest of my life. Our tiny house filled with art and the people we love the most. All the adventures. Even all the fights. I couldn't have asked for more than this. I'm not afraid to die. Not if it's for her. Not if it's for both of you." I had to stop as another contraction hit, stealing my breath and the time we had left.

Kai came closer and put a hand under my elbow, and held onto my hand, supporting me.

"But what about me, Sol? I cannot do this life without you. I *won't*."

"You must, Kai. For her. She will need you to be there for her. She will need you to love her as fiercely as you have loved me."

"I can't," he whispered, hanging his head. "Not without you."

"You *can*." I bit my lower lip as yet another contraction hit. It was almost time.

When the contraction passed, Kai watched me, and we both knew I didn't have much longer. "I can't say goodbye. I don't know how."

"I don't know how, either." I screamed as another contraction hit me. Kai held onto me, keeping me steady. Keeping me grounded.

As the contraction passed, I reached up and grabbed his cheek, brushing the tears away with my thumb. "You will see me again. In her eyes. In her fierceness. In her fire. Please don't ever forget how much I love you."

Kai let out a strangled sob. "I won't forget. I love you, Sol. More than you could ever know. And I will love her just as much. I will love her with my whole heart. I will not forget you. I will not forget what you sacrificed. And she will know your face. She will know your heart. Because I will *never* stop drawing you."

His words broke me, as the urge to push hit me strong and hard, and I screamed louder. Tears flowed from my eyes, soaking my shirt.

"I'm sorry, Kai. I'm so sorry," I sobbed, as the urge to push took over, my control completely slipping.

"You have *nothing* to apologize for, Sol."

"Tell my family . . ." I trailed off as I pushed again, unable to stop time. Unable to stop the inevitability.

"I will." His voice was quiet now—resigned.

I looked at him, one last time, willing him to see everything he meant to me. Willing him to remember. Willing him to be strong. Willing him to love despite what was handed to him.

Grabbing the link between us, I sent all the feeling I could straight into his heart, and then I took what I had left, every ounce of my life force, and began to channel it to her.

Pushing one last time, I felt her slip from me and the last of my life force drained out of me and into her.

My head fell back on the sand, and I heard her let out a fierce scream. The cry of a warrior. The cry of a survivor. The cry of my only daughter.

Then everything went black.

In the blackness, in the nothingness that followed, there was a single voice.

A familiar voice.

"Hello, Red."

Epilogue

Kai

S he had visions, just like I did. She even looked like me. The only thing she seemed to share with her mother were her glowing blue eyes.

Her visions were different from mine. I could already tell, even though Ephyra was only five years old. She spoke of her mother often, even though she'd never met her. The first time I knew she could see the past was a year ago, when she told me I kissed her mommy too much.

I had laughed, until I realized the only way she'd have known that was if she had seen it in a vision.

It should have comforted me. It allowed her to know her mother even though she was gone. But the reality was that I was terrified. Terrified of the power she held but also terrified I wouldn't be able to live up to the person she saw in the past.

That version of me had died when Solana did.

"Daddy! Come look at what we made!" Ephyra shouted with all the enthusiasm of a five-year-old, motioning through the door for me to come down to the beach with her.

I dried my hands on a towel, abandoning the dirty dishes, to follow her to the very spot I had lost her mother. The same spot Ephyra came into my life. The same spot where everything changed.

She skipped across the sand, humming a lullaby I didn't recognize. I suspected she'd heard it from a vision. She was normally a very quiet child, but when she was by the sea, she was joyous. It seemed to soothe her in the same way it did me.

Stopping just before the water line, Ephyra whirled around to face me. She had a huge grin on her face. It was a rare sight, seeing as she also inherited my grumpy disposition, as Sol had called it.

The sight of her smile wasn't what made the tears fall, though, it was what was at her feet.

A large sandcastle that was intricately designed lay on the sand. It was far too intricate for a five-year-old to have created by herself. But it wasn't the castle that caught my attention. It was what was written in the sand in front of it.

Chaos.

"We named it Chaos Castle," Ephyra explained, "because lots of crazy things happen inside the castle. There are even dragons!"

I wanted to form words, but I couldn't. All I could do was stare at the word in the sand.

Ephyra's face fell when she looked up at me. "Daddy? Why are you crying?"

"Who helped you make this castle, Ephyra?" I asked, though I already knew the answer. The handwriting was as familiar as the brush strokes she made across each painting that hung in our house. As familiar as the light in the eyes of the little girl in front of me.

"Mommy! She said she'd come back one day and help me build another one."

The End

Acknowledgments

This book was a whole different experience from writing my first one, and I mean that in a good way! This time around, I had more support and more collaboration, and loads of fun.

I can't thank my beta team enough for all the feedback and the countless group discussions that helped me mold this book into something I am genuinely proud of. To Tabitha, Ashley, Tess, Daph, Stephanie, Claire, Vanessa, Dana, and Allison. Without you, I'm not sure I would have had the courage to finish this book. No words can express my gratitude to you all.

To my book incubator writing group. You have all been a constant presence since book one, and your support and encouragement have been invaluable.

To my street team. You all have lifted me up when I felt like marketing was too hard. You helped bring my book into the world, and without you, it wouldn't have had the reach or the momentum. Whenever marketing feels too hard, you all go and post about my books, and it gives me the strength to keep going. I may be biased, but I believe I have the best street team out there!

To my spicy swap writing group. The way you've held me up and held me through the hard times. None of my books would exist without you all. Thank you for always being there, always encouraging, always listening to my random rants, and reminding me why we all write.

To my editor, Heather, at Simply Spellbound Edits. Your help, encouragement, adorable comments, and unwavering support made it possible for me to actually finish this book and get it out into the world. I sound like a real writer because of you!

To my sister, Carra. What can I say? You are my sounding board, my brainstorm buddy, my constructive criticism partner, and the person whose advice I trust the most. You are my go-to when it comes to writing, and I wouldn't be able to do this without you. Thank you a million times over.

Lastly, to my husband and kids. There are no words to express how much I love you all and how much your support has meant to me. AJ, I couldn't have done this without your silly comments that make me belly laugh, your encouragement, and our random brainstorming sessions, even when you hadn't even read the book yet! To my kids, this book holds a piece of each of you within it, and I hope you never forget how powerful you are, especially when you work together. You can change the world if you set your mind to it! I love you with my whole heart.

Also by

Also Available From Brilynn O'Neal

The Forgotten Earth Series
The Forgotten Earth

About the author

Brilynn O'Neal lives in California with her husband, three children, two dogs, two cats, ten chickens, and lots of honeybees. When she's not writing spicy, emotional stories, she's outside soaking up nature and saving bees.

Follow her on Instagram, TikTok, and Pinterest @forestsandfantasy

@FORESTSANDFANTASY